Praise for Arnold & Igor

"Part mystery, part love story, and part musical speculation, Howard Rappaport has written a novel that will certainly be of interest to musicians and music lovers. Featuring the two most influential composers of the twentieth century as the protagonists, Rappaport presents a world of what might have been, employing clever narrative devices to tell an engaging story."

—Leonard Slatkin, GRAMMY Award-winning conductor

"Howard Rappaport has written a fascinating and thoroughly engaging novel, wonderfully written with remarkable historical knowledge of two of the 20th century's most important composers, Schoenberg and Stravinsky. For the music aficionado, it is full of references to the greatest music of these two giants, but for the novice, the work is totally understandable as a great story told by a master storyteller. What a joy to read, as Rappaport brings us into the world of these composers, through their European years and, more intimately, into their time together in Hollywood. Congratulations to Rappaport for this important novel."

—Gerard Schwarz, Conductor Laureate, Seattle Symphony and
Mostly Mozart Festival, 8-time Emmy Award Winner.

ARNOLD & IGOR

A Novel

Howard Rappaport

Fomite
Burlington, VT

ISBN-13: 978-1-953236-92-0
Library of Congress Control Number: 2023946409

Fomite
58 Peru Street
Burlington VT 05401
www.fomitepress.com
06-20-2024

For Lisa
For Brenda
For Charlotte, Nathan, Andrea and Mel
And for Lida Beasley

"Even parallel lines meet—as mathematics assures us—at
such points, if one only has the patience to wait."
—Arnold Schoenberg, letter to Alban Berg

BOOK I

SIMON

Los Angeles, 1995

A PACKAGE WAS WAITING for him at the end of the day, a plain brown parcel beneath the grid of faculty mailboxes when he'd swung by the staff room to pick up his mail. No return address. *Professor Simon Grafton c/o UCLA Music Dept.* scribbled in spidery green marker.

Simon stared at it, urgently needing to get off campus, already running late for his wife's photography exhibition slated to get underway in less than an hour.

Leave it be until tomorrow, some rational voice in him urged.

But something about the parcel stopped him, its unknown sender, the surprising bulk when he stepped closer to examine it, intrigued for a moment then immediately beset by anxieties—Francine's exhibition a good thirty-five miles away and, as if this weren't enough, his most recent teaching evaluation, Dean Boderman's professional dressing down, to say nothing of the overdue Santa Fe commission—*good lord!*—the opera he was *supposed* to be wrapping up but somehow couldn't manage to finish.

The mysterious package was begging to be opened, the box too unwieldy to lug across campus to his car. Taking a deep breath, he looked around the staff room, thinking he ought to give Francine a quick call to let her know he'd be a little late.

Quickly! a different voice in him urged, *open it. Won't take but a minute or two.*

Grabbing a pair of scissors from the worktable, he leaned over to chisel through the packaging seal, pushing aside layers of newspaper, an earthy oily smell, vaguely sweet, faint hint of moldering as he plunged his hands into the box to exhume an immense leather tome.

Arnold Schoenberg
Brentwood, California
April 1947

Carefully, he hefted the document onto the worktable, pulling back the embossed cover, fingers trembling as they grazed the parchment, cologne, tobacco, sweat maybe, vestiges of the genius who'd created it.

Holy shit! Could it be?

Arnold Schoenberg's sketchbook. Was this, in fact, the final sketchbook, the one considered by scholars to have vanished long ago?

Transfixed, he turned gently through the vellum pages—musical themes, motifs, mirror inversions; a bricolage of lines and squiggles, circles, dots, squares and arrows; contrapuntal experiments, curious crossings-out, invertible counterpoint, abstruse instructions scrawled in German and other not-readily-decipherable arcana, Simon's head spinning with the implications of the manuscript before him. Contained within such hieroglyphs and cryptograms were surely the building blocks of epic themes—love, madness, murder, good and evil, God.

Schoenberg's lost sketchbook. The mere thought of it caused him to laugh aloud, the sound of his own voice jarring within the silence of the staff room. *My God, I mean, are you kidding me?* He stood frozen, wondering what the hell he was supposed to do. Who could have forwarded the document? And why to him?

The vibration of his cell phone startled him.

"Where are you?" Francine asked nervously. "They're about to present my award."

"On my way," he said uneasily.

Francine gave a breathless laugh. "I'm actually a little nervous."

"I'll be there soon," he said, squeezing his eyes shut, flustered, glancing out the window where menacing rainclouds were amassing against a darkening sky.

"Hurry, okay?" she said.

"You're gonna do great, France."

"Famous last words."

"Tummy butterflies," he reassured her, absentmindedly running his fingers along the edge of the manuscript. "It's just the butterflies talking."

Francine exhaled heavily. "I guess that's coming from the expert."

"At this point, I'm pretty sure I've encountered every last butterfly in the universe." He glanced up at the clock, stomach starting to burn as it occurred to him there was no way in hell he'd make it all the way over to Glendale in time.

"The boys," she said. "Don't forget to pick them up on your way over."

"Right," he said, prickling.

The boys. Shit. He'd forgotten they were over at the babysitter's.

"See you in a few minutes," he said, ending the call, staring stupidly at the sketchbook, muted banter from out in the hallway, the anemic hum from the photocopier, a lingering scorched coffeepot odor.

Get going! his wiser voice chided him.

Although, technically—*hypothetically*—he could still make it over to her expo, pedal to the metal, roaring up Wilshire to the 405, shooting up the diamond lane in a dash to Mrs. Larson's place then over to the college.

Pulse rushing, unable to resist, he peeled back a dense swath of pages for a final glance, surprised by the protruding corner of a small envelope, his own name scrawled across the front in tremulous handwriting identical to that on the packaging. He gazed up at the clock again, stomach knotting, beard prickling with sweat as he shifted his weight, marching in place with the letter like a hapless four-year-old.

Francine's event about to get underway, his overburdened brain doing some calculus to factor in the forty-five-minute commute, the fetching of the boys, all exacerbated by what was now looking like increasingly inclement weather, adrenalin skyrocketing, the onset of a panic attack as the wise, rational voice prodded him to gather up his musicological treasure and get the hell out of there.

Thrusting the envelope back inside the document, he grabbed at the newspaper packaging, bundling it frantically around the sketchbook, tucking the mummified array beneath his arm and bolting like an unruly running back, zooming around the corner only to hear his name being called from down the hallway, his department chair, Professor Demetra Kouras, waving a manila envelope as she made her way towards him.

"Your evaluation," Demetra said, pressing the envelope into his free hand.

"Got it," he said with a harried smile, less than enthusiastic about leafing through Dean Boderman's withering review of his teaching performance.

"I wanted to make sure you had a copy to read through and sign," she said, folding her arms, quizzical at first but then amused as she stepped back to stare at the newspaper disarray wedged against his arm, raising her eyebrows, inquiring if everything was all right.

"Of course," he managed, clasping the chaos of newspapers.

"You look white as a sheet."

Helpless, he stared at her, noting the paisley skirt and printed blouse she wore, her dark hair elegantly braided.

Running late, he explained, pivoting towards the glass doors across the lobby.

"Ah," she said, nodding, moving ahead of him to get the door, Simon thanking her as he stepped out into the late afternoon glare.

"Well," she said, "I'm off to another budget meeting. I hope wherever you're headed proves far more interesting."

"Let's hope I make it," he shouted over his shoulder, the document clutched at his side as he lurched towards Dickson Court and the parking structure looming beyond. Gulping in air, Simon gave the sketchbook another good squeeze, gearing up for the sprint of a lifetime.

Tableau I

Igor

"His eyes were protuberant and explosive, and the whole force of the man was in them…I was aware, nevertheless, that this was the most prescient meeting in my life."
—Igor Stravinsky

Berlin *Choralion-Saal*
December 1912

A TRICKLING CASCADE of piano notes, a plucked violin, a beguiling flute slinking into its low sultry register.

Confronted by Schoenberg's music—subsumed by its intoxicating perfume—Stravinsky realizes what he must do: after the performance, he must approach Herr Schoenberg, stolidly taking hold of the master's hand and making his introduction.

> *Den Wein, den man mit Augen trinkt*
> *Gießt Nachts der Mond in Wogen nieder*
>
> *The wine we drink with the eyes*
> *pours down in torrents from the moon at night.*

Pierrot Lunaire. Schoenberg's new song cycle. For weeks he's heard murmurings about this revolutionary music—*innovative, daring, outrageous*. Then, just last week, the phone call from Paris, Diaghilev shouting over the crackly phone line about an upcoming tour, *It's all set, Igor. Come with us! The Ballet Russes will be performing* Petrushka *in Berlin!* Diaghilev's laborious breathing as he went on to exclaim, *Mais, tu es le créatur! You, my dear Stravinsky, are the creator of* Petrushka *and* L'Oiseau de feu, *the very vessel, after all, through which such masterworks have passed!* adding with a sharp intake of breath, *And, Igor, while we're there, why don't we go hear that new Schoenberg piece everyone's been making such a fuss over?*

Now, bathed in the purplish cabaret light above the proscenium, the soprano gyrates snakelike, contorting her body as, alternately, she sings, declaims, oscillates, hisses, glides in glissando, and swoops in half-sung, half-spoken *Sprechstimme*. Costumed as Pierrot, the *Commedia dell'arte* clown figure, Frau Zehme (as she's named in the program), wears a tunic with oversized buttons, gaudy sequins, frilly collar and puffed sleeves, a patchwork of red, blue and green, a floppy hat, face floured in white powder.

> *Mit groteskem Riesenbogen*
> *Kratzt Pierrot auf seiner Bratsche,*
> *Wie der Storch auf einem Beine,*
> *Knipst er trüb ein Pizzicato.*
>
> *With a bow grotesque and monstrous*
> *Pierrot scrapes away at his viola,*
> *Like a stork on only one leg,*
> *Sadly plucks a pizzicato.*

He surveys Schoenberg at stage right, perched upon a stool in profile behind a scrim, intense and self-assured, the sonic inventor wielding his baton before a quintet of instrumentalists, flute, clarinet, violin, cello, and piano. Stravinsky notes that, like himself, Schoenberg is somewhat diminutive in stature. Viewing the great Schoenberg in the living flesh for the first time, an image of Napoleon comes to mind—robust, magisterial, domineering.

Laughter from somewhere in the audience perforates the music, tearing Stravinsky from its spell as Frau Zehme sings of Pierrot boring a hole into Cassander's polished skull, filling it with Turkish tobacco, tamping and puffing on it like a pipe, evoking further macabre images, a deathly moon…upon night's pillow, a drop of pallid blood tingeing a sick man's lips, moonbeams, disfigurement, eerie twilight, celestial flora, moths blotting out the sun.

The rustling around him is disheartening—stifled explosions of laughter, muted shock and outrage, the resignation of leaden bodies wedged like freight into stiff narrow seats. The bearded man to his left radiates sour body odor while, on the opposite side, Diaghilev is engrossed in the soprano's pantomiming, nearly gyrating, himself, to see past the gaping nebula of a hat worn by the woman in front of them. Pierrot, meanwhile, now in the fullest of hallucinations, swings a scimitar, intent on decapitating the moon as interweaving piano, cello and clarinet lines meet in sonic clusters.

But, my God, how could Schoenberg have possibly created such music? Ghoulish discordant clashes. Sustained dissonance resisting resolution. Anarchy. In one fell swoop, tonality eradicated, centuries of harmony and tonal order cast aside, the music sinister, harsh, grotesque, and yet at moments, dreamy, sensuous, tender even. No composer has ever dared to go *this* far in pushing the boundaries of music towards its outermost limits.

Confronted by such sheer musical power, Stravinsky recalls from his childhood in St. Petersburg the awe of colossal locomotives, combustion engines, the churning cross-rhythms of iron wheels, exhilarating anapests, the brutal bellowing of brakes, valves, pumps, blowers, pistons, blast pipes.

And he remembers the crackle.

The music of ice breaking along the surface of the Neva, the rasp and groan after a willful winter when warm weather wooed, the encrusted frozen layer swelling and then, in hairline fissures, relenting as the Earth yawned and stretched her limbs, he and his wind-burned little brother Gury patting snowballs as everywhere, with muted pops, the white-hot ice began to split, crumbling and releasing pent-up energy, *Slavnyy vesenniy. Spring!* Nature, in a balmy, fecund waft, disintegrating and renewing herself as, at last, from the frigid depths spring was unleashed.

No, for the love of God! He refuses to feel intimidated by Schoenberg, reaching deep within instead, for the courage he'd been unable to summon years ago at the St. Petersburg Mariinsky Opera House when, as a young boy, ten or eleven maybe, he'd stumbled upon his musical hero, Tchaikovsky.

His parents had allowed him to attend a Glinka semi-centennial, a special performance of *Russlan and Ludmilla* in which Stravinsky's father Fyodor, the famous Russian bass, was to sing the role of Farlaf. On a rainy night, Stravinsky sat alongside his mother in a lavish seat of apricot velvet, gazing out from the third tier into the dizzying blue and gold auditorium, the gilded tiers, crimson curtains, and blazing chandeliers beneath a scalloped copper dome all conspiring to make him feel like some nugatory pendant inside an opulent jewelry box. Enchanted, he'd taken stock of exotic ladies' furs, long gowns and perfumed clientele, focusing the mother-of-pearl lorgnette glasses upon his father, robed, helmeted and wielding massive saber as, from the stage below, he trudged around in ponderous boots bellowing his heart out.

And what was it like up in the theater's stratosphere, viewing his father down there? The seemingly infallible Fyodor Stravinsky, with his burnished bass voice and elaborate costume, Stravinsky recalling the estrangement he'd felt, even while very young, the father rarely deigning to speak to his sons, Igor and his brothers banished instead, kept out of sight whenever their father happened to be at home, reading or preparing for a role.

During intermission at the Mariinsky that evening, Stravinsky stood against the balustrade above the rear foyer, scanning the crowds through his mother's binoculars where, from the crest of the lobby's red-carpeted stairway, he'd spotted the legendary, white-haired and august figure of Tchaikovsky making his way across the marble hallway. Pulse quickening, he wanted nothing more than to rush over to his idol to proclaim his devotion. He wouldn't have a clue about what to say exactly, but what difference would it make, thrust against the very hem of the master—*anointed*—by such a god-like figure?

But instead he'd simply stood there, transfixed, frozen in his awe.

O alter Duft aus Märchenzeit.
O ancient scent from once upon a time.

Now Schoenberg's *Pierrot* reaches its culmination as conductor and musicians join the soprano to take their bows. Twenty-one brief songs performed in just over half an hour, Stravinsky too enraptured even to lift his hands to join the applause, affixed to his seat instead. Along the walls, gas lights flicker. A squall of winter air blows in from the opened theater doors to mingle with the warmth. A distant tram along the *Bellevuestrasse* groans while ascending the *Müggelspree*.

Slowly, the audience trickles off, leaving Stravinsky engulfed in an ocean of vacant rows, fingering his ticket stub while gathering the resolve to make his way backstage.

Bubbles in his stomach, he comes upon the scene backstage. A whirlwind of enthusiastic audience members orbiting the musicians, the cellist studiously loosening his bow as someone presents Frau Zehme with a bottle of *Kirschwasser*. Stravinsky recognizes a quartet of well-established composers, Strauss, Boulanger, Puccini, Ravel, huddled in one corner of the room, excitedly exchanging impressions of the performance. Wanting nothing more than to join their celebrated ranks, Stravinsky waves grandly at them though no one appears to notice.

Herr Schoenberg is surrounded by fawning students and other admirers, forehead furrowing as he raises a forefinger to emphasize a point, head tilting back to guffaw at some clever quip he's just made, Stravinsky waiting, eager, hesitant, emboldened, but then timid, bashful, fussing with his cravat, heart thumping in his throat as he calculates the ideal moment to make his way up to Schoenberg.

But why must he feel so ill at ease about approaching Schoenberg? After all, isn't Stravinsky himself now emerging as a formidable composer in his own right? Two seasons ago, his *Firebird* became an overnight sensation, reverberating across Europe, while *Petrushka,* his latest ballet, may be slated for a similar success. The thirty-year-old Stravinsky senses his own star might now be poised to rise, intensely curious, however, as to what Schoenberg might make of such resounding though arguably ephemeral success. The formidable Schoenberg, not yet forty himself, whose own notoriety and influence continue to proliferate: Ravel and Debussy speak of him with reverence; Strauss, de Falla, Busoni, Boulanger, all seem eager to weigh in on the implications of such a luminary.

Catching sight of the *Pierrot Lunaire* score on the piano, Stravinsky heads toward it instinctively as if magnetically drawn to it, extending a hand towards Schoenberg's music like a priest seeking the altar stone. Carefully, he nudges aside the baton, glancing around furtively before slowly pulling back the cover, enthralled to imagine an energy force field emanating from the score. Here before his own eyes, Schoenberg's astonishing musical blueprint. Captivated, Stravinsky reads through the score, reliving the performance he's just heard.

Remarkable. A new way forward. Pierrot, a leap into the unknown, stroke of genius, vatic glimpse into a new century inching towards chaos.

"I see you enjoy my *Pierrot*," a stern voice says from behind him in a subdued yet perforating Viennese accent.

Startled, he turns to confront the intense eyes of Arnold Schoenberg, his tuxedo forbidding, the dome of his head stark and gleaming, Stravinsky's shoulders tensing as he straightens and attempts to stand taller, dry lips parting to croak out a feeble *Guten Abend*.

"Herr Schoenberg, please, why, yes, I am Igor."

As he pauses to collect himself, he catches a whiff of Schoenberg's pomade, the leathery medicinal scent of his cologne.

"Igor Stravinsky," he continues, "from Paris." His tongue feels gritty. "Well, first Russia, naturally, why, oh yes, Russia, originally and—"

Schoenberg's bald dome is rimmed by a strip of fine dark hair, his stare unwavering, merciless.

"But, now," Stravinsky blathers, "yes, now, I reside actually in Switzerland, directly across the lake from Geneva." Clasping then unclasping his hands, he thinks to add, "Maybe you are familiar? Paris also. There I reside as well."

Lifting his eyes, slowly meeting the master's gaze, he wipes at his lips, dry-mouthed, waiting breathlessly for Herr Schoenberg to chime in.

"There I am working. As a *composer*." He swallows heavily. "Like yourself! And!" Nodding. "Well, recently, I composed some music for the ballet." Nodding more vigorously, "Very nice. And which everybody seems to have—"

"I happen to be familiar with your work," Schoenberg says.

SIMON

"I CAN'T BELIEVE how late we are!" Lincoln said, Simon's eleven-year-old son, overwrought with preadolescent angst, squirming in the passenger seat beside him, Simon, white-knuckled at the wheel, meanwhile, tearing through surface streets in a race to the community college.

"Hideously late!" six-year-old Luke chimed in from the back seat.

"We'll get there," Simon reassured his sons, aiming for both confidence and calm, despondent, though, as he glanced at the dashboard clock to confirm they were now officially half an hour late.

"What's the deal, Dad?" Lincoln said, narrowing his gaze when Simon turned to look at him, an array of his mother's freckles scattered over his nose and cheeks. "Where *were* you?"

"Work," Simon said with a little shrug, plagued with remorse about leaving Francine in the lurch like this. He admired the handsome turtleneck Lincoln was wearing, his hair, normally shaggy, carefully combed and parted. No doubt the diligent work of Mrs. Larson, the babysitter.

Lincoln groaned. "Mom said for us to be ready to roll at *five sharp*."

"On the dot!" Luke echoed breathlessly, Lincoln glancing over the back seat to ask his little brother to be quiet and to let *him* handle this.

Detained at a red light, fingers tapping nervously against the steering wheel, Simon flashed on the rare and exquisite document concealed in his trunk, exhilarated now by the sketchbook's magnitude and historical implications, its potential to change nearly everything in the world of modern music. At the same time, though, the notion he might be carting around ill-gotten goods was troubling.

And what about the letter personally addressed to him, its seductive corner peeking out at him? His breath quickened. He couldn't wait to inspect his find.

In a pleasing flash, he suddenly visualized his opera's completion, his status as *serious* composer elevated to some new zenith, his academic and professorial rank equally recompensed. For years he'd been struggling to complete his opera, a mammoth undertaking, easily the largest commission he'd ever been awarded, his own take on the contentious relationship between Arnold Schoenberg and Igor Stravinsky. Could the document's uncanny arrival, its unplumbed secrets, propel him across his opera's finish line, providing answers he'd long been seeking concerning Schoenberg and Stravinsky? Such revelations might result in some series of groundbreaking musicological articles he'd go on to publish.

Who could he contact for advice? First thing in the morning, he could put a call in to the Schoenberg Institute. Simply for a bit of direction. He needn't spill any beans just yet but, instead, toss out a small bone, a carefully-selected detail or two—*hypothetically-speaking*—just to feel things out as to how best to proceed.

"Mom's gonna kill us," Lincoln was saying.

"Brutally," Luke rasped.

Simon watched the languid windshield wipers do their work. Outside the window a festooned car dealership rolled by, a lumberyard, a judo studio.

"I'd say you guys are probably right on the money about Mom," he said, astonished—mortified—by how time had completely gotten away from him. He'd pledged to Francine he'd be there. The award was a real coup, a true honor—her photographic achievements officially recognized by the Glendale Community College Fine Arts Department. No doubt, were this *his* installment or recognition ceremony, Francine would be right there for him. The acute disparity, the blunt selfishness on his part, savaged him.

As if listening in on his private thoughts, Lincoln insisted, "We need to be there to support her."

"Yeah," Luke squealed, "Mom needs us!"

"Shut up!" Lincoln yelled, turning again to chide his little brother in the back seat. "You're just repeating everything I say."

"Am not repeating everything you say," Luke said.

"You're not helping."

"Am too."

Deflated, Simon said, "I'm really sorry about this, guys. I had every intention—"

"It's just what families do," Lincoln said, "help each other out."

Simon frowned, attempting to come to some conclusion about exactly what it was families *did,* a vague memory of his parents in Los Angeles emerging, followed by an even dimmer recollection of the years after his mother had passed away.

You actually knew both composers? he remembered asking his father.

Not yet five years old when his mom died, Simon was only able to recall a scant handful of details—his father's background in botany and agronomy and how he'd accompanied his wife, Helena, from England to Southern California where she was to become a leading soprano among the Los Angeles avant-garde. His father, Jasper, meanwhile, in order to make ends meet, began working as a fine gardener, employed by a number of renowned clients, Schoenberg and Stravinsky among them.

What was it like working for them? he'd asked his father, years later.

And that other question, the question rooted far back, mixed into a few of his earliest memories: *How was it possible that Mom could have simply vanished one day?*

But, despite the son's entreaties, the father remained tight-lipped, stoic and withdrawn, such topics deemed officially off limits, memories too fraught apparently, too painful for his father to dredge up.

Now, crestfallen, Simon watched the wiper blades screeching like excitable pigs across the windshield, thinking bleakly of all the work still hanging over him, the black cloud of his overdue opera commission intermixed with the increasing uncertainty of his teaching post.

But, in terms of specific job performance indicators? Dean Boderman had said during their evaluation meeting earlier this morning, *I'm seeing quite a bevy of red flags, indicators that things are starting to head south.* Watching Boderman read from his notes, Simon had stared at the dean's billboard of a forehead, his square-set equine jaw, long teeth like whitened stones while Boderman read through his bullet-point list of infractions and deficiencies: tardiness—somewhat chronic; failure to hold regularly-scheduled office hours; student work neglected, paperwork not returned in a timely manner.

"Dad," Lincoln said, "can we listen to the Shostakovich?"

Simon didn't respond, the question barely registering, his thoughts alighting instead upon Demetra, Chair of the Theory & Musicology department, the scrutinizing look she'd given him earlier during his deer-in-the-headlights moment while clutching the sprawl of unearthed treasure against his hip.

Dr. Demetra Kouras, PhD, Musicology (Princeton), distinguished scholar and, as it so happened, world authority on Schoenberg. Should he approach her, revealing his secret while soliciting her expertise in helping to decode the document?

"Hey, what's with all these meditation CDs?" Lincoln asked, rifling through the glove compartment for the Shostakovich. Clutching the steering wheel, Simon veered around the sluggish driver in front of him.

"We should listen to the Shostakovich," Lincoln said.

"Something's gonna hit the fan," Luke said, whistling a tiny *phew!* "I'm not allowed to say what, though."

"Be quiet, Luke," Lincoln yelled. "It isn't helping the situation."

"*You* be quiet," Luke shot back. "Who made *you* the boss of my brain, anyway?"

"*Luke-puke,*" Lincoln said under his breath.

"*Stinkin' Lincoln,*" Luke countered.

"*Luke-warm,*" Lincoln muttered.

"*Guys!*" Simon cautioned in something like a growl, "knock it off."

"Actually, you know," Luke said a moment later, "Dad's a really good driver."

"Now, that's it!" Simon said, "Now we're working together, guys, now we're playing ball like a real team." He smirked at Luke in the rearview, his towheaded son, comical in his tiny argyle vest, suited up like some cheeky old guy at a country club.

He couldn't suppress a grin. "Luke, where in the world did you learn that business about something about to hit the fan, anyway?"

"From Bradley," Luke said, blinking rapidly, the way he did under scrutiny whenever it dawned on him he might be on the verge of serious trouble.

"Bradley Hodges?" Simon asked. "In your class?"

"Bingo," Luke answered.

"Bradley gets it from his older brother, I'm sure," Lincoln said. "From Jeffty."

"Ah," Simon said "I see."

"Bradley's a natural born killer," Luke said. "At least that's what he likes to go around telling everyone."

"Good grief," Simon muttered. "What is he, around six?"

"Yeah," Lincoln scoffed. "Six. *Real tough.* "

"Shut up," Luke whined.

Simon glanced anxiously at the dashboard clock before punching the accelerator, whizzing through a busy intersection just as the signal was going red, clenching the steering wheel and, before he could stop himself, swearing helplessly under his breath.

Tableau II

Igor

> "World-fear is assuredly the most creative of all prime feelings."
> —Oswald Spengler, *The Decline of the West*

"IGOR!" DIAGHILEV CALLS BACKSTAGE, waving Stravinsky over to where he's conversing with a woman, zaftig, wearing green-tinted, bug-like spectacles and a beaded butterfly cloche.

Head tilted back, Diaghilev says, "Come say hello to Mademoiselle Rondo, journalist and music critic from the *Zeitgeist,* who's written so favorably about our Russian Ballet." Barrel-chested and avuncular, Diaghilev wears a close-fitting gray suit and a maroon bow tie, a monocle dangling from a chain in his vest.

"You're a far more reliable judge than I, Igor, when it comes to musical matters." Winking at Mlle Rondo, Diaghilev explains how his own talents, in heading an internationally-renowned ballet company, tend more towards the pecuniary, "taking care to lubricate each of the moving parts so as to prevent the entire train from derailing."

Mlle Rondo readies her notepad, requesting general impressions about the *Pierrot* performance.

"*Magnifique!*" Stravinsky responds, eyes darting around the room to home in on Schoenberg, nodding and laughing heartily among his admirers.

"I couldn't fail to notice how the audience was prone to squirming in their seats," Rondo says in a voice somewhat warbling. "The woman beside me plugged up her ears." She knits her eyebrows. "I suspect she may have been on to something."

Stravinsky smiles politely, the palm-sized black butterfly fastened to the front of Mlle Rondo's cloche reminding him of the enormous moths blotting out the sun in *Pierrot*. Listening to her Americanized French accent, Stravinsky now recalls meeting her in Paris some time ago, the anise on her breath, a faulty hip resulting in a ploddingly asymmetrical gait.

"What Schoenberg has accomplished is nothing short of remarkable," Stravinsky says, sensing Diaghilev's measured breathing beside him, stealing another glance at Schoenberg and eager to continue his conversation with him. But now, as he watches Schoenberg, wild-eyed and lunging forth like a puma to defend some assertion he's just put forth, Stravinsky feels his own nerve rapidly diminishing. Has he already missed his chance with Schoenberg, failed to put his best foot forward?

"M. Stravinsky?" Rondo asks with a puzzled look.

Suddenly, Stravinsky catches sight of a woman across the room, dazzling in her blue satin gown and speaking with Frau Zehme. Captivated, he's unable to take his eyes off her, the fine facial features, the serpentine coil of her chignon.

"Is he always so distracted?" he hears Mlle Rondo ask Diaghilev.

"Hello, Stravinsky?" Diaghilev hollers, rapping his walking stick upon Stravinsky's shoulder before leaning in to whisper. "*Es-tu, en bureau aujourd'hui? Arrêter de se branler!*"

"Revolutionary," Stravinsky mutters to Mlle Rondo. "Schoenberg's *Pierrot* may very well be the solar plexus of modernism."

Rondo looks up at him from her notepad.

"A deluge," Stravinsky continues, "a musical force which can no longer be ignored, one bound to thrust every one of us into the future, right along with it."

Leaning in again, Diaghilev indicates the woman in the blue gown. "Frau Vivian Růžek, if I'm not mistaken. A choreographer. The one in fact responsible for creating the Pierrot pantomime this evening." And, next thing he knows, Diaghilev is introducing Stravinsky to the scintillating woman in the blue gown, Frau Růžek's voice *dolcissimo*—light as a songbird—when she addresses him, Stravinsky taking hold of her hand, blushing, no idea what to say.

Frau Růžek wears a diamond choker. Her lips are delicate, cheeks flushed with high color. Before he can come up with the right something to say, he hears Schoenberg calling Frau Růžek's name, a beautiful wooden owl figurine in his hand.

"For your new baby," Schoenberg says to Frau Růžek. "For Elsa."

"But, you carved this yourself?" Frau Růžek asks.

"Black Forest linden." Schoenberg smiles. "A young sapwood begging, practically, to be whittled."

Bemused, Stravinsky finds himself wondering whether he too, as a composer just starting to find his footing, isn't akin to some young sapwood, impressionable, pliant, willing to be shaped by masterly hands. And when Frau Růžek steps in to kiss Schoenberg's cheek, Stravinsky feels his own face go warm.

Diaghilev informs everyone that, regrettably, he must excuse himself. "I'm afraid, there's still much work to do prior to the performance."

"*Performance?*" Schoenberg asks with interest, prompting Diaghilev to report with exuberance on the upcoming *Petrushka* performances slated to open this coming weekend at the Kroll Theater.

Turning to Frau Růžek, Schoenberg nearly beams. "But, you know, this I would very much enjoy hearing."

"I'm certain we can arrange tickets for you," Stravinsky pipes up. "Right, *Seryozha?*"

"By all means!" Diaghilev says with a theatrical clap of his hands. "I look forward to it."

The conversation reaches a lull, bowed heads followed by an uncomfortable silence.

Sensing Schoenberg's eyes upon him, Stravinsky holds his breath, too timid even to lift his gaze from his shoes.

Finally, with a sharp intake of air, Schoenberg announces, "But! After your performance." His eyes lock with Stravinsky's. "I insist. You must all come over to our home to dine with my wife and me."

SIMON

IT KILLED HIM to come face to face with Francine's look of keen disappointment when he and the boys finally stumbled into the exhibition gallery after barreling into the parking lot of Glendale CC, then bolting through the drizzle, frazzled, having missed the recognition ceremony altogether. Whatever crowd of appreciative supporters had shown up initially, the numbers by now had dwindled to mere stragglers, the hors d'oeuvres platter decimated to a stray trio of celery stalks and a few crackers.

"At least you're here," Francine said glumly.

Simon reached for her shoulder. "France," he said, screwing up his face, "I'm *really, really* sorry. Something came up at the last minute."

Shrugging, she looked away.

"Mommy, there's your pictures!" Luke exclaimed, pointing excitedly at the arrangement of photos across the gallery walls, black-and-white portraits of modern dancers, musicians, and visual artists captured over a span of several years. Simon admired the painstaking layout, the artful placement of each portrait.

Throwing a lanky arm around his mother's shoulder, Lincoln complimented Francine on her photos as well as on how nice she looked. She wore a pleated skirt and teal cardigan, her hair pulled back in a ponytail.

She did look pretty, Simon thought, younger somehow, wispy bangs, bookish eyeglasses, dimples prominent whenever she managed a weary smile.

"Wow, Mom," Luke said, twirling on a heel, "this is awesome." Francine bent down to give Luke a hug, pointing to a portrait she'd taken in their living room of Simon and the boys, the three of them stationed in the recliner that had once belonged to his late father.

"Remember, sweetie?" she said to Luke, "you helped Mommy set up that shot."

"When was that one taken?" Simon asked. "I had a lot more hair. Fewer wrinkles, a few trillion more brain cells probably."

"It wasn't all that long ago, really," Francine said. "Three or four years ago, it must have been." She shrugged. "Right around the time of the Santa Fe commission."

The commission. Twinge of panic. The anxiety-provoking muddle of an opera he wore around his neck. And now, good god, the sketchbook. He wanted to tell her about the package.

Instead he complimented her on the way she managed to capture the grainy light, mumbling something about f-stop settings.

Laughing, Francine said, "My gosh, remember how long it took to get that shot?"

"Dad hugged me and Linc forever," Luke said. "I thought we were gonna get smooshed."

"It did feel like forever," Francine said, shaking her head. "I swear I stood there for hours waiting for the shot."

Gesturing around the room, Simon smiled at her. "Everything looks fantastic, France."

"Really?" she asked. "I mean. Is it all right?" She blushed. "I felt a little weird, you know, putting some of the earlier shots up."

"Nah," Simon said, "they're great. I love the early pics. All those gritty black-and-whites of urban Philly."

"Dad was like totally late picking us up," Lincoln said, eyeing Simon uneasily.

Feeling the heat of his family's eyes upon him, Simon shifted his weight. "Crazy day. A strange package arrived today. Just as I was getting ready to leave campus."

"I can't believe we even made it over here," Lincoln said, shaking his head.

Francine's smile was stoic. There was so much he needed to explain to her. It was all he could do not to walk right over and throw his arms around her, reminding her that soon—before they knew it—all this opera madness would be over and everything could return again to normal.

"Dad truly gave it his all," Luke said, looking from Simon to Francine as if picking up on the tension between them. "He drove like a thousand miles an hour to get over here."

"Uh-oh," Francine said, her eyes widening as she played along. "That sounds *really* fast."

Lincoln scowled. "Apparently, not fast enough, though."

The sketchbook. Would now be the appropriate time to bring it up? Not a valid excuse for missing her show, certainly, but totally crazy, nonetheless.

Francine bit her lip, looking away, pointing out a photo to Lincoln and Luke of a female dancer in a mesh top, frozen in mid-leap beneath an overpass in downtown Los Angeles.

If he could just explain about the sketchbook—

"It's almost like she's flying," Lincoln was commenting about the photograph.

Gathering his nerve, Simon turned to Francine. "Hey," he said, swallowing. Francine stared at him. "Strangest thing you ever saw. This package sitting there in the staff room. And just as I was—"

"Simon!" a boisterous voice sang from behind them somewhere. "Finally. You are here!"

He cringed as a large and hot palm landed upon his shoulder, Carla's perfumed cigarette silage, Simon bracing himself as he turned to greet her.

"Everything looks wonderful," he told her.

"But this one!" Carla said, patting Francine's shoulder. "She is truly this night the star of our skies."

Smiling, he stood by helplessly as Carla ran her fingers through the side of his wife's chestnut hair, coaxing aside a few strands, Francine returning Carla's smile, pointing out how none of this would have been possible without all her support and generosity.

"Not true at all," Carla protested, wagging a finger and clicking her tongue.

Carla was Italian. She liked to use her hands effusively and had this habit of standing uncomfortably close during conversations. Whenever Carla was around Francine, there seemed to be a repertory of vague caresses, the type of affection reserved typically for cuddly pets. Was this anything he should pay closer attention to? Or was this merely the way certain Italian women chose to express themselves?

A moment later, Francine and the boys off to the restroom, Carla handed him a plastic cup of wine, effectively closing off the last molecules of personal space, eyelids coated in mint eye shadow as she proceeded to talk his ear off about all the *significant artistic progress* Francine was making behind the camera.

The wine was too sweet. He managed only a tiny sip, wanting nothing more than to spew the cloying substance back into its cup. Carla's taffeta blouse was starchy, incongruously formal it seemed to him, as she moved in a notch closer.

"It comes from *Eeetaly*," she said, grinning about the wine. "They produce it in Carvagna, near where my family comes from." Her breath was warm and herby. "Tasty, no?"

Drowning, he longed to extricate himself, anxious to be back at home, back to work on the opera.

And what about the Schoenberg manuscript stowed away in the trunk of his car? He'd barely had a second to fathom the document or consider what course of action he should take, whether or not to come forward and turn over his fortuitous masterpiece to the rightful authorities. Because, in continuing to hold onto it, wasn't he possibly implicating himself in some depraved criminal link that might only come back to bite him?

"You have been?" Carla was saying.

Huh? Christ, had she been talking to him the whole time?

"In *Eeetaly*," Carla said, rolling her eyes and blowing air up at her bangs. "You have been there?"

Yes, he told her, yes, yes, in fact he had—Florence, Venice, Rome, Naples, Pisa.

With a theatrical sigh, Carla complained about what an ordeal traveling could be. "Next week, they want to fly me to Chicago," she said. "Can you believe it? They hired me to do a shoot with the Joffrey Ballet."

He was hardly listening, nodding, though mainly trying to keep his head above water, coping with the surge of anxiety brought on by the commission, perversely curious as well—considering the way things seemed to be going with his teaching evaluations—how much longer he was destined to hold onto his teaching position.

"It's completely up Francine's alley," Carla was saying, Simon nodding, desperately scanning the restroom area for signs of his family.

"Wouldn't you agree?" Carla said.

Agree? He bristled, nodding profusely, ashamed to admit he hadn't heard a word she'd spoken, but telling her yes, absolutely, he completely agreed.

His family returned. Time to say their goodbyes, and head home. Settle in for a little while before putting the boys to bed.

At which point, he'd double back to the car, smuggling his delicious contraband into his study.

Dear Simon (Professor Grafton!),

Such a pleasure it was for me to be present at your Eastman graduate composition recital all those moons ago, (a full quarter of a century of 'moons ago,' as I now sit down to write to you!). And quite another distinct pleasure it was reuniting with your father, Jasper, at that very same moment.

Encountering your father, I was immediately jolted back to a time when my sister Marta and I first arrived in the States to live and work in the household of my cousin, Elsa Růžek, and her husband Claes. No doubt you've heard stories of how, upon their own arrival in California, your mother and father also lived for some time in that very house—stories of triumphs, travails, and misfortunes.

And as I listened to your concert that afternoon, I recalled the little boy, Simon, only three or four years old at the time, there in my cousin's garden alongside his father, armed with tiny trowel, while Father looked after various gardening tasks. There you were as well in Mr. Stravinsky's garden, the small boy with squat little legs barely capable of mounting the narrow staircase to Mr. Stravinsky's music studio upstairs!

I swear, I can still hear the clucking, the profusion of chickens behind the Stravinsky home, the bilious bleating goat tethered to a terrace post, braying about her milking, the jar of brown honey on the front stoop left by Rachmaninoff, a second-hand Dodge in the driveway and Stravinsky roaring off to Beverly Hills to meet up with Orson Welles, house cats amok, an operatic bloodhound they called Boris Good Enough, two dozen lovebirds in the parlor and one sadly-doomed parrot. The occasional garden parties there, or Mr. Stravinsky perched on his head, posed in Hungarian calisthenics, barricaded up in his studio to test out piquant polychords, my cousin Elsa enjoying tea and crumpets with Vera Stravinsky, brimming with the latest news of how her Orpheus project was faring over in Hollywood.

This I also remember fondly, Simon: the fun we all had during one particular afternoon when I happened to be

present, violin in hand, for an impromptu music lesson Mr.
Stravinsky was kind enough to offer. You were likely too
young to remember, but Mr. Stravinsky played some of his
own creations for us at the keyboard before assisting us in
'composing' minor creations of our own, offering me one
of his personal calligraphy pens and you a thick pastel, as he
guided your neophyte fingers in rendering "goose egg" whole
notes upon a scrap of manuscript paper: N.B., every good boy
does fine: this must surely have been Simon's first opus! (Ha!
Little did any of us realize then that this suckling apprentice
would himself one day grow into a proficient composer in
his own right!) Stravinsky played through our compositions,
alternatively singing and muttering in Russian, expertly
harmonizing our little pieces while all but transforming them
into full-blown symphonic gems!

Another "egg," no less amusing: the Fabergé Egg music
box Stravinsky took down from the mantel, winding the miniature crank to liberate an anemic 'Swan Lake' as we clasped
hands and danced like overjoyed crickets about the studio. If
I'm not mistaken, Stravinsky wound up presenting the very
same egg as a gift to your father. And so perhaps you were fortunate on later occasions to enjoy this wondrous musical ovum
and, for all I know, you may even still be in possession of it.

But, Simon, allow me now to come to the point of my
writing to you. I am forwarding to you a very special parcel,
a rather rare manuscript indeed, one long presumed to be
missing, a musical sketchbook belonging to none other than
Arnold Schoenberg. Mind you, this isn't merely another of
Schoenberg's numerous sketchbooks. But, rather uncannily,
this particular document appears to span several decades,
dating nearly clear back to the turn of the century.

I have no doubt you'll be a worthy custodian. Furthermore,
your musician's eyes will no doubt quickly gravitate towards
what I can only presume are unknown and undocumented
collaborations between Mr. Schoenberg and Mr. Stravinsky.

But, the professor will now be asking himself: How did
such a rare treasure find its way into the arguably plebeian
hands of a hapless violinist such as myself?

The sketchbook was, for a while at least, and for reasons yet to be explained, in the stewardship of one Solomon
Hersch, something of a musical luminary in his own

right—accomplished violinist, chamber player, and studio musician, who performed in prestigious string quartets with the titanic likes of Piatigorsky, Primrose, and Heifetz, appearing frequently in the 'Evenings on the Roof' music series in Los Angeles, and who was to become my own private violin instructor in Los Angeles. Sol owned a violin store over on La Brea you may happen to be familiar with.

When Sol passed away, I was among those charged with sifting through the various personal effects in the music shop, a lifetime's worth of delectable detritus—troves of books, scores, metronomes, violin parts, bow hair, plus all the other seemingly endless flotsam and jetsam which tends to proliferate over the course of a lifetime.

As you might imagine, when I came across such a manuscript while packing up boxes, squirreled away in a cabinet in the rear music studio, the hairs on my neck instantly prickled. Good lord, what in God's name was <u>this</u> doing here, I asked myself, while peeking through the pages to behold not simply a miraculous and fulgent musical assortment, but as well my cousin Elsa's numerous choreographic sketches for the 'Orpheus' screenplay and film project with which she'd spent so many assiduous hours in collaboration with Mr. Schoenberg.

Who exactly was to become the rightful custodian of such a priceless catalog? Should it remain in the hands of Gertrud, Arnold's beloved widow, or with one of the Schoenberg sons perhaps? With Nuria, the daughter, with whom Mr. Schoenberg and Gertrude escaped the Nazis? Or perhaps Georg and Trudi, progeny of the first marriage with Mathilde Zemlinsky? Should it be entrusted perhaps to the Schoenberg Institute at USC? The Library of Congress? The Music wing of the Austrian National Library?

Gazing surreptitiously about Sol's fusty studio, in need of further time to fathom such a wonder and come to a wise decision about its ultimate destiny, I watched helplessly in my own horror as, in one swift bite, the satchel I was holding appeared to devour the document. Perhaps it was I, then, who should become the rightful owner of my cousin's extensive work, after all, becoming, at least temporarily, its deserving inheritor and steward. Where else was the soul and spirit of Orpheus expected to go? And should I not do my utmost to ensure, by whatever means possible, that my cousin's creative legacy be preserved?

Whatever Sol may have been doing with the document, whatever curious circumstances may have led him to assume guardianship, I do not presume to know, though he may have been clinging to it while thinking along similar lines.

Years later, coming across your name in an ASCAP bulletin regarding your "Arnold & Igor" project-in-progress, I knew immediately what I must do.

I feel you are now to become the sketchbook's rightful protector, Simon, one, no doubt, who's telling a story about these composers in the opera you yourself are now working to bring to fruition. Perhaps then, this document might be of particular interest to you. Perhaps you can furthermore give serious consideration as to how such a sui generis treasure, "Orpheus," might someday embark upon its own deserving journey towards completion. In any case, I sense you would agree, further work is yet to be done before the sketchbook is to be forfeited to the appropriate academy, archival destiny, or other final resting place.

And so, you have my blessing, Simon. And I hope someday soon your opera will meet with all the success it deserves.

Yours,
Ingo Kohler

SIMON

Schoenberg in his hands. Arnold Schoenberg's final sketchbook, an historic treasure—Simon's personal Dead Sea Scrolls, his Rosetta Stone—now resting before him illicitly, upon the desk in his basement music studio.

Frayed and well-thumbed, the sketchbook's thick pages looked to be sewn into the worn spine painstakingly by hand; he'd had the pleasure of viewing other such hand-bound sketchbooks and scores in the Schoenberg Archives at the University of Southern California.

Turning eagerly through the pages of the document, Simon examined the vestiges of a keen and fervent mind at work, a chicken scratch of idiosyncratic hieroglyphics, melodic swirls, serpentine episodes and erratic counterthemes, leitmotives, vagrant chords, matrices and other formulae, endless decisions and indecisions, erasures, fresh starts, even miniature caricatures of various music critics etched into a few of the margins.

He came upon a familiar Bach chorale fragment, *Es ist genug*; fragments of Viennese waltzes and Ländler; and a smattering of various German words he was somewhat able to puzzle out with his academic German: *stöhnen, weinen, Verrat, untröstlich, Verklärung— to groan, to cry, betrayal, inconsolable, transfiguration.*

Then, several pages in, he zeroed in on an unusual passage.

Unlike the other hastily-scrawled examples throughout the sketchbook, this particular passage had been written out in a meticulous calligraphic hand, the contrast of its autograph so striking it almost seemed as if an entirely different composer could have penned it. Beneath the passage, Schoenberg then seemed to have begun playing around with the theme, developing several of his own variations.

Furthermore, Ingo had written, *your musician's eyes will no doubt quickly gravitate towards what I can only suspect are unknown and undocumented collaborations between Mr. Schoenberg and Mr. Stravinsky.*

As he examined the passage more closely, humming the pitches in his aural imagination to transcribe them from sight to sound, he was dumbfounded by a stab of recognition.

Stravinsky's *Petrushka.*

Uncanny! Oil mixing with water. Schoenberg tinkering around with his archrival's music, Stravinsky haunting the initial pages of Schoenberg's long-lost manuscript.

Heresy. Sacrilege. Madness. Why would Schoenberg devote a portion of his sketchbook towards manipulating the *Russian Dance* theme from Stravinsky's *Petrushka,* interweaving his adversary's vibrant rhythms and orchestral colors into some private variant all his own?

Thumbing through a swath of the document's final pages, Simon came upon rough fragments of Schoenberg's *Orpheus* project. His final project before he died—*le dernier cri,* the last echoes from the twentieth century's great musical mind, Schoenberg, whom some maintained breathed air from other planets, visionary (*prophet,* as his more stalwart apologists might even propose), whose musical ideas irrevocably altered the direction of modern music, influencing essentially every composer that followed, Simon himself no exception.

Even Stravinsky, the staunch apostate and turncoat from the Schoenbergian *Method,* would himself ultimately make his own way towards the *Method,* experimenting with serial procedures immediately after Schoenberg's death when he felt liberated finally to splash around in the chilly waters of dodecaphony.

Oddly enough—bizarrely—more than a few of these *Orpheus* passages suggested they too might have possibly been penned in a second, fastidious hand.

Stravinsky's? Simon's head was beginning to spin. Could it really be? The lost *Orpheus* passages. Might these pages imply some unique, creative juxtaposition, a synthesis of two musical geniuses never before revealed to the world? He flipped rapidly through the *Orpheus* sections, noting both the musical themes and stage directions from the screenplay/score Schoenberg collaborated on with choreographer Elsa Růžek.

*Prologue: When he played and sang Orpheus
had power over everyone and everything that
heard him; not only humans but animals,
flowers, and even rocks and water.*

Scene 1: Listening to him sing, she fell in love.

*Scene 12: He would go to the Underworld to
fetch her back.*

*Scene 23: And all around him darkness, the
howling of spirits in torment, and the fierce yells
of demons. When Orpheus played and told of his
love for Eurydice, Persephone wept, remembering
the world of sunlight above and begging her
husband to allow Eurydice to return.
 …but was Eurydice behind him?*

Then, in the midst of the *Orpheus* passages, Simon was puzzled to come upon a curious, five-word square scrawled in large block letters:

S A T O R
A R E P O
T E N E T
O P E R A
R O T A S

Some type of palindrome, the words readable from top to bottom, and from bottom to top; left to right, and then right to left, a Latin square of some sort. He couldn't fathom what it might be doing in the document. Tomorrow, he'd head over to Powell Library on campus to do some further investigating.

Exhaling heavily, he closed his eyes, massaging his temples.

A mysterious Square, adjacent to two distinct musical autographs.

Preposterous! some voice inside him reproved. *Foolish flight of fancy. Back to work, slacker! You're only looking for inventive ways to procrastinate while grabbing blindly at straws and whiling away what precious little time you have left on the commission.*

But what if this hunch about a link between the composers turned out to be legitimate? What might such a revelation portend—not only for Simon's own academic career and compositional aspirations, but also for the rest of the musical world? If this lost manuscript were suddenly to come to light, would it not have the power to change virtually everything, overturning accepted orthodoxy about the nature of the composers' estrangement and animosity? If proven, the suggestion of an underground collaboration between the composers could wind up upending conventional scholarship, all previous assumptions about the schism between the two composers' approaches essentially up for grabs, music history books needing to be rewritten, academic heads rolling—at least those reputations staked upon the virulent antipathy between Schoenberg and Stravinsky.

Now the muffled sounds of laughter, familial mirth from the kitchen directly above, thrust him from his reverie, reminding Simon that, indeed, *others* existed up there, Francine and the boys up fairly late on a school night, cheerfully inhabiting their home—chirp of the microwave as they enjoyed late-night popcorn while he toiled away down here in his dungeon, husband, daddy, mole, relegated to some lower stratum, wondering what his family made of their dutiful composer/breadwinner.

Or might *breadloser* be the operative term?

The basement was devoid of central heating, Simon beginning to shiver a little within the spartan confines of the makeshift netherworld music den he'd set up for himself, modest throw rug, starkly bare walls, an electric keyboard perched beside a desk strewn with page upon page of his magnum opus.

He went over to the geriatric space heater to crank up the knob, rubbing his hands together while the heater exhaled and sputtered out feeble heat, seating himself on a battered futon, furniture he was prone to collapse upon, emptied and exhausted, having sacrificed the better part of the night to his muse.

Bugaboo or boon? What might the sketchbook augur for the outcome of the opera he was having so much difficulty bringing to completion? He was, after all, writing an opera about the relation-ship of the two composers, an opera with no foreseeable ending. How was it all to conclude? And would it be possible for him to decode the sketchbook single-handedly in hopes of arriving at the answers he so badly sought?

He found himself thinking of Demetra again, wondering whether he should get in touch with her, mentioning how he just happened to stumble upon something *fairly significant*, something begging for her particular expertise, something he wished to discuss with her at her very earliest convenience: was this how an email to her should go?

He didn't actually know her very well, certainly not on any sort of personal level, though he'd always been sort of curious. A hard-working colleague, to be sure, a fastidious scholar and dedicated professor. Ambitious too—presenting papers at scholarly conferences in Evanston, New Haven, New York and Princeton, and abroad in Amsterdam, Oxford, Toronto, Vienna, Berlin. It wouldn't surprise him if other academic institutions were courting her. Within the scholarly realm of all things Schoenberg, Demetra Kouras was, after all, a *name*, a *preeminent* name.

Meanwhile, he felt as if he were groping through a strange fog, apprehensive about the moral and legal obligations of holding on to a priceless document, marching in place momentarily, unready as yet to come forward with his haul. At least not before he'd had the opportunity to thoroughly scour the manuscript and scrutinize its conundrums. For the time being, he would simply horde his find in an old valise, stashing it away here in his studio behind the bulwark of the old futon.

Plunging back into his swivel chair, he ran his fingers over one of the sketchbook's dry pages, wondering if perhaps Demetra would be able to account for the mysterious appearance of the Latin square. Would she be game for decoding its meaning? Should he entrust her with his secret? She might already come to the table with some knowledge about the *Orpheus* passages, after all, or be able to register a scholarly opinion about the uncanny appearance of the *Petrushka* excerpt. No doubt, she would be capable of shedding light on the document's separate musical autographs.

Turning towards his computer, he clicked open his email, conjuring some private meeting where he could present his case to her, a brief meeting—nothing heavy-handed—simply to get a feel for where her particular interests might lie, and in what specific ways she might be able to provide assistance.

Heartbeat pounding, he leaned forward to begin composing his message to her.

BOOK II

SIMON

MERCILESS TRAFFIC, the muddled terrain of the I-405 southbound, the final artery of four hellish freeways out of Glendale, his car lodged in an endless metallic waddage, a hostile glinting in the early morning sun, a million vessels all going nowhere. Doing nine miles per hour, he lurched into the Los Angeles basin, destination Westwood and still a ways away, already eleven minutes late for his morning lecture.

Simon's fingers plunged into the jumbo sack of M&M's wedged between his thighs (*your complete breakfast on the go!*), bringing to his lips a fistful of sticky disks.

Molto adagio e sostenuto, the flow of morning traffic constricted yet further, his foot hovering over the brake pedal as he crept through a larger geological landscape, atavistic canyons of the Santa Monica and San Gabriel mountains, slurping hot coffee from a travel mug, washing down jags of chocolate, surfing through the radio settings, not exactly up for the murine perkiness of a Telemann concerto on KUSC, or the traffic update's prophecy of his own demise, flipping past Mariah Carey to land upon glib analysis of the O.J. Trial and promptly hitting the *off* button.

A hopeless twelve miles still to go in unforgiving traffic to UCLA's Schoenberg Hall to present his morning lecture, a strenuous, three-hour presentation, *Twentieth Century Masters: Schoenberg & Stravinsky*.

Reaching for his phone, he keyed his and Stuart's office number, leaving a desperate voice message (*Delayed, running late in traffic from hell, I hate to ask—but could you do me a huge favor, Stu, and cover for me, let the students know I'll be a little tardy this morning? Sorry, but I feel like Boderman's got my neck in a vise over there and my ass is on the line. Thanks, buddy. I owe you big time.*).

And damn the absurd campus parking system designed no doubt to placate harried, commuting, junior faculty like him. The main problem being he'd again neglected to bring along his Staff parking sticker. In his funk—the morning funk he'd emerged from, having spent the better part of the night immersed in the sketchbook—he'd buckled himself into his car only to discover that his Camry was seriously lacking in the fuel department.

Well. He'd simply adjusted course, crossing two lethargic miles of surface streets, swooping into the parking lot at Glendale Community College, to conveniently swap vehicles before tearing out of there in Francine's Subaru.

Blinded now by the scimitar of morning sunlight, he took in the freeway spectacle, the miasma of stagnant, fuscous air cloaking Los Angeles, the five lanes of gridlocked cars entrapping him like the five-lined staves that held the notes of his own gridlocked opera.

A limousine slithered alongside, a loutish Lexus cut him off, rumbling big rigs belched out noxious fumes. Directly in front of him, a long trailer, perilously close, teetered ominously beneath its sloshing load of blue porta-potties.

Breathe. Relax, damn it.

Wasn't this step one in *Powerful Guided Meditations*, the CDs he'd picked up the other day at the Bodhi Tree? It was all about mindfulness. And letting go. *I am bigger than any of my problems.* Breathe. *Free yourself from the burden of expectation by surrendering completely to the present moment. Desire nothing and nothing will be lacking.*

Or so his portable lama had averred.

The opera commission, meanwhile, continued to sink its fangs into his neck, making it impossible and more than a little inconvenient, actually, to desire nothing.

We realize you're working intently towards completion, the recent email from Santa Fe's Artistic Director Ms. Lindsay Tundler had begun, *but we wish to be exceedingly clear about expectation regarding the terms of the contract agreed upon by all parties.*

At a quarter of a million dollars, both the financial incentive and pressures of the Santa Fe Opera commission were considerable. And, as conveyed in the email, the artistic board was in fact making itself *exceedingly* clear: firm due date in four weeks, no further deadline extensions to be considered. *Otherwise, regrettably, we will have no other option but to pull the plug on the project, rescinding our offer thereby.*

But, the thing was, he'd already squandered the better part of the advance Santa Fe had awarded him, the whole of fifty grand, splurging on a Steinway limited edition. Dropping into the piano store one afternoon a few months back, he'd managed to convince himself that such an inspiring instrument constituted a *professional necessity*, the Baby Grand irresistible, one humdinger of a write off, too, the very tool required for getting the job done. Brandishing credit card, he'd pushed aside concerns about the financial burden this would inevitably end up placing on Francine and family, the nest egg increasingly vulnerable these days, particularly now, given the possibly fatal repercussions of his recent teaching evaluation.

Thankfully, though, he wasn't all *that* far from wrapping things up with the opera. A sprawling three and a half years and running, though, with this current project of his, including three extensions on the deadline and sour partings of the way with two separate, tetchy librettists. Three and a half years.

Compared to, say, God, who'd managed to complete *His* creative project in only six days.

Working title of his opera: *Arnold & Igor.*

Seized with anxiety, he inhaled a *centering-and-fortifying* breath while focusing on the mantra.

May I be filled with loving kindness.

May I be peaceful and at ease.

May I embrace vehicular constipation.

Poco più mosso. Thanks be to God, the tempo of morning rush hour traffic picked up a click; only a few more miles to go. Surely, his students—in light of this morning's sluggish traffic problem—would be willing to wait a few minutes, no harm, no foul there. The universe would continue to unfold.

Be grateful. Count a few blessings while you're at it. The boys were safely off to school and Francine, after a display of contrite and princely behavior on his part, would eventually find it in her kind heart to cut him a little slack for his rash decision of exchanging cars. He resolved, right there and then, to sit down with her this evening, show her the document, and, no matter what was required, figure out how to make it up to her.

Leaning to the side, he placed a protective hand on the leather valise on the passenger's seat beside him, sensing the heady document inside, increasingly convinced that the sketchbook could actually *confirm* a secret collaboration between Schoenberg and Stravinsky.

And, if this were true, might the composers' relationship be in some way intertwined with his parents' complicated journey? Was this Schoenberg relic the missing link, the proof in the pudding he'd unknowingly been waiting for, that final puzzle piece that could determine the conclusion of his opera? The Latin palindrome, the *Petrushka* and *Orpheus* passages. If he could simply get a better handle on all of this, he sensed the ending of his opera would reveal itself.

Hallelujah! In his opera, Schoenberg and Stravinsky were destined to come together. Furthermore, he sensed strongly that all of this had something to do with the choreographer Elsa Růžek and the bizarre circumstances of her death—that Elsa's story, along with that of the composers, was somehow bound up with the heartrending story of his own parents.

Whooosh!

From out of nowhere, a diabolical bread truck swerved into his lane, Simon's car screaming to a halt as he hit the brakes, inches shy of a fender bender, slurry of obscenities, the coffee mug airborne, overturned, sloshing his pant leg and seeping into his sock.

Have you earned your bread today? the bread company slogan cheekily declared.

The Los Angeles Times

LAST DANCE:
ELSA RŮŽEK DIES; PILLS BLAMED

By DOROTHEA RONDO
July 31, 1947

Hollywood and the classical music world joined forces in mourning the loss of notable choreographer and motion picture artist, Elsa Růžek, whose funeral took place today at Rosedale Cemetery in the Pico-Union district of downtown Los Angeles.

Elsa Růžek, 37, ballerina, choreographer, set design consultant for several Hollywood blockbusters, was found dead in her Brentwood home last week due to a suspected drug overdose of sedatives and sleeping pills. Nembutal capsules were found around her bedside, as well as Secobarbital.

An investigation led by coroner Trevor B. Dalton and autopsy surgeon Dr. E. F. Geyer is still underway due to further speculation that a subdural hemorrhage may have occurred, possibly initiated by blunt head trauma. Růžek's husband, Claes Huylenbrouck, the well-known conductor who recently took up the helm as music director at both MGM and RKO film studios, was conspicuously absent from today's ceremony. Nor was he present earlier for questioning when Růžek's body was discovered by her cousins, Miss Marta and Mr. Ingo Kohler of Beverly Hills. Huylenbrouck remains presently at large and, according to Police Sergeant Percival Brooks, is currently being considered as a possible suspect in foul play.

Born in Prague in 1910, Růžek was raised in Berlin by a single mother, Vivian Růžek, a dancer and choreographer herself, who relocated to Paris to become a troupe member and assistant to Vaslav Nijinsky with Serge Diaghilev's *Ballets Russes*. The young Elsa Růžek studied ballet and film production in Paris, forming her own classical dance troupe before emigrating to Los Angeles with Huylenbrouck in 1933.

Elsa Růžek's artistry touched thousands of lives through a career that encompassed motion pictures, dance theater, and Broadway shows, including *Billion Dollar Baby* and *Lady in the Dark*. As choreographer/set designer, she worked on films such as *Ziegfeld's Follies*, collaborating with Fred Astaire and Ginger Rogers for RKO's *Follow the Fleet* and *Shall We Dance?*, and working alongside Rita Hayworth on *You'll Never Get Rich*. She has numerous other credits and achievements to her name.

The funeral brought together a formidable cast of musicians and musical luminaries acquainted with her through her work, or through her husband's work, among them conductors Bruno Walter and Otto Klemperer; composers Arnold Schoenberg, Sergei Rachmaninoff, Bernard Hermann, Cole Porter, Kurt Weill, Erich Zeisl, Jerome Kern, and Igor Stravinsky; and numerous musicians, including violinists Jascha Heifetz and Solomon Hersch, and singer Lotte Lenya. Present were writers W.H. Auden, Upton Sinclair, Henry Miller, Christopher Isherwood, and Thomas Mann; artists Man Ray and Salvador Dali, as well as Alma Mahler, Vicki Baum, Q. Chester Lund, and Howard Hughes.

A who's-who panoply of Hollywood notables was also in attendance, including moguls Louis B. Mayer, Sam Goldwyn, and Sid Grauman; actors Bing Crosby, Basil Rathbone, Douglas Fairbanks, Spencer Tracy, Harpo Marx, Errol Flynn, Edward G. Robinson, Paulette Goddard, Barbara Stanwyck, Jane Russell, Gloria Swanson, Ginger Rogers, Jean Harlow, Joan Crawford; and a smorgasbord of other celebrities.

"What indeed was the secret to her charm?" Sam Goldwyn commented. "How can one define the essence of that penetrating magnetism which seemed to affect so many people? She exemplified art and grace within the flow of her movements and, in transmuting form from script to screen, was able to render ideas fully alive, both on film as well as in the theater."

At the time of her death, Růžek was purpotedly collaborating with composer Arnold Schoenberg on an ambitious screenplay, film score, and choreographed sequences based upon the Orpheus myth and slated to be released by MGM. "She was certainly a woman of her time," Schoenberg commented mournfully after the funeral." She had a unique vitality and depth of artistic vision cut short by this shocking tragedy."

Every musician, actor, director, and dancer who knew Elsa Růžek personally or through her art is saddened today by the loss of one of the world's brilliant artists and choreographers. "The people of our city have suffered a great loss," Vera Stravinsky commented. "She was my great friend, and her life and career are a conspicuous part of the history of our own times."

Tableau III

Igor

"Anyone who wants to be a real musician must be able to
set a restaurant menu to music."

—Richard Strauss

FOLLOWING THE *PETRUSHKA* PERFORMANCE, Stravinsky, Diaghilev,
and the elegant Frau Růžek find themselves seated around the
Schoenberg dining room table at the Villa Lepcke, Schoenberg's wife,
Mathilde, hunched over a steamy skillet at the sideboard, Schoenberg,
at the head of the table, pouring wine into goblets, his eyes fiercely alive
in the glow of candlelight.

Stravinsky glances around the dining room, giddy and jittery—
gloating practically— still unable to get over the good fortune of actually
finding himself *here* at the Schoenberg Berlin residence. Accordingly,
he's spent extra time grooming, carefully parting his fine, coppery hair,
face impeccably shaven and glazed with eau de cologne. He wears an
expensive linen jacket, once his father's, a patterned ascot—indeed, an
almost dandified appearance, one might conclude.

The Schoenberg apartment is airy, fringed by walnut bookcases
and a decorative vase of dried coneflowers beside an upright piano.
Balmy heat wafts from the adjacent kitchen. Gold-rimmed souvenir
plates from Innsbruck, Salzburg, and Bavaria have been mounted to
the dining room wall. In one of the back rooms of the apartment,

Stravinsky can hear Trudi and Görgi, the two Schoenberg children, engaged in a game of checkers.

Gazing at the paintings hanging in the Schoenberg living room, Stravinsky is unsettled by how jarringly off kilter they appear, jostled and chaotically arranged. He zeros in on an askew Kandinsky fishing boat alongside a constellation of other smaller works, all of which are merely satellites around a central and sizeable self-portrait of Schoenberg. Drawn in blue crayon—thin lips, delicate chin, probing ears—the master's forbidding and unsmiling portrait scrutinizes Stravinsky from across the room.

When Schoenberg lifts his glass in a toast to *Petrushka*, Stravinsky smiles, basking in the adulation as he raises his own glass.

"An extraordinary presentation!" Frau Růžek says. She wears a long velvet dress, a choker necklace, a mantilla of dark lace. "I was captivated by the sets, by Nijinsky's astonishing dancing, and the way he seemed to completely inhabit the puppet character." She smiles. "And I'll admit I fell instantly in love with poor Petrushka, moved by his misfortune of falling in love with the ballerina."

With a hearty laugh, Diaghilev winks and says, "Well, we do strive to put on a good show, don't we, Igor?" He's dressed in a fine lavender suit, his jet black hair bisected by a white streak.

It's been quite a week. Schoenberg's stunning and unforgettable *Pierrot* performance and the opportunity to make his acquaintance, all further amplified by the favorable reception of *Petrushka*.

Mathilde scoops turnips with horseradish, fried cutlets, and meatballs in a viscid gravy onto plates, the three dinner guests murmuring contentedly as plates are handed around.

"Ah, *kotlety!*" Diaghilev exclaims, spearing a meatball with his fork and holding it up triumphantly. "Divine! My sister and I were practically weaned on *kotlety.*"

"My grandmother," Mathilde says dryly, "she instructed me on the recipe." She unfastens her apron, using it to pat at her brow then seats herself at the table. Stravinsky can't help but notice a certain dour expression, her face wan and enervated in the glimmer of the candelabra. Her head droops slightly, sinewy tresses of frowzy hair protrude from her hairpins. Wistful, Stravinsky thinks of his wife back in Morges, listless herself so much of the time, lungs worsening while coping with intensifying consumptive bouts, soldiering on, nonetheless, looking after the three little ones and running the household, polishing the silver, scattering flea powder over the bed sheets. By this time of year, even at lower climes, the Swiss Alps would be blanketed in snow, the frigid winter air scorching Katya's lungs. Last winter she was confined to a sanitarium at Sancellemoz upon the slope of a wooded mountain, undergoing a strict regime of *koumiss*, sipping the fermented mare's milk of the Tartars. He'd visited her there, shielded by a surgical mask, helpless as he watched her succumb to coughing fits, sallow and drawn, stooping weakly over her porcelain bed bowl to expectorate.

Now Stravinsky finds himself staring furtively across the table at Frau Růžek, admiring her high color and fine bone structure, her electric blue eyes.

Forks grate rhythmically against plates. Diaghilev attacks his cutlet with gusto, sampling the wine with a vague slurp.

"Now, Herr Schoenberg," Diaghilev says, dabbing his lips with a napkin, "do not protest at what I'm about to say. But I have an idea I think will amuse you."

Schoenberg sets his fork down with full attention.

"I'm wondering whether you might consider accepting a commission to write some sort of music for our *Ballets Russes*," Diaghilev says. The inquiry hits Stravinsky hard; never before has Diaghilev run any such proposal by him, though he shouldn't necessarily be surprised: the impresario-*bon vivant* is constantly casting out his net in search of newer and bigger fish.

"I'm afraid I am no composer of ballets," Schoenberg says.

"Bah!" Diaghilev responds. "Ballet, opera, symphony. All the same, really. It all comes down to staging in the end. And how one chooses to package it. *Es wird alle mit dem Badewasser kommen!*"

In the end, everything comes out with the bath water. Stravinsky notes how Diaghilev doesn't quite hit the mark with the German idiom. Turning to Mathilde, he asks about the paintings in the living room and her eyes appear to brighten as she indicates a cluster of paintings, a thickly-layered forest glade, a wide-eyed cat, a young girl poking a chary foot into a lake.

"Those over to the right I have painted," Mathilde informs him.

"They're lovely," Stravinsky says with a nod.

"And, there," Mathilde says, "on the other side, my husband has made his self-portrait. As well as more pictures."

Like expendable electrons orbiting around a central atom, the smaller paintings are dwarfed by the immense Schoenberg self-portrait. One painting features a pair of hands, another a tormented gray-haired woman with a black mouth and burning red eyes that appear to swirl within their sockets.

The incongruity of the paintings. He can't get over the way they seem to have been so haphazardly mounted, an unsettling disunion of *his & hers* artworks that make him want to get up from his chair to go over and straighten everything out.

"Forgive me," he says to her, "but I had no idea you and your husband were *both* painters."

For an unbearably long moment, Mathilde remains silent. Stravinsky follows the trickle of warm wax as it makes its way down the candelabra's silver branch, pooling onto the oil cloth. He stares into the candle's shimmering ghost, wondering whether he may have misspoken and inadvertently offended her, while conjuring a player piano roll upon which his remarks have been perforated and encrypted, and might therefore be redacted.

Mathilde's lips part. "I *was* a painter." She turns away, slowly shaking her head. "But. No longer." Abruptly, she stands, muttering something about seeing after the children before promptly departing from the room.

Frau Růžek and Diaghilev, meanwhile, are discussing some sort of project, Diaghilev enumerating the countless opportunities for dancers and qualified choreographers in Paris these days.

"And, with our own *Ballets Russes*," Diaghilev says, patting her arm, "why, someone possessed of your particular talents would, of course, in no time meet with fantastic success."

From the head of the table, Schoenberg scowls. "I should think one hardly need go scrounging around Paris for creative sustenance. Really, one need go no further than Berlin."

"Undoubtedly," Diaghilev is quick to respond with a diplomatic nod as he fiddles with his waxy moustache. "And while this may indeed be the case, I prefer to think that dance in Paris is currently reaching some new and enthralling apogee."

"Frau Růžek has already a slew of commitments in Berlin," Schoenberg says with a stony expression. "Maestri Furtwängler and Bruno Walter have both been pressing me for recommendations for the upcoming opera and ballet seasons."

Stravinsky steals a glance at Frau Růžek as she stares into her plate, kneading her napkin.

"Furthermore, there's her family to consider," Schoenberg says, puffing his cheeks. "I should think it rash, not to mention poor form, to uproot, *mitten drinnen*, exporting oneself over to Paris like some alien cultivar of potato."

"*Potato!*" Frau Růžek exclaims with a laugh. "But, Arnold, I insist: you mustn't flatter me! After the endless tribulations of my dancing career, I'm not sure potato's the commodity that readily comes to mind."

"Of course not, Vi," Schoenberg says with a wave of his hand, "though I think you see my point."

Opting for levity, Stravinsky pokes his fork into his plate of uneaten vegetables. "Although, an uprooted potato still maintains a status a notch or two above a dancing turnip."

Diaghilev and Frau Růžek chuckle, just as Mathilde reenters the room and returns to her seat.

"In fact, I'll have you know," Schoenberg says with a vague smirk, "Vivian and I have been discussing, between the two of us, a collaboration of music and dance. *Und so.* As I think now it may be only too plain for all parties present to—"

"Arnold," Mathilde hisses, "must you persist always in speaking for others?"

Schoenberg's glare is murderous.

Pointing at Mathilde, he says, "*You* have no right to judge." The veins in his forehead protrude and he clutches his serviette, twisting it in his fingers. "*You*, of all people, have no such right!"

Bristling, Stravinsky holds his breath, afraid to move.

"*Disgusting*," Schoenberg says under his breath, "*ganz widerlich. Es kocht mein Blut.*"

Mathilde gnaws her lip. The radiator hisses. A water droplet plummets into the kitchen basin with a terrifying, reverberant plonk.

From the rear of the apartment, the children giggle over something, Trudi reciting a bedtime story to Görgi, her five-year old brother, a fairytale about a cruel little boy who goes around delightedly torturing tiny animals and innocent people.

Finally, Diaghilev draws a sharp breath. "Well, it appears, for the time being anyhow, we shall be forced to table our discussions." He looks around the table then leans back to light a thin cigar. "In any case, let's none of us place the apple cart on top of the horse just yet."

SIMON

Schoenberg and Stravinsky secretly collaborated.

At the lectern, tortured and enthralled by such speculation, he was gripped by a queasy feeling, an acidic taste loitering in his mouth, his belly thudding as if some irascible percussionist were down there banging away.

Simon scanned the tidy rows of students, an array of Bruin beverage mugs and water bottles, morning pastries balanced precipitously upon the edges of wooden fold-out desks, sixty or so undergraduate eyeballs trained on him while their professor fussed with the laptop, eager for his PowerPoint (*SCHOENBERG/STRAVINSKY*) to boot, the students' expressions patient and understanding, yet expectant, eager for the professor to profess—for the composer to compose himself.

"During the 1940s Arnold Schoenberg and Igor Stravinsky, the two pillars of twentieth century music, immigrate separately from Europe to Southern California," Simon began. "And in so doing, the entire history of Western music, which has been percolating nicely in Europe for a good seven centuries or so, shifts right along with them."

He gulped a breath of air, the lecture hall balmy this morning, his beard and neck clammy. "Indeed, the entire core of musical modernism pivots, essentially, from Western Europe to Western Los Angeles.

"The political upheavals leading up to the Second World War force both composers to pull up roots and flee Europe." He continued, well aware of his slightly feral smell, his sock still soaked through, squishy from the overturned coffee during this morning's commute. "By the time the Nazi flag is waving in Germany and Austria in 1933, Schoenberg, a Jew, has already made his way out of Germany to settle in the U.S.

"Meanwhile, Stravinsky, displaced by the Russian Revolution and struggling to make ends meet during stretches of privation and uncertainty in Switzerland and France, makes *his* way to the U.S. only a couple of years later in 1939, giving the distinguished Norton Lectures in Music at Harvard before eventually settling in Los Angeles, not far from Schoenberg, in Beverly Hills."

He moistened his lips, feeling the pinch of his corduroys. His pores had become suction cups, miniature octopuses clinging to his starched Oxford.

"And so, there they are," he said, "our two great luminaries, living side by side, not all that far from where we are right now. They wind up residing a few miles from one another for more than a decade. And yet." Simon scanned his audience. "During all this time, the paths of these two geniuses essentially… *never… intersect.*"

He let the statement linger for a moment like a dust cloud, sickened by its over-simplification, his willful obfuscation, a part of him, meanwhile wanting to scream, *Don't listen to any of this, you people. They did in fact meet! And, by the way, everything I'm now professing to you is essentially up for grabs!*

His lecture, he knew, wasn't *the whole story.* Not even close.

Dogma and convention had conveniently painted these estranged rivals into two separate corners of the boxing arena, though Simon's own private opinion, his *gut feeling* about the way things really might have played out, contradicted this.

He glanced out at his students, impressionable, biddable, docile almost, beneath the blaze of fluorescents, immersed in their note-taking, digesting his fodder seemingly without further ado, the promising Pat Clark leaning across his seat to whisper some clever *bon mot* to Joy Rasmussen; Milton Arrillaga and Christine Bald, lovebirds dripping with affection, hands furtively intertwined beneath desktops; Anica Koren sprawled across her seat, glasses perched low on her nose, glaring his way per usual as if she'd just ingested a bad mollusk; while Randy Fox, no doubt savoring the final bobbing figments of some reefer-induced hallucination, blinked with terminal uncertainty, looking even more strung out than he had during last week's Mahler lecture.

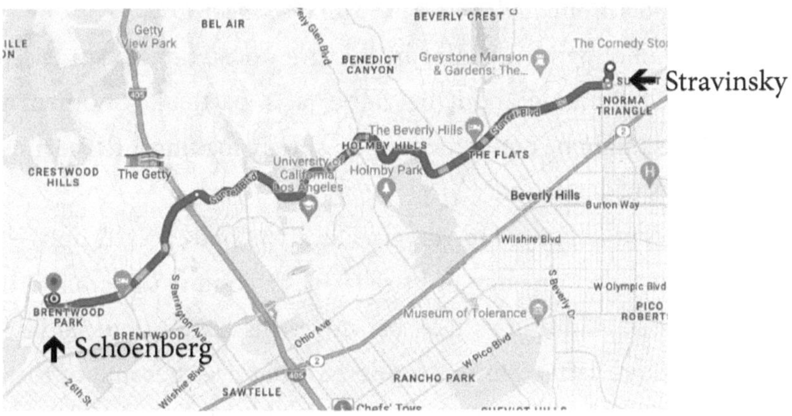

"Here's a map, laying out the eight-mile route between their two homes," Simon continued, "proceeding from the Schoenberg's Brentwood home at 116 North Rockingham Avenue (which—*ahem!*—FYI, happens coincidentally to be situated on the same street and a mere few houses down from the notorious O.J. Simpson house), to the Stravinsky home at 1260 N. Wetherly Drive in Beverly Hills.

"Take a good look at how close these two lived to one another for a good decade. Virtually within the same zip code. Had zip codes been around, fifty years ago."

Were they stirring in their seats, the students, a little restless? At the midway mark of the quarter, they must have been fairly worn down, tired, no doubt, of waiting for his frumpy arrival, miffed when he'd huffed in grimacing and twenty-three minutes late for the lecture.

He'd abandoned the car—*her* car—in a restricted, two-hour residential zone off Hilgard somewhere, consigning its windshield to another parking ticket, easily his twentieth or so in the last weeks. He'd left Francine a brief voice message, apologizing profusely for taking her car in his panic. Then, like some wounded ibex, he'd galumphed across campus in his coffee-drenched sock, laptop bag and valise alternately flailing and bucking on their shoulder straps like twin wrecking balls intent on tenderizing both sides of his torso.

After Mom died, where did you disappear to?

Fumbling to organize his lecture notes, he was surprised to find himself thinking about his father at a particular moment when all efforts might be better focused on simply making it to the finish line of today's presentation.

What happened to you guys, exactly? he'd worked up the nerve to ask his father one day, age twelve or so, coming upon his father at the desk of his upstairs study, bent over his leather journal beneath the gooseneck lamp. Simon wondered what ever became of that journal, remembering his father's cluttered desk and the ledger book in which Jasper kept a record of his gardening clients' accounts, Simon recalling, as well, the Fabergé egg, the gift Stravinsky had presented.

And what about me? this newly-intrepid young man had further ventured. *If you weren't around, and Mom wasn't around, then who was around to look after me?*

But his father, so often effusive when out working in some garden or another, now appeared to recoil, stiffening, nudging the journal aside, and retreating into reticence.

Simon, please, his father said quietly, *there's no need to do any further backtracking down that particular road. What's done is done. For everything there is a season, as the saying goes. All things in their own time.*

Now, suddenly the heavy vestibule door at the top of the lecture hall swung open with a sinister squeal, Simon glancing up, pulse ratcheting into a mortifying *allegro agitato assai* as the forbidding figure of Dean Boderman stepped into the lecture hall. The room now seemed to be charged with something akin to the entrance of the proverbial movie gunslinger, the unsettling figure outlined in the shadow of a swaying saloon door.

But what was this? His boss returning for a final surprise attack, extending surveillance and gathering additional intel—further evidence of his charge's professorial ineptitude?

Molto diminuendo e subito pianissimo. Suddenly the room seemed to have gone stone still, Simon locking eyes with Boderman, who stood tight-lipped at the top of the auditorium, folding his arms.

"Now. As I mentioned in class the other day," Simon croaked out, addled and frantically retracing his steps while gulping in a few good molecules of air, "it seems the composers *did* meet on rather amicable terms in Berlin in 1912." He swallowed hard. "But, by the 1920s, certainly, their artistic paths diverged, as Schoenberg unveiled his twelve-tone method—or *serialism*—precisely when Stravinsky began to look back towards older musical models of *neo-classicism*. Each composer was struggling to bring something new into the world, and perhaps could do so only with the thought that he alone was right."

Good God! Murmurings, restless rumblings, minor fracases now seemed to be breaking out in every sector of the room, a fugue of commotion, Boderman dolefully jotting detailed and no doubt incendiary observations into that official pocket-sized notepad he enjoyed carrying around, the same compact doomsday book Simon had noticed previously during official *scheduled* teaching evaluations.

Helpless, he stole a glimpse of his students, wondering whether—*possibly*—such a spontaneous rumpus constituted that critical benchmark of student engagement he'd been so set on achieving, or whether this particular teaching situation was in fact more akin to unvarnished anarchy. Was this particular level of engagement indicative of the *empowerment* and *self-accompanying learning modalities* Boderman loved espousing?

We'd really love to try and keep you aboard here on our team, Boderman had said to him the other day. *Among our Bruin family.*

Now, feeling as if someone had managed to squeeze his head into an unyielding tourniquet, Simon glanced around again before raising his voice.

"Please!" he hollered, tossing his hands in the air, "if we could all just—" His voice was unsteady, no more effective than a quaking shawm. He felt lightheaded, winded, his skin prickly. "If everyone could please—"

He stole another peek up at Boderman, who continued to stand there stonily, his towering frame, broad forehead, and king-sized hands looming over the lecture hall like Don Giovanni's *Il Commendatore.*

"We can spend a good amount of time *surmising,*" he struggled to articulate as, finally, the hullaballoo began to subside, "endlessly debating. What *might* have taken place." His tongue felt torpid, useless as a beached whale.

"But the picture that music historians portray," he managed, "is that of two eccentric geniuses existing on separate planes, their musical styles diverging into distinct camps by this point, and into two polarized schools."

Forwarding the slide on the screen to *The Second Viennese and the Neoclassical Schools,* he used his shirt cuff to swab at perspiration sluicing down his face. "And, as each grappled to define modern music, the two wound up on entirely different musical paths, paths which became— for many reasons we'll be examining more closely—irreconcilable."

For some reason—*fuck!*—his laptop screen had now gone completely black, Simon gnawing at his lip, temples throbbing, praying the thing had merely gone into sleep mode while jabbing hopelessly at random keys on his console as if performing in some nightmarish piano recital, imagining the wolfish smack of Boderman's lips among the fidgety students as he fought off a certain bilious lurching in his abdomen, intent on finding a little comfort within the stanchion his head had now been crammed into prior to the slaughter.

—⁓—

FLAMMABLE FLEM TRIUMPHS IN PASADENA

November 9 1941 | DOROTHEA RONDO

Despite a reputation for being challenging to get along with and an almost boorish tendency at times for placing his musicians under rather extreme emotional strain, Flemish-American Conductor Claes Huylenbrouck's performance of Alban Berg's *Lulu Suite* and Mahler's *Das Lied von der Erde*, presented last night with the Pasadena Civic Orchestra, was, nonetheless, a resounding triumph.

The Berg *Lulu Suite* featured highly refined musical moments, haunting and near-ecstatic, particularly throughout the fourth movement variations, the result, no doubt, of Huylenbrouck's decisive command and uncanny ability to consistently deliver vital performances, which are anything but commonplace.

Maestro Huylenbrouck, whose podium style with the orchestra some musicians begrudge as an intimidating amalgam of exacting surgeon and totalitarian dictator, accomplished an ethereal balance in the Mahler, exposing subtleties of timbre rarely achieved in performances, the Mahler further enhanced by incandescent vocal passages from rising mezzo soprano star Helena Dent.

Already at 39, Huylenbrouck's temper is legendary. He demands the utmost perfection from his players and will stop at nothing to achieve it. One anonymous musician in the orchestra commented, "Playing for him, one has the feeling of being utterly alone, and watched at every moment beneath the maestro's scalding glare."

SIMON

"There is nothing I long for more intensely, if
for anything, than to be taken for a better sort of
Tchaikovsky…Or if anything more then, that people
should know my tunes and whistle them."
—Arnold Schoenberg

"SCHOENBERG'S MUSIC might be considered anything but a toe-tapper, and certainly nothing you'd go around whistling."

A few minutes shy of wrapping up his lecture, Simon had just finished playing passages from Schoenberg's *Pierrot Lunaire* and his atonal melodrama, *Erwartung,* on the CD player, his presentation now fully retrieved and back up on the screen, thanks to the charitable Anders Björklund who'd hurried down the aisle to save the day, restoring everything via a judiciously minimalist series of six or so keyboard clicks, Simon thereafter spending the next moments going over further biographical details on the two composers—Stravinsky's Russian roots and French influences, Schoenberg's initial awe of Wagner and, later, Brahms.

"I doubt Webern or Berg went around whistling Schoenberg," Simon told his students, profoundly relieved when the door at the top of the lecture hall clicked quietly and Boderman vanished. "Nor was Schoenberg's own family *whistling* Schoenberg, I don't think. In fact, I'd venture to say, Schoenberg himself probably wasn't even whistling Schoenberg."

From the front row, Selwyn Khaw's hand shot up to ask what Schoenberg *was* whistling.

"A good deal of Brahms probably," Simon responded, amused by the question. "Haydn, Beethoven, Bach. Mahler! Plus a sprinkle of Schütz and Gesualdo for good measure."

"But, I mean, if you can't *whistle* Schoenberg," Kendra Lapenia asked, extending legs sheathed in spandex, "can you at least *dance* to him?"

"Interesting question," Simon said. "In general, Schoenberg's music may not be quite as *danceable and theatrical*, or even for some, as *palatable* as Stravinsky's. But, in terms of dissonance, I invite you to consider what a shocking and radical move such *unwhistleability* represented at the dawn of the twentieth century during a time when Tchaikovsky and Brahms had only been out of the game a mere three decades or so, and as composers like Elgar, Puccini, and Rachmaninoff—tunesmiths all—were meanwhile still churning out good old-fashioned melodies which lent themselves, unequivocally, to singing, humming, and, yes, whistling."

He sucked in a breath. "And all of this didn't represent just another ellipsis from, say, the Classical era to the Romantic. But something I would describe as much more radical. Something much more *threatening.*"

Christine Bald raised her hand. "But isn't it true things tend to change over time? I mean, *The Rite of Spring.* That was shockingly dissonant in its own day, right? But now look. It's totally part of the mainstream."

"Ah, so true," Simon said. "Amazing what a few years can do to help absorb the shock of modernism. When we look at a painting, the eye, for whatever reason, is able to assimilate new modes of expression more quickly than the ear. When Picasso famously renounced *perspective* in painting, this was embraced, at least by many, as a new visual language. But, at the same moment, people recoiled when Schoenberg bent all the rules of harmony while renouncing *tonality*." He shrugged. "In any case, Beethoven, Wagner, Picasso, Van Gogh; James Joyce, Virginia Woolf, T.S. Eliot. The list of artists who were initially misinterpreted, misconstrued, or rejected flat out is extensive."

"In a way, though, I sort of agree," Randy Fox said, sniffing. "Atonality, non-tonality, tunelessness. It sort of creeps me out, you know? It's like the man's willfully *trying* to ruin classical music or something."

"And I'd say you're not alone in that concern," Simon said. "Schoenberg has often been labeled as abstract, theoretical, and even an *archenemy of tune*. Though I would argue his intention was not to *shock* the audience but rather to reflect *shocking* times.

"That said, many music historians claim that Schoenberg's musical doctrine was responsible for one of the most revolutionary changes in the techniques of music that history has known, a doctrine that broke completely with the past, his twelve-tone system singlehandedly exerting the greatest influence of any system in music history, possibly, since the church modes were discarded centuries ago in favor of major and minor scales." He brightened. "In any case, certainly a composer worth getting to know more thoroughly."

Simon exhaled. "Ah, Schoenberg." He paused, allowing the heroic name to reverberate in the lecture hall within the very building on campus named for the composer.

"Mainstream? Music that's conducive to whistling?" Simon folded his arms with a little laugh. "Nah, somehow, I don't think so. *Nobody* whistles Schoenberg."

from the journal of Jasper Grafton

Beverly Hills
17 October 1943

Whistling! Whistling Schoenberg! And, of all places, in the Stravinsky garden.

Shoulder deep in shrub, wielding loppers in the war against Pittosporum undulatum, Victorian Box, & the Buxus hedgerow flanking the Stravinskys' Mediterranean-style villa, I cease my whistling when suddenly, out of thin air, it wd. seem, Igor Stravinsky materializes, rapidly torpedoing my way.

Stravinsky: bespectacled, short & spry, knitted cricket sweater, white slacks, sandals. Wants to know what I'm whistling. 'Whistling?' I inquire innocently, hoping to keep my secret under wraps, well-nigh mortified, meanwhile, by my indiscretion. Certainly, one should refrain from whistling Schoenberg in the Stravinsky garden.

Stravinsky undertakes a courtly bow. Heavy cough, scanty moustache, nose fleshy & protuberant, long-lobed ears. Waving the thin 'Gauloise' that lives between his knuckles, insisting I whistle the tune again, my cheeks coloring to a blush akin to that of Mrs. Stravinsky's plump heirlooms over on the other side of the garden.

Whistling Schoenberg for Stravinsky. No mean feat. Paralyzed by his certain half-starved avian stare, a penetrating glance beneath hooded eyelids, I'm aware of a mild glaze of sweat as I rest the pair of loppers upon the hedge while conjuring how my dear sweet Helena might render the phrase, her voice rising and steadily gaining in power while singing passages from Schoenberg's portion of the Requiem for Vivian Růžek.

My gaze roving over the garden to the spiky Bear's Breeches, Acanthus mollis, in need of intervention, Stravinsky tilting his head like a bird of prey when I've finished whistling, gnome-like, lips taut, inquiring with still more persistence about my whistling.

Quicker on my feet this time: 'Dunno, just some ditty from someplace, must have gotten lodged, you know, up inside the old noggin.'

Stravinsky, draws a deep drag from his Gauloise: 'Well, whatever it is, the good gardener seems to've planted some little seed, sparked something in me.' When I inquire about his portion of the requiem he frowns and looks away, thrusting his hands into baggy-kneed trouser pockets. The Requiem's performance is to take place in only a few weeks, Helena more than a little panicked having thus far only received Schoenberg's portion.

Stravinsky grimaces, eyes screwed up behind his pince-nez while complaining about insomnia and various other afflictions, providing a bronchial blow-by-blow, all the while puffing away on his cigarette, lamenting how the cough keeps him up at night, siphoning away all energy as next he recollects for me his nicotine poisoning years ago, and the typhus he contracted from an insidious oyster not long after composing Le Sacre du Printemps. 'Seven weeks in hospital at Neuilly,' he says, 'sick as a dog. Diaghilev stayed away, refusing to visit, terrified of catching something, though he was kind enough to take care of the hospital bill. Ravel, though, showed up and wept at my bedside.'

Stravinsky coughs. 'Fate can be cruel, Jasper. The gods send me the inspiration for The Rite of Spring then thank me by poisoning me.'

I suggest squill, Urginea scilla, the lily-like plant which grows from a bulb, nature's indomitable suppressant & expectorant, assuring him I'll do my best to try and get hold of some for him, along with a sprig of Motherwort perhaps for the jangled nerves.

Eager to get back to composing, Stravinsky bids me a good afternoon, flitting around flower pots on the tiered patio, mounting the wisteria-enshrouded brick steps of the loggia and, seconds later (would ya get a load of that?) plucking out on the piano in his upstairs music studio the very notes I've just whistled.

But how strange! What can he be up to in his studio, puttering around with Schoenberg's melody, turning it over as if searching for a personal foothold in his rival's music?

A dragonfly alights upon an umbel of bronze fennel as I kneel to assess the imperious tuft of quackgrass mounting an ambush of Myrtle and Eleagnus. Traipsing past Vera Stravinsky's art studio, in my dungarees and wellies, headed towards the kitchen garden, I'm pleased with the cabbage & beet rows, the trellises loaded with painted serpent cucumber, buttery crookneck with lime-green blossom ends, & tomatoes—bulging, blushing, beguiling—Cherokee Purple, Old German, John Baer, Hillbilly, Hungarian Heart, Tommy Toe.

Dutch hoe scratching the soil, my rastrum imprints a musical staff across the earth as I plow the loam beside old Fagus sylvatica, the stately beech with its gray elephantine trunk, the watchful white eyes of lavender larkspur, speckle-throated foxglove plumes, pendulous angel's trumpets, creamy orange & fragrant.

I guide my plow, accompanied by Stravinsky playing Schoenberg, Arepo's hoe combing the earth, keeping the work circling.

Sator arepo tenet opera rotas.

Busily nectaring, the honey bees do their work.

Two households both alike in dignity. Strange this bee I've become, fluttering to & fro between rival gardens, a hired hand employed by Montagues & Capulets.

Crouching, I run my fingers over the dusky velvety flowers, a voluptuous blue shawl of borage, the bees floating nearby in the warmth. Vast sky, fulgent sun, music of the earth. The bees pay me little attention. Legs loaded with pollen, they attend to their duty, amenable to sharing the flowers.

Dipping from flower to flower, the bees do their work.

Tableau IV

Arnold

WITH A JOLT OF excitement, Schoenberg unlocks the oak cabinet in the living room, lugging his sketchbook over to where Stravinsky's seated at the piano.

"But what an exquisite thing," Stravinsky says, running a finger over the cover. "Did you bind this yourself?"

Nodding, Schoenberg pulls open the book to a random page, fragments of a music drama, *Die glüchliche Hand,* he's been working on.

"What I wondered, though, is whether you wouldn't mind perhaps to jot down something from your *Petrushka.*"

"*Petrushka*?" Stravinsky asks. "Inside your book?"

Schoenberg waves a pen.

Stravinsky swirls an ornate treble clef onto a blank page, hesitant at first, Schoenberg exclaiming, *Wunderschön!* fascinated by the meticulous penmanship. They've been enjoying Turkish coffee from the samovar and a platter of Mathilde's *Mandelbrot.* Diaghilev departed earlier for another engagement followed shortly thereafter by Frau Růžek.

Demitasse nestled in his hands, Schoenberg studies Stravinsky's industrious notating, admiring the calligraphy and wondering about this guest, elegantly-dressed and leaning up against his piano in dark flannel trousers, prim cravat and studious horn-rimmed glasses. Eight years his junior, Stravinsky's a trim man, wiry and short in height like himself. Abundantly energetic and exuberant. Like a Mozart symphony. Prominent nose, lips somewhat oversized.

"I'm curious to know what you make of all this fuss between M. Diaghilev and Frau Růžek," Schoenberg says. "This talk of the Parisian ballet."

"One never quite knows what new trick Diaghilev may have up his sleeve. But, well, that's Diaghilev for you. Always on the lookout for new talent." Stravinsky smiles. "But, good God, you know, they say the man could charm a corpse."

When Stravinsky resumes notating, Schoenberg studies him with further scrutiny. Whatever Diaghilev may have up his sleeve, such wooing of Vivian must not come to pass. After all, why should he entertain the thought of sharing Vivian, his colleague, friend, and confidante?

The living room door clicks open and the two young Schoenberg children, all elfin grins, tramp across the carpet in woolen pajamas and yellow nightcaps to kiss their father good night.

Absolutely not, Schoenberg resolves. Under no circumstances will he sanction her traveling to Paris to pursue whatever outrageous idea Diaghilev may have up his sleeve.

"No, no, no," Schoenberg mutters, "This simply will not do."

Crestfallen, Stravinsky reddens. Indicating the passage he's just painstakingly copied down into the sketchbook, he shrugs. "You want I should stop?"

Later, the two share the piano bench, playing through four-hand arrangements of the Old Masters, Beethoven, Schubert, and Brahms symphonies, Stravinsky inquiring in between selections about Schoenberg's oil painting on the wall depicting Mahler's burial in Vienna last year.

"You knew Mahler well?"

"The world for me is an entirely different place now since Mahler departed it," Schoenberg says. "A true visionary. A source of solidarity and inspiration. I didn't fully realize it when we were both in Vienna, though now, in retrospect, it's only too plain."

"I was fortunate also to have such a mentor," Stravinsky says, "my composition teacher, Rimsky-Korsakov."

"Something of a spiritual father for me, Mahler was." Schoenberg shakes his head. "I don't think there's any getting around it. Somehow, we must find this essential father figure."

"Father figure," Stravinsky echoes, as now he proceeds to play various motifs from a ballet-in-progress, *The Rite of Spring,* pounding out on the keyboard a barrage of discordant sounds and palpitating cross-rhythms, percussive dissonances—E-major in the treble, thrashing against E-flat major-seven in the bass—the piano trembling as his compact body gyrates and the entire room seems to sway in discord.

"Disturbingly beautiful!" Schoenberg hollers above the noise.

"A sacrificial offering!" Stravinsky hollers back.

From out of nowhere, Mathilde appears, storming towards them, dressed in an old nightgown and violently jabbing at Stravinsky's shoulder, intent on breaking up the pagan ritual he's been reenacting in the Schoenberg living room, Stravinsky turning to confront his enraged aggressor, whose hisses prompt him to lift both hands from the keyboard as if it were a furnace, plunging his fingers into his armpits. *The Rite of Spring* reverberates before dissolving into silence as an embarrassed grin spreads over Stravinsky's face, the face of the schoolboy miscreant caught in the act of larceny.

"*Bitte!*" Mathilde says. Her hair is tangled in obstinate knots. "The children. These noises you make. You disturb their rest."

As if on cue, from the back of the apartment, little Görgi begins to wail, Schoenberg cringing instinctively, remembering the fateful day years ago in Vienna when the sick and tormented baby howled and howled and Mathilde was nowhere to be found.

Bowing his head, Stravinsky apologizes and, seemingly appeased,

Mathilde strokes Stravinsky's shoulder, petting the precise spot she's just pummeled.

"I assure you, Mati, we will be more careful," Schoenberg says.

Mathilde looks Stravinsky up and down as if considering a purchase. Then, glowering at her husband, she says, "For the love of God, control yourselves."

"*Ach,*" Schoenberg mutters once she's left the room. "Do not mind Mathilde. She is not herself." Sighing, he gestures towards the keyboard. "But, *sotto voce* maybe this time. And, if you wouldn't mind, maybe something now from *Petrushka.*"

Elated, Stravinsky places a foot over the damper pedal, demonstrating his *Petrushka* chord to Schoenberg, C-major juxtaposed over F-sharp major, launching into a muted rendition of the *Russian Dance,* the same excerpt he's penned into Schoenberg's sketchbook.

Schoenberg croons with enthusiasm, turning now towards the bookcase to nudge aside plump volumes of Balzac and Strindberg before locating a copy of his *Pierrot* score, along with an unwieldy manuscript, *Art and Scholasticism,* unpublished essays by a Heidelberg colleague, Jacques Maritain. He places both manuscripts on top of the piano as gifts for Stravinsky, who seems touched by the gesture.

Seating himself at the piano bench alongside Stravinsky, he begins to play his *Six Little Piano Pieces,* op. 19.

But a moment later, Mathilde swoops in again, fuming, predacious, snapping her fingers at her husband.

"Arnold Franz Walter Schoenberg!" she cries. "Your music continues to disturb us!"

Schoenberg exhales heavily, placing his trembling hands in his lap. "I am sorry," he says calmly, "for all your suffering."

Mathilde grimaces. "Do not patronize me."

"I am sorry my music causes you so much grief."

"Your music," she says with an acidic stare, "it suffocates me."

SIMON

Settling into the plush designer chair in Demetra's office, Simon admired the vase of orange tiger lilies on her desk, alongside a musicology book she appeared to be annotating. Atop the bookcase, a round wooden clock's frantic time-keeping was juxtaposed with the lush resonance of a brass ensemble rehearsing Gabrieli somewhere along the corridor.

He'd been up here occasionally for subcommittee meetings, textbook evaluations, budgetary discussions, her scholarly chamber easily four times the size of the water-stained subterranean hovel, the yellowing airless crypt in the bowels of the music building, he and Stuart shared.

"So," Demetra said, "how can I be of help?"

Her expression was serious, all business. It occurred to him she might have little interest in sacrificing valuable time to confer with the likes of some junior faculty colleague. Her hair was carefully braided. She wore a charcoal gray pencil skirt, a silk blouse with polka dots and a necklace of wooden beads.

"Your email the other night," she said. "It struck me you had something pretty urgent you needed to discuss."

Tongue-tied, unsure how exactly to delve into things, he fidgeted with the handles of the valise.

"What's on your mind?" she asked. "I'm all ears."

She happened to have lovely ears. Like perfect shells, Simon thought, spangled and adorned with silver and topaz.

He sat forward, "Listen," he said, glancing back at the closed door and lowering his voice. "No one knows about this."

Curious, she searched his face.

Simon swallowed. "All of this. It's— *confidential.*"

"Is everything all right?"

"No," he said, shaking his head, "yes! Of course."

Eyebrows knitted, she asked, "You're not in any sort of trouble?"

"No, no, nothing like that," Simon said, shaking his head as Boderman's carnivorous grin came to mind, his problematic teaching evaluation.

She smiled. "Well, that's good."

"Listen," he said. "What I'm about to say to you needs to stay right here in this room."

Demetra nodded, miming the zipping up of lips and raising three fingers. "Scout's honor."

"What if I were to tell you about a secret?" he said, leaning in closer so that their knees were nearly touching. "A few days ago. The weirdest thing happened." He glanced quickly at the valise beside him, explaining how he was still reeling, still trying to make sense of everything.

Demetra's green eyes got bigger. "The other afternoon! You were running late, hurrying off somewhere."

"Bingo."

Their hands momentarily brushed and he felt his face flush, the cool edge of her sterling bangle, ruffle of a sleeve, the softness of her skin.

Antsy, he said, "I seem to have stumbled upon something." He fumbled some more with the valise handles, studying her expression. They could hear the rubbery squelch of someone hurrying by, along the corridor.

Grinding his molars, he asked, "What if I were to tell you about a secret document, something which, for reasons I'm still struggling to understand, seems to have fallen into my hands."

She was staring at him, intensely curious now.

"A sketchbook," he said, unsettled by the word, and yet, noticing how rapt she'd become as she sat forward in her chair, ready to listen to whatever he had to say.

"I mean, there's a reason," he said, "a pressing reason, actually, that I wanted to meet with you." He drew in a great breath. "Because, I think, *you*—you, of all people—might be especially interested in hearing who this sketchbook seems to have belonged to."

She crept a few more inches forward in her seat, their knees nearly touching again.

Meeting her gaze, he said slowly, "Arnold Schoenberg."

"Jesus," she muttered.

"No," he said, "but close."

Narrowing her gaze, she blinked slowly. "Hold on a second. You're telling me you just *happened* to stumble upon—" Again she blinked, the floodgates of her vast intellect beginning to open, that incandescent musicological mind, Simon, meanwhile, grinning like the Cheshire cat.

"But—" she said with greater urgency. "Wait. I don't understand." Her brow furrowed. "What is this *document* you claim to have found?"

"The lost sketchbook."

She swallowed hard.

"I assumed you'd be interested," he said.

"Interested?" she cried, exploding with laughter. "My God, Simon. *The lost sketchbook?*"

"Crazy, right?" he said with a laugh, "I know."

He leaned over, plunging his hands into the valise, triumphant as he retrieved the document, setting it down before her on the table like a sacred offering.

"It's unbelievable," she said quietly.

"Welcome to *my* world."

She opened the cover very slowly, mesmerized, murmuring to herself, Simon watching as she leafed carefully through the opening pages, verifying immediately the sketchbook's authenticity and provenance.

He watched her examining it. He liked watching her. Willowy, studious, coaxing a wisp of dark hair behind an ear, poring over the manuscript, captivated, her mind focused and at full thrust, Simon sitting beside her observing the great scholar at work. It was almost as if he weren't officially conferring with her but, instead, spying on her. Electrifying. Her sweet fragrance and steady breathing, that way she had of sitting forward, provoked and yet calm, so engrossed in the manuscript now she seemed to have forgotten he was even in the room. Sitting this closely beside her, acquiescing to whatever this clandestine mission of theirs was destined now to become, he caught himself basking in the unspoken intimacy, intrigued by her powdery scent, her deeply-toned complexion, the striking contour of her jawline.

He allowed himself to sink back into the designer chair as he glanced around the room, noting a framed photograph on the filing cabinet, Demetra alongside some man who very well could have been her father. A bronze statue on the bookcase caught his eye, long and slender, a foot or so in length, a nude female with weathered face and skin.

"Ah, Giacometti's *Woman of Venice*," Demetra said when she noticed him staring at it, getting up to retrieve the statue and offering it to him.

He took hold of it with both hands, the base heavy, the woman's fragile and emaciated figure cool against his palms.

"A rather special statue, actually." She smiled pensively as she turned to place the statue back on the shelf. "It belonged to my father."

"The man in the photograph," Simon said, gesturing towards the file cabinet, Demetra nodding slowly, her expression a little wistful.

Then, indicating the document, she asked where on earth he could have stumbled upon such a thing, Simon disarmed and smiling tensely, anticipating such a line of questioning, of course, though uncertain about how much of his own personal family history he felt comfortable disclosing.

"Well, I can tell you one thing," he said, "none of this is due to any musicological prowess, whatsoever, on my part."

"No?"

"Long story," he told her, mumbling something about a friend of a friend, a tenuous family connection.

"But, your opera," she said. "You're writing about Schoenberg, if I'm not mistaken. Stravinsky as well."

"Right," he said, flattered she was familiar with his project. "Turns out this document may have actually changed hands a couple of times." He thought about Ingo's letter. "Tucked away in a drawer for a while in some music shop. But then found by someone, a violinist. Ingo Kohler."

"Not ringing any particular bell." She stared at him. "But, why you, Simon? And why just now? I'm still not clear on the connection."

"Me, neither," he said, looking away. "Honestly, I'm still trying to piece all of this together." She turned through more of the document, pausing when she came to the page with the Latin square.

```
S  A  T  O  R
A  R  E  P  O
T  E  N  E  T
O  P  E  R  A
R  O  T  A  S
```

"Ah, yes, good!" he said, "one of the many things I'd hoped to ask you about."

"Fascinating," she said. "Can't say I've ever seen it before. Definitely warrants investigation." Going over to her desk, she returned with pen and paper to copy down the palindrome. "I'd say we have our work cut out for us."

He glanced at the statue again. "Your father's statue, you had started to say?"

She pressed her lips together. "It was my father's longtime dream for me to become a scholar. Following in his footsteps." She gave a nervous laugh. "The man was rather insistent—cunning! Truth be known, rather obsessive. Finding clever ways to slip the term, *PhD*, into conversations, always prodding me, subtly and not-so-subtly."

"And here you are!" he said, indicating the lavish surroundings. "The scholar." He smiled at her. "Seems your father may have been right, all along."

"Well, Papa always said I'd make one *lulu* of a scholar some day. That was the word he liked to use: *Well, that was certainly one* lulu *of a book!* he would say, something like that." She shook her head. "Papa. Quite the scholar himself. Dr. Panos Kouras, PhD, Classical Literature—Egyptian, Greek, Macedonian." She bit her lip. "Right up until his dying breath, he pretty much expected the world of me."

Simon nodded, flashing upon his own father, wondering whether he'd ever felt that same paternal pressure of having to live up to any implicit or explicit set of expectations.

"Right out of the gate, I guess the bar got set fairly high," she said, her gaze far away. "No pressure or anything, right?" Frowning, she turned to stare out the window. "Always striving to live up to Papa's expectations," she muttered, "always intent on pleasing the old man." Suddenly, she groaned. "Good lord, Simon, forgive me! I really didn't mean to get sidetracked."

"No, no!" he said. "It's fascinating."

She moved towards him, touching his shoulder lightly and gesturing towards the manuscript. "This is quite something, Simon." He nodded, staring off at the bookcase, zeroing in on the nervous wooden clock, dismayed by how late it had gotten. Standing abruptly, he retrieved the document, sensing her eyes upon him as he slipped it back into the valise.

"To be continued then?" she asked.

"Right," he said, "to be continued."

Tableau V

Igor

"I'm glad we don't further trouble your family," Stravinsky says, settling into a rough-hewn bench across from Schoenberg at E.M. Leydicke, a lively tavern in Berlin's Kreuzberg district. He feels well here in the alehouse's *gemütlich* setting, the atmosphere both stimulating and relaxing.

"Art does not mind whether the artist himself acts well as a man," Schoenberg says, indicating the Maritain manuscript Stravinsky has brought along, quoting the passage from memory. *"The creative spirit is imbued with a sacred egoism."*

"To sacred egoism!" Stravinsky says.

A dour waiter appears, bowtie askew, bringing over a round of apple schnapps, taking up a stubby pencil to scribble the bar tab down onto a placemat.

While they set up chess pieces on a rosewood board, Schoenberg orders a hunk of German rye *(a little something maybe to nosh)*, dark and dense, delivered on a breadboard with a pâté knife and a congealed crock of sallow substance, which the two slather over their bread. Chomping away, Stravinsky suddenly tenses, thrusting out his tongue.

"Good God!" he cries in disgust. "What *is* this stuff?"

"Das ist Schmalz," Schoenberg says proudly, licking rheumy residue from the corner of his mouth.

Spitting the hateful bolus into his napkin and slugging back his drink, Stravinsky winces, fearfully working his tongue against the roof of his mouth. "But, please. If you wouldn't mind. Remind me, what is *Schmalz*?"

"Lard."

Vigorously, Stravinsky draws his napkin over his mouth. "But you know," he says with a shrug, "the bread here isn't half bad."

"Yes, a true German bread they serve," Schoenberg says, smacking his lips. "*Und*— with a crust so firm and indestructible you could kill a man, bludgeoning him over the head with it, were it to become necessary to do so."

"*Mais, le pain!*" Stravinsky cries with gusto, recalling the Parisian bakeries he enjoys frequenting, "*la manne des dieux!*"

Schoenberg narrows his gaze. "Yes, however. In terms of Frau Růžek. I'm afraid Paris simply will not do."

Stravinsky swallows. "In any case, I'm sure she'd first wish to discuss the matter with her husband."

"Husband, did you just say?" Schoenberg guffaws, launching into a story about Frau Růžek's foolish *involvement* with Karel, a military officer back home in Brno, her naive assumption that he loved her, never suspecting the cur was already married.

Schoenberg goes on to describe how she'd become pregnant with Karel's child—with Elsa—while, *plötzlich*, her little viper slithered off, back to wife and children.

"Like a worn pair of lederhosen." Schoenberg glares. "That's how he left her. All alone, and now with a small baby to contend with."

"A troubling story," Stravinsky says, disheartened by the details.

Raising his knight to take Stravinsky's bishop, Schoenberg is quick to assure him there's more where that came from—more *tsuris*, "further tales of abject misfortune I might choose to inflict upon you." Screwing up his face, he says softly, "Vivian and I—" He shakes his head, taking a gulp of his drink then closing his eyes as he backtracks momentarily, recounting for Stravinsky the Berlin Opera House where he and Vivian once worked together on a production of Monteverdi's *L'Orfeo,* the two of them discussing the work at length while dreaming of collaborating one day on their own original version of the Orpheus myth.

"She and I would sometimes meet up after rehearsals," Schoenberg explains. "*Hier! Ja,* very often right here in Leydicke! Like-minded souls were we. As alike as one egg is to another."

Stravinsky keeps his forefinger affixed to his rook while surveying the chessboard. He looks appraisingly at Schoenberg then, working up the nerve, gingerly broaches the subject of Mathilde, baffled when the name appears to cause Schoenberg to cringe.

"Earlier, though, during dinner," Stravinsky proceeds with delicacy. "You know, at one point, I was actually more than a little perplexed. I'd asked Mathilde about her paintings on the wall, such questioning seeming to have actually elicited sobs."

Schoenberg rubs his temples, staring wearily at Stravinsky for a long moment before quietly explaining how it was Vivian who'd once helped him through a serious crisis in his marriage.

"Some years ago, this was," Schoenberg grits his teeth. "But when it engulfed me, this *meshugas,* I was like a man drowning in an ocean of boiling water. Broken, uncertain whether even to go on living." He clucks his tongue. "For a time, when we lived in Vienna, Mati and I, we struggled to put food on the table. Scampering like gypsies from one living situation to the next. Forced to depend upon charity, never quite able to make ends meet." He purses his lips. "I made up my mind, however, I was going to be a composer."

"*Legche skazat', chem sdelat,*" Stravinsky mutters, "easier said than done."

Schoenberg's smile is sardonic. "Truer words were never spoken through false teeth."

"But, Mathilde—" Stravinsky probes, cautious and tense.

"*But Mathilde!*" Schoenberg parrots with a look of pure hatred. "Good God, Igor, must you hound me?"

Stravinsky colors. "You're right. I've no cause to pry." He sips his schnapps, pleased by the alcohol's burning fruitiness. His curiosity getting the best of him, he sucks in air sharply and asks about the paintings in the Schoenberg living room.

"I think you'd started to mention something," Stravinsky ventures. "A crisis of some sort."

Schoenberg closes his eyes momentarily. "It's not such a cheerful story. At any rate, I do think our evening might be better spent discussing *music*." He stares at Stravinsky. "Our rather diverging approaches to composition, for one thing." When Stravinsky's rook swoops in to make quick work of his knight, Schoenberg pouts and, wagging a finger, launches into a probing analysis of all previous moves leading up to this moment, explaining why, apparently, the error had been made.

"But your *Petrushka*!" Schoenberg suddenly cries. "Remarkable, isn't it, how in your *Petrushka* and in my *Pierrot*, we both gravitated at practically the same moment towards the *Commedia dell'Arte* stock figure."

"Sad and troubled clowns," Stravinsky says. "France and Italy. I too was struck by the coincidence."

Schoenberg explains how this sort of thing seems to occur often between himself and a handful of his closest students, Berg, Eisler, Webern, Wellesz, comparing their works-in-progress—*their various approaches in vitro, as it were*—only to discover with astonishment how they seem to be operating from an entirely similar perspective.

With a triumphant murmur, Schoenberg whisks his rook across the board to annihilate Stravinsky's bishop, reaching into his pocket for his cigarette case and lighting a thin cigar.

"One can't help wonder, though," Schoenberg says, "if your own composition style, too, wouldn't begin to shift gradually towards something—well—more *Viennese*. Or, at any rate, *Teutonic*." He scratches his skull. "Or, my god, Igor, at least something more *European*."

The assessment hits hard. Stravinsky lowers his gaze.

"There does seem to be a great many *able* composers out there," Schoenberg presses. "But truly formidable ones? Composers capable of distilling ideas down to their essence with true economy? *Bah!* The vast majority are fly-by-nights who merely gesticulate. Shouting in their desperation. Farting into the wind."

Glumly, Stravinsky glances around the tavern. Still curious about the Schoenberg paintings, he's been waiting for the right moment to gently nudge the conversation back in that direction, concerned, though, about blurting the wrong thing and only further agitating his colleague.

"I would, however," Stravinsky says tentatively, "be just a little curious, you know. He searches Schoenberg's expression. "To understand more about the paintings. More about—"

"Because," Schoenberg says, "Maybe I could be of some practical value to you in offering a musical suggestion, here or there. A few words of advice to point you in the correct direction."

Stravinsky raises his eyebrows, tormented by the barrage of follow-up questions whirling through his head concerning Mathilde and Vivian, the unsettling paintings in the living room.

"Apprentice painters," Schoenberg says. "Tell me, Igor. How do such younger artists manage to learn technique?" He clasps his hands, unwilling to wait for a response. "They study the masters."

Stravinsky stares into the chessboard, impatient now himself, and dying to ask Schoenberg point blank for his assessment of the *Petrushka* performance earlier today.

"Copying the masters," Schoenberg says. "This, I think, is critical."

Schoenberg describes his own rather unorthodox musical upbringing, an autodidact waiting eagerly for volume *S* of his parents' music encyclopedia set to arrive so that he could teach himself Sonata form, Stravinsky, meanwhile, slowly lifting his gaze, heart pounding while tiptoeing toward the subject of Frau Růžek.

"A moment ago," Stravinsky says, "you were saying how she helped you."

Schoenberg drums his fingers on the table top. "I might, for example, be tempted to suggest a style much more compact. Less *folksy*. More restrained. Surely, there are more effective ways for one to—" He sniffs. "Certain compositional techniques, I mean to say, which lend themselves more effectively to what you hope to express."

Glum, Stravinsky nods.

"And especially now!" Schoenberg says. "Post-Wagner and post-Mahler. Now, more than ever, it's critical to understand musical structure in terms of *economy*."

"Of course," Stravinsky says bitterly.

"After all," Schoenberg says, "one can only go so far with—how shall I put this to you plainly?—*peasant music*."

Schoenberg's assessment lands like an elbow to the throat.

"Folk-inspired, yes," Stravinsky says quietly. "But never sentimental. No less serious than your *German* kind of music."

Schoenberg scoffs. "But, can folk music actually ever be regarded as *serious*?"

"On the contrary," Stravinsky says, "such folk elements lend themselves perfectly well to variation and expressive possibilities." He forces a friendly smile. "It seems, though— You were just about to say something more about the paintings."

"For the love of God, Igor, can you not let it go?" Schoenberg huffs through his nostrils, tortured evidently while whisking breadcrumbs from the table. He drains the last of his grappa, squinting into Stravinsky's eyes.

"Very well then," Schoenberg says. "You asked for it." From across the table, Stravinsky can smell his medicinal breath, the hot acidic ferment of pressed marc.

"You want I should spoil your evening? Is this really what you desire?" For a long, unbearable moment, Schoenberg affixes his tart gaze on Stravinsky. "Very well then." He clacks his tongue. "So now I shall spoil it."

But where on earth was Mathilde?

As Schoenberg launches into his tale, Stravinsky quaffs the last of his drink, aching to hear what Schoenberg has to say.

The baby's condition was worsening—the barking cough, and with each additional rasped breath, the tiny dent just above Georg's breastbone threatening to cave in, his temperature continuing to spike.

Dear God, where was Mathilde? She'd promised to pick up the baby's medicine on her way home from her art lesson. All afternoon he'd been awaiting her return, looking after the baby while hoping to get back to the string quartet he was writing, concerned, now that it had begun to grow dark, that the apothecary would close before Mathilde was able to get there.

Desperate, he'd placed Georg in his pram, wheeling him over to the apothecary himself to pick up the medicine, standing now, upon their return, before the monolith of the stone building, the dwelling they rented above the ground floor brassiere shop owned by Frau Goubi, their landlady, an old Gymnasium associate of Zemlinsky, his brother-in-law.

Peering through the gossamer drapery of the brassiere shop window, he took note of the bald mannequin torsos, somewhat sinister, festooned with brassieres and smiling at him from their wooden mounting poles. He was hoping to locate Frau Goubi back there, wanting to thank her for loaning him the Kronen for Georg's medicine, wondering further if she might advise him about how to manage the baby's condition.

Alas, the store was empty and so, lifting Georg from his pram and unlocking the house door, he mounted the flight of stairs, imagining that during their absence Mathilde might already have returned home.

No, Mathilde was nowhere in sight, the apartment cavernous in her absence, and the baby beginning to wail again, as if also painfully aware of his missing mother, alternately wheezing and shrieking, ashen, clammy, contorting its tiny mouth for more oxygen.

But what could possibly be keeping her? What if something horrific had happened to her? Had she mentioned taking the train over to Linz to fetch Trudi, their five-year-old, who was spending the weekend at her grandmother's?

Mercifully, the medicine took effect quickly and he placed Georg into the awaiting softness of the living room crib. Peace finally. Now he might be able to get further work done on Hands, the oil painting he'd promised Kandinsky for the Blaue Reiter exposition only weeks away, as he searched around the apartment for the set of oil paints he and his wife shared, perturbed when the paints too seemed to have disappeared. Surely, Mati understood he was in the middle of a major project. Perhaps she'd only moved the paints somewhere temporarily while tidying and had neglected to mention it.

What in the world could be keeping her? Was she not in the least concerned about the baby? What exactly could she and Gerstl possibly find to talk about? She might be helping her teacher with an installment of works he'd been preparing to mount at the Secession Building. Yes, that at least made some sense. He'd visited Gerstl's studio himself on previous occasions, where both he and Mathilde had taken painting lessons.

Hunting around the apartment now, throwing open cabinets and drawers, he found himself standing before her large armoire, weighing whether to encroach upon her private space before stepping forward to unlatch the heavy wooden doors, confronted with the clutter of her belongings, stacks of correspondence, a toothless comb, a photo of her brother, Zemlinsky, performing on the cello, scarves, medicine bottles, perfume flasks, minerals, tins of talc, and—tucked away behind a few hanging gowns—a stack of painted canvases.

Rifling through her paintings, admiring a few of them while mindlessly tilting each one forward in pursuit of the paint box, his eye caught an unsettling anatomical blur—an ear, a lustrous shoulder, a white thigh, an ocher-tinted breast—

Rapt, Stravinsky watches Schoenberg swallow and squeeze his eyes closed.

"The bitter anguish I felt," he says to Stravinsky in a wavering voice, "upon discovering that Mathilde herself was the painting's subject." Mathilde, his wife, perched upon Gerstl's stool and gazing out blithely, fully naked with that certain look on her face: immodesty, acquiescence, provocation.

Schoenberg describes the primordial gasp that escaped him, the convulsion of panic while confronting his wife's stark bareness, Mathilde, at the center of the painting,

staring back at him, her coy smile, lewd red lips, whorish eyes, while her lover took his time in rendering every tinted and titillated pore—each intimate inch of her body.

The chair beside the mirror in the painting. This was certainly familiar; on numerous occasions Schoenberg himself had sat in it. The artist's palette was familiar as well, the coarse heavy brushstrokes—mauve, ocher, molten yellow and white for the skin tones—the feminine torso he'd managed to capture, bare breasts, shocking genitals.

Riveted, Stravinsky burns to know what happened next, Schoenberg detailing how overcome and utterly inflamed he'd become, possessed, storming into the bathroom, agitated and *tormented, quite out of his mind now, thrashing through the wicker basket of her soiled laundry, flinging socks and various garments to the floor, grabbing hold of a beige pair of her undergarments and burying his face deeply where, in his despair, he was able to confirm the presence of an unfamiliar scent, a scent decidedly not his own, nor his wife's pungent niff, but rather, the foreign stink of another.*

Mouth agape, Stravinsky says in a hoarse voice, "She betrayed you."

When Mathilde finally returned home it was past nine at night. He'd been slugging absinthe, nodding off in his state of nervous despair.

Richard offered to take me to dinner, *she reported to him, averting her eyes, folding her hands against the sash of her dress.* All the way in Donaustadt! You wouldn't believe how long we waited at the Bahnhof.

And how is Richard? *he asked amicably, blithe, careful to control his voice.* How is Gerstl? *he inquired once more, making his voice all the more treacly.* Tell me Mati: How is Gerstl?

Schoenberg narrates for Stravinsky how, throughout the evening and all through the next day, he kept putting the same question to her—*How is Gerstl?*—probing deeper and deeper as he watched patiently for some reaction, an eyelid's involuntary flutter, a tightening around the mouth, launching the very same question again and again, *How is Gerstl?* relentless, intent on prying her open as, indeed, he eventually began to sense within her the hint of a fissure.

How is Gerstl?

Oh, but wasn't she trembling now! Biting her lip, evading his gaze, slithering off into the baby's room to collapse in the rocking chair. Smoldering, he cried, How is Gerstl? rousing her, his own heart thudding, noting the way she recoiled in her rocker, attempting to comfort the baby and yet trembling so violently she wound up upsetting her tea, scalding her lap, even splashing the baby, she and the baby wailing in lurid duet.

Turning to glare at him, she shrieked, But am I really so disgusting to you? Getting to her feet, she deposited the baby back into the crib and, with no further explanation, fled the apartment.

He waited through the night for her to return, shredding up her canvasses the next morning and feeding the curled fragments to the incinerator.

Finally, on the third day, she returned, along with her brother, Zemlinsky, who'd managed to persuade Mathilde to leave her lover and return home if for no other reason than for the children's sake.

Schoenberg stops there, heavy-hearted, tortured, Stravinsky spellbound, meanwhile, as Schoenberg describes the macabre news headlines the next day, reports of how Gerstl burned the whole of the paintings in his studio, along with personal papers before plunging a knife into his chest and wrapping the telephone cord around his neck to hang himself.

"Dear God," Stravinsky whispers.

Schoenberg swallows, a faint wail emerging from the back of his throat.

"I tried to warn you." Schoenberg rubs his eyes with the heels of his hands. "But some people don't take *no* for an answer."

Stravinsky reaches across the table for Schoenberg's shoulder. "I can't imagine what horrors you've been through."

"For quite some time things have been strained," Schoenberg explains. "Maybe it's better Zemlinsky never introduced the two of us in the first place." He looks at Stravinsky. And then, brightening, he says, "But Frau Růžek. She, at least, came to my rescue. Offering solace. Friendship. Loyalty."

Stravinsky signals the waiter for more libations. A long silence passes between them while *Sperstunde*—last call—is officially announced and the place begins to empty out, guests shouting their farewells to the bartender at a copper till illuminated in the glint of beer steins and tiered liquor bottles.

Then, a moment later, as if seized by some furious pique of inspiration, Stravinsky reaches for the stubby pencil the waiter left behind, flipping the soiled placemat over to scrawl a five-line staff, Schoenberg watching attentively as, in a white heat, Stravinsky meticulously constructs a tower-like chord of eight distinct pitches.

"Voila!"

"But, what is this?" Schoenberg asks, sliding the placemat nearer to him and adjusting his eyeglasses as he examines Stravinsky's chord.

Then, wresting the pencil from Stravinsky's grip, moving the table candle closer, he pencils in a five-line staff below Stravinsky's chord, dashing off a musical rebuttal.

Stravinsky murmurs in delight as he takes the pencil from Schoenberg to add to their impromptu composition, the two composers parrying with gusto, the notes piling up as the germ of an idea is spun out further on the tavern placemat.

Handing the pencil back to Schoenberg, Stravinsky says, "I think we may be on to something here. What do you think?"

"Know what I think?" Schoenberg says with a little hiccough and a look of pure exhaustion. "I think it may soon be necessary to have the waiter bring over a fresh placemat."

SIMON

It was dark and well past dinner by the time he returned from his meeting with Demetra, twinge of guilt while pulling Francine's car into the garage before entering the house to confront her photographs hanging in the entryway, portraits of dancers and buskers. Across the living room, the Steinway accused him, an unpleasant reminder of the commission deadline and the blitz of emails and phone messages from Santa Fe pressing him for updates on the opera.

Setting the valise down in the kitchen, Simon climbed the hallway stairs, pausing at the top to catch his breath, *molto pesante*, aware of the extra pounds he'd put on during the travails of the past year, acquiring more than a hint of Falstaffian bulge over the belt. Exercise-deficient, to say the least, his nutrition execrable by any standard, his personal *staples* slash *binge items* tending more towards doughnut holes, M&Ms, salami sticks, plus a wide range of salted crispy foods (amazing, actually, what an unassuming vending machine these days could produce in terms of the quick fix), plus sodas, sports drinks, beer, etc., personal staples, he conceded, which probably were not getting the nutritional job done, weren't universally embraced as major building blocks of nourishment (although, technically, wasn't there a smattering of fiber in beer? Hadn't he read somewhere how blueberry muffins contained phytonutrients?).

Francine was propped up in bed when he entered the bedroom,

engrossed in *An Aperture Monograph*, a book on Diane Arbus's photography, wearing a peach-colored nightgown and humming along softly with the Billy Joel CD playing through her headphones.

He lumbered towards the bed his head heavy like a hulking mastodon, his side of the bed, forfeited of late, adding a further foreignness to the room, a space they hardly seemed to inhabit together anymore.

Francine removed her headphones and said hello, her large brown eyes gazing at him from behind her glasses.

Leaning in to kiss her forehead, he mumbled something about a meeting that wound up going ridiculously late.

"Luke was really hoping you'd make it to the game."

Game? He was drawing a blank. "Luke's soccer game!" he cried. "Shit!"

Strike one.

He looked away, glancing at black-and-white prints on the wall, images by Lange, Cunningham, and Leibovitz, alongside his Mahler print and a photograph taken during their honeymoon a lifetime ago, the two of them absurdly young, huddled against a majestic Big Sur coastline.

"I'm sorry about taking the car," he said.

Strike two.

Francine shrugged, her expression hard to read.

"I was late, I guess I panicked and wound up doing the stupidest thing possible."

"I stopped at the gas station after work to fill your tank."

"I really appreciate it," he said, sheepish.

The sight of his father's old leather recliner in the corner dismayed him, heaped now with women's clothing, a leather jacket, assorted undergarments, a mound of pull-on slacks with price tags still affixed. The chair was among the items they'd sorted through a few years ago when his ailing father transitioned from Ohio to a retirement home in West L.A. shortly before he passed away. Simon recalled the chair's prominent position in their living room, alongside the mantel, where pottery pieces and Stravinsky's elegant Fabergé egg were displayed. Whatever became of that egg? Simon wondered.

"Crazy day," he said, sitting down heavily on the edge of the bed, catching the lavender scent of her bath soap.

Tell her about the sketchbook! a voice inside him urged.

"France," he said, kneading his fingers. "The other night?" He chewed the inside of his mouth. "You know, when the boys and I showed up late for your show?"

Strike three.

She shook her head firmly. "You know, at this point, I'd just as soon forget about it."

"Sure."

"I mean, it's done now. Right? In the past."

He nodded. Then, sucking in his cheeks, he said, "But there is *one* thing. One other detail—"

Sighing, Francine hugged her shoulders, returning her focus to the Arbus book.

"There's something I need to show you," he said, sitting taller. "Super important. Won't take long."

"I'm really beat," she said.

"I know," he said, headed for the stairway. "But, just for a quick sec. I'll be right back."

The moment was hardly ideal, but he returned with the valise, holding the sketchbook in his lap as he sat beside her, flipping through the pages, Francine startled, not knowing what to say, asking him how and why, who, where, when—

"You're sure it's authentic?"

"This," he said, lightly tapping the opened page, "this is gonna change everything."

"You've got your hands full," she said.

"Full as ever. I need to get back to the opera after I check in on the boys. But, hey, listen," he said, placing a tentative palm on her knee. "Listen, France. I'll make it up to you, all of this, I swear." His face brightened. "This weekend, I dunno. Maybe we can take the boys out on a hike, head over to the beach." He smiled. "Wouldn't that be nice? Do something, you know, *fun* as a family, maybe go get a—"

"I won't be around this weekend," she said, sitting up straighter against the headboard, pulling the feather quilt off her knees. "Carla invited me to go with her to Chicago over the weekend."

Chicago. Hadn't Carla been saying something about Chicago the other night?

"Hold on," he said, "I'm not—"

"And I told her I would."

"You told her—? Whoa," he said a little too loudly, "Back up a sec. Carla asked you—?"

"The Joffrey Ballet," Francine said. "A photo shoot. They've hired her to oversee things, headshots, portraits, action shots, that sort of thing. It's a fairly big deal. Anyway, she asked if I could tag along, you know, to sort of lend a hand."

Simon closed his eyes, drawing a cleansing breath while counting backwards slowly from ten.

"You know, frankly, I was flattered to be asked," Francine said. "A jam-packed weekend, reasonable air fare, accommodations, meals, a lot of it pretty much taken care of."

"And—just like that—you *accepted?*" Simon asked, feeling the twinge of a headache coming on.

"You should see how nervous Carla is," Francine said.

"Perfect. And if I didn't happen to have a major commission due in three weeks—"

"I realize it's last-minute."

"My God, Francine!" he hollered, clenching at his thighs. "What about your work—Your classes?" He gnawed his lip. "And the boys. What'll we do with the boys?"

"I'll be using a few of my professional days," she said.

Simon gritted his teeth. "I'm under the gun."

"Believe me," she said quietly, "I'm well aware of *your* pressures."

"Jesus, France!" Simon said too loudly, "The flight alone must have cost a small fortune. And, well, the *timing*—"

"The timing's less than ideal," she said, biting the side of her finger. "But I need to grab this opportunity."

"I'm just not sure we can afford to spend the money."

"Last winter. The Stravinsky symposium in Baltimore? We sure managed to come up with the budget line for that one."

"My opera!" he practically screamed.

She shushed him, reminding him that Luke was already asleep.

Lowering his voice, massaging his temples, he asked, "Do you understand the pressure I'm dealing with?" He wrung his hands together. "The clock's ticking. Every second counts. This is it for me— do or die! My career on the line."

"I get it," she said, "I've lived through my fair share of commission deadlines with you."

"But—I mean, for God sakes, you know how *huge* this one is. A quarter of a million dollars." He laughed. "No biggie or anything. *Nooooo* pressure!"

Francine puffed air from her cheeks. "Let's not blow things out of proportion. It's only a weekend we're talking about. Things will work out. I mean, the world's not going to end if Carla and I—"

"And now Boderman's breathing down my neck," he said, wincing, clawing at his beard. "Things have gotten insane over at work. *Insane!* I feel like I can't do anything right over there and— and then! Okay, so now, unilaterally, you're running off with Carla?"

Again Francine shushed him.

"Francine," he said, "sweetie, listen." He raked his fingers through his hair. "Can we talk about this?" Maybe come up with a slightly different plan?"

"You're dealing with a lot," she said, patting his forearm. "Hey, I understand that."

He drew a deep breath, holding it in his chest for four counts, exactly as instructed on the meditation CD.

"All I'm asking is for you to help me get through the next weeks," he pleaded. "Once the opera project's all wrapped up, I swear—"

"I *need* to do this," she said. "Not just for Carla. But for myself."

He stared down at the carpet.

"And the boys? Just what do you propose I do with the kids all weekend?"

"Call Rita Larson," she said. "Or get someone else to help babysit if you feel you need the—" Her eyes suddenly got big. "Oh! Which reminds me. Super important. It seems Lincoln got invited to some sleepover or something this weekend." She shook her head. "Which I strictly *forbid* him to do."

"You're forbidding a sleepover?"

"It's over at the Hodges' place." Francine wrinkled her nose. "Under no circumstances will our kids be having a sleepover at the Hodges' house."

"I don't follow," Simon said. "Lincoln got invited but isn't allowed to go?"

"I don't trust these people," she said. "They're a rough crowd, a little out of control or something. And maybe you can get away with being, you know, a little wound up in school." She expelled air. "I can't put my finger on it. It's like there's something I just don't trust. Not when it comes to sending my children over." She shrugged. "Maybe it's excessive caution on my part, paranoia even."

"But, that older Hodges kid," Simon said, "the one that Lincoln likes. What's his name?"

"Jeffty."

"Jeffrey," he said.

"*Jeffty!*"

"Sure, all right," he said, rolling his eyes, "*Jeffty*. He was on Lincoln's soccer team last year. Striker, right? I mean, he seems like a nice enough kid."

Francine gnawed her lip. "A nice enough kid who just happened to get suspended last year for bringing a knife or some type of crazy homemade weapon to school. And, from the way Luke talks, the younger brother may be following fast in his brother's footsteps."

Natural born killer, Simon thought. "Well, they seem pretty normal to me. Jeffty and—what's the little guy's name?"

"Bradley."

"Bradley, right. I mean, Bradley's sorta cute, right?"

"Most definitely, these people are *not* cute," she said with a bitter expression. "I need you to trust me on this." She pointed her finger. "Promise me you won't cave in to the boys' begging and conniving. Because, you know they *will* resort to begging and conniving."

He shrugged.

"You hear things from other parents, too," she said. "Drugs. Something about a domestic incident awhile back, the police involved. Maybe it's the town rumor mill, but my gut's screaming *huge red flag* on this one."

"All right."

Her gaze was piercing. "Promise me you won't take them to that sleepover."

"Okay," he said, holding up his hands. "All right. Jesus, Francine!"

"Simon, promise me."

"I said, *okay*."

"Other than that, the boys won't make many demands. They know all about your deadline." Chuckling, she added, "Who knows? Maybe you'll wind up enjoying some quality *dad-time* with your kids. I'm sure they'd really enjoy that. In any case, I'll be back in town before you even know what hit you."

※

Lincoln was at his desk, hunched over a textbook and listening to music on his headphones when Simon stepped into the room, navigating around strewn clothes to exchange a high-five and ask how his day had gone.

"Yeah, good," Lincoln said, switching off the disk-player. His long hair drooped nearly to his shoulders, the *Chewbacca* T-shirt, tight across his chest, accentuating his lanky arms. Simon wondered if he might still be a little galled about missing so much of Francine's photo exhibition the other day.

Simon glanced around the room, admiring the incongruent patchwork of posters (Mötley Crüe, The Beatles, Paul Simon, The Doors, Shostakovich, Copland, Britten), interspersed with Lakers, Kings, and Dodgers pennants, a fold-up music stand and viola case in the corner.

Lincoln was studying a science textbook, *Understanding Our World*.

"Major quiz tomorrow," Lincoln said. "This one I'll need to ace." He pushed out his lower lip. "Otherwise, I'm toast."

"*Toast*," Simon said, drawing out the word. "What type of toast?"

"The finished kind," Lincoln said. "Doomed. *Finito.* Done! In terms of my grade. That's according to Mr. Laduke, anyway."

Simon expelled air. "Yeah, well I seem to be on intimate terms myself with *toast* and *doom* these days." He pointed to the headphones. "What were you listening to?"

"Hindemith," Lincoln said. "The piece I'm learning for the recital."

Searching Simon's face, he said, "You and Mom. What were you guys fighting about?"

"Not really *fighting*," Simon said, "just *adult* stuff."

"You guys were having an argument," Lincoln pressed.

Simon picked up one of the black pancake-shaped rocks on Lincoln's bookshelf, rocks he and the boys had collected in Santa Barbara a few summers ago where they'd rented a cottage on the beach.

"Sounded pretty intense, though," Lincoln said.

"Nah." Simon turned the rock over in his palm. "No big deal."

Lincoln raised his eyebrows. "You're pissed she's going to Chicago for the photography thing and the sleepover with Carla."

Oh, so she'd already informed the boys about Chicago.

Simon proceeded to explain calmly how no one was *pissed*, how *pissed* wasn't necessarily the operative term.

Lincoln's eyes brightened. "*Appalling!*"

Simon laughed.

"The timing totally sucks," Lincoln said, "and the whole thing's *appalling*, right?"

"What is this?" Simon said, laughing some more. "Where do you come up with the vocabulary?"

"It's on this week's vocab quiz," Lincoln said. "Check it out. We need to know a bunch of words for Mrs. Phillips: *Appalling*. Along with *destitute*." He thumbed through a spiral binder. "And *indigent*. Oh, and *conjugal, charlatan, ruffian, infidelity,* and *pathological.*"

He looked up at Simon with that gentle earnest look he sometimes got. "I know you're super busy, Dad."

"Running the gauntlet."

"What are you running?"

"Nothing," Simon said, "just some more vocabulary."

"But. I mean, if you have a little extra time, maybe you can quiz me, you know, since Mom won't be around."

Never enough time, Simon thought, hating how he was forced to constantly choose between work pressures and his family, telling Lincoln he'd make a sincere effort to carve out a little time.

"Guess what?" Lincoln said. "I'm writing a song. For viola. Mr. Diaz says he'll let me perform it on the next recital if I can make it, you know, *sing!* Maybe you'll give me a few pointers."

Simon shrugged. "Things are pretty nuts with the commission. And now, with your mother heading—"

Sulking, Lincoln said quietly, "Okay."

"We just need to get through the next couple of weeks," Simon said.

Again Lincoln frowned.

"Deal?" Simon said. Three more brutal weeks before the finish line. Then it would all be behind them. Things could finally get back to normal.

Lincoln buried his gaze in his science book.

Stuart, for example, Boderman had prodded him the other day during their evaluation conference. *No doubt Stuart wouldn't mind a little friendly nudge up the departmental food chain.*

Simon squeezed his eyes shut, thinking of Boderman and that pesky Bruin family of his.

Our team's currently a little bulky, Boderman was intent on informing him. *Plenty of* other *instructors out there waiting in the wings, jonesing to get in the game, you know? Beaucoup. Both in terms of associate faculty and adjunct pools. The team's fairly deep right now.* Grinning. *Deep!*

Simon looked over at Lincoln. "Hey, I'm proud of you for composing your own piece of music."

Gnawing at the side of his pencil, Lincoln said, "It's tough being a composer, though, right?"

"A little tougher every day," Simon said, thinking about the valise waiting for him out in the hallway.

"When I grow up?" Lincoln said excitedly. "I'm going to write an opera."

"Good for you."

Lincoln sucked in air sharply. "Oh, yeah. Dad! I promised Jeffty I'd come to his sleepover on Saturday."

Frowning, Simon said, "I know. but your mother—"

"Check it out, though," Lincoln said. "They just set up their Nintendo Virtual Boy. Jeffty says they've got an entire game room in the works. Awesome, eh?"

"Sounds great," Simon said. "Although—"

"Believe me," Lincoln said, "I already know what Mom has to say about it." His grin was conspiratorial. "Which is why God invented two parents instead of one."

Tableau VI

Igor

THROUGH THE HUSH OF nighttime Berlin, Stravinsky makes his way back to his hotel, shoes swishing over the pavement, the wind at his face an arsenal of tiny needles. He adjusts his muffler, wishing he'd brought along hat and gloves. Nestled in one arm, the score of *Pierrot*, the Maritain essays in the other as he passes beneath the yellow illumination of a lone dormer window, a rat scuttling out from a gap in a storefront window on the *Bülowstrasse*, trailed by a ropy tail.

The city feels dead, sealed up in shadows, the streetcars, cabaret-goers and prostitutes all vanished, even the rag-and-bone man off to wherever he goes. An abandoned chestnut roaster is stationed near the curb. Overhead, the branches of bare trees lurk against the night sky like eerie carcasses.

I was a painter. But no longer.

Mathilde's words during dinner continue to bewilder him. Schoenberg's portrayal of the Gerstl affair would seem to account for Mathilde's forlorn stares, the faint tremble of her lip when Stravinsky had pressed her for further details about the paintings on the wall, the prickly tension around the dinner table, Schoenberg's proprietary glances at Frau Růžek. The gloom enshrouding Mathilde, the alarming rictus, aglow in the candlelight, her puzzling hysteria as the evening wore on.

He can just make out the 4 a.m. hour on his twitching timepiece, an entire city to himself, tipsy, giddy, a lone somnambulant crawling towards a hotel bed in the midst of gloomy Prussia, staring up at the night sky's gossamer sprawl of stars, clusters of ragged clouds lit by a Pierrot moon, pale and shrunken, gaping between the pilasters as it follows him from one stone building to the next.

He remembers, not so long ago, huddling among companions on a rotting Montparnasse rooftop, gazing up at the starry sky in anticipation of Halley's comet, Debussy, Picasso, and Nijinsky awaiting its emergence with trepidation, Stravinsky wedged against a boyish and hirsute rabbi reeking of celery, Proust huffing up the rooftop stairs to join them, followed by the young painter, Chagall, Paul Valéry next, Sarah Bernhardt and Coco Chanel, all more or less in concord that this streaking firebird across the night sky would officially usher in the end of the world.

Now, crossing a bridge above the *Landwehr* canal and transecting *Potsdamer Platz*, he enters the imperial front doors of the *Hotel Adlon Kempinski*, the lobby silent as a morgue as he rings the bronze bell (*E-flat*) at the main desk, a sleepy concierge surrendering the room key, the lift droning up four floors (*F-sharp*), as he moves past a circus of snores from Diaghilev's room along the corridor before entering his own. Odor of gardenias, linens stiffly starched as, reverently, he lays the *Pierrot* score and Maritain book upon the small desk, a shrine housing last week's *Pierrot* program and the concert ticket stub he holds onto like a souvenir charm.

Retrieving his own pocket-sized sketchbook, Stravinsky props a pillow and climbs into bed, leaning back against the headboard to notate the first inklings of a new work, sound colors just beginning to take shape in his imagination, a set of Japanese Lyrics inspired by *Pierrot* and his interactions this evening with Schoenberg.

Darkness recedes, a garish vapor nudging the window as Stravinsky continues to spin his musical notes like an industrious sketchbook, noting a few fresh gestures he'd composed the other day for *The Rite of Spring* during the thunder and hiss of his train journey from Geneva to Berlin. Glancing over at the desk enshrined with various mementos, he thinks of Schoenberg's parting embrace, long and heartfelt as, one by one, the tavern lights winked out.

Schoenberg. Who by now would have reached his own home, possibly sitting down to compose something himself during this hypnagogic hour. Stravinsky imagines him at his desk, extracting the greasy placemat from a coat pocket, unfolding it like a map and contemplating how their *Orpheus* fragment might be further expanded, fleshing out some new and startlingly ingenious variation, nabbed from the ether—from the firmament of Beethoven, Mozart, Bach—a wizardly masterstroke woven into the musical tapestry that Stravinsky has now begun for him.

For them!

Schoenberg, pausing to muse upon this newfound fellowship of theirs while doodling a little portrait of his fawning Russian compatriot upon the Orpheus palimpsest.

Eyes closed, Stravinsky feels giddy, imagining his own visage taking shape from the corner of a begrimed tavern placemat.

SIMON

AFTER SAYING GOOD NIGHT to Lincoln, Simon ventured into Luke's room, his younger son breathing steadily as he slept. In the dim of the nightlight, Simon tiptoed over to pull the comforter over Luke's glow-in-the-dark T-Rex pajama top, comforted by the sight of his sleeping boy.

Alongside the bed, one of Luke's stuffed animals was propped up on a small plastic chair. Simon couldn't make out what type of animal it was supposed to be, but from the way it had been arranged on the chair, it looked as if the animal might have been poised for some type of discussion, placed there to read Luke a bedtime story, or to inquire about his day. In addition to missing the soccer match this afternoon, Simon was disquieted by the fact he'd been absent entirely from his sons' lives today.

He gathered up the stuffed animal, soft, chubby and astonishingly lightweight. In the dimness, he could make out streaks of blue and white fur along its back, a flat orange nose, glossy button eyes. A penguin maybe. No mouth—he inspected it another time to confirm this. How did it manage to eat? He'd definitely need to ask Luke about all this tomorrow.

He thought about his own father, working in one of the many gardens he tended. The garden Simon was now vaguely able to recollect may even have been Stravinsky's or Schoenberg's. This would have been during the 1940s, Jasper Grafton placing a strong arm around his four-year-old son, pulling him into the warmth of an oversized woolen work shirt, dusty moleskin workpants, scent of sweat and aftershave, pungent eucalyptus leaves, marigold, and the rosemary he would have been pruning. Jut of an elbow, bones, sinews, a powerful beating heart, the small boy cocooned in his father's embrace, a calloused hand, rough like stucco, settling along Simon's nape, knotty gardener's hands, soil-stained and branched with protuberant veins.

You know, Simon, you can do anything you dream of, his father told him, his British accent mellifluous and reassuring. *Become whatever it is you dream of becoming, a musician, if you fancy. Like your mum!*

But where is Mom? the little boy had timidly put forth, staring up into his father's gentle but guarded eyes, searching for some explanation that might possibly account for his mother's abrupt and seemingly permanent absence.

Now Simon stroked the stuffed animal's soft furry head. Luke adored penguins. And he could see why his son preferred its soft comfort to many of the other stuffed animals heaped in the corner. Locating an odd zippered pouch placed low on the penguin's back, he unzipped, surprised to discover the small battery-power pack attached to a wire.

Intrigued, unable to resist, he slid the button panel to the opposite side, causing the penguin to suddenly vibrate, white light frenetically flashing, accompanied by near-excruciating squawks, Simon muttering, *Shit!* under his breath, while jamming the button back to the *off* position, Luke sitting up abruptly and rubbing his eyes, his gaze pivoting from the vacant chair over to his father.

"Ned Spencer, go back to sleep!" Luke's groggy voice mumbled at the penguin, his eyelids already resealing.

Stifling a giggle, Simon stood frozen and silly, cradling the penguin, carefully backtracking in a slow retreat from the room.

Luke's eyes opened again as he mouthed with a sleepy grin, "Dad, what are you doing here?"

"I just came in to check up on you, see how your dreams were going."

"Fine," Luke said inside a yawn.

Simon stepped forward to smooth Luke's bangs. "Well, that's good, buddy. Hey, I'm really glad to hear that." Leaning over to kiss his son's cheek, he whispered for him to go back to sleep.

"All right," Luke said, "but, Dad—?"

"What?"

"I don't like it when you're gone."

"Yeah," Simon said, "I know. Sorry. Got stuck in a meeting."

"Me, Lincoln and Mom. We were waiting up," Luke said in the midst of another yawn. "We didn't know where you were."

Simon stroked his son's forehead, sheepish about taking Francine's car, guilty about his extended meeting with Demetra, thinking of Stravinsky and his unusual domestic arrangements, the slew of extramarital affairs, the double life he was said to have carried out.

Luke blinked several times. "We tried calling your phone."

"Hey," Simon said, "no need to be frightened. Adults—" He swallowed heavily. "It's just sometimes things come up."

Simon closed his eyes. When exactly had things gotten so complicated, so fraught? The clock was ticking on his commission, a thousand details yet to attend to, the ending of the opera still not clear to him.

In another few minutes, though, he planned to be back in his basement study, reorchestrating the 1916 collision of Arnold, Igor, and Vivian in Paris, thinning out the instrumental texture of the large orchestra palette he'd chosen to employ to fully dramatize the stormy confrontations of Arnold and Igor.

"Promise me you won't come home so late," he thought he heard Luke say, Simon lost in thought, thinking of the English horn motif in his opera that represented Stravinsky and the Schoenbergian music he was currently working on—conjuring in his imagination that moment in the rehearsal room of the Paris Opera House when Schoenberg presents Vivian with the score to one of the *Lieder* he's written for her.

"Otherwise, I'll get afraid," Luke said in a small voice, "scared you might not come back."

"I'm not going anywhere," Simon said, gently stroking Luke's soft hair. "Deal? No one's leaving you, buddy. Ever. Okay? Not Mommy. And not Daddy. I'll always be here for you."

"Okay," Luke whispered, yawning, already drifting back into sleep. Simon leaned in to kiss his cheek.

That time, the time his father vanished and then wound up in a mental institution, the time when Simon's world shattered, when the adults and caretakers in his world were lost to him, leaving him abandoned and orphaned and terrified. That time a woman named Elsa had taken him to visit his father at the ward, the scratchy sandpaper texture of his father's face pressed up against his own, the paroxysm of sobs from his father's body Simon had never before heard, a man grieving for his wife as his world descended into darkness and Simon, a small child, drowning while trying to hold on, unable to fathom how such deep sorrowful sobs could possibly be emanating from his father's body.

—⁓—

The Los Angeles Times
HUYLENBROUCK'S DISAPPEARANCE
STILL A MYSTERY

DOROTHEA RONDO
July 14, 1947

Nearly four weeks after dancer Elsa Růžek was found dead in her Brentwood home from a suspected drug overdose, her husband's disappearance continues to arouse further suspicion about his possible involvement in her death. By all accounts, however, investigators are bewildered, as they may now have reason to suspect husband Claes Huylenbrouck of being the person ultimately responsible for an accidental drug overdose or possible traumatic head injury leading to a fatal subdural hemorrhage. Coroner Theodore B. Dalton and autopsy surgeon Dr. EF Geyer continue to examine all evidence.

Huylenbrouck, meanwhile, remains missing or at large and, according to Police Sergeant Percival Brook, may have fled the country.

Maestro Huylenbrouck, known in musical circles as the Flammable Flem, has had his own share of recent professional downturns. Following differences with oil magnate and arts benefactor, Q. Chester Lund, Huylenbrouck's spectacular musical career took something of a nosedive, resulting in his prompt dismissal from several conducting positions, his own chamber ensemble, the Orchestra Imperiale, among them, as well as other key musical posts at MGM and RKO studios.

SIMON

In the arid chilliness of the bank vault's viewing room, Simon stood over a slate-blue drawer, examining the contents of his and his father's joint safe deposit box. Although Jasper Grafton passed away more than three years ago, Simon had never gotten around to combing through his father's old curios, timeworn gewgaws and various moldering documents in hopes of uncovering some sentimental artifact or stumbling upon unexpected treasure.

But Ingo's letter and the mention of Stravinsky's Faberge egg had piqued his curiosity; Simon found himself obsessing over the egg, as he tossed and turned at night, convinced that if he could manage to locate the egg among his father's things, it might help trigger a submerged childhood memory or two, memories surrounding the loss of his mother and the particular toll this had taken on both him and his father.

Could the egg itself help connect more of the dots, shedding further light on how his parents' path might have intersected with that of the composers? Unable to squelch this burgeoning curiosity, Simon wound up forgoing office hours and a subcommittee meeting, even forfeiting his afternoon Baroque counterpoint seminar, sneaking off campus instead after his morning lecture, and driving over to the savings bank on Wilshire Boulevard to exchange I.D. for the vault drawer's long silver mortise key.

The egg hunt didn't take very long. Sure enough, there, among the stacks of papers, various envelopes and bits of jewelry of the drawer's contents, he noticed a small, sturdy cardboard box, which he carefully unwrapped. Placing the gold and enamel egg in his palm, Simon unhinged its upper segment to reveal a miniature golden replica of the Gatchina Palace in St. Petersburg, embellished with flag, cannon, statue, and garden parterre, recalling his father's boyish grin and how he never seemed to tire of the pleasure of unfastening his egg.

Equally delightful was the egg's musical mechanism, tucked beneath a swath of velvet, which churned out a tinny rendition of the theme from *Swan Lake*. Fiddling with the long-lost egg, winding the minuscule key so that now Tchaikovsky became juxtaposed with the pneumatic puff of the vault's air duct, Simon closed his eyes, recollecting a medical clinic somewhere, his father slumped in a chair and surrounded by hospital orderlies.

Where did you disappear to after Mom died?

During that particular afternoon, his father had failed to show up at nursery school at the end of the day. Something was wrong. His father had never before failed to appear, forcing Simon to remain hostage in an office upstairs, inexplicably orphaned while Mrs. Endore ran a plump forefinger down the school's emergency contact numbers.

Coming upon his father at the hospital later that day, he felt relief wash over him. During all that time spent waiting after school, he'd remained a brave little soldier, capable of swallowing the panic which had been steadily building. Now, though, in the presence of his father, he gave full vent to the bottled-up sobs, the soles of his shoes squealing over a polished corridor, reeking of floor wax solvents, that seemed to go on forever. Confronted with his father's stony gaze, Simon looked into vacant eyes that revealed no hint of recognition, his father's hair wiry, shaggy as a roan bull, the statue of a father someone had stationed there in place of the real one, frighteningly inanimate and staring blankly at dun-colored hospital walls.

Now, as the Tchaikovsky melody wound down in the vault's viewing room, Simon swallowed his sadness, fingers shaking as he set the egg down on the marble countertop and rummaged through more of the drawer's musty contents, an old lease, a pile of bank statements, his mother's wedding ring, crinkled photos of his parents posed dramatically against the bluffs of St Ives.

He picked up a frayed book, a monograph, *An Agricultural Testament*, its flyleaf autographed by the author:

> *12 July, 1939. For Jasper, accomplished botanist, horticulturalist, and agronomist. Knee deep in muck (microbes!), you played a key role at our research experiment station at Indore in advancing efforts to transform mouldering straw and animal manure into black gold. All good wishes on your journey to the New World! Nihil in intellectu nisi prius in sensu.*
> *—Sir Albert Howard*

He flipped through several sepia postcards from India sent by his father to his fiancée, Miss Helena Dent, in Surrey during the 1920's. He combed over a silver bracelet and an exquisitely hand-crafted wooden owl carved with the initials, *AS*. Digging still further, Simon was dumbstruck to come upon a stone pendant on a leather strap with an engravement.

<pre>
S A T O R
A R E P O
T E N E T
O P E R A
R O T A S
</pre>

Nestling the pendant in his palm, he stared mutely at it, his head swimming with a flurry of questions. What was this five-word, Latin square—*the Magic Square*, or *Sator Square*, he had now discovered it was called—doing among his father's possessions? And what was the connection between the Sator Square, the composers, and his father?

He continued to peruse flaking newspaper clippings, a review of conductor Claes Huylenbrouck, *the Flammable Flem*, conducting in Pasadena nestled in an obituary of dancer Elsa Růžek, "*LAST DANCE: ELSA RŮŽEK DIES; PILLS BLAMED.*"

"Elsa Růžek," Simon said aloud. Had his father actually ever uttered her name? He and his father had relocated to Ohio in 1949. But what had it been like for his father earlier on, accompanying his mother to Los Angeles to eventually find himself toiling in the gardens of various Angelenos, Hollywood celebrities, and other notables, the likes of Schoenberg and Stravinsky, Franz Werfel, Harpo Marx, Thomas Mann, Cole Porter, Aldous Huxley, Vivian Leigh, Claes Huylenbrouck, and Elsa Růžek?

Plumbing still further, he noticed something at the bottom of the drawer, an archaic scuffed leather journal, its spine cracking, an assemblage of thick unevenly-cut parchment pages fastened together by a threadbare length of twine.

> *Beverly Hills*
> *17 October 1943*
>
> *Whistling! Whistling Schoenberg! And of all places, in
> the Stravinsky garden.*
>
> *Shoulder deep in shrub, wielding loppers in the war
> against Pittosporum undulatum, Victorian Box, & the
> Buxus hedgerow flanking the Stravinskys' Mediterranean-
> style villa, I cease my whistling when suddenly out of
> thin air, it wd. seem, Igor Stravinsky materializes, rapidly
> torpedoing my way.*

BOOK III

Tableau VII

Vivian

"Music can be unsettlingly prophetic, like a kind of
seismograph sensing the eruptions to come."
—Sir Simon Rattle, 'Leaving Home:
Orchestral Music in the Twentieth Century'

"Can you still play the old songs?
Play, darling. They waft through my woes."
—Rainer Marie Rilke, 'First Poems'

Wiener-Konzertverein Great Hall
31 March 1913

Vienna Concert Society,
Bösendorfer-Saal

LAUGHTER. SO ENTIRELY OUT of place, it seems to her.

And next, shouting, jeers, a restless audience whose stirring and commotion threaten to overtake the performance. From the gallery in the *Konzertverein*, Vivian listens to Schoenberg's newly-composed *Chamber Symphony*, Schoenberg crouching on the podium, jabbing the baton and shaking his arms like a wild man to elicit more energy from the twelve musicians before him onstage.

It's been months since her uneasy parting with Schoenberg, just as she was leaving Berlin to join Diaghilev's troupe in Paris. She remembers the well wishes, the friendly peck on the cheek but also the mournful look he gave her, the emotional complexity lingering as they said their goodbyes.

But this week the *Ballets Russes* tour has placed her in Vienna for performances of *Afternoon of a Faun*, *Prince Igor*, and *Till Eulenspiegel*. Coming upon the notice in the newspaper, she made a hasty decision to attend this afternoon's concert, catching the streetcar over to the *Ringstrasse* after her dance rehearsals.

The *Konzertverein* is a magical place for her, filled with happy memories. A Neoclassical concert hall with brilliant acoustics, narrow and intimate like a dollhouse. She's always loved the gilded ceiling, rectangular columns and pillars of caryatid figures, recalling the memorable trip she and her family made from Moravia years ago to attend the opera here. Watching Schoenberg conduct his own works while forced to contend with unruly concertgoers, she wonders what's become of the respectable bourgeois Viennese audience she remembers.

Now, as Schoenberg's music intensifies into punctuated angular thrusts, the shrill utterances of piccolo, bass clarinet, contrabassoon, and horns are met by laughter and catcalls. Vivian leans over to shush the uncouth young man sitting beside her, astonished when he stands to voice his dissatisfaction, astonished all the more when he turns to her with a malicious grin.

"But, you enjoy such vile puke?" he asks, producing a bruised piece of fruit from his pea coat pocket, waving it before her obscenely then flinging it towards the stage. Other audience members follow suit, whistling, booing, emptying their pockets and handbags to hurl personal items—stray coins, pebbles, a wadded-up concert program, an egg—heckling the musicians with contempt.

"*Madman!*" someone in the audience shrieks at Schoenberg. A few seats away, a woman blows into a skeleton key with a shrill screech as another woman bends to unclasp a shoe, launching it like a fusillade towards the podium. Overhead, against the balcony's balustrade, a fist-fight between two red-faced men has broken out.

Schoenberg slams the baton onto the rostrum, turning to confront his detractors.

"Anyone who continues to disturb the performance," he hollers breathlessly into the black maw of the auditorium, "shall be forcibly removed by the police!" Turning back towards the musicians on stage, he attempts to resume conducting, though the melee only intensifies.

A portly man stands to point an accusatory finger at Schoenberg.

"*Shoot him!*" he hollers.

The dread in her belly turns to icy terror as it occurs to Vivian that her safety may be in jeopardy—Schoenberg's safety even more so, exposed in the crossfire like a sitting duck.

When a few audience members storm the stage a trio of policemen emerges from somewhere, attempting to quell the ruckus as they hurriedly usher Schoenberg and the musicians from the stage.

Sandwiched in the hemorrhage of panicked and fleeing concert-goers, Vivian nearly collides with Dorothea Rondo, the music critic, who ceases her disjointed wobble up the gangway, resulting in an even greater bottleneck, as she jots something down onto her reporter's pad.

Freed at last from the throngs, Vivian steps outside into the gloom of a late afternoon drizzle, looking around desperately for Schoenberg, pinpointing him beyond the parterre fountain, coattails flying as he tears away like a thief.

"Arnold—" she cries, hurrying after him, "Herr Schoenberg!"

When she catches up to him Schoenberg turns in mute horror, shoulders tensed. A slant of heavy drizzle pelts the top of his head. He's fled the theater without his overcoat, his tuxedo ravaged, wilted in the damp.

"Arnold," she says, out of breath, stepping forward to embrace him, bombarded by the sourness of perspiration. "Dear God," she whispers, "I'm so sorry."

"*You?*" he babbles, "Vi!" His face is still perspiring. He indicates the *Konzertverein.* "But, you were *there*? *Inside*?"

Clasping his arm, she leads him down the *Domgasse,* away from the theater.

When they reach the Austrian National Library moments later, Schoenberg pauses to catch his breath. "Here," he says with a fretful expression while probing the surrounding *Josefsplatz* for lurking concert hall assassins. "Here's where I thought to seek refuge. Anonymity. Protection from the sharks."

"But, can you believe it?" he continues, glancing up at a statue of Charles VI seated on horseback. "Such pernicious scorn. The way they sat there mocking the music. If it weren't for the police, I'm certain they would have all enjoyed gnashing me up into little giblets back there and gobbling me up."

"Thank god you're all right."

The rain intensifies. Vivian secures the kerchief around her head.

"But," he says with wild eyes. "I had no idea you were in the audience! Had I known you were there—" His face colors. "I might have mustered a little more fortitude."

He asks what she's doing in Vienna; on tour, she's quick to respond, the *Ballets Russes.*

He raises his eyebrows. "With Diaghilev?"

She nods, uncomfortable under the scrutiny of his gaze as she turns towards the square, scanning the white stone and imperial marble columns for shelter from the rain.

"And *Stravinsky*?" he asks.

Moments later they sit across from one another in the stuffy comfort of a crowded coffee house amidst the murmur of conversation. A languid plume of cigar haze rises slowly like a cloud against the replica of a gilded Klimt frieze.

"I'm tickled you attended the performance," he says.

"I was curious to hear what you've been up to, your latest compositions."

He reaches across the marble tabletop for her hand, placing his own over hers, warm, a little clammy, the skin translucent and deeply veined beneath the bald light of the chandelier. Vivian draws a tense breath, advising him to put the unpleasant business of today's concert behind him.

"You know how such things go," she says, carefully freeing her hand. "The audience needs time to catch up to your vision, adjust its ears to new colors and sounds."

"Yes, all right," he says, "if you say so."

She thinks of her own undertaking in Paris. Stravinsky's *Rite of Spring*, a project she's currently steeped in with the *Ballets Russes*. What should she say to him about this? She's become absorbed with Stravinsky's ballet, obsessed—everyone has, Nijinsky, Diaghilev, Roerich, the production crew, the enormous troupe of dancers. A work-in-progress fraught with its own shocking dissonances, primordial underpinnings and atonal primitivism, the ballet set to premiere in less than two months' time.

She longs to tell him about Paris, highlighting her artistic world, the stimulating collaboration within a role as both dancer and choreographer under Diaghilev's visionary leadership. She wants to describe what it's like assisting Nijinsky, drawing upon her background in *Dalcroze-Eurythmics* as a conduit between Stravinsky's fiendishly complex score and Nijinsky's equally cumbersome choreography, the distorted pretzel shapes of the dancers' bodies.

Moments ago, as they crossed the mannered green of the *Volksgarten*, she nearly confided in him about her life in Paris, the spartan yet endearing flat alongside the *Jardin des Plantes* she found for Elsa and herself, she and Schoenberg strolling the rose bushes and prim hedges of the garden's grand pathways like an aristocratic couple, admiring neo-Gothic columns flanked by deities and winged chariots, the Triton fountain, dramatic reliefs carved into the marble of the *Grillparzer* Monument, her lips parting at the Mozart Monument, though they made no sound, and their stroll continued past the *Hofstallgebäude's* imperial stables and Empress Sisi's grand, octagonal riding hall.

Now they order *Sachertorte*, dense cake coated in dark icing and laced thinly with layers of apricot jam. She wraps her hands around a steamy mug of *Kaffee mit Schlag*, finding comfort in the hot, bitter liquid beneath a sweet cumulous of whipped cream.

"You've been a loyal friend," he says to her, his ears reddening as again he reaches for her hand, Vivian alert this time, folding her hands in her lap while ladies on either side of them, dolled up in smart veiled hats with prickly feather quills, plunge their forks into the meringue peaks of *Spanische Windtorten*.

"Forgive me," he says. "But I find in me— Certain feelings."

She looks away, gazing at the parquet floor, brocade drapery, the leaden light seeping in from the tall window.

Placing both palms on the table, he pleads for her to return to Berlin in a voice that strikes her as disconcertingly parental. He sips his coffee, describing a new piece he's begun work on, "part of a song cycle, I think, eventually this will become."

She should probably finish her coffee and bring their meeting to a close.

"I'm happy for you," she says finally.

"A song," he says, "which, *ja*, I think it's fair to say you yourself have inspired."

Leaning forward, he again gropes for her hand but, vigilant, she wrenches it away with so much force she thwacks his coffee mug off the table, flustered, dabbing at the hem of her spattered dress while avoiding the disapproving glances of blue-haired-bouffant Viennese women—haughty old things, tightlipped in powdery blouses, setting down cups of tea to peer and then scowl between dainty pink bites of *Punschkrapfen.*

Schoenberg frowns, wipes at his lap, lays his linen over the puddle on the tablecloth as a waiter hurries over to attend to the mess.

"Things continue to go rather poorly for Mathilde and me," he says somberly, screwing up his face. "Can you believe it? Mathilde actually propositioned one of my composition students recently. I stumbled upon them in the living room, Mati, for all intents and purposes, groping the poor, unsuspecting ox." He snorts. "Preposterous! The things the woman feels compelled to do, simply for attention." He breathes heavily, she can hear him wheezing, a rasp in his chest.

"For the sake of the children. This is the sole purpose we remain together. United by a shared burden. Eternal misery."

Vivian refolds her napkin, placing it on the table.

"But everything dear to you is in Berlin," he says. "Your parents. Friends, colleagues." His gaze bores into her. "Your *brother.*"

Oh, so now he'll opt to play the sick brother card, she thinks, *Jiri's worsening polio.*

"Your brother's many needs," he says, twisting the knife in further. "And what about friends? The theater—cabaret! The restaurants you and I used to enjoy." He tilts his head to smirk at her. "The Leydicke Tavern!"

She should never have come. Not to the concert. And certainly not here with him. There will be no graceful way for her to extricate herself, she now sees.

"And Elsa?" he asks, leaning forward to appraise her, adopting the guise of ardent solicitor while she exhales heavily, wishing to God he would stop.

"Tell me, if you would, please," her prosecutor begins in that reproachful, somewhat subtle but unmistakably patronizing voice of his, "how it is you think you may *possibly* maintain the pretense of raising a daughter, given the precarious situation you now find yourself in?"

"We manage."

"A woman all alone in Paris. *Bah!*" He clucks his tongue. "Not so very nice to think about. Working until all hours of the night. And with no family around." He wrinkles his nose. "Certainly, you must recognize, this is no way to raise a small child."

Raising children. Does he honestly consider himself the expert, prepared to parcel out pithy advice? Now she's fuming, forced to defend the life she's chosen for herself and her daughter, closing her eyes as she thinks warmly of Tamara, her closest friend in Paris, her big-hearted colleague from Diaghilev's troupe, whose doting, extended family has all but adopted her and Elsa.

"There *are* people in Paris who care about me," she insists, sitting up taller. "People more than willing to step in to assist."

"*And Stravinsky?*" He puffs his cheeks.

"He's created a new ballet."

"I know all about it."

Exhausted suddenly, she looks at the row of newspapers suspended from a wooden rack, struck by easy laughter from the young couple in the adjacent billiards room.

His face softening, he informs her he's been giving more thought to *Orpheus*. "This, Vi, I would very much like. Getting back to the *Orpheus* music you and I once spoke of."

"Now is not an ideal time."

She stands, saying she must go.

"If only I could make my feelings better known to you," he says.

She moves towards the coat rack, slipping into her coat, glancing back at him from the doorway.

Pelting of rain. Chin down as she steps into the chilly breeze of the alleyway, clothes filling with wind, feet meeting the hard cobblestone. She continues to feel the gravitational pull, some relentless force directing her back to the coffee house.

Forward, she tells herself, *keep moving forward*, as now she joins the surge of passersby along the street, jostled, and yet resolved, marching forward, away from Schoenberg, into her own steamy breath.

SIMON

```
S  A  T  O  R
A  R  E  P  O
T  E  N  E  T
O  P  E  R  A
R  O  T  A  S
```

"It's called the Magic Square," Simon said, indicating the Latin Square in the margin of the sketchbook. "Or, more specifically, the Sator Square."

Demetra nodded approvingly. "I see you've done your homework."

"I spent a couple of hours over at Powell the other day, hoping to work through a few issues."

They were back in her office for another meeting. They'd agreed to meet twice a week on an ongoing basis to chisel away and decode the sketchbook's mysteries.

"Naturally, I did a little investigating myself," she said, her finger hovering just above the manuscript page, tracing above the Square's contour, horizontally and then vertically.

"This is what's known as a *boustrophedon*," she said.

"*Boustrophedon?*"

"An ancient type of document creation used for inscription into stone. The practice dates all the way back to the Ancient Greeks."

"Ah, the Greeks," Simon said, smiling, "your people!"

"Exactly," she said. "This square is a bi- or multi-directional form of inscription, readable both forwards *and* backwards." She clasped her hands. "But, instead of reading like a book—left to right and then, next line, left to right again—" She traced her finger above the square in a continuous 'S' shape. "It reads instead like a snake! Left to right for one line. But then, for the next, right to left. And so on."

```
S A T O R
A R E P O
T E N E T
O P E R A
R O T A S
```

"Every other line is flipped or reversed," he said.

"Nifty, eh? The letters can be read in reverse. Rather than left-to-right in English or right-to-left in, say, Arabic or Hebrew, the alternate lines can be read in opposite directions. And, since word order is free in Latin, the meaning stays the same."

He gasped quietly, struck by a sudden insight. "The oxen and the plow."

"What do you mean?"

"Oh, nothing," he said. "Forget it." He was thinking about his father's journal, the image of the toiling farmer. "It's just— Watching the way your finger moved over the Square reminded me of a farmer plowing a field."

"And I can see why," she said. "Sowing, reaping. *Sator Arepo Tenet Opera Rotas* translates, roughly as, *Arepo the sower keeps the work circling.*"

"Or, in another guise," he added, recalling some of his own sleuthing, "something like, *the farmer Arepo guides the wheels of the plow.*"

"Yes, right, Simon."

His father's journal containing the reference to Arepo. And then the torn book page in the safe deposit box which had also contained the Square. In terms of everything he knew and understood about his father, the farming metaphor certainly seemed apt—gardener, farmer, man of the earth, plowman of the soil, seed-sower, cultivator. How, he wondered, had his father stumbled upon the Magic Square, and why did he refer to it in his own private musings? Anxious, he looked over at Demetra, wondering if he should tell her about the journal.

"But the palindrome," he said, leaning over to trace a finger up and then down over the square. "It works vertically, as well."

"It's what's known as a quadruple Latin palindrome," she explained. "I was reading about how the stone tablet was buried in the ashes of Vesuvius, unearthed among the ruins of Pompeii, dating back to 79 AD." She smiled. "It's all so fascinating. My father. I mean, can you imagine? Honest to God, Simon, the man would have had a field day with all of this."

"One *lulu* of a field day," Simon said, grinning.

Demetra laughed then blushed slightly.

But, good God, he was certainly antsy! Impatient, the dread brought on by his deadline bubbling away inside him like an acid.

"All right," he said, sighing. "So, what have we got? A Latin Square of some sort that reads forwards, backwards, up, down, bottom to top, top to bottom." Grinding his teeth, his deadline mocking him, he looked over at Demetra, barely able to stifle his sarcasm. "Impressive. Heady stuff. But why was Schoenberg so interested in it?"

For a moment, Demetra stared back at him before launching into a description of a few of Schoenberg's demons, his rampant super-stitions, and how he suffered from *triskaidekaphobia*, the fear of the number thirteen, "Routinely skipping right over that measure in many of his compositions," she said, "and, upon reaching page thirteen in his score, quite often simply renumbering the pages." Demetra sniffed. "He feared turning seventy-six, because the two numbers added up to thirteen. Prophetic, though, his fear: he died at seventy-six. And on the thirteenth of July, a Friday."

"Fascinating," Simon said, unconvinced as yet, worried they could be wasting precious time chasing their own tails.

"He had plenty of other hang-ups, as well," Demetra added, "premonitions. Visions. Certain feelings of foreboding—these sorts of things."

"And you're making a connection," Simon said, "between the Square and superstitions?"

"Apparently, the Square was once also used as a kind of occult symbol, scholars associating the five Latin words with Christ's five wounds upon the cross." She tugged at a loose strand of hair. "And there's a long tradition of people who believed the Square contained magical powers that could protect people from the devil."

"A form of protection then?" Simon asked, wondering again about his father and the journal. Was his father superstitious or mystical in any obvious way he might recall? Had his father been intent on protecting something or someone?

"Most scholars agree the name Arepo is probably only a common name," Demetra said. "It's what's known as *hapax legomenon* or, in other words, a term that appears here, but nowhere else within the Latin literature. However—" She traced over the word TENET, which formed a cross within the center of the square. "Get a load of this."

```
S  A  T  O  R
A  R  E  P  O
T  E  N  E  T
O  P  E  R  A
R  O  T  A  S
```

"*Tenet,* the central underpinning, can be taken to mean *holds, keeps, possesses, preserves,*" Demetra said. "But a peripheral meaning might also possibly be, *protects.*"

"All right," Simon said, "Arepo protects. But, *protects whom?* Protects *what?*"

Demetra shook her head. "There's some thought that this *Sator* figure is not only a planter or sower, but also a kind of *progenitor,* possibly even a divine being, a type of *parent* figure or *creator* of something." She crossed her legs. "A prognosticator perhaps, as well, someone capable of seeing into the future."

"Protection, creator, visionary," Simon clenched the arms of his chair. "We seem to have a smorgasbord of possibilities here. But what's the connection to Schoenberg? What's it doing in the sketchbook?"

Demetra shook her head. "I'm afraid, I just don't have a good answer for you. Not yet, anyway. I'd need more time to examine the document."

"Understandably," he said.

She tapped the sketchbook. "Because, we do have our work cut out for us." Folding her arms, she sighed. "I don't know whether it's possible for us to meet more often, or—I don't know—how you'd feel about my keeping it overnight to examine. Or over the weekend, possibly—"

He gnawed his lip. "Honestly, I'd have to think about it." He closed his eyes, placing the tip of his tongue against his hard palate while she continued to scan through the document. Drawing a deep breath, he focused on that slow and controlled *cleansing* breath from the meditation CDs.

What a pickle this was now turning out to be. Down to the wire with the opera but at the same time sensing how the Square itself might supply the very key to the answers he sought. Could the Latin Square be connected in some way to his private hypothesis, the affirmation he'd been searching for, that the composers had something more to do with one another than the official record showed? *Hang tight,* some voice of reason was whispering inside his head. *Stay the course a moment longer.*

But, come on, I mean, really! another bigger and more adult voice now intervened. Just what in God's name did he think he was doing, *gambling* on some crazy Square? *Unconscionable,* he concluded, *utterly irresponsible, frittering away precious composition time, swiping at straws essentially, all in some desperate hope that such sleuthing might magically result in outwitting his deadline.*

All debating aside, though, the uncanny coincidence of the Square's appearance in both sketchbook and journal could not be denied. He stole a peek at her, the pleasing oval shape of her face, the vibrant Mediterranean complexion; lush, short-tailed eyebrows and deeply-set green eyes. And, if this weren't enough, she'd asked him about his opera earlier, curious about how the project was proceeding, keenly interested in what might have originally drawn him to the subject. It was a pleasure to discuss his work with another musician, someone intelligent and curious, someone sympathetic to the creative process, the endless roadblocks, frustrations and occasional breakthroughs, the mood swings, second guesses and prolonged episodes of self-doubt, all of which came with the territory.

"No doubt, though," Demetra said now, fingers gently tapping the Latin Square in the sketchbook, "the notion of divine creator, a progenitor creating original works of art or shepherding some larger artistic movement, would really have resonated with Schoenberg. He certainly thought of himself as a visionary of sorts, the father of a broader modernist movement."

"That makes sense, I guess."

She stared intently at him. "But, Simon. I just don't get it. Why all this fuss over the Latin Square?" She gave a little shrug. "I mean, wonderful as it all seems, I'm sure you've got more pressing matters you're dealing with."

He thought again about the journal— this *other little secret document* he also happened to be harboring. *Go on now,* some animus in him urged, *full disclosure, team work.Come clean. Tell her about the journal.* He could feel his neck and shoulders tensing, one *lulu* of a headache coming on.

"The other day," he said testing the waters, "you spoke about your father." She shook her head slowly, another wistful smile slowly forming. "You know, it's funny," he ventured. "My father. I remember, growing up, he kept a journal."

She looked at him askance, and he shrugged, explaining how, recently, he happened to come upon it, describing the safe deposit box, how he'd put off dealing with certain tasks after his father had passed away.

"Those types of things can be trying," she said. "Believe me, I know."

"But, wanna know a crazy thing?" he said. "The other day I was flipping through the journal when I happened to stumble upon the *identical* Magic Square."

Demetra knitted her eyebrows. "But, how can that be possible?"

"My father was a farmer and a trained botanist." Again he shrugged. "So, maybe the Square appealed to him or caught his attention some-how." Simon explained how his parents had emigrated from England to Southern California in the 1940's to allow his mother to follow her dream of a professional vocal career while his father took on various gardening clients. Quite a few famous clients, as it turned out.

"I was probably only four or five at the time, too young to remember," Simon explained. "But, crazy as it sounds, it just so happened my father at one point wound up working as a gardener for both the Schoenberg and Stravinsky households.

Demetra laughed. "Well, Simon!" She smiled and then mock-frowned at him. "And how long were you planning on keeping this a secret?"

He shook his head, searching for the words. "It wasn't intentional."

He swallowed. "It's a difficult subject. My parents fell upon some really difficult times in Los Angeles. My mother died when I was very young."

"I'm so sorry." She asked about his mother's music career.

"My mother's name was Helena Dent," he said. "A soprano. Rather well-regarded, apparently, among LA's avant garde during the 1940's, though, I doubt you would have heard of her."

When he looked up she was grinning at him.

"What?" he said, smiling, embarrassed.

"Well, Simon Grafton, it turns out you seem to have all sorts of secrets up your sleeve."

～

Evenings on the Roof

Hollywood, CA
16 November 1939 8:00 p.m.
Peter Yates, Artistic Director, presents:

Helena Dent Grafton, Soprano
Claes Huylenbrouck, Conductor
Franz Josef Haydn, *The Lady's Looking Glass*, H. 31
Igor Stravinsky, *Three Japanese Lyrics* for high voice
Franz Schubert, *Winterreise*, D. 911
Arnold Schoenberg, *Pierrot Lunaire*, Op. 21,
    a Melodrama for reciter, piano, flute/piccolo,
    clarinet/bass clarinet, violin/viola, and cello,
    choreographed by Elsa Růžek

Tableau VIII

Vivian

"Woe to him who seeks to please rather than to appall."
—Hermann Melville, *Moby Dick*

"The pagans on stage made pagans of the audience."
—Thomas Kelly, *First Nights:*
Five Musical Premieres

The Rite of Spring premiere
Théâtre des Champs-Élysées

Paris, 29 May 1913

As the zero hour approaches, Vivian lingers backstage, pacing in bast shoes amidst the frenetic preparations. A carpenter hollers instructions to a trio of stocky stagehands inspecting sections of the set, an electrician switches lamps on and off while crew members work on portable floods and drag lengths of cable across the floor towards square traps in the stage. It's all slowly coming to life—spotlights checked, backdrops wheeled into place. In the pit, a trombonist warms up with slow arpeggios, a piccolo player detonates the same four shrill pitches while, backstage, the dancers navigate around wooden planks, stray props, and other debris.

She wears a coarse-fibered tunic of red, yellow and brown earth colors, the bands along her skirt and top streaked with white and blue, accentuating breasts and hips while affording stark glimpses of bare leg whenever she moves. Like Nijinsky's choreography, the costume evokes the erotic.

During the past few days, an electrical force has slowly been accumulating. Among other Parisian cultural gossip, advance press reports have forecasted a sold-out house. What will unfold tonight is anyone's guess.

Vivian's reassured to come upon Tamara backstage, warming up in the corner.

"Are you frightened?" Tamara asks, dark eyes, robust lips.

"Only mildly mortified," Vivian replies with a nervous giggle as they execute *échappées* and *changements*, flexing to make the muscles supple and elastic. Around them, fellow troupe members follow suit, grabbing at a vertical batten, stray pieces of scenery, or a fixed ladder for support while undertaking similar stretches. They assemble into small groups, chatting nervously as they pull on tights or fasten purple tunics and prehistoric bearskin costumes, bathrobes, pointed bonnets. Several dancers pace around with dour, funereal expressions, trepidation in their eyes, mild panic even, as they work in a pair of new ballet shoes and consult strips of paper, cheat sheets containing the complex asymmetrical counts of the choreographic sequences.

The conductor, Monteux, paces backstage among the dancers, deep in thought, his face ashen and stern, a general steeling himself for what is to come. The baton in his hand is a stiletto, which in mere minutes will launch the proceedings—slowly, ominously, at first, before slicing through the air to evoke terrifying sounds.

Pulling the heavy stage curtain back an inch or so, Vivian peeks out into the auditorium, wondering if Schoenberg could be out there among the throngs, wishing he *were* out there.

The house lights flicker, signaling the ten-minute warning before curtain time, Stravinsky streaking by backstage, pale and harried, oddly winsome in his tuxedo. Vivian can't help but feel admiration for such a colorful and spry leprechaun, the impish sorcerer responsible for the brilliant musical score. She finds Stravinsky fascinating—the energetic angularity, chocolate eyes, delicate facial structure as now he leans over the battered rehearsal piano to pound out a knotty passage from *The Ritual of the Rival Tribes* in a last-minute consultation with Nijinsky.

Diaghilev waddles by, adjusting the pince-nez over his nose and muttering to himself, momentarily distracted by a male dancer's derrière, his neck craning to gaze high up into the rafters as if propitiating the gods.

Remain vigilant! Maintain your focus! Monsieur Diaghilev warned everyone at the conclusion of last night's rehearsal, cautioning them to be prepared for potential audience resistance, if not, possibly, a more hostile reaction. *This will be our show, not theirs,* he reminded them, insisting, no matter what, the show must go on, exhorting the troupe as if preparing them for battle—a theater of war, rather than one of dance.

Several months of rehearsals have led up to this moment, exhausting ordeals often extending late into the night, Stravinsky parachuting into the dance studio from time to time, slamming his fists on the keyboard lid and otherwise flying into a rage about unacceptably sluggish tempos, sweeping the rehearsal pianist aside while pouncing upon the piano keys to demonstrate various polyrhythms, hollering at a petrified Nijinsky and losing all patience with the dancers in their struggle to navigate demonic rhythmic patterns.

I must treat each individual dancer like a sculpture, Nijinsky confessed privately to Vivian. *I will risk breaking them if I must.* Nijinsky drilled his dancers almost without mercy, painstakingly working with each individual to twist and contort their bodies, molding them into near-lifeless objects, explaining to Vivian how the ballet was the incarnation of Nature itself—*the life of the stones and the trees*—as he continued to shape his dancers into symbols of the tribe's life force before piling the whole of the cast into frightening human pyramids.

"Places, everyone!" Nijinsky now cries, clapping his hands.

The house lights dim, then a melody emerges from the orchestra pit, a lone plangent bassoon, tense and wailing in its highest tessitura, mingling with the uneasiness of an audience unready to settle down.

Anxious, the dancers wait backstage, unending stillness, the wing dark and drafty, lit only by the glow of a ghost light. Her stomach is in knots, her fellow troupe members equally anxious, she can sense, jittery, swathed in flaxen scarlet smocks, their maiden legs wrapped in cross-gartered strips of cloth, hair twisted into long braids, cheeks crudely daubed with swirls of blue and red makeup.

At last, Nijinsky cues the maidens to take the stage as the curtain lifts and Vivian, dry-mouthed, files out quickly among her group, falling into formation against Roerich's spare backdrop, a barren hilly land-scape of painted trees, a lake, copses, rocks, the sacred hill surrounded by smaller rises, a predawn gloom evoked from dark violet lighting.

Confronted by the circle of pagan dancers—not a tutu anywhere in the house—whose stomping only intensifies in sync with Stravinsky's frenetic score, the audience's reaction is a collective gasp. The crowd's restlessness is palpable. Their unruliness drowns out the orchestra, several audience members still on their feet, refusing to take their seats, sparring among neighbors in various shouting matches while others boo and holler obscenities.

It's nearly impossible for Vivian to hear the music, her group struggling to execute sequences without access to the instrumental textures, forced instead to rely upon vibrations from the orchestra pit. In the midst of the hullaballoo, the orchestra fights to carry out folk melodies and rhythmic displacements, their stalwart determination spurring the dancers on, Monteux wielding the baton with terrific concentration, self-possessed, nerveless as a crocodile.

Posed in tense angularity, the dancers point their toes inwards, right elbow resting on left fist, right fist supporting sideways-leaning heads. Flat-footed and straight-legged, they jump downward instead of up like unwieldy pachyderms, eschewing all traditional lightness or daintiness. The heat from the rafter lights overhead is searing. Vivian's shoulders and legs ache, her costume feels grotesquely heavy, as if it might drag her to the floor.

But how preternaturally deformed we must appear, she thinks, the line of the body deliberately distorted, knees turned inwards, heels pointing out, fists clenched, wrists contorted, elbows pulled forward sharply so that gnarled hands twist in towards the body with palms flat and open. Shoulder to shoulder, the dancers drop to their knees, lowering their heads until their painted cheeks graze the floor.

Now the eight maidens within her circle activate like puppets, jerking into life, hopping in unison to disjunct pulsations in *The Augurs of Spring*, squatting, rising on tiptoe, shivering, trembling, right hands falling to their sides, heads jerking to the left.

As one orbit of the stage is completed, every other dancer leaps out from the ring formation—out, and then back again—the stomping convulsions of the wild *khorovod* circle dance vibrating thunderously over the stage. Hips and thighs lifted in pelvic thrusts, feet flexed in wide second-position pliés and jarring backbends, the stampede of anarchy further agitating the audience as the chaos intensifies into shouts, whistles, catcalls, lurid insults, the terrifying rumbling of what now begins to feel like a riot.

Then they're up again, the dancers circling, whirling, the timpani unleashing further violence, troupe members joining hands then crossing their arms, five groups of eight dancers bending to roll onto their bellies as the character of the old woman appears...

The troupe resumes pouncing, debris hurtled at the stage, wadded up concert programs, coins, stones, pieces of ripe fruit, the dancers feeling their way by osmosis, guided by pounding drums or the errant screech from trumpets and horns. In the wings, Nijinsky stands on a chair, pounding a cane as he hollers dance counts in polysyllabic Russian numbers—thirteens, seventeens—neither he nor the dancers can keep pace with. The house manager flicks the lights on and off, officers of the gendarme sweep in to eject unruly audience members.

"But! I beg you!" Diaghilev howls into the mayhem from center stage, "allow them to finish the performance!"

Suddenly, Tamara stumbles, ankle collapsing, knee buckling grotesquely as, with a sharp cry, she tumbles to the floor, reaching out for Vivian just as Vivian's formation pulls away, yanking Vivian along with it, Vivian, panicked, wanting to come to her friend's aid, her fingertips grazing Tamara's for a moment before she's thrust away again by her formation, a single mechanical unit robotically intent on hitting its mark at the opposite end of the stage.

The tribal elders stretch their palms to the sky, guiding the Sage to kiss the sacred earth, the first tableau rushing towards conclusion, a whoosh, thud, Vivian fleeing from the stage beneath the falling curtain.

SIMON

"So fascinating," Demetra said, handing Ingo's letter back to him. "I'm flattered you shared this with me."

Simon turned through the sketchbook pages to the *Petrushka* passages, gathering the nerve to broach the subject of Stravinsky with her, "a burning issue for me, actually," as he explained while steeling himself. The topic was delicate, he knew; not once during any of their meetings had Stravinsky's name come up, though surely she would have noticed the *Petrushka* insertions as well as the distinctly contrasting autograph.

Demetra went over to the thin Giacometti sculpture on the bookcase, lost in thought as she ran her fingers lightly over the slender neck and shoulders of the Woman of Venice.

"I don't know," Simon ventured, "I feel like maybe it's the elephant in the room here. Something tells me you aren't all too eager to discuss Stravinsky in relation to any of this."

"Well. I *am*, after all, a Schoenberg scholar," she said with a shrug.

"Naturally," Simon said, "a Schoenbergian, amen!" He smiled. "But, taking that fully into consideration, of course, I guess I was hoping—especially after reading Ingo's take on everything—you and I might take a step back for a second and think about Stravinsky's possible role."

Demetra expression was doubtful.

"Because, it seems to me," he said, "I *do* think we need to at least consider Stravinsky."

She folded her arms. "Schoenberg, you know, is a rather rarefied focus. All-consuming. And in the scholarly work I undertake, you really can't afford to stray too far from the matter at hand, or allow yourself to be sidetracked by distractions."

"Distractions?" He laughed in disbelief, pointing to the document. "This Stravinsky passage? Rather uncanny. I mean, wouldn't you agree? Page after page of Schoenberg sketches. But then— What do you suppose it's doing here?"

"My expertise is in Schoenberg," she said flatly.

"You have to concede, though, just how bizarre it is, the Stravinsky passage. Smack dab in the middle of Schoenberg's private sketchbook. Don't you find it at least a tad incredible that this document not only *suggests* but, to my mind, *confirms*, that something—*mysterious,* something very much *behind the scenes*—may have been taking place between the two of them?"

Demetra knitted her brow. "What are you suggesting exactly? A covert collaboration? I'm sorry to say, there just doesn't appear to be any *other* documentation among source materials in the Schoenberg archives that would point to any such *collaboration.*"

"But, don't you see? That's what makes this—this *thing*, this document—unlike anything else!" He laughed. "I mean, it's remarkable! Ground-breaking potentially."

"Listen, Simon, don't get me wrong, I love the enthusiasm." She gazed up at the ceiling for a moment. "I'm just not prepared to *go* there myself."

"But a *collaboration*," he said, "between the two greatest composers of the twentieth century. This could *potentially* change everything. Were I—were *we*—to come forward with this kind of discovery, history books would need to be rewritten." He placed his fingers lightly upon the sketchbook. "We're talking about entirely fresh terrain no scholar's ever uncovered." He swallowed. "In fact, everything scholars *have* asserted about the development of modern music would be up for grabs, essentially, our entire *conception* of the last fifty or sixty years—"

"Believe me," she said. "I've combed through every last crumb of documentation at the Schoenberg Institute. And I've personally examined every shred of source material that's passed through our doors here at UCLA." She expelled air. "I can't tell you how many hours—indeed, years of my life, at this point—I've spent in Vienna and Berlin, at Yale, Harvard, the Library of Congress, knee deep in autographs and source materials." She sucked her lip. "I hate to burst your bubble. But there's simply nothing out there to corroborate the claim you're making. And, well, an undoubtedly spurious claim at that, one lacking historical or biographical testimony, nothing in Schoenberg's letters or theoretical writings to support it, no eyewitness or personal accounts from close associates, students, family. Zilch." Again she shrugged. "And, to the best of my knowledge, nothing whatsoever in the Stravinsky archives, either."

"But the *calligraphy!*" he all but shrieked. "How do you explain *that*? *This* is clearly a *distinct* calligraphy, unique. An entirely *different* calligraphy from anything else in the document." He scratched his head. "And it *does* resemble other Stravinsky sketches I've seen. Other *Petrushka* sketches anyway. As well as autographs of other Stravinsky works."

"You're right about that," she said. "In the case of *Petrushka*, this particular insertion in the sketchbook could in fact date all the way back to 1912 when the two composers met briefly in Berlin as *Petrushka* was premiering there." She nodded. "So, yes, it's conceivable, I suppose, that Stravinsky could have somehow—and for whatever crazy reason—penned something into Schoenberg's sketchbook." Her eyes grew larger. "Almost as if Schoenberg marched right up to Stravinsky after the show, flipping open his sketchbook to ask Stravinsky for his autograph."

"And the *Orpheus* section?" Feverish, he turned through pages. "These notations. They're mostly pencil. And yet, distinct handwriting. Is this not Stravinsky's hand once again?"

Yes, Demetra conceded, parts of the *Orpheus* section might appear to be written in an autograph different than Schoenberg's.

"But, an entirely different composer's handwriting?" She tsk-tsked. "I'm sorry. I'm just not prepared to stick my neck out that far. There's absolutely no documentation from the 1940s for this, when Schoenberg was embarking upon the *Orpheus* project with Elsa Růžek." She sucked in air sharply. "But, what we *are* certain about—what's *incontrovertible*—is the fact that by the 1940s, the two composers had succeeded in cementing an acrimonious and irreconcilable rivalry. Simon, these two pretty much *hated* one another."

But, my God! All the more reason then for the two of them not *to want to be transparent about the sketchbook and their meeting,* Simon ranted to himself, light-headed and beginning to perspire beneath his sweater.

"If I told you how long I've been living with this idea," he said, working to control his voice. "That the two may have had something secretly to do with one another—"

"Which, don't get me wrong," she said with a light laugh, "is an absolutely *wonderful* conceit. Extraordinary by all accounts. Dramatically-speaking, and coming from a fictional point of view, it gets right to the crux of exactly what opera should be." She smiled. "Total creative license. I love it! Yes, in this type of scenario, it's certainly compelling and even a little fun to think about. Deviant. As a dramatic construct, mind you, a kind of fairy tale, a flight of fancy."

"It's more than that," he said with a bitter taste in his mouth.

Demetra seated herself, turning through a few more pages, navigating—to his utter dismay—*away* from the *Orpheus* sections.

He took a chance. "Demetra. What if—?" He looked at her tensely.

"Look. I need you to listen for a moment. Because. What if scholars have gotten it all wrong? What if this really *is* Stravinsky's hand here, mixed into the *Orpheus* sketches?

"It isn't," she said.

Groaning, he said, "I just don't get how you can be so mulish."

"Fair enough," she said. "I'll explain how I can be so *mulish*." She gnawed her upper lip. "Though you may not like what I have to say. Simply put, and in the baldest of terms: Schoenberg would *never* have compromised his own artistic standards through any sort of *dalliance* with *Stravinsky*." She allowed her comments to settle. "It would be an impurity of sorts. Anathema. Musical contamination. I mean, in view of all we know about the degree of enmity between these two figures, what you're suggesting is the Montagues breaking bread with the Capulets, for heaven's sake; Hutus and Tutsis hooking up after hours as bedfellows; Arabs and Jews sitting down, shoulder to shoulder on the West Bank to nibble matzoh together at a Passover Seder.

"And, I'm afraid, what this does," she continued, "is simply to distort and, well—to my way of thinking, anyway—*adulterate* Schoenberg's legacy." Her disgust was unmistakable. "*Petrushka* passage notwithstanding, by the 1940s, Schoenberg essentially disdained and disowned everything about Stravinsky. If he wasn't actively denying the very existence of Stravinsky, he was only too quick to excoriate."

But, the evidence, he silently lamented. *There it is, right in front of your nose!*

"And so, were I now to suggest something so perverse as a behind-the-scenes partnership, I'd be turning my back on generations of loyal Schoenbergians, spitting in their eye, essentially." She sighed heavily. "To say nothing of the dismantling of decades of my own work."

Dejected, he watched helplessly as she thumbed through more pages, navigating somewhere towards the middle of the document, playing with a strand of hair, sucking on the tip of it while zeroing in on a particular passage.

"Ah, yes," she murmured, captivated now by some altogether fresh discovery, "an early fragment of the String Trio, opus forty-five. Schoenberg's graphic depiction of his own heart failure. Would you get a load of that?" She giggled to herself. "Uncanny!"

Gazing up at him, starry-eyed, she said, "You realize no one's ever laid eyes on these source materials before."

"Exactly," he said, stirred again.

"Unbelievable," she said, touching her fist to her lips, sighing, her thoughts wandering.

"Although," he said, "let's not get ahead of ourselves? If you wouldn't mind turning back to the *Orpheus* sections for just a—"

"Pittsburgh," she said in a whisper. "The International Music-ological Society. This'll truly knock the ball out of the park at the spring conference."

"Listen, I really don't think we should—"

"I mean, it's all here," she continued, transfixed. "The missing Schoenberg sketchbook. Page after page of puzzle pieces. Clues, a map to the treasure. Lord almighty. *Ha!* Who would have ever imagined?" She cackled. "This is gonna make a few waves. You can be sure of that. I'll need to get in touch with Rodinsky—Alvin—over at the Society for Musical Theory."

"But what I was actually hoping to propose," he said, throat burning, "was that we could focus our efforts, first and foremost, on the *Orpheus* sections."

"We'll want to move swiftly on the proposal," she said, looking past him. "The abstract will have to be put together fairly soon if we want the paper to be in contention for the conference."

"Because," he said, "*Orpheus* is where I presently am, you know, in terms of my opera, the nut I've been hoping to crack. That repeated series of notes that keep cropping up, those same pitches, over and over again."

"But what exactly is my angle going to be?" she said, glancing up towards the ceiling.

"*Orpheus*?" he repeated more loudly. "That's where I think you and I ought to be focusing."

"There's so much material here." Slowly, she nodded. "An overwhelming number of sketches and musical propositions, really, to contend with."

Releasing a cleansing breath, he stared at the framed photo of Demetra and her father on the filing cabinet, a delicate Japanese vase beside it, his gaze roving towards the bookcase where the bronze Woman of Venice stood, arms stiffly at her sides, like a sentry appraising him with a dubious expression.

"These kinds of things, they often take quite some time to work through." She sniffed. "When you come across original source material of this caliber, one *does* have to live with the material for quite a while, day in and day out."

"Sure," he said, "I get it."

Laughing, she tossed her head. "This is going to sound terribly maudlin. But it's almost as if the source material begins speaking to you, revealing its secrets in faint whispers. Scholars, Simon. True scholars. They practically become married to a find this big. It can start to take over your whole life." She frowned. Then, breathing in sharply, she stared hard at him.

"Which is why I need to ask you something," she said.

He fidgeted, his palms clammy.

"A request," she said, looking at him for a long uncomfortable moment. "Simon, I'd like your permission to duplicate the manuscript."

He felt himself recoil, almost as if she'd kicked him, steadying himself as his fingers dug into the chair arms.

"With your permission," she continued with a grave expression, "I'd very much like to have my own working copy on hand."

My God, had she really just asked if she could copy the document?

"I mean. Let's not kid ourselves here. I think we both realize this could take years. At the pace we've been going, examining maybe a handful of pages at a crack." She expelled air forcefully. "And I, for one, know you don't have that kind of time. Not with a rapidly approaching deadline in—what—three weeks is it?" She narrowed her gaze. "And, quite frankly, nor do I."

Sick to his stomach, he sat affixed to the chair.

"I need time," she explained. "More time with the manuscript. To put it more baldly: *vast* amounts of time."

"Right," he said, queasy as he dared to imagine the series of acclaimed scholarly articles she'd go on to publish, elucidating the sketchbook's wonders, articles penned solely and exclusively by Dr. Kouras herself, slated for high-ranking music journals, the keynote or plenary address she'd wind up presenting worldwide at various prestigious musicological conferences while continuing to ascend the academic ladder towards a crowning professorship at some top-dog institution, Harvard, Princeton, Brown, Yale. Or, her winsome photo beneath a *New York Times* headline:

Rare Schoenberg Document, Assumed by Scholars to be Missing, Reclaimed by Brilliant Leading Musicology Scholar

Giving his knee a pat, she said, "Imagine how much *more* we'd be able to explore and accomplish during our sessions together. How much faster things would begin to move. I'd have a much better handle on things, a greater depth of knowledge I'd then be able to offer you." She looked him up and down. "Don't you see? That way, I could be that much more of a help to you."

Hedging, he said, "It's not that I don't trust you." He nodded. "Honestly, though, I'm just not comfortable with the thought of some duplicate manuscript floating around out there. It's too risky.

"Look, Simon. My main priority is to help you with your opera. That's all I want. Wouldn't that be something? Whatever it takes to cross that finish line you've been chasing for a long time. Too long." She crossed her legs. "I'd very much like to help you accomplish that."

Leaning a little closer, he caught a glorious whiff of her scent, a fruity aroma, honeysuckle or grapefruit, hint of vanilla, musk.

"No one would ever have to know about the duplicate," she said quietly. "*Total secrecy—our secret.* We'd still continue to meet privately."

Then, changing tack, she asked about his recent teaching evaluation as he slumped in his chair—into a much smaller version of himself.

"Oh, yes, that," he said.

 "Bernie and I spoke about it at length."

"Perfect," he muttered, deflated as an image swept the scene of Dean Boderman, lifting his eyes from the teaching evaluation the other day.

Not exactly a stellar report, is it? Boderman had said, prompting Simon to apologize, baring his soul about how tumultuous a quarter it had been for him. *Yeah?* Boderman said. *Well, that and a dollar'll get you in the subway.* This, followed by a grin of impeccably white teeth.

Now Demetra was nodding. "A bit of a snag, the evaluation. A few significant adjustments, no doubt, to be made on your part." She clasped her fingers. "Certainly not the end of the world, though."

"If you say so."

"And, I'll have you know, I put in a great word for you. I sang your praises, Professor Grafton." She smiled. "Teamwork, right? We're all in this together. I figured you could probably benefit from a little wiggle room. Particularly now during crunch time."

Because, this report? Boderman had said at the close of their meeting. *It appears to be telling a kind of story. And the story it's trying to tell?* Boderman pushed out his lips, shaking his head pitifully. *Well, kemosabe, this ain't the kind of story I want to be spending any of my time reading.*

"At any rate," Demetra was saying, "I think I've managed to persuade the dean to refrain from breathing down your neck. At least for the foreseeable future."

"God," Simon said, "you have no idea what a relief that is."

"Bernie and I go back a ways," she said. "I'm privileged to enjoy something of a special and direct channel to the dean. I've no doubt, if the tables were turned—if I needed something pretty badly from you—you'd go to bat for me."

Dazed, head swimming, he went over to the window, hoping to steady himself, gazing into the courtyard below where students hurried by beneath the vivid purple canopy of jacaranda trees.

Turning, summoning his nerve, Simon said, "I'm sorry. But duplication just isn't an option."

"You know," she said a moment later, "I might also manage to make a few things happen for you here in the department. Open a few doors, that sort of thing." Her smile was pleasant. "Boderman would no longer pose any sort of concern, whatsoever."

Simon raised his eyebrows.

"*Tenure,*" she said, spelling it out for him. "Job security. I'm not exactly sure what I'm able to do in terms of helping you wrap up your opera. But, with regard to your standing at this particular institution, well, suffice it to say, it wouldn't be too much of a stretch for me to sort of nurture and enable certain *career* advancements on your behalf."

He suppressed a laugh, biting his balled fist.

"What?" she asked with a little pout.

"It sounds to me as if you're leveraging—"

She shook her head firmly. "I just want to be absolutely clear about things. The teaching evaluation. Undoubtedly, this needs to be addressed." She gave his shoulder a pat. "And I can certainly help to ensure that it does *exactly* that, while moving in the right direction. A negative review, on the other hand." She wrinkled her nose. "That could really have a detrimental impact on things and wind up making life terribly unpleasant for you."

Tail between his legs, he closed his eyes, sensing the edge of some bleak sinkhole she seemed to be leading him towards.

Demetra went over to her desk, retrieving a business card, bending to jot something down.

"Here," she said, pressing the card into his hand. "I've given you a lot to think about. Why don't you sleep on it?" She indicated the business card. "That's my home number." She met his gaze. "Just in case. If, at any point, you know, you felt you wanted to discuss further, or, really, Simon, we could talk about anything you'd like. Anything at all."

Tableau IX

Igor

After the performance, Stravinsky and members from the ballet company reconvene at *Café Cheveux Sur la Poitrine* in the sixteenth arrondissement where a disinterested waiter delivers flutes of champagne among cigarette haze and lively banter.

They're all here, Stravinsky thinks as he glances around the table at notable personages—Diaghilev, Nijinsky, Benois, Roerich, Karsavina, Coco Chanel, Isadora Duncan, Cocteau. Gertrude Stein converses with the writer, Comtesse Anna de Noailles; the choreographer and dance critic, Princesse Amedee de Broglie, sits beside Dorothea Rondo to compare notes. A handful of dancers are present as well, everyone keen for a celebration, despite the premiere's hostile reception.

"Exactly what I wanted," Diaghilev cries, "just the reaction I was hoping for!" He strokes his moustache. "Friends, there's no going back now to the ballet company from some exotic and far-off culture we were once presumed to be. *Non!* Now, certainly, they'll take us seriously, no longer batting us aside as mere picturesque bazaar. *Au contraire! Paris et le monde entier, prendra note!*"

A momentary lull. Then an outcry with everyone eager to chime in all at once. *But, what lunacy from the audience!* they holler at Diaghilev. *Was such a hostile reaction truly what you'd been hoping for? You must be a masochist, or perhaps mad yourself! Exactly what Diaghilev wanted?*

Stravinsky himself was outraged by the collective outcry, seething midway through the performance and then fleeing his seat in the stalls to take in the remainder of the performance from the wings of the stage. He'd managed to find his path towards the music through *rhythm*—not *melody!*—as the creative lifeblood of modern sound. Meanwhile, all around him, the world appeared to be radically transforming while the art world attempted to keep pace.

Smiling now, Diaghilev shakes his hands, hoping to quell the uproar.

Nijinsky hollers at Diaghilev, who shushes him, explaining how it was absolutely his intention to shake up the establishment—*ruffling a number of feathers, stirring up controversy.* "Why, think of the publicity alone," Diaghilev says. He narrows his gaze. "*Barbarism* is good for box office."

"*Divine!*" Diaghilev cries, winking at Dorothea Rondo. "I won't sleep a wink while waiting for tomorrow's batch of reviews. I can assure you, I'll be the very first customer in line at the newstand for *Le Figaro* in the morning."

"Nothing like a few well-placed shock waves to rouse the opiated masses," Roerich chimes in.

"Indeed," Diaghilev responds, giving Roerich's head a fraternal pat.

"Oh, but the audience was pernicious tonight!" Nijinsky objects, shaking his head. "Bloodthirsty like bats. There's simply no call for brutality."

"But, on the other hand, Vaslav," Stravinsky says, "nearly every pore of the *Sacre* oozes with brutality."

"*Oui, mes chers,*" Diaghilev says, "a new era is dawning. Out with the *démodé,* and in with the new. *Au revoir, la belle époque!*" Satisfied, he sighs. "The modern period has now been launched and, friends, mark my words, there'll be no turning back."

Stravinsky steals a peek at Vivian, admiring her pleasing neckline, alabaster complexion, her quiet intense eyes.

Diaghilev stands, raising his glass to toast Nijinsky. "And to our dear Vivian, and the exceptional work she's accomplished in helping our dancers assimilate Nijinsky's inscrutable imagination and machinations." Amidst her cheering colleagues, Vivian's smile is timid, overwhelmed, seemingly, by the recognition, as now Diaghilev turns to Stravinsky with raised glass.

"Last, but certainly not least," Diaghilev says, "*le compositeur ne plus ultra,* the incomparable, irrepressible—Stravinsky!"

"Hear, hear!" the others holler, clinking glasses.

As the night wears on, the troupe slowly trickles away, leaving Stravinsky and Vivian alone among the last of the revelers. And later, when she glances at him with a look that seems sultry to him, possibly, a familiar shiver jolts through his body, the stage now set for certain transgressions. Caught up in the flurry of too much excitement, it occurs to him he may betray Schoenberg before the evening's over, soberly confronting the fact that he may be no better than a Judas. Or a Richard Gerstl.

"My family is away," he says to her as they step outside to hail a cab. "Off to Geneva to visit my sister-in-law." He scratches his head. "With all the strain I've been under—all the strain I've placed them under—I fear I may have driven them away."

"But you must be missing them," she says.

He shrugs. He's conflicted in terms of Katya, towards whom he feels the purist of affection and the absence of any longing. He stares down at his polished shoes, lighting up a filtered *Gitanes* and offering her one with a devious grin.

Taking a drag from the cigarette, Vivian says, "Your music. It's intoxicating."

"You're very kind," he says with a mannered bow, casting aside further thoughts about his family or about Schoenberg and what his relationship with Vivian might entail.

Schoenberg. Truly an onerous Teutonic monkey upon one's back. How dare he stick his Semitic snout in anything Stravinsky wishes to accomplish as an artist.

"The energy!" Vivian exclaims. "All that raw, primitive power. Visceral. Primal. I can't fathom how you managed to find such sounds." She takes another drag from the cigarette. "I felt its power tonight as I danced, Monsieur Stravinsky. I felt—" She looks into his eyes. "Transformed by the music."

"But you must call me Igor," he says in a velvety voice.

"*Eager*," she pronounces the name, probably not unaware of his poorly-concealed swooning as he hedges his bets, sensing that now is the moment to lean over and, with the gentlest of pressure, caress the side of her face.

Art does not mind whether the artist himself acts well as a man. He recalls the Maritain essay. *The creative spirit is imbued with a sacred egoism. If he sins as a man, he does not sin as an artist.*

They share a cab, bumping over rutted side streets past tall buildings, striped awnings, gas street lights, the cab pulling up to the corner near her flat, Stravinsky handing over the fare, insistent upon escorting her every step of the way to her doorstep. The perfect gentleman, slipping an arm through hers as they approach her door, clutching his catch, preening, exhilarated.

At the entrance of her flat, when she turns to thank him and bid him good evening, he kisses her.

from the journal of Jasper Grafton

Los Angeles, California
11 August 1939

As the train shrilled to its final halt beneath the canopied platform,
Helena & I shared a bedraggled look before succumbing to giddy
laughter. Official émigrés we now were, moments away from
disembarking into unfamiliar territory, into chapters of our lives wholly
unwritten.

'I'd gladly give my eyeteeth for a proper bath,' Helena sd. & I advised her
not to trade in on those precious eyeteeth just yet, though the thought of
a sudsy plunge did hold a certain appeal, following the weeks of cooped-
up fustiness, long nights spent negotiating unforgiving sleeping berths &
an abject sustenance of insipid succotash & intractable mutton chops.

Helena's blouse & jumper top looked tousled, the dull & eerie slant of
light from the compartment window underscoring weary brown eyes
& general wraith-like appearance. Through the window, we witnessed
a commotion of train passengers newly disgorged, Helena commenting
on our epic journey while retrieving a looking glass, her comb smoothing
over her yellow hair, a de Havilland or Bergman in profile, albeit a
quieter beauty w/ high forehead & classic square jawline.

'If I weren't so bone-tired,' she sd., 'I'd be inclined to pen a Homeric epic
about our adventures.'

'That,' I replied, 'or a letter of complaint to the Union Pacific's
management beseeching them to construct their sleeping berths from
steel far more pliable.'

During the Atlantic crossing that preceded our train journey, we'd sequestered ourselves in the inner sanctum of the steamer's commodious dining saloon and smoking room, amidst the relentless to-&-fro-ing of fellow travelers, crew members & stevedores, Helena immersed in her music scores, marking passages, vocalizing softly & communing with the friendly souls of German poets—long since deceased, of course—Rilke, Wedekind, Buchner, Altenberg & Hartleben, authors of the song texts she'd been studying. Her chief focus: 'Pierrot Lunaire,' the formidable Schoenberg song cycle, which in only a few short weeks will mark her Los Angeles debut.

Behind the closed doors of our cabin, a narrow room smelling persistently of disinfectant, Helena & I sang folksongs to one another to pass the time, My Heart's in the Highlands, Black is the Color of My True Love's Hair, Danny Boy, The Bells of Aberdovey, Scarborough Sands, relishing the intimacy, our familiar & cherished regimen in light of the many unknowns lurking on the opposite shore, a soothing tonic against the slap of the bitter wind, the ashen sky swollen with fog & the sea itself wine-dark, scrotum-tightening—as Mr. Joyce wld. have it— white foam sloshing the porthole as, accompanied by the ocean's damp roil & persistent swell, the two of us made our lovely music.

Stepping from the Union Pacific now, crossing the threshold of our awaiting lives, we found ourselves tattered & torn with, as they say, little more than the clothes upon our back, displaced, downtrodden, a vagrant duo, partners in grime, negotiating our cumbersome luggage trunks, a prickly pair of everyday escapees we were, direct from the local circus side show.

Amidst the congestion of languid somnolent travelers, we pulled our weighty baggage across a majestic & cavernous train station lobby, Helena stopping & setting down her bags, head tilted towards the high Palladian windows where sunlight streaming through the slats imprinted prisms across the travertine marble floor.

'Jaz, listen,' she sd., closing her eyes, mesmerized by the echoes swirling overhead in the Art Deco chandeliers, her clairaudient ears attuned to the polyphony of voices, the beckoning of sirens.

Did the shimmer of decanted sunlight in such a chthonic vault, accompanied by the motet of ethereal spirits up there, mark our propitious entrance into some mystical underworld of transmigrating souls?

No matter, Sator Arepo, etc., I'm here to protect & look after you, dear sweet Helena.

We searched the train station lobby for our hosts when suddenly, in the midst of the crush, a petite woman emerged, elegantly-dressed in long blue gown & a stole the hue of deep moss, standing alone & bearing a cardboard sign upon which the name Grafton had been most carefully engraved, making her way towards us, lithe & graceful as a sylph, her copper hair pinned up in a chignon, dangling onyx earrings, jewel-studded handbag.

'Helena?' she uttered in some knotty Eastern European accent, Helena beaming, 'Why yes! You must be Elsa!' & Elsa taking hold of Helena's hands to welcome her:

'Allow me please to kindly welcome you each in the United States & to California both!' Elsa sd. before turning to me, heavy scent of corsage as she extended a braceleted hand so smooth and delicate I felt rather self-conscious about my own unsavory getup.

'And, surely, you must be Chosper,' she sd.

Chosper! That's how she rendered my name, an evocation so rich I was loath to suggest any form of correction, rather hoping she'd go on gorgeously mispronouncing it.

'But, you know,' she confessed with a wave of the hand, 'sometimes my English comes with difficulties. Please permit my nuisance.'

Beyond the train depot, the sun's ecstatic blaze had been waiting to bombard us, a phalanx of slender palm trees extending from the station's entrance towards a wide boulevard humming & snarling with passing automobiles.

A few feet in front of us, a tripartite whiteness: a tall, white-haired figure wearing an oversized white blazer stepping towards us from a colossal white motor car w/ the intention of dutifully collecting our belongings. This wd. be Ferguson, the valet, hefting our luggage into the trunk of the car, a Chevrolet Coupe with chromium grille & trim, the whole get-up resembling some modern chariot sent by Mr. Zeus himself.

'But, my word,' I murmured as Helena & I were settling ourselves into the voluptuous back seat, 'what an astonishing machine. Can't say I've

seen anything quite like it back in London among all those Wolseleys, Daimlers, Rovers and the like,' Elsa turning from the front seat, saying, 'Yes, one of my husband's recent pursuits. Claes sends both regards & regrets, by the way, a busy rehearsal schedule this day prevents him, unfortunately, from greeting you more personally.'

And then we were in transit once again, making our way along an immense, gold-lit boulevard beneath a canopy of swishing Arecaceae, prehistoric fibrous husks of dry, airy palm stalks & no turning back now. A final parting glance at the train depot as the grand monolith of Spanish Colonial & Art Deco vanished into the background.

But hardly had we passed through the gates of Valhalla when we realized w/ perfect terror that Ferguson, our somber ferryman, appeared to be navigating the vehicle from the wrong side of the road &, come to think of it, from the wrong side of the car where—rather than on the proper, right side—the steering wheel has been erroneously mounted on the left.

Peril! Helena's face drained at once of all color, her frightened eyes confirming our imminent demise, as I sat forward on the verge of voicing some theatrical or otherwise hysterical objection (Avast and brace about, Ferguson! For the love of God and country, I beseech you, my good captain, belay and adjust course directly!)

But the flow of traffic, as ever ubiquitous & quotidian, Ferguson's languid smirk from the helm of the vessel & the serene way in which Elsa turned to offer us a tin of jam & shortbread cookies reassured us that, indeed, all was well in our travel-weary utopia & that we might as well sit back, close our eyes & settle into the dream.

Tableau X

Vivian

She wakes up beside Stravinsky, fretting about Schoenberg.

Stravinsky's bare back is to her while he snores off the previous evening, sunlight seeps into her flat through a crack in the curtains, early-morning Montparnasse pulsating with motorcars, passersby, the clang of a trolley along the *Boulevard Saint Michel.*

Moments ago, she'd been having a dream about Schoenberg who, midway through his performance, laid down his baton suddenly, turning to search among the hostile audience, pinning his gaze upon her and then hollering something she was unable to decipher. She wonders what he might have been attempting to convey. Would it have something to do with Stravinsky?

She pulls the bed covers aside gently, extending her limbs and assessing the ache in her joints, her muscles tender from last night's ordeal. Wincing, she recalls the sound of Tamara's stifled moans when she took a fall during the first tableau, already on her way to the hospital by the time Vivian was able to make her way backstage, resting, as M. Auric assured Vivian, in the finest of care.

She glances over at her bedmate, at the freckly bare shoulders of a slumbering Stravinsky, the fiery Russian kobold, disarray of fine coppery hair, the great mastermind, architect of the madness, immobilized in an ursine snore. The bedside timepiece shows ten o'clock, her daughter due back shortly from Tamara's mother's apartment.

Naked, she slips out of bed, muscles smarting as she navigates around the sprawl of tuxedo vestments on her way to the water closet.

This ephemeral coupling with Stravinsky: she has no hopes or illusions, no presumptions, no designs as to any sort of a future relationship. After the intense weeks of preparation and the tribulations of last night's opening, her surrendering to Stravinsky had offered up its own thrilling release. Swept up in the Dionysian fervor, she'd let down her guard, allowing the moment to unfold, permitting him to seduce her—a befitting, sizzling flambé to cap off the experience, accompanied by the bodily resonance of *Le Sacre's* awakening of nature, the writhing of birds and beasts, the raw energy, sensual and sexual. Their lovemaking, then, was its own form of rebellion and release, uncontrollable tingling, erotic thrashings, the violent shudder of orgasm.

As she takes hold of a flaking lump of soap to wash at the basin, her thoughts return to Schoenberg. No doubt he'd frown upon her spartan living conditions, the grubby *trop bohémienne* apartment in a musty Montparnasse garret, the improvisatory earthenware sink basin propped up on planks, the tempermental cast iron stove, eccentric plumbing, dilapidated scrollwork and dull wainscotting. And everywhere a heap of battered dance slippers and jettisoned leotards, errant lingerie, dog-eared novels, stacks of poetry, choreographic notebooks.

Schoenberg. She hates the way he maintains some vague hold over her, or that she owes him any form of allegiance. And now, this tryst with Stravinsky, this little mess she's made for herself which must quickly be straightened out. Never mind. She refuses to feel guilty or beholden to anyone back in Berlin. Not now anyway, not during *her* moment while riding the crest of an invigorating if somewhat reckless adventure.

She slips on undergarments and a simple dress, opening a dresser drawer to come upon Maurice, a tiny mouse she's tamed, a companion of sorts, sniffing up at her from a maroon serviette.

Across the room, Stravinsky awakens. Sitting up in bed, he squints at the clock, exclaiming how late it is. "Gorgeous day!" he mumbles, rubbing his eyes. "What shall we do to take advantage of the nice weather?"

"I'm not sure," she says, thinking of her various errands, flowers for Tamara, Elsa's return soon.

"But we must celebrate," he says, eyes brightening as he wraps the duvet around him. "The *premiere!*" he says with a breathless laugh. "Why, the show, of course. If nothing else, the very fact of our survival." He flashes a grin. "But, also, the good fortune the heavens have bestowed upon us in choosing to bring the two of us together, the fortuitous confluence of a Vivian and an Igor."

When she pulls open the curtains Stravinsky shields his eyes, patting the bed for her to sit beside him.

"I'd like to get hold of *The Times*," he says, "to see what the critics have to say about *Le Sacre*. I'll bet the news even traveled to a number of international papers."

Resigned, she seats herself upon the edge of the bed, folding her hands in her lap.

"Let me take you to my favorite café," he says, "*De la Muette*, just off the *Bois du Boulogne*. They serve brutally strong coffee there and fresh croissants. We can stroll the *Tuileries* afterwards, taking in the cherry and apple blossoms."

"My daughter's due back soon."

"We can all go," he suggests, stroking her hand. "A happy trio."

"Tamara. I need to check on her, over at the hospital."

He hangs his head. "Later this afternoon then."

She looks away.

"Some night it was, though, eh?"

She's aware of her exhaustion, a desperate desire for some time alone.

"But really," she says, "I seem to be little more than a pagan in all of this."

"An exquisite pagan, though," he says, retrieving his glasses from the nightstand then announcing they'll go for oysters; he knows the perfect place, nestled beneath the *Arc de Triomphe.* He mentions an equestrian show in town Elsa would enjoy.

She tells him she's meeting with Diaghilev and Nijinsky this afternoon; she'll need time to prepare notes for the dancers before tomorrow's performance.

"I'll accompany you to the meeting."

Does he not give up?

"And then, afterwards," he says, "there's a queer little bar on the *Rue Duphot."* He searches her face. "Which I absolutely must take you to! This wonderful negro musician there, playing Gershwin and Cole Porter on banjo and saxophone."

"I need to rest up for tomorrow's performance," she says, getting up to gather up stray pieces of his tuxedo, thinking of *Orpheus* and the grandiose plans she and Schoenberg once made.

"Perhaps you'll compose a ballet for me some day," she says to assuage some small tiny bubble of guilt about her standoffishness. "Maybe even an opera. Orpheus. Forbidden to look back at Eurydice. The dance of life and death. So powerful."

He murmurs his assent.

"I'd change the roles around, though," she says. "Have the Orpheus character be a woman, who then descends into the underworld to rescue her deceased male lover."

He raises his eyebrows. "Ah, interesting."

"The story could be told through music, dance, song and spoken words," she says. Again she thinks of Schoenberg, their unbegun Orphic project they'd long spoken about.

He groans faintly. "Dance and song both within the same musical form? Mmmm, this I'm not so sure about."

"Clearly, you thrive in collaboration. We could enlist Diaghilev, Nijinsky, Roerich, Benois."

"Music can be married to gesture or to words," he says with a little scowl, "though not to both without bigamy."

Tense, she holds her breath, consumed by the implications of their betrayal, unable to purge Schoenberg from her thoughts, always thinking of Schoenberg, already imagining the letter she intends to send him, the letter she'll soon write but never send.

BOOK IV

SIMON

In the world of solo-parenting, one could do worse than chips and soda for dinner— hell yeah, way worse. Along the continuum of parental negligence, there were far more egregious acts, it seemed to Simon. One meal of unadulterated junk food wasn't going to tip the scales one way or another.

Just like that, Francine was gone! Her departure obligated Simon and the boys to fend for themselves. Not much of a cook, he might have at least put a few eggs up to boil, or ventured over to the Courier Café to pick up Dagwoods. But the Lakers were playing. Maybe at the half, he could scrounge up something. In the meantime, he tore open the top of a family-sized bag of chips, setting it down on the coffee table.

"Fresh from the sack," Simon said. "Dig in, hogs."

All grins, the boys applauded and cheered while settling into the L-shaped sofa in the living room. He and the boys adored chips, the pleasant primal gnashing of absurdly-salted textured triangles.

There's plenty of stuff in the freezer, Francine had assured him before leaving—*tacos, fish sticks, frozen peas.* When the airport limo pulled up earlier in front of the house, Carla rolled down the window, waving a tanned and braceleted arm from the back seat.

"This is awesome, Dad," Lincoln said now as a dust storm of neon orange crumbs settled onto his *Star Wars* shirt. Luke was nodding in agreement, cheeks loaded like a blowfish, fingers and lips dusted in artificial cheese.

During a Laker timeout, Simon sat forward to examine the goatee of crumbs on Luke's face, muttering in a crotchety old man's voice, "Hey, why don't you do us a favor, kid, and go get yourself a napkin?"

Luke's grin was perverse, his teeth and gums coated in orange sludge. "That's a funny voice, Dad. Do it again."

"*Whuhhhh*?" Simon moaned.

"That cranky old voice," Luke said laughing, swiping at his lips then running his fingers over the tops of his shorts, Simon blinking several times, puckering and speaking in the old man voice, "So, who do you *tink* you are, a human napkin or *some-ting*?"

Luke fell back in a squeal of giggles and Simon leaned in to tickle him.

"Dad," Luke said, squinty-eyed between breathless giggles. "Is this our dinner, for reals?"

"Hmm," Simon muttered, placing a finger on his chin, "no man or woman on this entire wondrous planet of ours can truly know the answer to such a question. Ask me something easier."

"Like what?" Luke said.

"Like the square root of the hypotenuse," Simon said, displaying a triangular chip before gnashing it like the Cookie Monster.

Lincoln rolled his eyes while inhaling his own horde from his cupped hands.

"I seriously doubt Mom would be very impressed," Lincoln said.

"Right," Simon said, taking the feedback to heart.

Luke shook his head. "Mom might even get mad and curse you under her breath."

Simon laughed. "Seriously, Lukey? Mom doesn't do that."

Luke's eyes widened. "One time she did."

"Luke, dude," Lincoln said, "chill, okay? It's fine. We just won't mention it to Mom. Right, Dad?"

A discussion between the boys followed, Luke concerned that Mom would want to know every last detail of what exactly was consumed, Lincoln suggesting they could simply tell her they couldn't remember, or report they'd had sandwiches or something that sorta tasted like chicken.

As he listened inattentively to the boys' discussion, Simon found himself wondering what Francine and Carla might be up to. He *should* get up right away and give Luke's face a good wipe-down before proceeding to ferret through the fridge for a carrot or something sufficiently green and fibrous. Pasta. He could certainly put some noodles up to boil.

Actually, what he really *ought* to do, though, *subito*, was to get up from the couch to resume work on the opera, polishing the scene in act two, 1916, the moment when Schoenberg, Stravinsky, and Vivian converge in Paris.

Yesterday, while cocooned in the basement studio, he'd expended the better part of the night perusing the sketchbook, piecing through the *Orpheus* sections for hours, fascinated by its streaks and smudges, frenetic erasures and workings-out as he outlined the basic prime form of the twelve-note tone row.

He'd become particularly intrigued by the first four pitches of the row, the notes, *E-G-E^b-A,* which kept appearing. Clearly written initially in Schoenberg's autograph, but then, abruptly, the notes seemed to be drawn in by a completely *different* hand, the calligraphy both more assiduous and more decorative.

E-G-E^b-A. During last night's stuporous trance, he'd begun to imagine the two composers side by side, sketchbook opened before them as they scribbled out experiment after experiment, the four notes interwoven throughout.

E-G-E^b-A. Why those four notes, again and again?

"Dork brain!" Luke was shouting at Lincoln with tiny clenched fists.

Simon blinked, glancing over at his sons, both bodies tensed like wildcats.

"Hey, hey," he said, waving his hand, "what's going on?"

Luke pointed at Lincoln, glaring. "He drank like half my Sprite!"

"Moron breath," Lincoln said, rolling his eyes, "bird brain."

"Doofus!"

"Hey!" Simon barked, "knock it off."

How would Francine go about handling the skirmish? First of all, she'd turn slowly with a Zen-like calm to address the boys like young adults.

"Dum-dum brother!" Luke shouted.

A model of pure patience and self-control. Unflappable. That was Francine for you; grace under pressure, phlegmatic, saintly.

"I barely drank any of your lame soda," Lincoln hollered. "Stupid obsequious butt-muncher!"

Francine would then explain to the little mercenaries, in that absurdly patient and mollifying *Mr. Rogers* voice, how it was never a very good idea—or, indeed, very kind at all—to belittle or disrespect another human being.

"How would you like it if I drank all your soda?" Luke shrieked, red-faced and apparently on the verge of convulsing.

It is just plain wrong, she would instruct the children, *to use disparaging names, slurs, or any other epithets—*

"Tattletale, little goo-goo baby—" Lincoln was taunting.

"My soda!"

"Shut up!"

"No, you shut up!"

Head exploding, the blood whooshing in his ears, Simon roared, "Shut up, you little twits! Both of you!"

That seemed to do the trick. Both boys promptly slackened, turning back in blissful silence to the basketball game.

Exhausted, Simon squeezed his eyes shut and rolled his shoulders back, ruminating on the four Orpheus pitches, *E-G-E^b-A,* sensing something urgently important there. Something had to be there, he was sure, something beyond the notes themselves, a code of sorts; he felt it in his gut, the key possibly to unlocking the mystery of the *Orpheus* passages. And if he could unlock the Orpheus mystery and this glimmer he had of an Arnold-Igor collaboration, would it also then be possible to discover the ending of his opera?

But how would he go about decoding the manuscript, and how much longer could he keep this up, sniffing desperately among runes while hoping to stumble upon a few good answers? What if he were simply wasting his time, throwing away the precious final moments he needed to devote to the opera?

The game was back on now, Magic at the foul line, a side-by-side analysis on the screen of Del Harris's and John Lucas's coaching stats, Lincoln belching from the build-up of carbonation, his delicate eyelashes blinking in surprise as he muttered, *excuse me,* with a blush of modesty.

"What about the sleepover tomorrow over at Jeff's?" Lincoln turned to ask.

"Please, Dad?" Luke begged.

"Wait!" Simon said, turning to Luke. "*You* weren't invited. I thought this was a big-kid venue."

"Yeah, Dad," Lincoln said, "but, check it out. Jeff's little brother, Bradley. Same grade as Luke, right?" Lincoln nodded confidently. "So, we thought we could both go."

Eyes wide, Luke said, "Sleepovers are mostly for big kids, though. I hope it's not scary."

Lincoln rolled his eyes at Simon.

A jolt of excitement went through Simon, a wee shaft of daylight, some small bundle of grace staring him right in the face. With the boys out of the picture temporarily, who was to say how much composing he could accomplish? Untold amounts. He'd been chewing on the thought of a babysitter to help free him up. Boys, opera-writing. Both were full-time endeavors requiring time as well as psychic and emotional energy.

The sleepover party was perfect, really, a godsend. And without the headache of having to coordinate babysitter logistics, or yank himself away from his work to go referee the boys or have to contend with feeding the troops. He would simply drop the boys off at the Hodges' place, and—*voila!*—get right back to the commission.

"*Please?*" the boys pleaded.

"Your mother—" Simon said. "She's got a list of concerns a mile long."

Both boys huffed and lowered their heads at the same time, an identical pout emerging on their faces.

"Mom should play for Golden State," Luke said.

Lincoln groaned. "What are you even talking about, mung bean?"

"Golden State," Luke said, "the Golden State *Worriers.*" He pressed his tiny lips together. "Mom's a total worrier."

"Luke, watch it!" Simon said, "you're getting chips all over the place."

"Sorry," Luke said, sitting up and swiping at his mouth with his soiled fingers, Simon wincing at the sullied pillow, the avalanche of crumbs along the sofa.

"But, well, it's only fair," Luke said, inadvertently twisting the knife in. "Mom gets to have *her* sleepover with Carla."

Flinching, Simon chewed his lip, putting his focus back on the Laker game as the Laker defense stole the inbound Sixers pass, converting on a Magic-to-Divac alley-oop.

What exactly was up with Carla? he dared to wonder. Close associates, two women with a mutual passion for photography. Why was he having so much difficulty accepting things at face value? Professional colleagues, plain and simple. Cut and dry, no need for him to be Encyclopedia Brown or Hercule Poirot, sniffing around for clues, or reading into nuances in order to expose scandals that more than likely weren't merited. Two colleagues. End of story.

Who at this moment happened to be holed up for a languid and intimate weekend together in some palatial love nest halfway across the country.

I cringe whenever I see Lincoln around that Jeffty kid, Francine had said the other night. *I swear, my blood begins to boil.*

Now, raking his fingers through his hair, Simon apologized to his sons about the sleepover, explaining how he just didn't think he could override their mother on this one.

"*Pleease,* Dad," Luke moaned from the sofa, giving Ned Spencer, his stuffed penguin bedtime companion, a hearty squeeze.

"I promised Jeffty," Lincoln said.

"And I promised your mother," Simon snapped back.

"We won't tell Mom," Lincoln reasoned, eyeing his brother, "will we, mung?"

Wide-eyed and folding his arms, Luke said, "Heck no. No way, brother. No way will we."

---

15 September 1913
Paris

Dear Arnold,
I hope this letter finds you well. I have been working on several new compositions, fortunate to have secured a few ballet commissions, thanks to the good will of Diaghilev. I very much enjoy collaborating with colleagues and sharing ideas with other artists, choreographers, costumers, designers, dancers and musicians.

I work as much as possible and manage to get a lot done.
It's quite something, however—I'm sure you might agree:
facing an utterly new composition in a fresh style, conceived
of without the benefit of precursors or other guides. How
nerve-wracking all of this proves!

Thus, not without a bit of trepidation, I am now enclos-
ing a copy of a section from my latest score-in-progress, 'The
Nightingale,' the story of a dying Chinese emperor redeemed by
the appearance of a magical nightingale. I hope you will find a
little time to review my work, presented here only in a crude and
unfinished draft. Perhaps you will make suggestions. Perhaps
you yourself will become something of a magical nightingale!

Sincerely,

Igor

p.s. enclosed you will please find our Café Leydicke
"manuscript," the Orpheus fragments we hashed out in Berlin.
But how quickly our menu appears to be running out of space!
Accordingly, I have taken the liberty of attaching an additional
sheet of manuscript paper with the hope of dropping a few
more appetizing crumbs onto it.

• •

17 May 1914
Vienna

Dear Friend,

I must say I was overjoyed to hear that you like the one
piece I've shared with you. And I sincerely hope that you will
later come to like the other one.

I inadvertently forgot to post this letter for a few days.
Meanwhile, I have been preoccupied in developing an entirely
new and potentially groundbreaking "theory" as to how musical composition must proceed. I will be interested to hear how
it appeals to you.

I am uncertain as to what contact you presently keep
regarding Frau Růžek. But I would kindly ask that you send
along my regards, conveying how she remains always in my
thoughts. Perhaps you will be good enough to inform me how

she fares in her new ventures there. Also: would you kindly do me the favor of forwarding me her address?

Meanwhile, enclosed once again is the Leydicke Orpheus fragment, returned to you post-haste with the spinning-out of a few further musical ideas.

With friendly greetings,
Arnold

• •

9 February 1915
Vienna

Dear Igor,
To date no word from you as to Frau Růžek or her whereabouts. I am certainly pleased, however, that a few of your compositions will be performed on an upcoming program for our Society for Private Performance, namely the string quartet and the four-hand arrangement of your scintillating 'Petrushka', both scores residing securely upon my desk.

I am furthermore delighted you have chosen to program and conduct some of my own works—the 'Five Pieces for Orchestra,' 'Hergewächse,' and the 'Four Orchestral Songs'— on an upcoming performance of yours.

My main stipulation will be to insist that all tempo markings and indications of musical expression, naturally, be regarded as sacrosanct. They must be followed to a T. Regrettably, all too often I find my best musical intentions disfigured rather hideously by the "interpretations" (well-meaning, albeit something less than competent) of other musicians, e.g., conductors, who frequently end up missing the mark entirely. All of which results, naturally, in a less than satisfactory performance and, in fact, more often than not, a significant dismemberment of my original intentions.

I beg you therefore to observe such indications exactly, if you wish to remain on good terms with me!

Yours,
Arnold

9 March 1916
Paris

Dear Arnold,

I am elated about your decision to travel to Paris so that we may soon resume our discussions face to face regarding musical projects. I look forward to share the progress of my Nightingale with you, as well as other works-in-progress. M. Diaghilev has helped push all the necessary paperwork through to grant you the proper visas and other necessary documentation for crossing 'enemy lines,' thus making your Vienna-Paris journey possible via governmental sanction in some official capacity as cultural attaché.

Meanwhile, I'm re-enclosing our Orpheus notes with a few further elaborations. What may simply have begun as late-night, grappa-induced scribbles now seems to have morphed into the genesis of a promising composition!

No doubt, Frau Růžek will be highly pleased to reunite with you around the demands of her rehearsal schedule.

Thank you for the suggestions you have already been generous enough to provide regarding my Nightingale.

I eagerly look forward to our meetings in a month's time.
Kindly,
Igor

Tableau XI

Arnold

"I feel air from another planet.
The faces that once turned to me in friendship
Pale in the darkness before me.

...and your light,
Beloved shadow—summoner of my torment—

is now extinguished quite in deeper burning flames."

> —Stefan George, *The Seventh Ring*
> *Entrückung (Transcendence)*
> *trans. Richard Stokes (2005)*

"You respect me; but how if one day your respect
should tumble? Take care that a falling statue does not
strike you dead!"

> —Friedrich Nietzsche, quoted by
> Carl Jung to Sigmund Freud, 1912

Paris

April 1916

The journey from Vienna to Paris necessitates twice the time it normally would, the train forced to circumnavigate the perimeter of the Western Front. Schoenberg gazes out the window at a war-scorched landscape lit by a smoldering sun, a world descending into chaos and madness as he conjures up the stench of mortar beneath clumps of low clouds, the din of *Mausers* discharging, birch trees denuded and blackened, the sky irradiated for miles by grenades. He thinks of sword-wielding infantrymen and flamethrowers advancing through the tangle of barbed wire, entire villages decimated, a pile-up of dismembered bodies.

You are unfit to serve in the corps of the Kaiser's army, the baby-faced, OF-4 lieutenant-colonel had informed him during officer's training in *Bruck an der Leitha,* during which he'd suffered physical collapse brought on by an asthma attack. A second attempt at military service in Vienna proved no more successful, due to unstable health.

The apprehension he feels about his reunion this afternoon with Stravinsky and Vivian is juxtaposed with further unsettling images of war—refrigeration units withdrawn from the streets in order to transport blood; the soot-blackened oil lamps of hospital trains; filthy water buckets for scouring blood and muck from the carriage floor; windowless freight carriages to transport piles of the dead; men lying on hard straw or other makeshift stretchers, torn to bits by shrapnel, blood-soaked, bleeding through ears and nose, moaning, dazed and helpless, gasping for breath against the dense musk of excrement and iodoform antiseptic; young doctors calling ahead to oncoming stations for morphine, cotton, wool, clean bandages—to no avail, all such supplies long since depleted.

In the lavatory of the *Gare du Nord,* he splashes cool water on his face, arranges wisps of dark hair around his gleaming pate, primps his tweed suit, fusses with his necktie. Carefully, he refolds the handkerchief in his lapel pocket, turquoise silk, a gift from Vivian years ago, a token of support during Mathilde's extramarital escapades with Gerstl.

He sinks a few centimes into the station payphone, placing a call to the opera house, hoping to confirm that Vivian will be there this afternoon, the receiver pressed to his ear as he waits for the receptionist to locate her in rehearsal.

"Hello?" Vivian says.

The sound of her voice freezes him.

"Hello?" she says again, "who's there?"

He closes his eyes, incapable of responding as a train pulls in nearby with a bloodcurdling squeal. Porters heave luggage onto carts, an official announcement sounds over the loudspeaker in a garbled French he's unable to parse.

"Who's there?" Vivian demands. "Igor? Is that you?"

On the *Rue de Maubeuge* he purchases long white lilies for Vivian, riding the Metro to the *Théâtre du Châtelet* for his meeting with Stravinsky.

"It's nice we meet again," Schoenberg says to Stravinsky, setting Vivian's flowers down and gazing at a poster for a forthcoming ballet, *Parade*, written by Cocteau, with music by Satie and set designs by Picasso.

Stravinsky's dressed in a stylish linen suit, beaming with pride beside a mound of music scores arranged across the table surface of the meeting room.

"Somewhat of a quiet year," Schoenberg explains as they seat themselves. "The war has all but shuttered most of the concert halls and theaters. The cabarets even."

"Desperate times," Stravinsky says. "Here, people scamper about with the sole intention of filling their bellies. The total collapse of things." He shakes his head. "The end of culture."

Schoenberg asks about the *Rite of Spring*, the riots he's read about, providing an account of his own *succèss de scandale* at the *Bösendorfer*, the ensuing lawsuit during which a doctor testified that Schoenberg's music was injurious to the nervous system and a probable catalyst for mental illness.

But the war isn't solely responsible for Schoenberg's lack of productivity. Rather, the new theory of musical composition he's been feverishly puzzling out has consumed him as now he elaborates upon the set of procedures he's devised, "a system of musical laws for how melody and harmony must proceed. Dodecaphony, a method of composing with twelve tones, which are related only with one another."

Stravinsky mulls this over while Schoenberg presses further, explaining how the twelve different notes within the octave can be arranged in a certain order, a basic tone row, resulting in a kind of fixed template for the melodic and harmonic material, determining how this then unfolds throughout the entire piece.

"Heavily legislated, though, *n'est-ce pas?*" Stravinsky bites his lip. "The music already determined, even before it's had the chance to air out?"

"A way to ensure that all twelve notes of the chromatic scale receive *equal* emphasis," Schoenberg explains.

Stravinsky's grin is impish. "Sounds almost Marxist."

"The doing away with the hierarchical system of major and minor scales." Schoenberg folds his arms, declaring how the accepted procedures for melody, harmony, tonality, and consonance have now outlived their usefulness as Romanticism suffers a slow lingering death.

Stravinsky straightens in his chair. "I don't know whether I'll agree that melody and harmony have outlived their usefulness."

"Obsolete!" Schoenberg nearly shouts. "Reger, Strauss. Romantic harmony has nowhere else to go and can only collapse. If music is to survive, new theories must be imagined."

"New theories for *saving* Music?" Stravinsky laughs. "Maybe you should just get back to the humble business of composing." He smacks his lips. "At any rate, I doubt one must go quite so far in *revolutionizing* or *reinventing* entire systems—systems, which I don't need to remind you, have remained intact for centuries." He waves his hand. "After all, Herr Schoenberg— there's still plenty of good music to be written in C major."

Turning towards the mound of music on the table, Stravinsky pulls a composition he's been working on.

"*L'Histoire du Soldat*," Stravinsky says, "*The Soldier's Tale*. For small chamber ensemble, inspired no doubt by your magnificent *Pierrot*. A story about a soldier who, while on a brief furlough from the army, encounters the devil."

"The devil," Schoenberg mutters, screwing up his face as he thumbs through the score, struck by the rhythmic precision and pointed articulations, the artfully-woven tapestry of clarinet, bassoon, trumpet, violin, and percussion.

Moments later, while reaching into his dossier to retrieve the Café Leydicke placemat, Stravinsky beams.

"You've still got that oily doily from Berlin?" Schoenberg asks, amused by the curled and frayed parchment souvenir, the palimpsest of chords, melodies, countermelodies and other musical gestures they've exchanged numerous times through the post during the past couple of years.

"*Un duo de génie!*" Stravinsky exclaims with a smile, waving the placemat. "A poem-in-progress, despite its greasy splotches and lingering sebaceous remnants."

There's a knock at the door and Vivian enters, lissome, her face flushed, a towel draped around her shoulders.

"*Bonjour, messieurs!*" she says brightly. "I hope I am not appearing at the wrong moment. We have a break in our rehearsal schedule."

Breath quickening, Schoenberg presents his bouquet of lilies to Vivian, relishing the exchange of kisses on the cheek, reacquainting himself with the softness of her skin, the familiar lilt of her voice..

"Hello, Eager," she says, blushing as she turns to greet Stravinsky, Schoenberg noting Stravinsky's gallant bow, the exaggerated way he kisses Vivian's hand. Vivian fiddles with the silk turquoise handkerchief sprouting up from Stravinsky's lapel pocket, a handkerchief identical to the one he wears in his own lapel pocket, Schoenberg's mortified to confirm.

Dizzy, short of breath, he blinks into the bright lighting, bending with a sharp gasp, the fiendish eyes of Gerstl overtaking his imagination.

"Arnold?" Vivian asks in a panicked voice.

It's too late. He's already in the throes of a violent asthma attack, body tensing as he wheezes and gasps for breath. Vivian and Stravinsky hurry to his side to guide him into a chair. Vivian brings him a glass of water, inquiring whether they should call for a doctor.

Waving them off, Schoenberg focuses on restoring his breathing, slowly calming himself, as, eventually, the burning in his chest and throat subsides.

Stravinsky recounts for Vivian the profitable advice Schoenberg's offered on a few of his scores.

"Bravo!" Vivian says, her eyes roving between both men. "It's nice the two of you were able to meet and confer with one another—no easy undertaking in the midst of a war."

"Such splendid advice!" Stravinsky says with a nod, swiping perspiration from his forehead with the back of his hand before pulling out his handkerchief to daub at his brow.

Coughing heavily into his fist, closing his eyes, steadying his breathing, Schoenberg rests his throbbing head in his hands. He coughs again, swallows. Then he glowers at them. "I do not care for music about devils."

"So now you know," Vivian says to Schoenberg with a sullen look. They share a bench in the upstairs atelier, a cavernous space, palely-lit and reeking of solvent, the floor cluttered with oversized canisters of pigment and paintbrush pails. Large overlapping swaths of cloth imprinted with Picasso's designs for *Parade* line the floor.

"Igor and I—" She shakes her head.

He studies her full lips, the contour of her cheek. Her hair is pulled back in a red headband. He inhales the scent from her dancer's body, lilac, earthy, musky.

"We are nothing, Igor and I," she insists as she gazes off at stacks of unfinished canvasses tilted up against the walls. "Nothing."

His breathing is shallow. He continues to wheeze, incapable of taking in a proper breath.

"Your parents," he says, staring at her. "We happened to cross paths at the *Weihnachtsmarkt* in Charlottenburg not so long ago."

She frowns, her body stiffening.

"Naturally, they were concerned about you," he continues. "Your brother. His condition seems only to have worsened, requiring more and more of your parents' attention."

He tsk-tsks, pressing further. "One can only imagine how difficult things must be for your family, neither you nor your sister around to assist."

"I have other obligations," she says.

"*Obligations*," he scoffs, his voice booming operatically in the spacious room. "*Bah!*"

Bristling, she scowls at him.

"Family!" he says with a wave of his finger. "This must always come first."

"I have a family *here* now," she's quick to say. "And the ballet—"

"*The ballet!*" he shouts, ready to mock her, ready to roll up his sleeves and earnestly put forth his opinion on the matter. "This ballet dream of yours is barely afloat, gasping for its final breaths." His coughing continues, jaw clenching as he gasps and struggles to clear his throat and lungs. "It won't even manage to outlast the war before sinking into oblivion, taking your smug Russian philanderer and every other fly-by-night along with it."

"Once the war ends," she says, "things will return to normal."

"Let me help you. You and Elsa. You shouldn't feel compelled to exist the way you do, timid, always a little *hard up*. Desperate, ready to throw yourself, it would seem, at the first suitor who happens to come your way."

Now she's red-faced; now he's gotten to her.

"The people, Vi," he continues with a gentler tone, "friends, family, the opportunities you've left behind in Berlin, my goodness, the plans you and I once made!"

"Are you *mad*?" she asks. "Your family. Your children—your *wife*! You're acting as if these things don't even exist."

"A few adjustments, if necessary, can always be made, so that—"

"Ho, I see!" she says with a derisive laugh. "And so, this *commitment* business, the importance of one's family, turns out to be rather equivocal. Flexible. *Well!* How *convenient.*"

"Sometimes," he says quietly, "in extenuating or *extraordinary* circumstances. Certain types of commitments must unfortunately be broken."

Reaching into his valise, he presents her with a rolled-up manuscript, waiting patiently for her to undo the ribbon, pulse quickening as he watches his composition unfurl in her hands.

"For you," he says, leaning back and crossing his legs as she looks over the manuscript.

He gazes at her. A slant of grainy light from the circular window above perfects her. "For you, Vi, I made this composition."

The bench creaks a little as he inches nearer to her. "A song setting of Stefan George's poetry." Staring off, he quotes softly from the George poem, "A tempestuous wind overwhelms me." He swallows. "In sacred rapture where the—"

She stands suddenly, flinching, squirming away when he reaches for her arm.

"I must return to rehearsal."

"Yes," he says, "But, please. Allow me to explain."

With great care, she rolls the manuscript up and hands it back to him.

Getting shakily to his feet, he confesses how he tried writing letters to her. "To attempt to convey what is in my heart."

"Sometimes," she says, "things happen for a reason."

He hates her for saying this. For her calm and aloof disinterest. For not seeing what he sees or feeling what he feels. For not needing him the way he needs her.

"I'm afraid," she says, "in all your despair—in all this wild inventiveness and tireless melancholic yearning. You seem to have invented a *me* that simply doesn't exist."

The door creaks when she pulls it open and steps towards the landing, glancing back at him with what he'll remember as a mournful look, footsteps hurrying away, fleet dancer's feet descending the stairwell in a resounding rhythmic patter.

At this moment, in the grip of turmoil, he's unaware that her dancing descent, plaintive and harrowing, will form the central plodding rhythmic motif of a string quartet he will one day compose. More significantly, at this moment, he has no way of knowing that this will be the last time he and Vivian ever see one another.

Quickly, quietly, her footsteps trail away, *morendo,* vanishing…*bis zum Nichts.*

SIMON

THE HODGES' PLACE WAS undergoing considerable construction, the front lawn a maze of rubble and gaping pits overlaid haphazardly with plywood planks, the area roped off with yellow tape like a crime scene.

Simon and the boys made their way past a backhoe digger truck in the driveway, sidestepping a ripped out pathway and cinder block debris, creeping along the garage, a dog growling at them, rearing its massive menacing head through a side window, paws thumping and scratching as they inched towards the front door.

Lincoln rang the bell and they stood on the porch awhile, until finally the door was opened by a mousy woman, hair matted, her face puffy, slightly sallow, as if she'd just gotten up from a nap. She wore black lipstick, spandex pants and pool shoes, her navel exposed beneath a clinging tank top.

"Hey, I know you," she finally said, groggy and staring out from behind the screen door. "You guys go to Foothill with my kids."

"That's right," Simon said.

"Patsy," she said, pulling back the screen door and taking hold of Simon's hand, "Patsy Hodges."

Lincoln waved the gift they brought along, a few comic books and a scary-looking claw-glove they'd picked up at a party supply store on their way over.

"We're here for the party," Lincoln said.

Patsy stared in miscomprehension.

Luke asked if Brad was there.

She smiled. "Bradley! Of course he is, sweetie!"

They stepped into the dark-paneled living room, a battered sofa littered with plastic army soldiers, the armchair rubbed smooth and smelling of dog. Ripped out ceiling panels revealed sooty beams and exposed wiring.

"We're in total construction mode around here," Patsy explained. "And on top of that, I'm finishing up a major project with work. *Crayyyyy-zy!*" She shuffled over to a card table heaped with dozens of hand-painted greeting cards with brightly-painted gumballs on the front.

"You made all those?" Simon asked.

"I'm an artist," Patsy said.

Lincoln told Patsy his dad was a composer.

"No kidding," Patsy said. "Sounds like a tough way to go. My clients make endless demands of me. I can barely keep up."

Simon picked up one of the cards from the table, examining the carefully-rendered gumball then opening to the message inscribed inside: *You are your best you! Have an awesome day!*

"My dad's scrambling to finish his opera," Lincoln explained to Patsy.

"Sounds serious," Patsy said. "Pressure with a capital *P*."

The dog began barking again in a low and barbarous growl, Patsy stepping outside to quiet the beast while the boys wandered over to the sofa, rummaging around the cushions for buried army men.

Last night he'd experienced something of a breakthrough on the sketchbook. The *Orpheus* passages, with their Schoenberg/Stravinsky juxtapositions, became a kind of musical blueprint for what he'd been striving to achieve sonically in his own opera. Why couldn't he *borrow* some of these Arnold and Igor sketches and musical inventions for the project he was creating, essentially *lifting* Schoenberg/Stravinsky *in situ* for his own purposes? *Good artists borrow*, Picasso had famously said, *great artists steal.* Working deep into the night like a crazed epidemiologist, he was able to isolate and extract what he suspected was a Stravinsky strand among the *Orpheus* passages, playing a musical line on his electric keyboard *simultaneously* with a neighboring passage by Schoenberg, marrying the two composers' styles, in effect, while stumbling upon a unique and dazzling musical *synthesis*, music never previously heard.

Inspired by an Arnold-Igor collaboration, he'd continued to fuse melodies and phrases, transplanting musical DNA while funneling the recombinant results into the pages of his own work. Transformation. An alchemist smelting his philosopher's stone from the rich amalgam of the two composers' separate styles.

Now the Hodges boys appeared, emerging from some mysterious nook as they stood among the kitchen's ripped-out flooring and exposed pipes.

"Lincoln Log!" Jeffty hollered from beneath a paint-blistered alcove, pumping his fist and then awkwardly extending certain fingers in some bizarre pattern of what Simon could only intuit was some sort of gang signal. Bradley waved at Luke. He was dressed in a grimy tank top and short underwear he'd long since grown out of.

"Yo, Luke Skywalker!" Jeffty shouted, pointing at Luke. "Showtime, rugrat." An AC/DC T-shirt, several sizes too big, draped over his thin frame. "Time to meet your maker, little man."

Leaning in towards Lincoln, Simon asked, *pianissimo*, just what the hell all that was supposed to mean.

"Shh," Lincoln whispered back, "It's just how we express ourselves sometimes."

"Happy birthday, Jeffty," Simon said, prompting Jeffty to blush and lower his head with a guilty grin.

Patsy returned to the living room. "Yep, major league renovations.

Plumbing unhooked every time you turn around." She exhaled heavily. "Been peeing in a bucket half the time."

A broad-shouldered man wearing a leather vest and tool belt lumbered over from the back of the house, grabbing hold of Simon's hand with a merciless squeeze.

"Dane Hodges," he said, chomping on a wad of gum. He had a bushy moustache. "We've been busy around here. Pipes, electrical, masonry." Watery-eyed, he looked Simon over, hand on hip while pulverizing his chewing gum. "You do pipes?"

Simon shook his head.

"Putting in a koi pond where the front lawn used to be," Dane said. "Should be fairly sweet, when she's done. Outdoor lighting, small deck." He shook his head, lowering his voice. "Meanwhile, rewiring the whole fucker of a house." He pouted. "Doing the whole thing myself. Hell, know what? Why should I throw money at some bloodsucker handyman? I can get the job done, hell, I don't need some sorry-ass contractor to show me how to do things."

"Right," Simon said, taking in the house's gaping viscera.

"Just finished installing a three-quarter-inch pressure vacuum breaker," Dane said with a gravelly laugh and a nod, "the gooseneck so old it cracked clear on through the gasket putty, and I'm going, *shit, do I plumb a whole new sink wasteline or just tie the fucker into the toilet and be done with it, or what?* Got maybe three feet tops between the two, you know, to work with back there."

Simon whistled. "Sounds rough."

"What would *you* do?" Dane asked, staring at Simon.

Simon shook his head, smiling politely. "Quite some job."

"I asked what *you* would do," Dane said.

"Sorry," Simon said with a shrug, "haven't a clue."

"It's a *sonabitch*," Dane said, brow furrowing, "I'll tell you what. A real *sonabitch*."

Simon asked where the other kids were.

"The sleepover?" Simon said, raising his eyebrows. "The birthday party—?"

"Mister," Dane said, "I'm actually having a little problem following you there."

"The special party, Pops," Jeffty cut in. "*Daaaaad! Remember?* The sleepover you and *Moms* said I could have."

Dane licked his lips, staring off.

"Look," Simon said. "Obviously there's been a misunderstanding." He narrowed his eyes at Lincoln. "I'm so sorry." Lincoln and Jeffty shared a smirk.

"This is actually a little embarrassing," Simon said.

"Stop," Patsy said to Simon, thrusting out a hand. "Just stop it. Don't be ridiculous. Hey, we're all friends here."

"Boys are welcome to stay," Dane said nodding in a basso voice. "No issue there."

Glancing back at the door, Simon thanked them, head whirling. "But, actually, you know, we were—"

"They can sleep out in the garage with Tar," Dane said.

The four boys nodded feverishly.

Tar. Man's best friend, Simon reasoned. *Cujo. How reassuring.*

Shifting his weight from one leg to the other, Simon struggled to come up with the best pretense for scraping up the boys this very instant and getting the hell away from the Hodges' place. Should he fabricate some previous engagement, explaining how he'd completely forgotten all about dinner with the grandparents?

"The garage is where the new Nintendo is, right?" Lincoln was asking Jeffty.

"All things considered," Simon said, "I mean, with all the construction and, with everything else going on. I'm sure you guys already have your hands full."

"We sleep out there all the time," Jeffty insisted. "Anytime we friggin' feel like it."

Simon held his breath.

He might leave the boys here—*temporarily!*—Only for a few hours max. No harm in that. Returning around dinnertime to fetch them and make his excuses. Boys get to hang out. No rude exits or awkward scenes. Everybody wins.

"Please, Dad, can we?" Lincoln asked.

Simon shrugged. "Sure. Yeah, all right."

"Come on, people!" Lincoln said. "Showtime, roaches! Let's get the gear from the car."

Removing a business card from his wallet, Simon scribbled down his cellphone number, handing it to Patsy, telling her to please get in touch right away if anything came up.

"You got it," Patsy said, giving him the thumbs up. "And good luck with your opera. Hope you beat that deadline." She laughed. "Hope you kick the shit out of it."

Tableau XII

Arnold

"I always called it one of my greatest merits to have
discouraged the greatest majority of my pupils from
composing. There remain, from the many hundreds of
pupils, only six to eight who compose. I find such who
need encouragement must be discouraged, because only
such should compose to whom creation is a 'must,' a
necessity, a passion, such as would not stop composing if
they were discouraged a thousand times."

—Arnold Schoenberg

"Of what strange alchemy was this man [Schoenberg]
compounded that the sources of his inspiration flowed
most freely when stemmed and checked by legislation of
the most stifling kind?"

—Glenn Gould

Mödling, Austria
March 1922

AT HOME IN HIS study, seated at the secretary he built last year,
Schoenberg hears the front door click open unexpectedly down the
hall, footsteps plodding along the corridor.

Then a whistled folk tune, *Alle Vögel sind schon da*. His son, Georg,
he confirms, home from *Gymnasium* hours before the local school
normally lets out. Shrugging, he returns his attention to the Stravinsky

score open before him, *Three Children's Tales* for voice and three clarinets, miniature pieces he's been considering for an upcoming concert for his *Society of Private Musical Performance* series.

Admittedly, he'd written earlier this morning to Berg, Stravinsky's music resembles virtually nothing of the "modernist" approach and, even more disconcerting, the Russian rogue seems intent on glancing <u>backward</u> to earlier styles, to the primitive and démodé. Frustratingly simple, his music can be. A brash disregard for established European modalities with its perversity of polytonal harmony—

But, privately, on some deeply personal level, Schoenberg struggles to reconcile a certain fascination with Stravinsky's approach, bowled over at times by the creative animus at play.

It's been some time since they've seen one another; not since Paris have he and Stravinsky crossed paths. They keep up a collegial and business-like correspondence from time to time, negotiating performance expectations each has about his own work, nary a mention of Paris, Diaghilev, Orpheus and, particularly, Vivian.

In a few weeks, Schoenberg's new composition, *Orpheus Fragments*, will be premiered in Paris with Milhaud conducting. And although prior commitments prevent him from attending, he can't help but wonder whether Stravinsky might attend.

Now commotion from the kitchen distracts him, raising his hackles. The clatter of dishes, cabinets, drawers, the sink faucet gurgling, Georg's ham-fisted bumbling, until finally, nearly driven mad by the relentless metronomic thwack of the meat cleaver, he gets up uneasily from his desk, storming the kitchen to come upon his son leaning over the table, intent on devouring the pork loin he's just ravaged.

"Why home so soon?"

With a good-natured smirk, Georg looks up at his father, fine facial features, searching eyes, locks of unruly brown hair.

"School's over for the day," Georg says with a shrug.

"School children should be in school."

Prüfungsordung, Georg explains, examinations schedule, as Schoenberg appraises his son's somewhat pimply complexion, the unassuming smile on his lips, the contemplative expression of a poet.

"You can make use of the extra time by practicing your French horn," Schoenberg says, gesturing towards Georg's room.

Brushing unruly locks from his eyes, Georg mentions his mixed feelings about attending the music academy next year.

"Genius isn't plucked from trees," Schoenberg says. "Talent must be carefully nurtured."

Georg frowns, resting his chin in his hands.

"Practice," Schoenberg says, "*Übung macht den Meister*. Diligence, discipline. You do not work hard enough."

"But this is exactly what I've been trying to explain," Georg says, "the other interests I have. Other— priorities."

"Do you intend to produce *nothing* in your life?" Schoenberg asks. "Is it your desire only to be lazy and to achieve nothing?"

"Literature," Georg says gently.

"Literature," Schoenberg scoffs. "*Quatsch!* You only waste your time."

"Anna and I," Georg begins to say, Schoenberg wincing while swatting away the absurd reference to the former serving girl they'd hired when Mathilde fell ill. As Mathilde's health worsened, Anna had stepped in to help manage the household, her involvement intensifying once Mathilde had been confined to the sanatorium in Gmuden for depression, anemia and malnutrition, the family reeling while attempting to adjust.

"Why do you insist on making everything so difficult?" Schoenberg asks.

"We love one another," Georg says carefully as Schoenberg stares harshly at the wayward and irreverent son before him, Georg's slender fingers and tender lips much like his mother's, Görgi, the helpless and sick baby Schoenberg had looked after in Vienna, while Mathilde carried on with Gerstl.

What does one do with a recalcitrant child? He only wishes success and fulfillment for his son, he's already made all the necessary arrangements for Georg to attend the *Musikakademie* next year.

Georg searches his father's face. And, although Schoenberg looks upon such an ardent gaze as sadly and touchingly beautiful somehow, he maintains a stony mien. Overcome with affection for this creature before him—the light curly locks, docile smile, eyes filled with wonder and dreams—he feels possessed by an urge to go over and embrace him, pelting him with kisses.

Thinking better of it, he instead summons will power and strength from within, unyielding strength, no wavering, an iron will. After all, is this not the father's mandate: to guide his son and enable him to correct course? No, a line in the sand must be drawn, his paternal duty, noblesse oblige, faithfully carried out.

from the Journal of Jasper Grafton

6 February 1945

*Meningitis has now been confirmed, Helena's battered body continues
to stiffen, neck, face & body rigid, even while resting calmly in bed.
Stale breath of the hospital, pent up air, the chair dragged over to her
bedside, taking hold of her cool hands & singing to her, 'My Heart's in
the Highlands,' the ballad she & I sang to one another a lifetime ago in
St. Ives.*

> *Farewell to the Highlands, farewell to the North,*
> *The birthplace of valor, the country of worth.*
> *Wherever I wander, wherever I rove,*
> *The hills of the Highlands for ever I love.*

*Schoenberg stops by the hospital w/ his wife, Getrud, & Elsa. Excitedly
places a copy of Orpheus' Lament into Helena's tremulous hands.*

*'For you,' he says to H w/ a wistful smile. 'I want you should learn
it, to sing it one day when the screenplay & score are at last ready for
production.'*

*After the visitors depart, Helena, propped up on pillows, reads through
the Schoenberg song, humming pitches then singing of Orpheus' descent
into the Underworld, strumming & coaxing his lyre, captivating all who
listen to his song. Helena sings quietly w/ breathy voice & wavering
tone, against the backdrop of birds beyond the hospital window, their
birdsong florid, profuse, timeless. The Orpheus seems to lift her spirits.
She wants to sing it for the film, she informs me. Yes, when you're better,
I respond, unsure of what more can be sd. & in the days that follow,
more & more she desires to sing it, whenever exhaustion will permit.*

Helena sings & I hum along or whistle sometimes, & later when I bring Simon along, Helena & I sing for our bright-eyed boy.

SIMON

E-G-E♭-A-B-F-D-F♯-C-A♭- B♭-D♭

Simon sounded the notes upon the Steinway in the living room, the twelve-pitch series of the *Orpheus* tone row. E-G-E♭-A. The tone row's first four pitches continued to accuse him, appearing over and over again throughout the passages. Why did both composers appear to be spinning material throughout the *Orpheus* passages, musical phrases centered seemingly around a kind of motto based on these four initial notes?

He'd presented lectures to his students on the "*mortar* of motif and motto," building blocks of musical composition, demonstrating how such composers as Bach, Mozart, Haydn, Schubert and Mahler used scraps of melody, recycling and restating the material like a refrain.

Brahms, for example, incorporated the three-note motto, *F-A-flat-F*, throughout his third symphony, F-A-flat-F: <u>*Frei* **a***ber* *froh*</u>—free, but joyful! Brahms, the eternal bachelor, free and unattached, yet joyful. Or so he'd wanted to portray himself.

And what about Shostakovich? During his lecture, Simon sounded the *signature* notes, *D-E-flat-C-B* on the keyboard to illustrate how, following Bach's example, musical pitches could correspond to letters of the alphabet. Dmitri Shostakovich, in some of his works, had made use of the four pitches, *D-E-flat-C-B* to spell out his own name; the pitches *D-E-flat-C-B*, represented <u>*D. Sch*</u> (with *ess,* the letter S, represented by the note *E-flat* in German; *and H* represented by the note *B).*

Now, as he examined the sketchbook passages, Simon couldn't help but wonder whether some similar practice wasn't in operation here, whether Schoenberg and Stravinsky weren't also embedding some musical allusion or hidden code.

Returning home a short while ago from the Hodges' house of horrors, he'd rolled up his sleeves, eager to get to work on the opera, wandering from basement workspace to the Steinway upstairs, side-stepping the train wreck the boys had managed to create in less than twenty-four hours—a nuclear fallout of food debris, a furry maroon splotch on the linoleum, inexplicable streaks in the carpet; an impressive laundry pile-up; backpacks, stray toys; shoes seemingly everywhere (an irreconcilable disparity between number of household shoes and number of human feet).

Now as he situated himself in his downstairs burrow, he trolled through the pages of his opera score on his laptop, adjusting a solo vocal line for greater delineation within the orchestral texture, altering the colors within the orchestral palette by mixing a low flute into the viola texture, muting the horns in one passage, thinning out the percussion in others.

The composers coming together, laying down arms to join forces in collaboration: this was how his opera would end.

And as he read through more pages of his father's journal, he wondered what conspiring adventitious forces could have compelled the composers to put aside differences and come together, a crisis of some sort maybe, that could have drawn them together?

E- G- Eb- A.

There had to be an answer. The hourglass sands of the deadline were rapidly dissipating. Desperate, he sounded the pitches on the keyboard *ad infinitum,* squeezing his eyes shut and wondering about an associative or extramusical meaning to the four pitches.

He needed Demetra's input.

Removing her business card from his wallet, he glanced at the home phone number she'd scribbled down. One or two questions, nothing more. Would she be home? He imagined her nestled among various research projects, domiciled, exactly as he now was, a kindred soul, steeped in noble scholarly pursuits.

What about the boys? some paternal voice nagged.

Hold your beans, he told the voice, telling it to take (as the boys were fond of saying) a chill pill. After all, the boys would be entertained and joyously distracted over at the Hodges' place. It was still early. Plenty of time later—after he'd gotten more work done on the opera—for a heroic descent onto Chez Hitchcock to rescue the kids.

My home number, just in case, Demetra had said, pressing her business card into his palm. *Or, really, Simon, we could talk about anything you'd like.*

He dialed her number from the kitchen phone, anticipating her voice while the phone rang, visualizing the Westwood townhouse she might reside in, heart sinking when the answering machine clicked and the voice message recording came on, her husky alto register so different from Francine's lighter mezzo soprano voice.

"Oh, hey," he said, collecting himself after the ring had beeped, "Simon here," blathering on about how he'd decided to take her up on her offer, how he'd stumbled upon something quite interesting but perplexing he very much wanted (needed) to run by her.

"This evening," he added, "if you happen to be around and it isn't too much to ask." He left a call back number.

He was seated at the Steinway with the sketchbook moments later when the kitchen phone rang, Simon's heart beating in his throat as he scrambled to answer it.

"Sime," Francine said, Simon's breath catching as he barely managed a croaky hello, Francine asking how the opera was proceeding, how the boys were managing.

"Good," he said, "all fine here."

"It's after ten in Chicago," she said. "We're beat. Long day. Getting ready to turn in."

He asked how the shoot was going.

"The Joffrey's a dream. We've been shooting in Lincoln Park and all around the Loop. You should see the lake. Gorgeous!"

"Well, that sounds good," he said, distracted, wondering if his voice sounded particularly peevish.

She told him she missed everyone then asked about the boys.

Uh-oh— Shit!

"Tell me what those crazy kids of ours are up to," she said. "Can I speak to them for a sec?"

Mouth dry, he squeezed his eyes shut, scrambling to come up with what to say.

"You still there?" she asked.

"They're already asleep," he said.

"*Asleep!*" Francine said with a gasp. She giggled. "This early and already *asleep*? On a weekend, yet. Did you hypnotize them or something?"

"Cough syrup," he said. "Worked like a charm." They shared a laugh. "Actually, we were up late last night watching the Lakers. We played some Scrabble, watched a movie."

She asked how the project was coming along.

He glanced at Demtra's business card on top of the microwave.

"Coming along, I guess."

"I told you you'd be able to get some work done."

Tail between his legs, he nodded.

"Well, listen, I won't keep you," she said. "I'll call again tomorrow some time."

Later, when he was downstairs at his desk, the phone rang again.

"I hope I'm not calling too late," Demetra said.

"Not at all," he said, swallowing, catching his breath from the trot up the stairs.

"How's *Arnold & Igor* unfolding?"

"I'm chipping away over here," he told her. "But. The basic row, the prime for *Orpheus*. I had a few questions." Simon described the four-note motif throughout the *Orpheus* passages, the initial pitches of the row, repeated over and over again in the sketchbook.

"Ah, a tetrachord," she said, explaining how the twelve notes could be broken down into smaller units, three groups of four, for example, four groups of three or, as hexachords in two groups of six.

With a little laugh, Simon admitted how ridiculous all of this was, attempting to hash through thorny details over the phone without the aid of the manuscript between them.

Clearing her throat dramatically, Demetra said, "I needn't say, *I rest my case.*"

"I guess I never imagined we'd be dealing with any of this over the phone," Simon said. "At any rate, chalk it up to a crazy hunch. But I keep going over the four pitches—*E-G-E-flat-A*. I feel like there's something there, Demetra." He closed his eyes. "Like something might be embedded within those notes, I don't know, a code of some sort."

"Sounds like all this sketchbook-sleuthing is turning you into a full-fledged musicologist."

"I don't know about that. But I *do* get the feeling somehow, these pitches weren't just selected at random, simply for purely expressive reasons alone."

"Meaning?"

"Could there be something else?" he asked. "Something *symbolic* maybe, something—"

"You're talking about an *extramusical* association of some kind." Demetra explained how it wouldn't be at all unusual for Schoenberg to do something like that. She sighed. "But, these things, you realize, they can sometimes get knotty, requiring quite a bit of unraveling."

"Sure," he said.

"I'm really glad you called," she said.

"Yeah, me too. I guess, I just wish—"

"Simon, listen. Are you hungry?"

Tableau XIII

Igor

"Schoenberg's music is among the most expressive
ever written."
>—Charles Rosen

"My childhood…was a period of waiting for the moment
when I could send everyone and everything connected
with it to hell."
>—Stravinsky, *Memories and Commentaries*

Paris
May 1922

AT A BUSTLING CAFÉ off the *Square des Épinettes*, Stravinsky and his mother sit down for lunch. They've come from a concert featuring the music of Schoenberg, Webern and Berg.

"*Incorrigible!*" Anna Kyrillovna Stravinsky weighs in with a snort, a one-word indictment of the entire performance. Stravinsky adjusts his beret, squinting into the late afternoon sun, determined not to let *Mamochka* provoke him.

"Alarming what passes for music these days," his mother says. Her translucent cheeks are scribbled with veins.

The Old World conventions are out, he explains, for better or worse, no longer relevant.

"Scriabin!" Mrs. Stravinsky says loudly. "New world, old world.

That's beside the point. I promise you, if a composer like *Scriabin* were still writing music today, the music would have some meat on its bones."

"But, exactly to my point, *Musechka!*" he says. "Scriabin's no longer around."

"Just because it claims to be *modern* doesn't mean it has to end up sounding like curdled milk."

With a pale smile, Stravinsky suggests that wine may be *la métaphore appropriée*, a little time required for fresh music to age properly, the audience needing time to assimilate new art.

"Sour milk is sour milk," she says, narrowing her gaze. "And the same goes for wine. Down the basin. That's where sour wine goes."

"But my *Sacre*," he says. "The Parisians vehemently rejected it. Ah, but then." His eyes brighten. "Following a relatively brief reevaluation, suddenly there's consensus as to its legitimacy." He shrugs. "A decade passes, then—inexplicably, magically—the music gets absorbed into the mainstream."

Mrs. Stravinsky shakes her head. "With such things, Igor, one knows immediately whether it's art."

"Give it a decade."

"I haven't got a decade." She appraises her son through cool blue eyes. "And, in any case, you know already how I find *Le Sacre* no more satisfying than a cat scampering over piano keys while clumsy people make fools of themselves attempting to dance to it."

"They booed Wagner's *Tannhäuser* at its premiere," he's quick to defend, listing off other artists—Monet, Van Gogh, Cezanne, Gaugin, Toulouse-Lautrec—whose work encountered similar rejection. "El Greco. Vermeer!"

"Well, it's no Scriabin, your music."

Stung, he stares off across the *Square des Épinettes* at a *papeterie* and antiquarian bookstore, flagging down a waitress for a Cointreau and seltzer water for her, Armagnac for himself.

In addition to the Schoenberg piano pieces this afternoon, Schoenberg's new wind septet, *Fragment from the Journey of Orpheus*, was premiered, Milhaud conducting while Stravinsky listened in shock, unaware that such a work even existed, the music he and Schoenberg originally cobbled together from the tavern placemat, mailing it back and forth for further invention.

It's called dodecaphony, Schoenberg explained to him nearly five years ago at the Paris Opera house when they'd last seen one another, *a method of composing with twelve tones which are related only with one another*.

Stravinsky's forced to admit that such a mathematical approach continues to confound him.

Slowly, achingly, his mother pronounces the name, *Glazunov*, articulating each excruciating syllable—*Gla-zu-nov*—three poisonous darts that pierce his heart.

"Now, *there* was a composer who understood beauty," she adds as Stravinsky swirls his aperitif, exasperated and already eagerly antici-pating her departure from Paris and return to Ukraine.

Upon arriving by ship from Hamburg the other day, she immedi-ately insisted he accompany her all the way over to Lourdes to pray and partake of the holy therapeutic water trickling form a narrow spring in the grotto. A ten-hour train journey, Stravinsky waiting as she kneeled at the high shrine of Catholicism to offer up gratitude to the Virgin Mary for her safe passage.

Now, leaning forward in her wicker chair, his mother reaches for his hand. "You know, Igor, they adored your father. All of St. Petersburg. They all adored your father."

He manages a cordial nod, wincing, holding back the bile rising in his throat as he thinks of his late father, pressuring him continuously to put aside any musical aspirations, focusing instead on academic pursuits.

You are a poor pupil, his father, evidently disgusted, liked to remind him. *Why do you waste your time always tinkering at the keyboard?*

Stravinsky recalls how he must have swallowed the torrent of emotions within while bowing dutifully to the towering man clad in black cape.

A leading bass singer at the Imperial Opera, his father had certainly been ensconced in the music world. All the more reason then—it might seem obvious to conclude—for the father to recognize and acknowledge the son's talents. As a child, young Stravinsky had spent countless hours at the piano, composing rudimentary songs and otherwise keeping pace with his father when the two of them sight-read four-hand arrangements of Beethoven and Schumann symphonies.

I will try harder, he'd vowed to his father while anxiously broaching the subject of his weekly music lessons. How tense the domestic setting, he and his brothers slinking around the house at *Oranienbaum,* their dwelling filled with sacred relics and inscrutable religious images, medicinal-scented candles, odor of sanctity, the ongoing invocation of saints.

Stravinsky had recently begun piano lessons at the conservatory in St. Petersburg, intent on continuing, though his father had waved the family's raskhodnaya kniga, his personal account book in which expenditures were obsessively recorded.

These lessons of yours, his father announced, *they're costing me the eyes off my face! Two rubles a week, nearly.* He stuck out his lower lip. *Next year, you will matriculate at the university in Law. A livelihood. This is what is required.*

His father's glabrous pate, the archipelago of pancake-shaped liver spot splotches that reddened when his anger rose, Stravinsky, meanwhile, mute, trembling, burning as he glanced hopelessly around the airless room, the godforsaken nursery isolated from the rest of the household in the family's second-floor Victorian, uncertain whether his meekness or his obedience was the more shameful.

And what form of musical guidance was the great Fyodor Stravinsky able to provide to his son? The father's colossal ego rendered him all but blind to the son's inborn talents, as Fyodor, in his spectacular private library—a collection that rivaled the largest in all of Russia—silently mounted the ladder to retrieve a much-loved book.

Or the fraught evening ritual at the dinner table, nerve-wracking silence, glances averted, heads bent in the solemn spooning and slurping of soup, Mother rigid, scarcely emitting a sound, cowering along with the rest of them.

Now, distinct warbling from a nearby table thwarts Stravinsky from his reverie as a woman in an outlandish straw hat and thick, ermine stole waggles her fingers at him.

"Monsieur Stravinsky!" Dorothea Rondo exclaims, making her way towards their table in stiff and masculine tweed trousers, her cheeks powdered like fuzzy moth wings. "I thought that might have been you I saw earlier at the concert."

Stravinsky introduces Mlle Rondo to his mother, indicating the vacant chair, Mlle Rondo seating herself, eager to hear Stravinsky's reaction to Schoenberg's new septet.

"My position," he tells her, "is not to *think* about music, but to respond to how music makes me *feel*." He sips his drink, uneasy still about memories of his father. "Though, I'll confess I found this afternoon's musical offering wholly incapable of eliciting any sort of emotional response."

Already regretting his knee-jerk reaction, he stops to mentally edit, wishing he could retract the statement. In all honesty, Schoenberg's *Orpheus* did in fact provoke a certain undeniable emotional response in him. Not due in any way to its unfathomable twelve-tone technique per se, but rather some chill of recognition as his ears prickled at a single repeated chord.

His chord! The eight-note chord he himself had scribbled out on the tavern placemat nine years ago in Berlin, the *Orpheus* germ, leading to the impromptu collaborations between him and Schoenberg.

"Do I have this right then?" Rondo asks with a smirk. "Inscrutable. And, as you point out, also wanting in any sort of musical substance?"

"Hold on there!" Stravinsky protests. "That isn't at all accurate, I made no such assertion."

"*Au contraire,*" she says as she taps her reporter's pad with a fiendish grin, "I've got it all down right here. All the juicy details fit to print."

Changing tack, Rondo requests a response from Stravinsky regarding Schoenberg's recent searing assessment of his *Symphonies of Wind Instruments,* published in Rondo's *Kultur und Kunst* column for the *Zeitgeist,* Rondo apparently delighted to jog Stravinsky's memory about certain catchphrases from Schoenberg's analysis—*hopelessly nationalistic, folksy, repetitive, jejune.*

She's cornering him, Stravinsky compelled to defend himself, asserting how the opinions of other composers hardly concern him as Rondo, meanwhile, painstakingly records his responses.

Cubism on a very bad day, she's amused to remind Stravinsky, quoting more of Schoenberg's responses, grinning with what strikes Stravinsky as *Schadenfreude*, some wicked inclination to stir up the pot between him and Schoenberg.

"I may never live up to the standards of an Arnold Schoenberg," he says bitterly.

"Spoilt milk," Mrs. Stravinsky says, glaring at her son. "Every last dreg of it non-potable."

SIMON

Molto Fortissimo e Vivace. Westwood's Village Café. Hardly the appropriate place to whip out a rare and delicate manuscript while attempting to carry out scholarly commerce, not quite the hermetically-sealed, climate-controlled haven for exposing priceless documents to the elements.

For the time being, Simon kept the manuscript beneath the table, encased safely in the valise's leather scabbard, the café bustling on a Saturday night, flamboyant Spanish guitar music strumming over the loudspeaker, the table he and Demetra shared tottering like a tipsy galleon whenever either one of them lifted a beer glass or shifted position.

"By the way," Demetra said, "I think I may have figured out why Schoenberg would have been so intent on fiddling around with some ancient Latin palindrome about a gardener."

Simon leaned forward, eager to hear what she had to report while she rummaged through her handbag.

Her look this evening was casual, he noticed. An entirely different kind of look, non-bookish, jeans and a leather jacket, a turban-style hairband slipped over her dark hair.

Strictly business. That's what he kept telling himself, justifying their meeting as a necessary and urgent professional consultation. A quick drink, an occasion for some badly needed sleuthing on the document. After which he'd be on his way to fetch the boys. Nonetheless, he'd upgraded his wardrobe—corduroys, suede shoes and a red cable sweater, the precautionary mint he'd nibbled still lingering pleasantly.

Demetra retrieved a slip of paper with the palindrome written on it.

```
S  A  T  O  R
A  R  E  P  O
T  E  N  E  T
O  P  E  R  A
R  O  T  A  S
```

"It's an analogue for dodecaphony," she said. "A metaphor for what Schoenberg was attempting to do in his twelve-tone method."

She traced the Square, fingers moving horizontally, forwards and backwards, and then vertically.

"Four separate directions," she said. "Four musical possibilities." Demetra smiled at him, waiting patiently for him to make the connection.

"Of course!" Simon said, heartbeat shifting into high gear, *doppio movimiento*, "the tone row and its four permutations."

She nodded.

"Schoenberg was conceiving of music in four separate directions," he said, laughing, giddy about the discovery. "Holy shit! The basic row. The same sequence of notes, proceeding forward, but also backwards."

"Yes," she said, "the same series of notes which can proceed sequentially, forwards, but also in reverse."

"Prime and retrograde," he said.

She traced the Square's rows vertically once more. "But also, in inversion."

"And then retrograde inversion," he said. "The four permutations of the twelve-tone row. My God, it's perfect, the Sator Square. Elegant."

"It's exactly how Schoenberg must have visualized his twelve-tone procedure," she said. "And precisely as he would have wanted it to be understood." She tapped the slip of paper on the table. "The Sator Square acts as a visual metaphor for the mechanics of serialism. As Schoenberg once proposed, *A hat remains a hat, whether viewed from above, below, or from one side or the other.*"

All right, Simon thought to himself, *wonderful, lovely, peachy keen— But, then why would Schoenberg bother to pencil the Square into the* Orpheus *sections of the sketchbook, if in fact he himself already grasped the concept? What would be the point?*

Unless—

Unless, he'd scribbled it down with the intention of sharing it with someone else.

Stravinsky!

With a pallid smile, Simon swallowed, raising his glass to the Square and to dodecaphony.

"I can honestly say I've never toasted to that before." Demetra sipped her beer and then raised her glass with a kittenish smile. "And here's to *teamwork.*"

"*To teamwork,*" Simon said, clinking glasses while mulling over the likelihood of an Arnold and Igor teamwork.

Could Arnold have conceivably made use of the Square in order to illustrate his twelve-tone theory to Igor, holding his colleague's hand, essentially, while leading him through the formidable labyrinth of his own musical imagination?

Simon refilled their beer mugs from the pitcher on the table, wondering now about the reference to the Sator Square in his father's journal.

Guiding my plow. That's how his father appeared to view his own work, *guiding my plow, accompanied by Stravinsky playing Schoenberg.* And: *I guide my plow, Arepo's hoe combing over the earth, keeping the work circling.* And, in a recent entry, *Arepo, the progenitor, protector.*

By this point, he'd read through quite a number of the journal's pages, wondering whether he'd ever get to the bottom of his father's boundless fascination with the Square.

Demetra was looking at him with a serious expression. "Over the phone, you mentioned some questions had come up regarding the *Orpheus* tone row."

"Right," Simon said, leaning over to unlatch the valise, surveying the teetering table, the cluttered surface space.

He furrowed his brow. "Not sure I want to risk bringing the manuscript out in this—" He glanced doubtfully at the table. "I mean—"

"Listen," she said, "I live nearby. We could head over for a while." She shrugged. "It's quiet. Far more conducive to the task at hand. We'll be able to spread out and examine it undisturbed."

It made sense. Taking in the cafe's crowded chaotic ambiance, Simon thought things over. It certainly made sense. These were essential questions about the document, after all.

"I'm only a few blocks away," she said as they were leaving the café. "Might as well leave your car wherever you parked it. We can walk over."

Casual though it was, it was exquisitely nerve-wracking somehow to find himself strolling through Westwood Village alongside the winsome Dr. Kouras, sketchbook safely sheathed, while they hurried past a pizza joint, a pulsing pub, and a frozen yogurt shop, threading their way through hordes of college students, Simon recognizing Shay Wintrob, one of his students, surrounded by an argyled cluster of fraternity boys, grinning deviously at Simon as they passed.

Wending around a long queue of moviegoers, Simon thought he heard his name being called, turning to see Monique Krause, Stuart's wife, alongside her daughter in the movie line, waving and beckoning him over.

Shouldn't he go over and say hello?

"I'm sure the two of you probably know each other," Simon said smiling at Demetra, when they'd gone over to say hello.

Mo thrust out her hand, introducing herself and her daughter. She was dressed in a terrycloth sweatsuit, pale orange like a throat lozenge, her stringy gray hair wound tightly in a scarf.

Taking Mo's hand, Demetra smiled warmly, Simon groping for some plausible explanation of how he and Dr. Kouras just happened to run into one another at a nearby restaurant, Mo scrutinizing them, meanwhile, inquiring how Francine's shoot in Chicago was going.

"Well, *that* was a little awkward," Demetra said with a light-hearted laugh once they'd gotten away.

"She and my wife are pretty close," Simon said. "They share a few creative interests."

Demetra grinned conspiratorially. "You're out for barely an hour or so, and already you may have landed yourself in the doghouse."

They reached her townhose, a dark glass building off of Wilshire, Demetra leading him into a mirrored lobby, stench of solvent, bright lighting spilling over the waxed marble floor, a doorman with a bulbous nose greeting Demetra as *Ms. Kouras*.

"Good evening, Edgar," Demetra said.

Green track lighting cast a murky garish film over the lobby, an odd glow reflected in the indoor pond, a gurgling water fountain, glossy shoreline rocks, a few languid koi floating by. In the mirrored walls surrounding them on all sides, they could see their reflection, he and Demetra infinitely duplicated—a series of husky middle-aged Simons dressed in replicating red cable sweaters alongside an equal number of Demetras, dressed in glossy leather coats, snug designer jeans and smart sandals.

The elevator ride up to the seventh floor was excruciating, standing this close to her. Self-conscious, he averted his gaze, the elevator groaning as it slowly ascended. The beer had gone to his head. Her perfume, the scent of her—hair, skin, body lotion—the alluring outfit she wore. Smiling cordially, tingling, he found himself wondering what it might be like to kiss her.

"Almost there," she said, Simon's eyes wandering furtively to peek at her unzipped jacket, the open collar along her blouse, her tantalizing neckline. She caught him glancing at her and he blushed, clearing his throat, his gaze focused on his loafers.

"So, how long have you lived here?" he asked through a gauzy mouth, his voice awkwardly formal inside the elevator, booming with farcical self-importance as if he were interviewing her before a live audience.

"Eight years, just about," she said. "I'm on the waiting list for one of the penthouses."

Impulsively, she reached in front of him, pressing the elevator button for an unscheduled detour to the eleventh floor.

"Come on," she said, "I'll show you."

They emerged from the elevator onto the top floor, a dramatic view from the window along the corridor, an endless streak of car headlights sweeping along Wilshire Boulevard, the cityscape nestled against the twinkling hillside.

"Spectacular," he said, astonished, exhilarated, sneaking up here and alone with her, high above the city.

Demetra grabbed his arm, yanking him down the corridor, Simon laughing as he struggled to maintain balance.

"Whoa!" he said. "What the heck are you—?"

"Come on," she said, pulling him towards a gray service door, "I wanna show you something." Turning to him with a roguish grin, she pulled open a heavy stairwell door beneath a sign, *Emergency Evacuation Use Only*.

"Demetra," he said breathlessly, "where on earth are you taking me?"

Finger to her lips, she whispered how, technically, they weren't supposed to be doing this.

"No kidding," he said, huffing as he trailed behind her up the steep unlit stairs.

When he caught up to her on the landing, she asked in a whisper if he was ready, pulling open the latch to the rooftop door, kneeling and wedging her handbag into the door jamb to carefully prop open the door, singing, "Ta-dah!" as they ventured out onto the roof.

Reluctant, he set the valise down, unsure how safe it would be up here. But even while waffling, he had to admit it felt thrilling, prowling around with her, breaking the rules, her lovely laugh, the wind whooshing against his face and ears, flurry of street lights, a glimmer off the neighboring high-rises.

He negotiated the torpor brought on by the beer, its salty aquatic aftertaste, anchoring his feet, skittish with a sudden fear of plummeting over the edge.

He watched Demetra take a few adventurous steps towards the edge of the rooftop, turning to smile at him. He ventured a tentative step forward, fingers still grazing the doorway for security, glancing down at the valise, paranoid it might get blown around, the document swept away by a gust.

Demetra motioned him forward, and with a deep breath, he let go of the doorway, managing a single baby step forward, terrifying actually, no railing around the edge, a fragrant evening breeze blowing across the top of the building, kicking up dust. He could feel his legs locking, protesting any additional step, Demetra egging him on while inching closer to the edge.

"Careful!" he shouted, his feet obstinately affixed to the gritty surface of tarpaper. But this only provoked a fresh mischievous grin from her beautiful mouth, enticing smile.

"I love it up here!" she sang against the backdrop of what he imagined might be the brink of oblivion. "It's like climbing to the pinnacle of the world. *Aquillae.* Up among the eagles." Her arms circled in the breeze. "That's what I love to imagine. High up over the world, all petty pressures blown away by the wind god."

Stomach fluttery, eyes affixed to his feet, he negotiated an additional tentative step.

"*You know you want to,*" she called in a teasing tone, standing in profile and closing her eyes, chin tilted, hair billowing in the breeze.

Another step towards her, his toes, the soles of his shoes, assessing every last pore of roofing paper, nerves jangled while wondering about structural integrity and undetected engineering vulnerabilities, his timid brain calculating the risk of plunging right through the roof, his entire overactive nervous system highly alert to the faintest rut or gradation change below his feet.

"Almost there," she said, extending a hand towards him.

At last he reached her, planting his feet as if bolting them down, a distressing mere couple of inches from where the roof abruptly ended, or so it seemed, gasping, as he reached for her hand, adamant about not venturing one millimeter further. Queasy, he squeezed his eyes shut, expelling from his imagination the Thanatos of an oafish plummet as Demetra gently tugged at his hand, nudging him one final step.

"*No!*" he hollered, "*Jesus—*" heart exploding in his throat. "That's far enough!"

"Okay, okay," she relented, "no further, I swear."

They looked over the southern edge of the UCLA campus, traffic humming below, a scurry of ant-sized pedestrians, the medical center aglow in the background, a bird's-eye view of imposing brick structures against the lush canopy of trees.

"Wow," he said.

"My special place," she said, holding his hand. "Close your eyes. Listen to the music the wind makes."

"Mmm, yes," he murmured, "lovely."

"Aeolus," she said. "The wind god, fashioning his symphony."

"I like it."

"You know," she said, "for your next symphony, or whatever musical form you choose to write, you could try capturing the distinct colors of the wind."

"Interesting," he said, opening his eyes, glad to be discussing music with her, sensing she understood what it was like to live inside the world of sound, something he felt somehow he was never quite capable of conveying to Francine.

"Reminds me of growing up in Chicago," she said.

Chicago, he thought, *how funny is that? Francine and Carla together there now.*

"My father would take me all around to these amazing places in various pockets of the city, Greektown and the Polish Triangle, the symphony and every other musical venue in town, naturally. I distinctly remember the wind sculptures at the Standard Oil Building plaza on Michigan Ave. Often he'd bring me there. We'd spend hours just sitting and listening."

"I can't get over how much of the campus you can see from up here. An entire world."

"Well," she said with a strange smile, "it may pale a little in comparison to a lost Schoenberg sketchbook." She squeezed his arm. "But, at least I got to share one of *my* secrets with you."

...excerpted from concert reviews by Dorothea Rondo in Le Temps Moderns, *Paris*

(1921) "Music is powerless to express anything at all," Stravinsky insisted....

(1922) "Schoenberg is one of the greatest spirits of our era," Stravinsky commented, "a remarkable artist. I feel it!"

(1922) ...For his part, Mr. Stravinsky has gone so far as to refer to Mr. Schoenberg's most recent compositions as *sterile,* and even *useless* while quick to add, "I *detest* modern music."

In response, Schoenberg openly challenged Stravinsky to join the ranks of modern *forward*-looking composers, "rather than remaining struthious, head buried in the sand," Schoenberg further rebuked, "producing some crudely primeval form of music, which only looks backwards...Stravinsky eliminates tonal chords, proceeding clumsily, merely by the most barbaric rhythmic movement..."

(1923) ...Regarding recent comments made by Mr. Stravinsky, Schoenberg then went on to say, "My objection remains with all who seek their personal salvation by taking the middle course, merely nibbling at dissonance, wanting to pass for modern but too cautious to draw the consequences."

Tableau XIV

Igor

"I have never been able to compose unless sure that no
one could hear me."

—Igor Stravinsky

Venice, Italy
International Society for Contemporary Music Festival
7 September 1925

THE HOTEL VIEW OVER Porto San Nicolo is impressive. Campanile
chimes from the square at Santa Maria Elisabetta proclaim the 10
o'clock hour while, across the Lido, metropolitan Venice shimmers like
a watercolor.

Alone with the open score before him on his desk, pen in hand,
Stravinsky undertakes the finishing touches on his piano sonata, more
than a little curious as to how his new piece will be received by the
festival audience tomorrow.

But just as he's preparing to notate a few accents and staccato articulations in the score, he's ambushed by sonic disturbances from the
neighboring hotel room, scuffling, shouting, keys jangling, the squeal
of a luggage cart clumsily wheeled in. Over the commotion, he's able
to detect a familiar voice, a mumbo jumbo of mangled Italian and
corrosive Viennese German, distracted, unable to focus on his piano
sonata, he's attuned agonizingly to the tapestry of luggage unzipping,
noisy dresser drawers, throat-clearing and a quiet belch, a transistor

radio's crackle, a toilet flushing, the muted drumroll of flatulence. A chair dragged across the adjacent balcony and Schoenberg settling in, affording Stravinsky the partial glimpse of a hairy broomstick leg.

He strolls the Piazza San Marco, the canals nearby lacquered in vibrant green. Venice is his favorite city; he has fond memories of touring here with Diaghilev and the ballet troupe. And he recalls a sightseeing trip with Picasso, the antiquarian bookshops, galleries and balconied bordellos, courtyards filled with heat-soaked red stones as they navigated the labyrinthine canals, slugging Tuscan wine from a flask, Picasso, beside the Ponte di Rialto, producing a pastel crayon from his trousers pocket to eke out a miniature portrait of Stravinsky.

But in the present moment, the ink on Stravinsky's piano sonata has barely dried. After two more successful ballets with the Ballets Russes, *Pulcinella* and *Les Noces,* the new piano sonata's neoclassical style represents a departure—an entirely new aesthetic, a radical experiment. Rather than look forward towards the future of modernism, the new piano work looks backward instead, an homage to past classical masters, Beethoven, and even Bach, an attempt to impose order onto chaos. As he walks along the sun-illuminated canal, he can't help wondering what his colleagues may make of such an abrupt stylistic about-face.

Inside the Music Academy, a posted schedule affixed to a marble pillar indicates that Schoenberg's *Serenade* is currently in rehearsal on the auditorium stage, Stravinsky's rehearsal scheduled to follow immediately thereafter, at two o'clock. Behind the stage door, he can hear Schoenberg's music, an energetic march, angular and jagged, demonic for a moment but then folksy, jazzy, riddled with unresolved dissonances. Stravinsky's keen ears home in further, picking out precise instrumental colors—clarinet, bassoon, cello, bass, mandolin, guitar,

and baritone voice in Schoenberg's music—the way a master chef
might detect subtle fragrances in a bouillabaisse.

At two o'clock, Schoenberg and his musicians have officially gone
beyond their allotted rehearsal time, no sign of letting up. Anxious,
Stravinsky paces backstage, thinking of Vivian in Paris, an aloof cool-
ness after their romantic interlude had only begun to get underway.

We must move on, she said to him. Sting of a snub. Though,
certainly, he has moved on. As his marriage to Katya continues to
languish, he carries out a few trysts with various fawning dancers, cos-
tumièrs, and other professional attachés, Coco Chanel among them,
and recently, apple of his eye, the irresistible Vera de Bosset.

By 2:15, all patience eroded, he pummels the immense double
doors of the stage, a violent drubbing that's easily swallowed up by
the ferocity of Schoenberg's music. Hot under the collar, he pounds
more insistently, four-thudded groupings like the fate motif from
Beethoven's Fifth, his delicate pianistic hands throbbing as he wanders
into the lobby to retrieve Edvards, the tall, gray-bearded manager.

Edvards unlocks the ponderous backstage doors, revealing a manic
and red-faced Schoenberg leaping about on the podium like a banshee.

"Eins, zwo, drei!" Schoenberg hollers at the seven musicians before
him, whirling his arms. "Immer aufgeregt!" he cries, "Geschwindig,
nicht schleppen! Ja, gut. Aber, Schwungvoll!"

Smoldering, Stravinsky storms the stage, brushing past Schoenberg
on his way to the piano, flustered as he lays out the score to the piano
sonata.

Waving his thick conductor's score at Edvards, Schoenberg fur-
rows his brow. "My *Serenade* requires additional rehearsal time, due to
its complexity."

"Rehearsal times have been clearly posted," Stravinsky says with a scowl.

"But you perform only a piano sonata," Schoenberg says to Stravinsky,
"a mere solo work requiring minimal, if any, rehearsal."

"Rehearsal time is rehearsal time," Stravinsky says with a huff. "Non-negotiable."

With a shrug and ironic smile, Schoenberg scoffs sotto voce to his musicians, "A mere piano sonata, of all things!"

Stravinsky slams his palms against the top of the piano. "My god! Can you really be so self-absorbed—so— delusional!—so thick, to presume that you happen to be the only composer present at the festival?"

Schoenberg nods. "Yes. This is correct. But this is exactly what I presume."

—⁓—

At the Festival's culminating gala, he watches Schoenberg across the room, swarmed by composers, musicians, and audience members, each eager to discuss his innovative *Serenade* and the unveiling of his system of twelve-tone dodecaphony. Alone at the reception table, Stravinsky nibbles tiny grapes and pungent Italian cheese, maintaining his surveillance of Schoenberg and his proliferating adherents—Schnabel, Grosz, Ruggles, Szymanowski, Cassado, Hindemith, Villa-Lobos, who continue to flock over like blackbirds at the feet of the overweening, gesticulating Jew on the other side of the room.

Stravinsky's piano sonata has received a considerably cooler reception, the half-hearted applause petering out well before its composer had even completed his bow. Afterwards, a handful of colleagues approached to lavish modest praise, though their sentiments struck him as something more like pity, Nadia Boulanger effusive in her *bravos!* Ansermet, Florent Schmitt, Ibert and Honegger pumping his hand with enthusiasm while peppering him with blandishments about esoteric invention, clever construction and keyboard pyrotechnics.

Now, like a raptor, Dorothea Rondo swoops in from somewhere, gesturing at Schoenberg's buzzing corner across the room.

"Would you look at that?" she says, goading him, he feels sure. Costumed in a glittery vermillion dress with clownish yellow buttons, she wears an outlandish straw hat which resembles an upside-down lampshade, or something pilfered from the head of an unsuspecting monk.

Rondo shakes her head. "He's got them eating out of his hand."

Stravinsky puts on his best smile, wondering why this particular critic always seems to have it out for him. And when Rondo yammers on a bit too long about Schoenberg's *music of the future*, Stravinsky has had enough.

"The music of the future is completely useless to me," he says with the wave of a hand. "I live neither in the past, nor in the future. I remain in the present and can only know what the truth is for myself *today*."

"But Schoenberg's magnificent *Serenade*," Rondo says, giving the dagger another little twist. "I'm sure, on some level, you must have admired it."

"I *detested it!*" Stravinsky says, throwing down his hands. "Nothing more than convoluted formulae, this twelve-tone hogwash. Like a pre-formulation of the material on the artist's palette, which then fails to appear in the painting itself."

"But surely, you'll concede that, in sniffing around for inspiration from *past* masters, you're essentially looking *backwards* in your own music and, therefore, *not* writing music for *today*?"

Rondo gives a warbling laugh. "I tell you, these finicky little ears of mine detect in the Schoenberg *Serenade*, of all things, the faintest echoes of a Mozart serenade. Ironic, isn't it, how Schoenberg *also* relies on older, *past* Classical *structures*—marches, minuets, variations—even as he forsakes traditional harmony in focusing his sights upon the future."

"I would be pleased to discuss my piano sonata," Stravinsky says.

Rondo smiles. "And, allow me to say, these little ears of mine detect in Schoenberg's *Serenade* the faintest allusion to some of *your* own music."

Stravinsky laughs derisively. "*My* music? Utter *hooey!* He and I are incompatible, aesthetically, in every regard." Glum, he steals another miserable glance across the room.

With a look of pure mischief, Rondo scribbles away in her notepad, rolling up her sleeves and settling in for the entertaining battle she's busily stirring up: *Neoclassicism* versus *Dodecaphony.*

—∿∿—

That evening, Stravinsky rests in his hotel room, sprawled on the bed and listening to boisterous celebrations in the Schoenberg room next door. A champagne cork pops, someone makes a bawdy joke greeted by muffled laughter. For a moment, he considers taking the high road, going next door to join his associates for a nightcap.

Instead, he remains splayed upon the mattress, staring up at a water-stained ceiling, regretting that he'd forgotten to pack votive candles for the expunging of lingering evil spirits.

Cringing, forced to listen in on his colleague's haughty victory party, he reaches over to shut off the lamp, soured by a suspicion that Schoenberg's daring new musical approach may in fact be *ruining* classical music. Exhausted, prostrate on the bed, he gathers up the corners of his pillow, wedging them forcibly over his ears.

—∿∿—

…excerpted from concert reviews by Dorothea Rondo
in *Le Temps Moderns*, Paris 1925-33

"I do not know what I am supposed to like in *Oedipus*," Schoenberg commented about Stravinsky's latest ballet. "At least, it is all negative: for example, unusual theater, unusual setting, unusual resolution of the action, unusual vocal writing, unusual acting, unusual melody, unusual harmony, unusual counterpoint, unusual instrumentation—so much 'un' without being anything in particular."

One movement of Schoenberg's recent *Three Satires for Mixed Chorus* features an unmistakable diminutive Russian drummer (and who might this be?) with an old-fashioned haircut, drumming away, the astute Neoclassicist, dappling in dissonance, but essentially too timid to meet it head on. "Stravinsky's musical ideas are crudely juxtaposed," Schoenberg commented, "one idea following after the next in seemingly random fashion, with the uncanny intention not to expand upon or otherwise develop such ideas."

"Stravinsky is among the great creative spirits of our era," Schoenberg commented when asked about recent performances of Stravinsky's *Persephone, The Fairy's Kiss, Symphony of Psalms,* and Violin Concerto.

"…that truly outstanding artist of our time," Stravinsky stated with regard to Schoenberg's Violin Concerto and *Variations for Orchestra.* "That he is a genius, I acknowledge."

SIMON

Settling into Demetra's leather sofa, Simon suppressed a little smirk, never having dreamed he'd wind up *here* in the posh and scholarly sanctuary of Dr. Kouras, the sunken living room, handsome Persian rug, her bookcases lined with heady musicological monographs and opulent art books. What a story he'd have for Stuart on Monday!

Demetra lowered the dimmer switch along the wall, casting a soft glow over the living room. Simon smelled pleasant notes of mulled wine, cinnamon and nutmeg, a sweet, warm, aroma permeating her townhouse.

"Moussaka," Demetra said. "My mother's recipe. She'd often prepare it. I don't have much time to spend in the kitchen, but I love having these comforting scents wafting from my childhood."

While unsheathing the sketchbook, setting it down carefully upon the teak coffee table, he turned to see Demetra smiling warmly, a shot glass in each of her hands.

"Ouzo," she said after he'd tossed back a translucent, bluish substance, his eyes watering.

"Potent stuff."

"Authentic Greek liqueur," she said, draining her own glass. "An acquired taste, no doubt. My father was rather fond of the stuff, teasing my sister Eleni and me that it would wind up putting hair on our chests." Demetra rolled her eyes at the thought. She gestured towards the dining room. "Come. Let's enjoy the moussaka before it gets cold."

They ate dinner together in her dining room, delicate morsels of eggplant topped with béchamel and accented by cinnamon and wine-drenched raisins. Demetra filled their glasses from a dark bottle of Retsina, plying him with all sorts of questions about the Santa Fe commission, curious as to how he was negotiating all the pressure. Sipping from his wine, digging into the savory moussaka and farmer's salad, Simon found her interest reassuring and heartwarming.

Demetra refilled their wine glasses as they returned to the living room to delve into the sketchbook, seated beside one another on the sofa, heads bent together over the manuscript. Immersed in analysis, Demetra scribbled out calculations and musical formulae on a small notepad.

"I think you may be right about the encryption," she said, looking up at him. "Schoenberg *did* love a good musical game, puzzles, ciphers, jokes, acrostics, that sort of thing." Moving the pad in front of him, she said, "And, yes, I would agree with you that the pitches here could very well be representative of *names*."

"*Names*." He narrowed his eyes. "Okay, but *what* names?"

"*Three* names, actually." She pointed to the configurations she'd jotted down on her pad. "Here's the prime. *E-G-E^b-A-B-F-D-F$^\#$-C-A^b-B^b-D^b*, the original set of twelve notes forming the basis for all musical material that follows."

He watched her arrange the twelve pitches into a pattern of 4 + 6 + 2:

| E-G-E^b-A | B-F-D-F$^\#$-C-A^b | B^b-D^b |

"We can group the notes," she said, "to reflect how they most often appear in these sections." She looked at him with an avid professorial gaze. "But here's where things start to get interesting. The substitution of alphabetic characters for musical pitches."

"Like Bach loved to do," he said.

"Exactly. Bach embedded his own name and signature into some of his compositions by having the names of musical notes correspond with alphabetic letters."

"Or like Michelangelo," Simon said excitedly. "Embedding his self-portrait within *The Last Judgment* of the Sistine Chapel."

Nodding, Demetra jotted something down.

"*B*," she said, "the letter, which we know in German musical nomenclature actually represents the note *B-flat*. Next, the note and alphabetic character, *A*—in which the note *A* corresponds to the letter *A*, a simple, one-to-one correspondence between alphabet and pitch. Same for *C*. But then, for the letter *H*—"

"*H* represents the note *B* in German," he said.

Nodding, she pressed her pen to her lips. "But, nearly two centuries later, Schoenberg and his disciples—Webern and Berg, namely— became terribly fond of cryptic musical puns, injecting allusions, innuendo, and other sorts of wordplay into their scores." Demetra explained how this particular *Orpheus* cryptogram wasn't perfect, necessarily. Since the musical alphabet contained only seven possible alphabetic characters, one needed to adopt a flexible approach when matching note names with letters.

E-G-E^b-A

Demetra pointed to her manuscript pad. "If we take the first grouping, *E-G-Eb-A*, those four pitches you were so concerned about, we can match the note *E* directly with the letter *E*. And, bypassing the note *G*, just for a moment and moving on to *Eb*, we wind up with the letter *S*. Since Schoenberg spoke German, and within the German and Latin nomenclature—"

"*E-flat* corresponds to *ess*," he said, "the letter *S*."

Demetra nodded, matched the final note *A* with the letter *A* writing out the pattern on her notepad.

$$E=E \qquad G=? \quad E^b=S \quad A=A \quad E?SA$$

"Elsa!" he shouted, blood rushing to his head. "Holy shit, Demetra. My God. Elsa Růžek, of course!" He laughed. "The mastermind behind the *Orpheus* film project."

"Which would explain why you kept noticing the recurrence of these particular four notes."

"Like an homage," he said excitedly, "Elsa's name announced with those initial pitches and woven throughout the entire fabric."

Demetra pointed out there was no way of arriving at any exact musical representation for the letter *L* in Elsa's name, since the musical alphabet stopped at the letter *G*. "So, we *do* need to allow for some creative leeway in our deciphering, making do, in this case, with substituting the missing *L* for the note *G*."

And what about the two distinct handwritings within the *Orpheus* sections? She couldn't simply ignore or dismiss that. He burned to pose the question but then, thinking better of it, quashed the impulse. Now wouldn't be the moment to throw any sort of wrench into things.

She was staring at him. "What are you thinking about? I can hear the wheels spinning over there."

"The *Requiem for Vivian Růžek*," he said, remembering the portion of his father's journal he'd recently come upon, how his father had been the one who initially suggested to Elsa that she commission a requiem for her mother. "I came across an old review of the Requiem recently that mentions a repeated, two-note motif. I take it you know something about that work."

"Quite an unusual case." Demetra nodded. "*Both* Schoenberg and Stravinsky were commissioned to contribute though, sadly, no extant score or parts seem to have survived."

"Wonder what became of it."

"I doubt anyone really knows for certain," she said. "And I think I'm correct in thinking that the piece never shows up in the catalogue of either composer's collected works." She shrugged. "It appears to have been performed only once before mysteriously vanishing."

"Vanishing."

"Up in smoke," Demetra said. "Likely having to do with the peculiar circumstances surrounding the death of Elsa Růžek."

Again, she stared at him. "Your face, Simon. What is it? What's wrong?"

He tried to shake it off, but the sudden swell of emotion caught him off guard, the tragic loss of Vivian Růžek at the hands of the Nazis, followed not long afterwards by the harrowing fate of Simon's own mother, leading to his father's mental breakdown and incarceration in a mental hospital, leaving Simon in a fragile state of limbo—orphaned, essentially—for a period of time until his father was eventually able to recover, but this then followed soon after by a third tragic blow, the peculiar and puzzling death of Elsa Růžek.

"Simon?"

He looked away, tugging nervously at his beard, closing his eyes against the initial burning sting of tears, willing away the emotions, forcing them into some storage vault of non-feeling, a holding place for trauma within his body that enabled him to at least function and carry on, however modestly.

With the wave of a hand now, he indicated he was fine, insisting they continue.

Tentatively, Demetra placed her attention back on the *Orpheus* tone row, pointing to the sequence of notes in the middle of the row.

B-F-D-F#-C-A♭

"So, for the alphabetic character for the note *B*, using German and Latin as our starting point—"

"*H*," Simon said, "the note *B* represented by the letter *H*. Like with the *Bach* motif."

"Right." He watched as she continued to work things out, squinting at the *H-F* combination, two consonants that appeared not to align, positing that *F*, however, might also be thought of as *E-sharp*, its enharmonic spelling, resulting in the letter *E*, while still satisfying Schoenberg's strict twelve-tone dictum in which no pitch could be repeated until all other pitches had been utilized within the row.

Note B = letter H
F = (E#) = letter E

Demetra set aside the third note, *D*, temporarily, unsure how *D* fit into the puzzle, proceeding to the fourth letter, *F-sharp*, reasoning that it too, as in the case of *E-sharp*, could be considered enharmonically as *E-double-sharp*.

B becomes H
F becomes E
D - ?
F# (as E^x) becomes E

"And the same goes for *A-flat* at the end," she said. "We simply remove the flat sign and have the letter name, *A*."

Simon glanced at Demetra's manuscript pad:

H- E -?- E- ?- A

Simon stared in shock as Demetra completed her calculations:

$$\textbf{B-F-D-F}^{\#}\textbf{-C-A}^{\flat} =$$
$$\textbf{H-E-(L)-E-(N)-A}$$

The sight of his mother's name broke open the floodgates. "Helena." Demetra murmured triumphantly. "Helena Dent. It has to be."

His chest had caved in, insides pulverized, turning quickly to soup, trembling and praying his poker face would hold out, helpless against a new welling of tears.

"Your mother," Demetra said. "She'd been slated by Schoenberg—handpicked to sing the soprano role in the *Orpheus* score, hadn't she?"

An errant tear, maddeningly slow, burned down his cheek as he described the entry in his father's journal about how Schoenberg and his wife had visited his mother at the hospital where she lay ill and in decline. Elsa was there as well that day, exactly as his father had recorded it, leaving Simon with the undeniable intuition that his parents and Elsa must have come to be on fairly intimate terms. Apparently, Elsa's husband Claes was the nexus and conduit for events, a longtime mentor of his mother and then musical partner, in Europe initially, and later California.

"I can see how all of this must be hitting close to home with you," she said.

"My father wrote about the day Schoenberg came to my mother's hospital bedside," Simon said. "He handed her a copy of *Orpheus'*

Lament, an aria he'd just finished writing for the *Orpheus* project."

"It appears in the sketchbook!" Demetra said. "I recall seeing the sketches."

"Years later," he said, "that same aria was performed during Elsa Růžek's funeral, an event which, incidentally, brought Schoenberg and Stravinsky together for the first time after decades of estrangement." Simon screwed up his face. "Had fate been more kind, *Orpheus* might very well have ended up among Schoenberg's greatest masterpieces. Wouldn't you say?"

"Hard to say," she said. "This is truly my first encounter with it. Unfortunately, upon Elsa's death, the film project seems to have completely fallen by the wayside."

But it didn't end there! Simon burned to tell her.

"But really," she said, "who's to say what *might* have been, had the *Orpheus* reached completion."

"But it didn't end there," he said, surprised when the words slipped from his mouth. "Not with Elsa's death."

"What do you mean?"

He lowered his head. "Nothing."

"No, Simon, tell me. I want to know."

Shaking his head, he said, "Really, nothing. My head's fuzzy." He was thinking of the *Orpheus* passages in the sketchbook, the Arnold and Igor collaboration that might well have taken place after Elsa passed away. He'd been on the verge of blurting this out to her, though now, coming to his senses, he reined in any such delusional suppositions.

"Just a few crazy thoughts," he told her, gazing off at the white mantel and tall bookcases beside the alcove, the walls covered with Expressionist prints—Schiele, Klimt, Marc, Beckman, Schoenberg— her desk across the living room piled with books and papers.

Demetra tapped at her notepad. "Well, shall we have a go at the final name?"

Simon swallowed, exhausted but intent on completing the mission as Demetra explained how the last two notes proved toughest to decode, no apparent workable encryption letter to use as a starting point, prompting her to instead turn to the obvious, weighing possible biographical details to help determine who *else* might be integral in some way—what other name essential to *Orpheus*?

Indeed, *who else*? What *other* name might be missing from the puzzle? A two-letter name, or nickname perhaps, fundamentally important to Schoenberg and connected possibly to Helena, but certainly to Elsa.

"Some other name Schoenberg may have been intent on embroidering into the *Orpheus*," Demetra said, "someone dear to him he would have wanted to commemorate. Or immortalize."

"Vi," Simon said quietly, "of course. Vivian Růžek."

B♭ = (B) stands for V   D♭ = ?

Demetra wrote out the deciphered row.

| E - L - S - A | H - E -L -E -N - A | V - I |

Overcome, he could no longer restrain himself. "You, Dr. K., are a friggin' genius!"

Demetra laughed, blushing a little. "I go by many names."

"I'm blown away," he said, laughing, hugging his shoulders.

"Invigorating business, isn't it?" she said with a wink, getting up and heading into the other room to retrieve their wine glasses while Simon closed his eyes and in an intense flash suddenly understood how his opera could end.

The opera would conclude with Elsa's *Orpheus* project, both composers—after decades of estrangement—coming together to collaborate on it.

The *Orpheus* row.

It was all making perfect sense: the three interwoven names—Elsa, Helena, Vi—to whom Schoenberg would have wanted to pay homage; *Orpheus*, the handiwork of two genius composers, the marrying of their separate stylistic approaches, in some completely new musical guise.

"Mission accomplished," she said, handing him a refilled wine glass and easing beside him on the sofa.

"To the sketchbook," she said, smiling and clinking glasses.

"Hey, I'll drink to that," he said, sighing, lightheaded and relieved.

She set her wine glass down upon the coffee table, gazing at him now with a serious expression.

"You were saying a moment ago how you felt there might be something more to the sketchbook." She pressed a finger to her lips. "I've been doing more thinking about the contrasting autographs you pointed out. Asking myself what might be going on."

Riveted, floored by her sudden about-face, he set down his wine glass, eager to hear what she had to say.

"I've been asking myself some pretty tough questions." She shrugged. "Of course, I wouldn't feel comfortable as yet committing one hundred percent to anything." Smiling at him now—*Dolcemente e teneramente.* "But, look, I did want you to know how intrigued I am by the idea that both composers might have had a hand in the manuscript's *Orpheus* sections."

So, she's changed her tune, she's finally coming around.

"I can't begin to tell you how reassuring that is."

"Mm," she said, "I thought you might find that—*enticing.*"

She continued to stare at him, smiling pleasantly, maddeningly, while she studied his face, her own face inches away from him, perilously close, irresistible, Simon flattered, blushing now, on edge and completely out of his mind, heart pounding.

He needed to get up, politely say goodnight, and get himself home. So much work still ahead. Plus, the boys—

Reaching for his hand, she said softly, "Really, Simon, I want to do everything I can to help you."

He pulled her close, kissing her.

"Whoa," she said, "*What* are we doing?"

He kissed her again. Out of control, the room spinning, he needed to make the spinning stop, turning away from her, anguished, enraptured, mortified, sound of her breathing, sedate, beside him.

A moment later, modest now, restrained, she asked whether he'd given any further thought to her proposal. Simon searched her face.

"The manuscript," she said, her fingers brushing over the sketchbook. "Granting permission for me to make my own copy."

"I don't—" he said, blinking, "that's not— I mean, at this point—"

She touched his lips to silence him. "Hear me out a minute. Let's think about this. How much faster I'd be able to decode, for example— how much faster your opera might come together."

He suggested they could meet more often, a few more times during the week. He sucked in air sharply. "But, I'm just not comfortable, you know, with the idea of—"

"Then let me hold onto it."

He laughed. "Hold *onto* it? Oh, so now I'm simply supposed to surrender the document over to you?"

"Of course not!" she snapped. "Let's be smart about this. You're under the gun with your deadline. But every time you hit any sort of snag with the sketchbook, you're forced to stop composing." She glanced sideways at him. "But, what if— well, what if you had someone to do that part for you? An assistant of sorts." She gave his knee a friendly pat. "I'd be working ahead. At my own pace. Anticipating the next obstacle."

"You don't give up," he said with a groan.

"No one would need to know," she said. "A couple hours tops, and it's done. I'll take the utmost precautions with the spine, naturally. No worries, whatsoever, about damage." Demetra placed her face in her hands. "The two different autographs in the sketchbook, for example. That might be something you and I could begin to work on together." Searching his face, she said, "Wouldn't that be something? The two of us going in as a team to shake up the music establishment! How does that grab you, Simon? The scholarly team that makes the major breakthrough and winds up shattering all previous assumptions regarding Schoenberg/Stravinsky."

He sat forward, grabbing at his knees. "I *really* need to get going."

"Do you?" she said, standing, thrusting out a hand, signaling for him to stay put, an inscrutable smile moving over her face as, abruptly, she drifted from the room.

Exhaling heavily, he allowed himself to melt into the perversely snug sofa, easing out of his loafers, tipsy and giggling helplessly.

My God, he was tipsy!

Blinking, he lifted his heavy head, gazing up at her when she returned and stood astride him, planting her feet on the zebra-patterned rug. She was cradling an acrylic bubble bong in one arm, easing off her jacket with the other, Simon's hungry eyes roving her chest and shoulders, the partially unbuttoned blouse, skimpy tank top beneath, Demetra leaning over to kiss him roughly on the neck, nibbling an earlobe and then, with a sly smile, tilting the bong to inhale.

"*Whoa!* he exclaimed, followed by a helpless flurry of giggles, "whoa, whoa, whoa, Nelly!"

She offered him the bong, Simon grinning as he took a hit, Demetra leaning over to kiss him again.

Several more goes with the bong, the room now cloaked in silence, Demetra slumped beside him smiling, time grinding to a halt.

Then she got up, shuffling over to the bookcase, Simon dizzy, admiring her backside, watching as she hunted around for something, turning towards him with a naughty grin, a digital camera aimed his way, its shutter clicking.

"Smile, Professor Grafton," she said with a sinister giggle, "you're on *Candid Camera!*"

"Please!" he protested, clumsily waving his hands in front of his face. "Don't! Stop doing that. What the hell are you—?"

"Documentation," she said coolly, the word sending a shiver while she leered at him, rather drunk herself, stoned and half naked, giggling with an eerie breathiness.

"Capturing the moment," she told him.

Pointing at her, tortured by an unbidden image of Francine, he said angrily, "Look, I'd really appreciate it, if you would stop doing that."

"A night to remember."

Overcome with panic, forehead and neck perspiring, he struggled to sit upright, desperate to get the hell out of her apartment.

Francine, the boys—my God, what have I done?

He patted his pockets for his phone, throat parched, licking his lips, inebriated—wrecked—no way he was getting behind the wheel, put a call in to Mrs. Larson to ask for her help, praying she'd be able to come to the rescue, call someone—*anyone!* Stuart maybe, alerting him about the *situation* with the Hodgeses, begging him to go retrieve the boys.

He stared at his phone, thinking again of Francine, how he ought to place a call in to her as well, telling her how, despite everything—despite this *complete train wreck* he'd now allowed to happen—he still loved her, reassuring her that, yes, despite all of this, in the long run, everything was still going to work out.

Demetra moved across the room, dimming lights before trailing off down the hallway, headed for her bedroom, he suspected.

He should follow her. Get what he'd come for. Wasn't this *really* why he'd played along with her invitation to come over tonight, accepting such hospitality without further thought. *Get up, go ravish her in her bedroom,* a virile voice was now braying, Simon imagining their bodies entangled in satiny sheets while the two of them went at it mercilessly on some imagined heart-shaped and enchanted waterbed.

Whoa! Shit. Crazy! *Had he just dozed?*

Jesus.

Ha! Weirrrrd. Had he really just dozed off for a sec?

Heavy-eyed, he could feel himself slipping, succumbing to exhaustion, dissolving more deeply into the delicious sofa where gentle, blissful dreams awaited, his thousand-pound eyelids now aching to slam shut, if only for a moment, a wee power nap, why not, before the arduous trek home, head dropping like a great stone, eyelids closing, heavy heavy heavier.

BOOK V

Tableau XV

Arnold & Igor

"Los Angeles is a *Tabula rasa* where my music is concerned… Los Angeles, with the distinction that those wonderful films are produced here, whose extremely curious plots and wonderful sounds—as everyone knows—I love so well…. I am universally esteemed here as one of the most important modern composers, along with Stravinsky, Gershwin, Copland, etc."

—Schoenberg to Berg (1934)

"Hollywood and its unmitigated tripe of background music."

—George Antheil, composer

MGM Studios
Culver City, California
August 1935

SCHOENBERG WANDERS AIMLESSLY THROUGH the MGM Studios lot, no idea which direction to head in, late for his meeting with Irving Thalberg. A phalanx of palm trees leads to a dead-end loading dock. Then he stumbles upon an octagonal water fountain moments later, offices with low terra cotta roofs in the distance, a tall building flanked by Doric columns. Is this where he's supposed to meet with Thalberg and his executive team to discuss the film score for *The Good Earth?*

For a long time he's thought about writing movie music. He's always loved the theater, the notion of music and drama existing side by side. Before being officially notified (by a German government hardly predisposed towards Jews) that his *lifetime* contract at the Berlin Academy had been revoked—and not long after this, forced to flee Germany for his life—his composition, *Begleitmusik zu einer Lichtspielscene, Accompanying Music to a Film Scene*, was received favorably at Berlin's Kroll Opera House despite its twelve-tone dissonance. Berg remarked to Schoenberg after the performance how the piece might be all the more compelling if heard synchronically with a film that Schoenberg could also create.

Now up ahead, Schoenberg spots a dozen or so people led by a woman in a gray blazer. Some type of welcoming committee, he deduces, sent to personally escort him over to Thalberg's offices. Hurrying over, he joins up with the group as they enter a door marked *Stage Nine,* a spacious room with a three-legged covered wagon and spindly tumbleweeds, the façade of a cowboy saloon alongside mountain and cloud backdrops, floodlights mounted onto tripods, a pair of *Wild West* overalls encrusted with fake blood. The woman in the blazer is rattling off movie titles, *Grand Hotel, Dinner at Eight, Dr. Jekyll and Mr. Hyde, Tarzan, Love on the Run.*

"Well, I'll be damned," the man standing beside him mutters in a Texan drawl as, instinctively, Schoenberg widens his stance, hands on his hips, exactly as he's seen characters do on television and in the moving pictures.

Raising a palm, Schoenberg smiles broadly at the man. "*Howdy, partner.* It's nice you tour me around a little before introducing me to Thalberg."

For a moment the man stares at Schoenberg. Then he doubles over in laughter, slapping Schoenberg's back with a Texan-sized palm. "Good one, mister."

Meanwhile, in a dark-veneered reception room on the MGM lot, Stravinsky thumbs through an issue of *Life* Magazine, glancing at ads for Top Flite deodorant, Motorola, Overholt Whiskey and Chesterfield cigarettes while awaiting his appointment with Thalberg.

Why not write music for the moving pictures? Honest work, steady income. For the second time, he's come to the States, performing his music in New York, New Haven, Philadelphia, Cincinnati, Chicago, San Francisco, and Los Angeles. Samuel Dushkin, the violin soloist Stravinsky happens to be touring with, has put him in touch with a few of the studios. Some new, lucrative commission would not be an unwelcome prospect, particularly in light of the succession of tragedies he's recently endured, the loss of his first daughter, Ludmilla, and his wife, Katya, both from tuberculosis; and after this, his mother's passing.

"Let's get right down to brass tacks, shall we?" Thalberg says to Stravinsky from the helm of the conference table. He wears a well-pressed white shirt and crimson necktie, his dark hair neatly coifed.

"We're prepared to offer you twenty-five thousand dollars to provide music for *The Good Earth*. Which, yes, I realize is quite a sum." Thalberg looks at his team around the table. "But the picture's bound to be a smash. I can feel it. I've got my finger on the Hollywood pulse." He offers Stravinsky water from a chilled goblet, sliding over a platter of breath mints and candied nuts.

"And, well, given the fact that you happen to be *the* world's greatest composer," Thalberg says, "I like to think our offer's a prudent one."

Stravinsky smiles, taking note of photographs along the walls, Tyrone Powers, Barbara Stanwyck, Laurel and Hardy, Vivian Leigh, Myrna Loy, Errol Flynn, Bette Davis, Orson Welles, Shirley Temple, William Holden, and several others.

"After all," Thalberg says, "that *Soccer* of yours is absolutely terrific."

Stravinsky cups his ear. "Excuse me? My *what*?"

"That *Soccer* music you wrote," Thalberg says with a nod.

Baffled, Stravinsky offers a thin smile until, finally, a young man with curly hair and tortoiseshell glasses leans forward.

"*Le Sacre*," the young man says. "I believe that's what Mr. Thalberg is referring to, *Le Sacre du Printemps,* your *Rite of Spring.*"

"That's the one!" Thalberg says.

"Ah, *mais oui!*" Stravinsky says with a cordial laugh. "*Le Sacre!*"

"That sort of music strikes me as exactly what we may be looking for." Thalberg rubs his hands together. "A Chinese epic. Picture it! Sweeping landscapes, a fierce storm brewing, thunder, lightning, floods. Wheat fields swaying mightily in the wind, peasants under every rock, mass migrations of peasants!" Thalberg swallows. "But then, suddenly. And in the midst of an earthquake, yet. Oo-Lan giving birth to her baby!"

"I'm happy to offer my musical services," Stravinsky says.

Thalberg slaps the table. "Music to my ears!"

"Which can be availed for sixty thousand dollars."

His face pale, Thalberg points out that such a figure is nowhere within the budget. "Sixty-thousand?" Thalberg coughs. "Our offer of twenty-five thousand still stands." Nothing to sneeze at, Thalberg explains, payment for three months of contractual composition time, services beginning as soon as next week, a deadline set for early November.

"I will require one year," Stravinsky says

Thalberg flinches. There's a collective sign from around the table.

"But, Mr. Stravinsky," Thalberg says. "We're on a fairly tight timeline, you see. What you propose would only wind up delaying production. Why, you'd need to get the music into the arranger's hands in plenty of time to extract what we'll need for the—"

"*Arranger?*" Stravinsky cuts in. He narrows his gaze.

"Arranger. Exactly."

Wincing, Stravinsky assures Thalberg this will not be at all necessary.

"When my compositions are finished," Stravinsky says, "they are complete. Perfect nearly, not a note in need of alteration, abridgement, or—" he can feel himself cringing— "*arrangement*."

Deflated, Stravinsky leaves the meeting, turning the corner in the hallway corridor to nearly collide with a harried Schoenberg as the two gawk at one another in disbelief. Stravinsky's unable to fathom how the rabid serialist back at the Venice Festival a decade or so ago, intent on talking everyone's ear off about twelve-tone procedures, would sign on for so much as a single note of music written for the likes of Hollywood.

"I didn't know you were in Los Angeles," Schoenberg says.

Stravinsky mumbles something about concert appearances, standing taller as he rattles off his list of repertory, the violin concerto, *Perséphone*, his recent ballet, his *Symphony of Psalms*, studying Schoenberg's odd get-up, meanwhile, the tired woolen brown coat he wears draped over his small frame, the plaid hunting cap wrapped snuggly over a shiny egg-shaped head, conjuring up the image of Elmer J. Fudd, the Looney Tunes character Stravinsky gets such a kick out of watching.

"I am quite busy myself, you know," Schoenberg insists, only too eager to rattle off his own list of recent and impressive achievements, a chamber symphony, violin concerto, his fourth string quartet, "though, naturally, when I received the nice telegram from Mr. Thalberg summoning me personally to Hollywood to retain my services as a composer, well, how could I refuse?"

"Well, I certainly hope you brought along your *arranger*," Stravinsky says in a huff.

"We want to do a big picture," Thalberg begins to explain as Schoenberg settles in at the conference table, into a seat still warm, vacated only moments ago by Stravinsky. "Big budget, big cast, big everything!"

Schoenberg smiles agreeably, thinking of Stravinsky and how he must have shown up today with similar aspirations and intentions. Irascible Stravinsky! Whose spruce gabardine coat, baggy slacks and slip-on loafers remind Schoenberg of J. Wellington Wimpy, the pitiable hamburger-loving tramp *(I'll gladly repay you Tuesday for a hamburger today!)* from the Popeye shows he loves watching

"Luise Rainer," Thalberg says. "I'm sure you saw her in *The Great Ziegfeld*. Our talent scouts, after all, were the ones who discovered her." Thalberg's eyes appear to twinkle. "And, I'm here to tell you, that gal's star is only gonna continue to rise. We want her to play the part of the poor Chinese farm wife. Victor Fleming's already signed on to direct. Plenty of action scenes. Epic components, sweeping storms, thunder, flooding, trees uprooting, peasants running amok. The whole nine yards." Thalberg nods at the team around the table. "We'll need a big soundtrack."

Why not write a score for an American picture? Schoenberg thinks. The movie business looks to be promising, Hollywood's unlimited resources difficult to resist. He's adopted a more liberal view in light of propaganda, conceding to the idea that, in hoping to promote his music to a wider audience, certain additional effort may be required. He struggles to make ends meet, lecturing at UCLA on a modest salary, settling into a comfortable home in Brentwood Park where they're surrounded by vacant lots burgeoning with pastel fields of seasonal flowers.

Theater's in his blood: *Erwartung, Die glückliche Hand, Von heute auf morgen*. Discussions with Kandinsky years ago about the intersection of music, color, images, and drama. Student days in Vienna caught up in the fervor of Wagner, mesmerized by his concept of *Gesamtkunstwerk*, "total work of art," Schoenberg and his chums standing in line forever for opera tickets, then standing hours more to watch the performance.

"That piece of yours you did, Mr. Schoenberg, *Transfigured*—uh, something or other."

The curly-haired young man coaxes his tortoiseshell glasses further up the bridge of his nose. "*Transfigured Night*. I believe that's what Mr. Thalberg may be alluding to, *Verklärte Nacht*."

"That's the number!" Thalberg cries with a clap of his hands. "Hot dog! That's the one! Oh, but it's morbid. And yet—" Raising his eyebrows. "*Luscious*." He beams a smile at Schoenberg, sliding over the platter of breath mints and candied nuts. "That's exactly what the doctor ordered—catchy, rapturous!"

"But," Schoenberg says with a shrug, "you see, I no longer compose such music." He sucks in his lower lip. "This piece you mention, I wrote nearly forty years ago. In a previous century, this music was composed."

"Seems to've stood the test of time, though," Thalberg says. "Still a classic. Why, I happened to hear it the other night during the New York Philharmonic radio broadcast and, I tell you, the moment I heard the *lovely* music you'd written—"

"I don't write *lovely* music," Schoenberg says.

Thalberg interlaces his fingers. "Anyway, we're prepared to offer you fifteen thousand dollars." He glances around the table. "Now, I realize that's quite a lump of change. But we really do want the best man for the job."

Thalberg points out how droves of movie-goers will soon be flocking to see the picture. "Why, in no time and before you can say, *Gesundheit!* the name *Schoenberg* will become a household name. Right along with Ritz crackers and Motorola!"

"Forty thousand dollars," Schoenberg says. "This is the fee I shall require for my services."

Thalberg coughs. "*Forty thousand*." He scratches his head, groping for the water pitcher.

Schoenberg explains his idea for creating all the dialogue for the actors himself. In *Sprechstimme,* a form of sung speech.

"A new way for the actors to deliver their lines," Schoenberg says. "All of which will match the music I compose. Naturally, I'll work with the actors myself, teaching them how to speak the dialogue on pitch."

Thalberg and his team stare in disbelief as Schoenberg stipulates how he'll want to have the last word as well on lighting, staging, cinematography, editing.

Thalberg's laugh is shrill. "What you're proposing, Mr. Schoenberg, is that, essentially, it would be your contention to *direct* the picture yourself."

"What I propose," Schoenberg says a little dreamily, "is a kind of symphony accompanied by a film. The story, setting, and other elements all created around the music in such a way that the entire production can then be unified." He thinks again of Wagnerian operas, every element on stage derived from the music itself.

"But, in the greater scheme of things," Thalberg says, "the music represents only a single aspect, a small slice of a much larger pie." He nods. "That's just the way we do business around here."

Schoenberg frowns. "Perhaps the time has come, however, when music no longer exists as merely *accompaniment* to film."

"What you suggest sounds more like opera than a moving picture," Thalberg says. "A fascinating concept." He leans forward in his chair. "However—and take it from someone who knows the business inside and out—it ain't gonna fly, Schoenberg. Not in Hollywood it won't. In the picture-making industry, this kind of thing'll fall flat on its face before anyone can even begin to yodel, *Brunhilde!*"

Thalberg details the storyline of *The Good Earth* to Schoenberg, the Chinese refugees and peasants, the suffering of women and children, the bombings, fires, swarms of invading locusts that decimate all the grain from the fields.

"*The Good Earth* is a story about China," Thalberg explains. "Think *big Chinese* themes."

"*China*," Schoenberg mutters, screwing up his face, "*themes.*"

"So, now that you know of this great story, Mr. Schoenberg," Thalberg says. "Now that you've heard of the people's suffering, I think, as the greatest composer, you just may have stumbled upon the occasion to compose your greatest music yet."

"But." Schoenberg nibbles his lower lip. "The suffering of such people. This was truly terrible, no?"

"Absolutely!" Thalberg says, "terrible, indeed."

Schoenberg gets to his feet. "In that case, I refuse to do the music." He gazes around the table. "Apparently, they have all suffered enough."

SIMON

The vibration against his hip jolted him awake, pulse rocketing, his phone's buzzing infiltrating his dreams. Face welded to the sofa cushion, lower back smarting, he opened an eye in an unfamiliar place, just able to make out the white mantel's cavernous outline, the silhouette of an ottoman, bookcases in the murk of Demetra's apartment.

The radiator was hissing away, the room much too warm, as he pushed up into a sitting position, the ache in his back intensifying, his sinuses draining, prying phone from pants pocket and squinting at the screen, 5:09 a.m., a barrage of messages from Patsy Hodges, a message from Francine, a warm dread spreading over him.

The boys!

Unsteady, sick with fear, he tapped the most recent message.

It's me again, still trying to get a hold of you. Not sure why you're not answering. They're saying Luke's condition hasn't worsened. So that's good.

Patsy Hodges's voice sounded strange, sluggish for a moment then frantic.

Listen, they need to get a hold of you, Simon. Over at the hospital? The doctor wants to do a CT scan. But you're not exactly the easiest person to get hold of. So, hopefully, you're getting these messages.

Luke? Luke's *condition?*

Heart in his throat, he staggered to his feet, head throbbing like something deep inside his brain was trying to scratch its way out, blue glow down the hallway, a nightlight, Demetra's bedroom door closed.

The hospital.

He desperately needed to urinate.

Which hospital, though? Jesus, which hospital? Had she said? Glendale probably. Glendale. Forty minutes away.

Okay. Slow down, breathe, pull yourself together, okay, okay, okay, okay, okay— call Patsy, first of all. Get more details, find out exactly what's happened to Luke and, and then—his dread intensifying as he dared to wonder about Lincoln as well. Where was Lincoln— God! Did something also happen to him? Was Lincoln okay?

He selected another message, the image of the Hodges' flooring, the exposed circuitry, coming to mind, the man-eating hound.

The boys were playing out there, Patty's next message informed him. *But Luke, I don't know. He fell into the hole. On accident. You know, right through the planks on the front lawn— Or what used to be our lawn, I mean. They were playing* who-can-jump-over-the-trench *or something, jeez, I don't really know. Lord only knows what those little devils may have been up to. Dane and I, we were like totally asleep, out cold. We've warned the kids again and again not to play out there. Like a friggin' broken record. But you know boys. They're gonna do the opposite of what you tell 'em and have to learn the hard way. But, wait, hold on, hold on a sec— Okay, so now Jeffty's telling me it was mercenary soldiers the boys were playing out at the trench, not pirates. Mercenary truth or dare or something. (Sigh.) Whatever!*

Patsy Hodges: first responder.

He dug his loafers out from beneath the sofa, forcing his feet into them.

Luke, I guess, was trying to cross over. You know, over the planks. Ugh! I guess the other three may have commanded the poor little guy to walk the plank—

Panicked, he patted his pants pocket for his car keys, dazed, moving through the apartment towards the front door and negotiating the deadbolt, stepping out into the corridor's blare as he pulled the door closed, nauseous, jabbing numbly at the elevator's unresponsive call button and what he really ought to have done, for God's sake, was used her bathroom, his bladder writhing, swelling, threatening to burst, as he scampered back to grab at her doorknob which, not surprisingly, was locked, stumbling down the corridor towards the stairwell, focused on clunking down the metallic stairs without breaking his neck, recalling the vertiginous rooftop that had started things off, Demetra beckoning him—*You know you want to*—a grinning siren coaxing him closer and closer towards the edge.

He plodded down the stairwell, *Luke, oh my God, sweet Mother of Christ, hold on there, buddy, I'm coming, Lukey, I'm coming, I swear to God, I'm on my way—*

Pausing to retrieve another message.

…because he must've, you know, slipped and fell straight down into that hole. I guess the other boys tried to pull him out from the trench but I think his leg was probably already pretty fucked up by that point, pardon my French. We— I'm telling you he was trapped in the trench for some time, and we heard the screams, poor kid, Dane and I shooting out of bed like bats, going over and yanking the little guy out of the hole, though we could already tell his leg was sort of, you know, duh! obviously, I mean, by this point, twisted all out of whack. We knew that definitely wasn't a good sign, so we hightailed it over to Emergency. Glendale Memorial.

His shoes squelched over the lobby's glossy floor. Oppressive. No doorman on duty, no Edgar at this forsaken hour.

They're not telling us anything, Patsy's panicked voice continued hollering in his ear, echoing in the cavernous lobby. *They just don't know enough yet about whether the skull itself may have gotten fractured, or even crushed partially, or—*

The lobby mirrors reflected the lurid green of the pond—the

mossy bilge odor, the sluggish gurgle of the fountain, the anemic swirl of koi all conspiring to send his stomach lurching, as, dizzy, blinking, teetering, he made an oafish attempt to get his body across the lobby, bilious and swaying now, double, triple vision, hoping to hold it together but helplessly succumbing, doubled over as, with a volcanic lurch, he leaned over the eddying pond to vomit.

Gasping, wheezing, swiping slick gobbets from his lips with his sweater sleeve, he crunched over the glistening white pond stones like some wretched forest creature behind the rubber banana tree to relieve himself.

While exiting her building, it occurred to him with a fresh injection of panic that his car was parked several blocks away.

Which hospital had she said? And where the hell had he parked? Which God damn hospital was it?

God, Simon, I just pray you're near your phone or something, and you're getting my messages. Hurry!

Legs aching, he shuffled along Wilshire, an October breeze kicking up while the early sun nudged a cloud or two aside, people out and about with cups of take-out coffee, dogs on leashes, a young man in sweats gearing up for a run.

Fuck! Where exactly had he parked the god damn car? Near the restaurant, dumbshit. Which direction, though?

He hurried down endless blocks in a dream state—never in his entire life had he covered blocks of such length. They felt gargantuan to him, out of proportion to any conceivable human scale, as if, on top of everything else, he'd somehow turned Lilliputian, scurrying past darkened shop windows and shuttered movie theaters, stench of garbage cans, newspaper strewn over the curb, veering around a homeless man with a shopping cart, a figure even more zombie-like than himself, his shoe settling into something decisively squishy, a gooey carton of orange, chili cheese fries.

Where the fuck are you? It's Patsy again. Patsy Hodges? Hello! They think he may have gotten a concussion. Skull could be fractured. Those tightlipped bastards over at the hospital aren't telling us squat. Worse case scenario— I mean, they say he's awake now, so, that's a plus. Listen, Simon, I'm sorry to tell you this, but you need to get your sorry ass over here. Okay, sorry, sorry about that! God. I apologize, okay? I'm a little— Tense. (Sigh.) Frustrated, I guess. They're waiting to do a CT scan, waiting on parental consent, proof of insurance, stuff I can't really offer these people— They're concerned—like I say—he may have a concussion.

He huffed another block before it dawned on him, bleakly, unthinkably, he'd been racing all this time in the wrong direction, pivoting one-eighty now as the nightmare continued to spool out beneath towering high-rises, adjusting course, backtracking, dizzily retracing his steps, time now moving in rewind.

Fingers trembling, he dialed Patsy's number, signal roving then ringing, ringing, no one there.

Scrolling through more of his phone messages, he pressed the one from Francine.

Where are you, Simon?

The sound of Francine's voice—her panic, the portrayal of pure and intense pain— slapped him.

*Luke, he's—*Francine's voice croaked, *I can't understand why you aren't there—* Never before had he heard that agony in her voice. *Why aren't you picking up the phone?* the voice was hollering between sobs. *What's wrong? I just spoke to Lincoln, and with Patsy Hodges. They told me they've been calling the house but can't get a hold of you—*

Just up ahead now he could see the Village Café, his car parked a block or two beyond.

I'm on my way home, Francine said, *on standby at O'Hare, hoping to get on the next flight.*

He reached his car, the first blaze of morning light piercing the sky, early morning birds, a bicycle bell's shrill jangle, a flock of student joggers, a breakfast joint setting up against a backdrop of greasy haze, fumbling with the car keys, dropping them in the street, groaning while bending down to retrieve them, fingers shaking, jabbing the goddamn car key into the goddamn ignition socket, heart blasting away in his chest, engine revving, peeling off into the blinding sunlight, swerving around a bus towards the freeway on-ramp of the 405, holding his breath, wishing he could turn back the clocks, praying to God Luke would be all right.

—◦—

3 August 1943
Beliebtesten Enkelin, Most beloved granddaughter Elsa,
We are writing with sad news about your mother,
Vivian, and your Aunt Margi, whose deaths this week at the
Sachsenhausen concentration camp were confirmed through
reports. Apparently, the two were detained and arrested at
the French/German border while attempting to make their
way from Paris back to us here in Berlin. Needless to say, your
grandfather and I are devastated. Please know how much your
mother loved you. I pray you can find some strength and solace
in the great life she led as a dancer, as well as in the abiding love
she held always for you.
We will write to your cousins, Ingo and Marta, through
separate correspondence with the sad duty of having to inform
them about their own mother's death.
We keep you in our thoughts and prayers, meanwhile.
Zay gezunt,

Oma

SIMON

He stormed into the emergency room, possessed and running on sheer adrenalin, heart in his throat as he bolted towards the reception desk.

"My son!" he shouted at the nurse. "They— An accident. He was admitted—"

The nurse stared placidly, Filipina, he guessed, a little plump and much too young for the serious business of saving lives.

"Last night," Simon tried to say, wishing the woman's expression would register something close to concern. "They brought him in."

"Why don't we start with your son's name?" the nurse said in an even-keeled tone, disconcertingly calm, her gaze professionally disinterested.

"Grafton," Simon blurted, overcome with panic, looking wildly around the partially-filled waiting room. "Luke Grafton! My God, where is he? Please— Can't you help me? Is he all right?"

"Let's try and stay calm." She turned to her computer, stifling a yawn. "Let me see what I can find out."

He gritted his teeth, desperate to see Luke.

Pushing a clipboard across the counter, the nurse told him she'd managed to locate his son, explaining that Luke had been transferred over to Surgery.

Surgery?

He stared at her, searching for a clue of Luke's prognosis.

"We'll need you to fill out a few forms," the nurse said. Her hair was pulled back, cheeks and nose acne-scarred, the name *Fordeliza* printed on her badge. She gestured towards the waiting room behind him, suggesting he take care of the paperwork there, assuring him she'd let the doctor know he was here.

Taking hold of the pen, he furiously scrawled information into various boxes, squeezing his eyes closed while trying to recall date of birth, scribbling in *peanut allergy, no previous health problems,* scratching *N/A, N/A, N/A* across conditions like *Pregnant, HIV, FAS, TB, Hepatitis,* rummaging through his wallet for his insurance card.

He glanced up at the clock, replaying how he'd flown up the 405 freeway, a bat out of hell, shooting over to Glendale and arriving in under twenty-two minutes—record time, never once going below seventy-five, the speedometer grazing ninety-five, maybe even a hundred, a few times.

From the moment his phone had jarred him awake, he'd been operating in acute stress response mode, cortisol spiking as he'd groped around in the murk of Demetra's apartment, fumbling underneath the sofa for his loafers, bolting out of her apartment and then—

The sketchbook.

The sketchbook!

Oh my God, the sketchbook! He'd left it behind in her apartment. Had he even noticed it there on the coffee table in the living room's oppressive gloom? Had it been lying there the whole time while he slept, or had she nabbed it, bringing it with her into the bedroom after he'd passed out?

You snapped into action but left the sketchbook behind! Hahahahahaha! How crazy is that?

Someone was jabbing at his shoulder. He turned to see Patsy Hodges, melted eye shadow, hair in disarray, glaring at him.

Crinkling her nose, she said, "You look like total shit."

Lincoln hurried over, shouting breathlessly, "Dad!"

Simon threw his arms around Lincoln, cleaving tightly to him, glancing down at the checkerboard pattern of Lincoln's slip-on canvas shoes.

"We were just playing around, the four of us," Lincoln struggled to say.

Simon ncould only manage any ugly groan.

"Is he going to be okay?" Lincoln asked, sobbing.

Dane, Jeffty and Bradley wandered over, a trio of zombies holding paper cups of cocoa, Jeffty staring catatonically, Bradley sucking his finger, Dane's eyeballs bulging while his jaw worked a wad of gum.

The double doors opened, a doctor in a white coat emerging, lean, African-American, late twenties, he looked to be.

"I'm Doctor Maxwell," he said, "in charge of your son." He nodded. "Things are looking pretty stable now. He was admitted with a fractured femur. Couple of scrapes and bruises. Nothing I'm too concerned about. CT scan came out fine. No concerns there, whatsoever."

Simon exhaled heavily, overcome with relief. "Thank God. Thank you, I—"

"We gave him some medication for the pain," Doctor Maxwell said. "We've just finished setting the leg. If you'd like to follow me, I can take you to see him now."

Luke was resting calmly in his hospital bed, leg set in a splint and propped on a stack of pillows. A few minor cuts and scrapes across his face. He was staring at cartoons on the TV screen, the sound muted.

Simon went over to the bed, leaning over to kiss Luke's forehead tenderly.

"Hey, there, bud," he said, "how you doing?"

Luke smiled faintly. His chin was bandaged, his delicate blonde hair matted where a gash along the hairline had been cleaned up.

"I'm just glad to be out of that hole," Luke said groggily.

"I'll bet you are." Simon sat down heavily upon the edge of the bed, overjoyed at the sight of his son, seized by affection, reassured that the worst was now behind them.

He rested his head on the edge of Luke's pillow and closed his eyes while memories, emotional impulses, came at him unbidden, the traumatic afternoon, held captive at nursery school, worried that his father might have vanished, just as his mother had.

Luke was whimpering, Simon attempting to soothe him.

Between gasps, Luke said, "I really fell. A long way down." His eyes grew big. "It felt like I was falling forever down that hole."

Simon stroked Luke's head, his chest burning with bitter remorse that his own choices could have put his son right in harm's way.

"I thought I was probably gonna fall straight through the earth," Luke was saying. "And, after that, I'd probably have to live under the earth, all alone. *Probably.*"

"You're safe now," Simon whispered, stroking the sides of Luke's head. "It's all gonna be okay. I'm here, buddy. Your brother's here. I'm not going anywhere."

Blinking, Luke told Simon they'd taken a scan of him.

"I know," Simon said, "that's what the doctor told me."

"But it didn't hurt," Luke said.

"I'll bet they were just checking everything out. Making double sure you were okay."

Luke's eyes brightened. "Sort of like when they scan your baggage."

"Something like that."

Simon flashed on Francine, scrambling across the country in a panic to get to her son. He closed his eyes, dreading the scene, the hideous tableau, that Francine would soon come upon, their precious son, practically in traction, beside the sheepish foolhardy father.

But Luke was going to be all right. That's all that mattered. The other stuff would all get sorted out. Luke was okay.

He sensed in his gut, though, that this harrowing episode might merely be the opening act in some larger unfolding catastrophe he'd managed to set in motion.

When his sons asked when their mother would arrive Simon bristled for a moment before reassuring them it wouldn't be too much longer. His profound relief about Luke was juxtaposed with a prickly anticipation of what Francine's wrath might look like.

"What's the deal with your phone, anyway, Dad?" Lincoln asked, screwing up his face. "We were trying to get a hold of you, like, for hours."

Looking over at Lincoln, it occurred to Simon he'd been too panicked about Luke, and then further mortified about having left the sketchbook behind, even to have begun to formulate any sort of plausible alibi to account for the past twenty-four hours.

"I'm not really sure," Simon told Lincoln. "I must've been sound asleep (*true*). I dunno. Maybe my phone wasn't even on (*untrue*)."

"But we kept calling the house phone, too," Lincoln said, nervously whisking the hair from his eyes. "That's the thing. The house phone must have been working. It must have been ringing off the hook."

Simon shrugged. "I guess I was working. Engrossed. Must not have heard it from the basement."

Lincoln narrowed his gaze. "What's up with your hair, Dad? Looks like you just climbed out of bed or something."

"Got here as fast as I could."

"And what's with the sweater?" Lincoln frowned. "Mom gave you that about a hundred years ago." His face went sour. "Phew!" he said, leaning closer to sniff Simon's sweater. "Ouch, Dad! Dude, ew with a capital E. That's some serious stench. Raunch-o-rama city."

A few hours later Francine showed up, dragging her suitcase behind her as she raced into Luke's room.

"Hi, Mommy," Luke said, looking up from his bed.

"Hello, Lukey," Francine said, laughing with exhaustion and barely able to catch her breath as she leaned down to give his forehead a thousand kisses. "Hello, my sweet, sweet darling boy! How are you, little one?"

Simon went over to Francine, placing a tentative palm upon her shoulder. "He's gonna be okay."

As she turned to greet Simon, she recoiled.

"My God," she said, sniffing, looking him thoroughly up and down, exhausted, staring in miscomprehension at his sweater and soiled trousers.

Sucking in his cheeks, Simon tried for a neutral, disinterested expression.

"*What?*" he said.

Francine's look was hateful. "Have you been drinking?"

"Certainly not. I have *not* been drinking."

Francine wrinkled her nose. "And what's with the smoky odor?"

"I'll explain," Simon said, "I—"

"My God," she cried, "you reek of smoke!"

"Calm down," he said with a wave of his hand. "It's all good. I can explain. Everything's fine."

Francine glowered. "You look like you just slithered out of a sewer."

The room went silent. They were all staring, accusing him, waiting for some sort of explanation.

"You know," he began, forced to think on his feet, "Strangely enough. I mean." Panicked and drawing a blank. "It's funny, but—" Swallowing heavily, he shifted his weight, hoping to control the annoying tremor in his eyelid. "Long story." He hated the sound of his voice, jittery, waffling, culpable.

"I actually wound up over at Stuart's place last night," he said, his gaze moving from Luke to Lincoln to Francine. Stuart. That could probably work. A sturdy alibi he could begin to improvise upon like a twelve-bar blues.

Slowly lifting his gaze, he looked over at Francine to get a sense as to whether or not such subterfuge might have legs.

"Stuart called me," he began vamping. "Some sort of crisis at home. Or. I don't really know how things started over there." He tsk-tsked. "I'm still not all that clear on the details. An argument of some kind, you know, between him and Mo, apparently."

He and Francine locked eyes. His sensed she wasn't buying it.

"I went over for a while," he said. "Over to Stuart's place. Just to, you know, help put out the fire, try and console the poor guy." He stared down at the floor. "He was pretty bad off, Stuart. We ended up having a few. A few too many, as it happened." He licked his dry lips. "I must've conked out on his couch at some point."

His head had begun to pound. He sucked in air, waiting for her to say something—anything!

The silence was unbearable. He stood immobilized, three sets of eyes affixed to him, wondering which of his executioners would be the one to step forward to pin the donkey tail or pin the scarlet letter upon his befouled sweater.

Francine folded her arms. "Wait a second," she finally said, "I don't get it. You're facing a pressing deadline. But you wind up spending the evening with Stuart, the two of you getting ripped?"

"No," he said, blinking rapidly, "it wasn't like that. Listen. Out of context. I know it all probably sounds a little nuts."

Francine looked angrily at him.

"What does *getting ripped* mean?" Lincoln asked in a polite voice.

Simon reached to tussle Lincoln's hair. "Adult talk," he said, making a mental note to phone Stuart as soon as he could to fill him in on the situation, coordinating and corroborating timelines and other details, if need be.

"Stuart needed a friend," Simon said in total defeat. "All right? I did what I thought needed to be done."

"What about your sons?" Francine said with murderous eyes. "Did it ever enter your head *they* needed you?"

"Of course!" Simon hollered. "Jesus. Of course, France. Of course, it entered my head!"

—∿—

The Los Angeles Times
Requiem For Vivian Růžek: Montagues
and Capulets, or Two Peas in a Pod?

DOROTHEA RONDO
December 7, 1943

Yesterday's performance of *The Requiem for Vivian Růžek* drew a considerable standing-room-only crowd at the Synagogue of Hancock Park as audience members encountered a novel modernist work commissioned to honor a prominent Parisian dancer and choreographer whose life was truncated abruptly by the tragic forces of war.

The new requiem is the musical brainchild of Elsa Růžek, the surviving daughter of Vivian and an accomplished dancer/choreographer in her own right, the project underwritten by prominent oil magnate, businessman, and philanthropist, Q. Chester.

The tribute instigated an improbable comingling of two preeminent Southern California composers, Arnold Schoenberg and Igor Stravinsky, estranged and sometime belligerent artistic adversaries whose works have not appeared side-by-side on the same concert stage in quite a number of years.

Noted conductor Claes Huylenbrouck expertly led a chamber orchestra whose musically-sensitive presentation was matched by a radiant performance from mezzo soprano soloist Helena Dent.

The Schoenberg sections which opened the Requiem were, as one might expect for a musical threnody, doleful and heartfelt, characterized by lyrical and rubato string passages, reminiscent of Samuel Barber's *Adagio for Strings,* and enhanced by musical references to the Brahms Requiem, most strikingly his setting of the psalm, *Ihr habt nun Trauerigkeit* ('Now is your time for grief' John 16:22).

Curiously enough, this listener's ears detected subtle and nearly subliminal Stravinskian echoes within the Schoenberg movements. Whether this was unconscious on the part of the composer or some clever parlor game of musical allusions, one certainly had the feeling that, at least in this particular instance, Schoenberg in his homage managed to out-Stravinsky Stravinsky himself.

The other half of the Requiem was composed by Mr. Igor Stravinsky. Consistent with the Russian composer's predominant stylistic approach, the musical mien was often ebullient and scintillating, rhythmic and muscular, persistently dance-like at times, making for an intriguing contrast to the pensive gravitas of the Schoenberg sections and an apropos tribute to a woman who devoted her entire life to dance.

Given the solemnity of the occasion, however, one can't help but wonder about the suitability of such a jaunty and carefree musical approach. But again, were this listener's ears playing further tricks? The Stravinsky portions also contained what might be construed as oblique Schoenbergian references, most notably in a two-note (*B-flat-D-flat*) motive presented in various guises throughout portions of both composers' presentations. Creative coincidence? Or might the two rivals have been communing somehow, each tapping into some ineffable Zeitgeist while anticipating the other's musical predilections?

As the concert concluded to heartfelt audience applause, Maestro Huylenbrouck was stymied while attempting to join hands for a collective bow with the composers on either side of him. Instead, the composers maintained a mulish distance from one other, bowing independently in rather an ungainly, grammar-school-production manner, each meanwhile vying for the lion's share of the applause.

SIMON

"Is this my room now?" Luke asked. He was seated sideways along the couch in the living room, leg propped up against some cushions.

"For now it is, moon pie," Francine said. "For a little while, at least, until your leg gets *all* better." Crouching beside the fireplace, Francine was arranging some things she'd brought down from Luke's bedroom, storybooks, bedding, and Ned Spencer, the penguin.

"You won't have to worry about stairs," Simon said, hoping Francine would turn around and return his glance.

But, since leaving the hospital, Francine hadn't made eye contact. The car ride home had been strange after Luke had been discharged. Before Simon had even gotten the car out of the parking lot, Lincoln surrendered to exhaustion and Luke, strapped to his booster seat, nodded off a moment later. With all the strain of the previous several hours, an uncomfortable tension settled between Simon and Francine. Lowering the radio volume during a news update of the O.J. Trial, he'd asked about Chicago. But Francine had only stared out the window, saying she was too wiped out to chat. Now, getting up from the chair, Simon offered to heat up some soup.

"What kind should I make?" he asked Francine.

She had her back to him still while attending to Luke.

"France?" Simon asked.

"I dunno," she said in a monotone. "See what's in the pantry."

The kitchen was a disaster, a Superfund site of polluted cups and plates, strewn food wrappers, and an overflowing waste bin, cupboards ajar, a phalanx of plundered yogurt cartons, a mysterious pink-slime archipelago on the countertop beside a sack of furry greenish bread, a small but busy colloquy of ants strategizing around the perimeter of the fridge.

Stomach gurgling, he stood, mindlessly stirring clam chowder on the range, concerned about all the composing time he'd forfeited over the blur of the past twenty-four hours while fretting—devastated—about the mislaid sketchbook and his utter carelessness in leaving it behind.

Or had it been her game plan all along to steal the document, luring him over, getting him drunk and otherwise incapacitated, while carrying out her nefarious scheme?

The phone on the kitchen wall rang. Immobilized, he stared at it. Then, setting the soup spoon down on the trivet, he went over to answer it, halting in his tracks when Francine hollered from the other room she'd get it.

He turned down the burner, thoughts darting, sickened to imagine how the sketchbook would now become *her* ticket to professional triumph, opening up bigger and bigger doors—scholarly publications, guest lectureships, appearances at a circuit of impressive international musicological panels, academic conferences and other venues.

Francine's entrance startled him, Simon looking up to note how flustered she was, boiling, murder in her eyes.

"Soup's ready," he said, aiming for drollness.

"That was Mo on the phone."

He felt the blood draining from his head, recalling the look Mo had offered him and Demetra last night.

"Funny," Francine said. "When I asked how things were between her and Stuart, she had no clue what I was talking about." Francine's expression was pure disgust. "And when I mentioned you and Stuart getting together last night, she acted like I was bonkers, explaining how Stuart had met up with her and Terri for dinner over at El Cholo right after the movies."

Ensnared, sensing she was closing in for the kill, he looked away.

"I don't know exactly what's going on with you," Francine said, "but I don't appreciate being lied to."

"Are you sleeping with Carla?" he blurted.

"Priceless!" she said, placing her fists on her hips. "At this point, I think *I* need to be the one asking the questions here."

"Fine."

"Beginning with you telling me where you were last night."

"I went out," he said. "Out, for God's sake." He snorted. "I'm an adult. I reached this point of complete frustration. I had hit a snag and was feeling stuck. I went out. I took a break."

"Apparently you wound up traveling pretty far for a nightcap." Francine huffed. "Mo said she saw the two of you in Westwood. *You*," she added with a sneer, "and your *colleague.*"

"It wasn't like that."

"The whole thing looked pretty dicey, according to Mo. *You*, with an attractive colleague at your side. You and— *Demetra.* That's what Mo had to say."

"First of all," he said, stomach in knots, "Mo needs to mind her own goddamn business."

"You and Demetra— The two of you aren't—"

"Hell no!" he shouted.

Francine had gone pale.

"Listen, all right?" he said. "I'd run into some fairly thorny questions. Regarding my opera. Questions having to do with Schoenberg and his theory. Passages I've been going over and over in the Schoenberg manuscript. A subject, it would be fair to say, Demetra just happens to know a thing or two about." He swallowed. "I gave her a call. Simply to—"

Francine took hold of a soup bowl, turning to bring it to Luke.

"Want to know what happened?" he called after her. "I'll tell you, I'll tell you everything." He clapped his hands together. "But before I do—before any of this is going to make one wit of sense—you're gonna need a little more context. So, why don't the two of us just sit down and—?"

She turned.

"Because," he said, "without context. Without detailed and accurate information about a few burning issues in the sketchbook, anything I'd now have to say would sound absolutely ludicrous."

"You know what I think?" she said, her voice menacingly calm.

"What?"

"I think it's been one *hell* of a day."

"Right. Well, hallelujah and praise Jesus," he said, "I mean, at least we can agree on that." He gestured towards the seats at the counter. "Please. Let's you and I talk this through."

"No more talk," she said, eyes dilated. "No more bullshit."

"*I didn't sleep with anyone!*" he shouted.

Swatting down his confession, she turned towards the door. "I can't do this right now."

"Because, you know, I could have used the same reassurance," he yelled. "Going off with Carla to spend the weekend. You call *that honesty*?" He licked his lips. "How the hell do I know what to make of things? Where's *my* reassurance?"

"I'm going to go check on Luke now," she said, her voice serene.

Grabbing up a soup bowl too rapidly, he sloshed chowder on his loafer, frowning at bits of carrot and potato as he moved toward her. "Here. Let me—"

"When I come back from checking on Luke," she said, "I want you gone."

"Please," he said. "We can discuss this. God, if you'll just let me explain a few things." Tense, he nodded. "You're tired, sweetie, I know, I know that. It's a lot to expect. I'm sorry. I'm *so* sorry. God, I've put every-one through so much." He bit the inside of his cheek. "*Inadvertently,* though, I swear to you. I know I can convince you of that, if we just— And, God. I'm tired, too, so tired." He took a step nearer to her, reaching for her shoulder. "But please. Please, France, don't jump to conclusions. Not without—" He sniffed loudly. "Tell you what. Let's take care of Luke. That's first, of course." He clasped his hands. "Then we can sit down together. Straighten out this whole mess."

Her expression was pure hate.

"We'll have soup!" he said in desperation.

"I trusted you."

He lowered his gaze. "I screwed up. In terms of the sleepover, I completely— But, hey, hey. Let me walk you through everything. Step by step."

She stood, staring off, her lip quivering.

"Once you hear the whole story," he said, "*my* version of things—"

"I need you to leave."

"Things are already chaotic enough."

Francine sucked in air sharply. "I'm not sure what'll happen if you're still here when I come back from checking on Luke. I swear to God. I'll call the police if I have to."

BOOK VI

Tableau XVI

Igor

*"'I shall not compose music in accompaniment to a
photoplay. The story and the setting and all the rest
will be written around the music, and the music will be
composed in terms of the sound film. Thus, the whole
production will be conceived as a unit.'* Stravinsky told
the San Francisco Chronicle if he had to comply with
Hollywood contractual terms, he publicly announced,
he would refuse the project; he would write the music
with total independence and *'Hollywood will take it or
leave it...'* He adopted an inflexible stance diametrically
counter to that of other successful classical composers
writing for films. He would have nothing to do
with music 'puncturing' films (as William Walton
once described the secret of his own successful film
scoring)."*

—Charles M. Joseph, *Stravinsky Inside Out*

March 1944

STRAVINSKY IS ON HIS head.

Elsa comes upon him in his studio, forearms splayed sphinxlike on the floor, fingers clasped behind the back of his skull as a little gasp escapes her lips.

"But this is perhaps a bad time," she says, peering into a single upside-down eye, unsure what to make of the inverted pose he's concentrating to maintain, tennis shorts, shirtless upper torso, his thin and muscular legs extended.

"*Bad time?*" he grunts, anchoring his bare heels against the wall, focused on keeping his balance.

She compliments him on his balance, suggesting jokingly that he consider joining up with the troupe of dancers at Paramount she's currently working with.

"Hungarian calisthenics," he announces, his torso shaking. "*Shirshasana*, the supported headstand."

Then, drawing a deep breath, he lowers his knees slowly, exhaling forcibly as he somersaults to the floor, bounding to a standing position.

"*Voila!*" he exclaims with a clap of his hands, knees bent, thighs splayed like a fencer taking guard, Elsa applauding, impressed, he likes to imagine, by the compact birdlike man before her.

Grabbing a towel, he wipes his glistening head, taking up the cashmere shirt draped over the back of a chair and throwing it over his shoulders.

The inverted poses help increase the flow of blood to the brain, he explains.

"Each day I try to keep up a modest routine of such poses," he says, slipping into a pair of sandals and going over to the smoking table. "Gymnastics in the morning, sunbathing at noon. Followed by a bit of bathing in the sea."

Elsa seats herself beside the window, eager to share some news, he can see, while admiring the miniature etchings and paintings by Picasso, Braque, Klee, Tanguy and Miro along the wall. She has on a stylish yellow dress, a chiffon sweater and quaint bonnet. Stravinsky's amused by the stark contrast of his own informal garb.

"Sam Goldwyn has just given the green light on the *Orpheus* project," she tells him with a rush of excitement, folding and unfolding her hands in her lap. "He wants to produce the picture."

"A long time in coming," Stravinsky says. "Wonderful news." He smiles. "I'm happy for you, Elsa."

He gulps ice water poured from a pitcher on the smoking table, offering her some. She shakes her head, mentioning Vera had served her tea earlier.

Elsa describes the original screenplay and choreographed sequences she's been working on, mentioning Mr. Lund, businessman, oil magnate, benefactor, how over the moon he seems to be, glad to fund the bulk of the project.

"What I wondered, though," she starts to say, studying him with a serious expression. "What I've come to ask, Igor." She laughs nervously, coloring and shaking her head then staring down at her hands.

Stravinsky refills his glass of ice water.

She takes in a sharp breath. "I wonder—" Full of nervous energy, she stands abruptly, holding her breath for a moment before smiling and blushing. "I'd very much like you to consider writing the score for the project."

He crosses the studio to his oversized desk adjacent to two boxy upright pianos alongside one another.

"Film music," he mutters.

She tells him more about the screenplay, "only a rough idea, of course, but a beginning, at least—something! Numerous sketches for dance sequences. All to be married eventually with the original music." She smiles at him. "*Your* music, Igor."

He sifts through various clutter on his desktop, calligraphy pens, inkwells, pencils, protractors, rulers.

"Hollywood and I," he says quietly. "You know, we haven't proven to be any sort of match made in heaven."

"The budget, Igor. I'm told it's robust. Well worth considering." She looks over at him. "Vera seemed to think the opportunity might have come along at precisely the right moment for you."

He's not sure what to say as he fiddles nervously with compasses and styluses, running a finger over the face of a stop watch, picking up a wheeled roller, his own invention for drawing music staves onto blank paper.

"Igor?"

He sets a wooden metronome in motion, closes his eyes, the pyramid clicking at one hundred thirty-two beats per minute.

"Mr. Goldwyn," she says. "He was so tickled, you know, by the requiem for my mother you and Mr. Schoenberg created."

Tick tick tick tick. The metronome beats frantically.

He's unable to purge *Fantasia* from his thoughts, its lingering bitter taste. The way Mr. Disney and his bandits succeeded in strong-arming him, appropriating *The Rite of Spring* with the nefarious intention of reducing his efforts to schlocky background noises for colorized, animated dinosaurs. Creatures rising up out of prehistoric slime, his masterpiece co-opted, predigested and chopped to bits, spliced, diced, edited, regurgitated.

Was this to be the fate of his magnum opus, music reduced to mere accompaniment for some god-awful spectacle?

"Seventy-five thousand dollars," Elsa says with greater urgency. "This is what Mr. Goldwyn's prepared to offer you."

He whistles in disbelief, leans over the table to silence the avid metronome, tense now, flustered by her mention of Schoenberg, Schoenberg and his endless musical experiments. Unsettled as well by Disney—by the whole Hollywood enterprise, actually—with its ruthless moguls and tycoons, glitzy dinosaurs, flying lizards.

He shakes his head, saying how he has other irons in the fire, other commissions he's already currently committed to, concerts, recordings, important work to be done. Discussions with Auden about a new opera based on Hogarth's series of paintings, *The Rake's Progress.*

Seventy-five thousand dollars—*ha!* He won't earn anything close to this figure in the foreseeable future. He glances at sheets of manuscript paper he's affixed to the wall, a sequence of musical sketches he's been struggling to complete. Tacked to an adjacent wall is a map of the Allies' progress, with small flags and push pins depicting the unfolding of various current European battles.

An émigré again for the second time, caught between the vicissitudes of yet another war, he follows the terrifying siege and destruction of his native St. Petersburg these days from the safe haven of Southern California. How he misses his sons, both consigned to the French army, misses other family members in Europe as well. Years ago, the Revolution cut him off from his homeland. He hasn't returned.

Old Russia. How he pines for *Mariinsky Square*, its tapestry of transport sounds, horse-drawn trams, coachmen hollering and cracking whips, the rattle of droshkies over cobbled streets, cries of tradesmen, clamor of bells from Nikolsky Cathedral. That unmistakable city stench, the pleasant explosion each day at noon from the cannon miles away, at the Peter and Paul Fortress. The Bridge of Kisses where he and Katya once held hands dreaming about their future.

Gathering stray erasers on his desk, he considers her offer, piling the erasers into towers. Great music is made *'avec le gomme,'* he's fond of saying.

Slowly, he shakes his head. "I'm certain there are *other* composers who would only be too happy to lend a hand."

She narrows her gaze. "I've come to ask *you*."

Again, he shakes his head.

"A chance to be part of something big," she says. "Something —extraordinary."

When he looks up at her she's smiling at him.

"Like in Paris," she says.

"Such fond memories," she continues. "I can still remember—even as a very young child—my mother practicing and performing. And me dancing, just for fun, for Nijinsky."

"I'm afraid I must decline," he says, too gallantly perhaps, or with too much bitterness.

He refuses to compose musical accompaniment to a screenplay. Even a project as intriguing as what Elsa's now suggesting.

Still a spectacle, he concludes. He'll have no part in it.

Defiled by clunky colorized dinosaurs, musically-mangled accompaniments, and that miserable image he can't get out of his mind of Maestro Stokowski cheekily descending a color-lit staircase to shake hands with Mickey Mouse.

SIMON

Parting the curtains at Guillermo's Roost, a long-term-stay motel in Pasadena, Simon looked out at the crumbling courtyard where a child's inflatable pool had been left behind, strewn with leaf debris and empty beer bottles. Years ago, he and Francine had set up a kiddy pool in their backyard, Simon and the boys tossing a beach ball back and forth while Francine circulated with camera in hand.

As a small child himself, Simon recalled splashing around in a similar wading pool, his father nearby on hands and knees, pulling weeds and tamping down mulch in the herb garden, his bare shoulders striped by sunlight filtering through the dogwood tree. Had his mother been around then, or had it only been the two of them?

Now he closed the motel curtains, resigned to *roosting* in such a godforsaken place—*temporarily!*—relegating himself to making do, forced to improvise while biding his time. At least for now and until things had a chance to cool.

The mislaid sketchbook, his harsh exile from Francine and his boys. These things remained unthinkable, the pain intensified still further by the realization he'd hurt the people he cared most about.

Rubbing his eyes with the heels of his hands, he took in the full flavor of his surroundings, his sudden internment in an unfamiliar cell with its sagging mattress, peeling, salmon-toned walls and unpleasant curtains. The yellowing lamp shades and portable wheezing refrigerator and, above the headboards, kitschy fluorescent paintings of giraffes and flamingos.

Resting on the nightstand, his father's journal was begging for further attention. This made for wrenching reading at times, descriptions of his mother's illness, the full tragedy of his parents' journey unfolding across the journal's pages.

He'd been reading recently about the gardens his father tended and about Claes, his mother's apparent tyrannical musical partner, events he'd never fully comprehended, stirring up emotions in him.

He showered in the dilapidated bathroom, eager to get back to work on *Arnold & Igor,* dragging the breakfast table in his motel room across the carpet so that he could compose away from the distractions of the courtyard, missing the sketchbook, desperate to have it back safely in his hands again, desperate to finish decoding the *Orpheus* pages, now that more of its mysteries had been unlocked.

The computer booted, page after page of his opera score now before him.

His priority was to iron out more details in Tableau Sixteen, Elsa brimming with excitement about the go-ahead on the *Orpheus* project she'd just received from Sam Goldwyn as she approached Stravinsky, asking him to consider creating the musical score.

Scrolling to the scene in the score, Simon read through the stage directions in his libretto (*Stravinsky is on his head/ forearms splayed sphinxlike on the floor/ fingers clasped behind the back of his skull.*).

He hadn't said a proper goodbye to Lincoln and Luke, having found no opportunity to express how deeply sorry he was. Departing quickly instead, a handful of belongings stuffed into a suitcase, a few essential items from his music studio, his father's journal.

By the time he'd loaded his car, both boys were asleep. Headed down Orrington Avenue, racing farther and farther away from his kids in the search for lodgings not too far away from home, the sudden pang of severance had eaten through him like an acid.

from the journal of Jasper Grafton

Newberry Psychiatric Hospital
Los Angeles
July 1946

*Overcooked egg warm porridge gruel served up to captives from steel
trollies. No, thank you, ma'am, I prefer jam roly-poly, bubble & squeak.
Visiting hours. A woman called Elsa there to rescue me, though it's no
use: Helena gone.*

*Elsa's eager to share news of the Orpheus project. When I point out
the dusty gramophone in the common room she returns the next day
with a stack of Schoenberg recordings, Verklärte Nacht, the Solo Piano
Variations, op. 11, Erwartung, Gurrelieder, Pierrot, needle of the
phonograph pine needle needle of injection Dr. Pinkerton needling me.
None of Elsa's recordings features Helena.*

*Helena heavenward, communing from a sphere unseen, a place between
realms, the thin place, the Celts called it, numinous threshold, meeting
point between the visible & invisible Nihil in intellectu nisi prius in
sensu.*

*Elsa mentions a son, a little boy in their custody whom she & Claes look
after. 'At least until you're all better,' she says, 'until you're ready to come
home,' insinuates it might be possible during a future visit, to bring the
boy along. 'He learns every day more and more words, a few words even
in Czech! He's learned names for all the keys on the piano.' Proud smile.
'Claes has been showing him.'*

*Son? My son son son & the courtyard's primrose rows, snapdragons,
flox*

Love-in-a-Mist, Johnny-Jump-ups, calendula, verbena, solidago, Black-eyed Susans,

                       Meadowsweet Filipendula, Jupiter's Beard &
Helena hiding

                            somewhere in the flowers while Elsa
fondly tells of her and Schoenberg's co-creation of Orpheus. Suddenly,
Elsa w/ stern look:

                       'You can't remain here forever, you know. Your
son needs you.'

Somewhere along La Cienega, parched & sun-stricken, that's where
they found me, Leopold Bloom wandering forlornly, miles from home
beneath a scorching sky all the blue leached out

                          her blue eyes closing, her
final breath I

                               reached for her hand

                                     they

wheeled Helena off

a kindly priest guiding me gently from her hospital room

                       the Stravinskys trying to get a hold of me,

                              Cole Porter Harpo
Marx Thomas Mann   wondering where I was, wanted

in the Stravinsky garden goats chickens lovebirds, cats, Rachmaninoff's
honey on the stoop

                 Ingo & Marta—the niece & nephew—over for a visit

                           Stravinsky's
Hungarian calisthenics upon his head, Simon by my side

clenching tiny trowel among dragonfly Monarch firefly carpenter bee
roly-poly lacewing fungus

                         gnat scimitus syrphid

                            & up to the music
studio

to eke out a mini symphony,

                               Fabergé Egg

& music box on the mantel

Sol & his violin shop, the Orpheus screenplay & Elsa

                                                   this time waving
both hands furiously in front of my face

w/ greater urgency: 'Chosper, are you even hearing what I say to you?'

Tableau XVII

Arnold

"If it is art, it is not for all, and if it is for all, it is not art."
—Arnold Schoenberg

"I'm a stranger here, myself."
—Kurt Weill

Voice from the Burning Bush: Be God's prophet!
Moses: O, God, ask not thy servant to be thy prophet.
—Arnold Schoenberg, *Moses und Aron*

March 1944

THE CAT HAS GOTTEN out again.

A bright morning. Schoenberg, in long underwear, threadbare slippers and a silly hat amidst a modest thicket of pink-flamingo ornaments, stands on his front lawn searching for it.

"Kundry?" he calls out, stooping beneath a hedge, *"Liebes Kätzchen, bist du da?"*

Gertrud will not be pleased to discover the cat missing from his dozing spot on the dining room chair. He'll be forced to confess that its disappearance was caused by his own negligence, the front door left ajar when earlier he'd stepped out to retrieve the newspaper and milk bottles.

Now a mechanical groan startles him, a local tour bus, *Hollywood*

Legends, as it strains up Rockingham Avenue, moving beyond the iron gates along his driveway. His first instinct: a quick retreat back towards the house, the undergarments, slippers and Davy Crockett coonskin cap he has on hardly appropriate for confronting a busload of gawkers.

But who does he think he's kidding? By no stretch, can he or his home be considered tourist attractions. The *cause célèbre* he was once regarded as has been left behind along with nearly everything else in the Old World. Here, his music simply isn't played; the Los Angeles Philharmonic appears to want nothing to do with it, despite whatever connection he has with Maestro Klemperer.

In order to make ends meet, he teaches a handful of private students, demanding a mere fraction of the thirty-dollar fee he charged a decade ago in New York. Approaching seventy, he'll be forced to retire next year from UCLA on a meager pension of only thirty-eight dollars per month. His health is declining: asthma, a chronically ornery stomach, his heart slowly wearing down.

"And here on your left, ladies and gentlemen," a boyish voice crackles over the intercom as, further up the street, the bus squeals to a halt. "Why it's Hollywood's very own bright-eyed little princess, Miss Shirley Temple! Yes, that's right, our curly-topped darling resides just over to your left there, in that dandy good-ship-lollipop of a home while continuing to tug at the very heartstrings of each and every one of us."

Ms. Temple, his neighbor just up the road. Rather a different sort from himself, her oversized celebrity casting its towering shadow over Rockingham Avenue as now the bus continues its steep ascent, headed (ah, but the route is all too familiar) for the Cole Porter residence near the top of the block.

Now, while vaguely following the progress of the tour bus, Schoenberg daydreams about the *Orpheus* score Elsa has asked him to compose, vacillating about whether to take on such a project and unable to quash a suspicion that the bus may soon be making a stop over at the Stravinsky residence a few miles away.

Igor Stravinsky, bon vivant and gadabout, is everywhere these days. Photographed among the likes of Edward G. Robinson, Hedy Lamarr, Orson Welles, Charlie Chaplin, Huxley, Auden, Mann, Isherwood, Dylan Thomas. Enjoying abundant air time on both radio and television; appearing on *Information Please*, on NBC's Maxwell House hour, and on the new radio program, *Music that Satisfies*. Interviewed relentlessly, Stravinsky, cultural ambassador de facto, is asked to weigh in on inane cultural matters such as his favorite TV animal shows and cowboy pictures, where in town one might find the most succulent steak sandwich, or what his Sunday morning routines are typically like.

He was stunned the other night, while tuning in to *The Voice of Firestone* on television, to find himself confronted by a puckish Stravinsky, smiling broadly alongside Schoenberg's former pupil: musician, entertainer and host, Oscar Levant, both men willfully insinuating themselves into the sanctity of the Schoenberg bedroom.

But the clincher, the real stab to the heart. The recent issue of *Time* magazine Schoenberg keeps secreted away in his desk drawer, the single devastating sentence he's heavily underscored:

*At age 62, Igor Feodorovich Stravinsky, if not the greatest
living composer, is certainly the most influential.*

More and more these days, he ruminates upon what exactly his legacy will be, what the name *Arnold Schoenberg* will come to mean for the future. Expunged from his homeland, he dedicates considerable efforts to addressing serious musical and *moral* matters, issues deeply personal to him: the uncertain future of European Jews, and Jews throughout the world; the unfolding national movement of Zionism, and *Aliyah*, the process of immigration related to the foundation of Israel.

Cultural dislocation, the dissonance of Jewishness, have become mainsprings for creativity, a withdrawal into a lonely isolation from his God. Plagued by an uncertain financial future and the wholesale rejection his music has encountered—extending back more than three decades to his *Gurrelieder*—his journey has been nothing but uncertain, the recently rejected Guggenheim Fellowship a major setback, an award which would have allowed him to compose full time, devoting all energies towards the completion of a massive and all-consuming work-in-progress, his opera, *Moses und Aron*.

Now, heading back into the house, he comes upon the elegant wooden owl on the breakfast table, the figurine he'd carved a lifetime ago in Berlin for Vivian, the figurine Elsa brought over the other day.

Here, take it, she'd said, surprising him when she pressed it into his hands, her mother's wistful smile.

A memento, she said, *a small token of the dreams you and my mother once shared.*

SIMON

Immediately after his morning lecture, he burst into Demetra's Form and Analysis seminar, Demetra and a dozen graduate students seated around a table with pocket scores open before them, everyone shocked by the frazzled interloper shoving a chair aside and baring his teeth while making his bee-line towards her.

"I need to speak with you," he said.

Demetra looked up at him, calmly coaxing a wisp of hair from her face. "Professor Grafton, good morning."

"*Now,*" he said under his breath.

Excusing herself, she followed him out into the hallway pulling the door closed behind her.

"Where the hell is it?"

"I have it."

"*Where?*"

She sucked in her cheeks.

"I need it back." He stared past her at the succession of fluorescent lights curving around the corridor. "Is it here with you?"

"I can assure you it's perfectly safe. No cause for alarm.

"Stop!" He swallowed hard, the first inklings of a blinding headache coming on. "Stop patronizing me."

"With all due respect," she said, "that sort of response is hardly professional."

"Don't," he said.

She met his stare. "Don't," she said, curious, searching his face. "Or you'll *what*, exactly?"

Smoldering, he stood in silence.

"You don't really intend on threatening me."

"I need it back." The headache pulsed at the base of his skull.

"I understand," she said. "But, there's no call for hostility." She gathered a breath. "I mean, frankly, that sort of tough-guy aggression might wind up landing someone in a whole lot of trouble."

"Is it up *there*?" he asked, jabbing his thumb towards the ceiling. "Is *that* where it is?"

"Hey, hey, easy there," she said. "Honestly, Simon. I'd hate to see your career go up in smoke over a misunderstanding."

He glanced up at the ceiling. "Upstairs in your office. Is that where you hide it?"

"I told you. I have it. Under lock and key."

"All right, good. Fine then, I'll wait. Right here."

"I'm in the middle of class."

"Two-thirty then. Two-thirty sharp. Upstairs at your office."

"*Ho-no!*" she burst out. "That isn't going to work." She coaxed a strand of dark hair behind an ear. "Given the unforeseen turn of events. The decisions you've made— decisions you refused to make."

"Why?" he asked. "Why are you doing this?"

"I'm due back in class."

He laughed uncomfortably. "Unbelievable!" He shook his head. "I confided in you. Went out on a limb."

"*Limb*? Is that how you'd describe it?"

"But you went right ahead and copied it. Helped yourself to it."

"I regret we couldn't figure out how to work things out more gracefully between us."

Retreating, she pulled open the classroom door, sullen, exhaling heavily then ducking inside.

Tableau XVIII

Elsa

"Why should an ugly time need expression?"
—Maurice Ravel

25 July 1947

"I must speak to you," she says from the alcove.

Claes is stationed in the French armchair with a tumbler of Scotch when she comes upon him in the darkness of the living room. Feeble glow from the hearth, the drapes drawn, the chandelier fixtures along the wall in shadow.

He turns towards her with a hateful face. "If it concerns that heel, Grafton, we've nothing to discuss."

Carefully, she moves to the sofa, seating herself across from him, dreading the confrontation she's long been anticipating and delaying, until finally there's no other option.

"I've reached a decision," she tells him.

Claes swirls his drink.

"Please," she starts to say, but he waves her off.

She thinks of her mother, Vivian. An artist until her final breath, admired, influential. But unlucky in love. Though perhaps her mother would not have considered herself as such.

But Elsa's luck has finally begun to change, the family she's always longed for irrevocably coming into focus. She hadn't planned to fall in love with Jasper. But now he's come back from the hospital, rescued from the loony bin, Elsa practically bringing him back from the dead during untold visits. There's Jasper. And then there's the little boy, Simon. It's no longer possible to imagine living apart from them.

"I'm leaving."

Claes scoffs. "We have an agreement."

The fireplace crackles.

"Honor thy husband," he says. *"A wife of noble character is a crown for her husband."*

She pities him.

"But she who brings shame is like rottenness in his bones." He points at her. "Shame is what you bring."

Her eyes burn. "You're upset."

"Stop!" he says. "You will stop such imbecility."

"I'm leaving," she says more firmly. "It's only fair that I inform you."

"Fair? Is this what you think?" He winces. *"Shrew. Ungrateful whore."*

Her temples throbbing, she takes a deep breath, gathering the courage to look him square in the eye.

"I've come to discuss the situation," she says.

"And where would you be?" he says in a mocking voice. "Just where do you think you'd be if it weren't for me. My connection with Chester Lund—*Ha!* To say nothing of my ties to Sam Goldwyn and the rest of Hollywood?"

"I've worked very hard," she says.

"You've done nothing, Elsa. Accomplished nothing."

Trembling, she gets up, moving unsteadily up the stairs to the guest room she's been holed up in during the past weeks, avoiding him, taking meals on a separate schedule or skipping meals altogether, skulking behind the closed door of the guest room, biding her time while creating countless choreographic sketches and diagrams for

Orpheus, meeting with Schoenberg, looking after Jasper and Simon, spending quality time in their company.

With care, she folds the last of her dresses, placing them in the suitcase on the bed.

Strange noises from downstairs startle her, Claes bumbling around down there, muttering. Then a distinct sound. Paper ripping, pages being torn.

Cracking open the bedroom door, she tilts her head to listen, venturing a few tentative steps along the stairwell.

He's standing at the hearth, she sees, wrenching paper from a music score, feeding the pages into the billowing flames.

Her mother's requiem.

Panicked, hurrying towards him, she screams, gropes for the manuscript, Claes thrusting out an elbow, turning away and, with a deranged look, fending her off as he flings the last of the pages into the fire.

She turns towards the hearth, watching the sole copy of the Requiem for Vivian Růžek vanish forever.

With a grunt, Claes stumbles over to the stairwell, headed for the guest room, she fears, towards the suitcase, the keepsake box with photos of her mother, Vivian's staging diagrams and dance sketches, Stepanov notations, sketchbooks filled with Vivian's vision for *Pierrot, Orpheus*, and countless other projects, Elsa's own dossier tucked behind the bureau, her notations and sketches for the Orpheus film project.

Racing after him, she manages to catch up to him at the top of the stairwell, clenching for his shirt collar, Claes swinging around, slamming into her and knocking her backwards, airborne then crashing with a thud, a cracking noise, blood.

She lies very still, unable to activate her limbs. Eyes open but only to blackness. More blackness. Like a fog pressing down over her as Claes's panicked cries become increasingly muffled, further and further away, *Elsa, Elsa, Elsa, Elsa!*

SIMON

"Now, what sort of masterpiece you say you left behind in here?" Dobson, the night custodian, asked, giving Simon an appraising look as the two stood outside of Demetra's office.

"A manuscript," Simon said, "*Really* valuable." He expelled air heavily. "I can't believe I was dumb enough to leave it behind."

"A manuscript." Dobson nodded. He was dressed in slate-colored work coveralls, a miniature skullcap over his graying Afro. "Well, all right."

While Dobson mulled the situation over, Simon eyed the tantalizing set of master keys dangling from his waist.

"I got all the way home and realized I'd left the document behind," Simon said.

"I got you," Dobson said with a tobacco-stained grin as he removed the key ring, in search of a skeleton key.

Simon held his breath.

Scalded still from his encounter with Demetra, he'd returned to campus this evening with idea of somehow gaining access to her office, peeking through the dark glass of the administrative office downstairs, scanning various desks where an extra key might be stowed away, giving the locked door handle a futile tug before wandering through the music building in search of Dobson.

Ill at ease now, Simon watched Dobson sifting through his key ring, accompanied by the sonic backdrop of practice rooms, an Ivesian collage of Hanon exercises, Chopin Mazurka, an oboe concerto, scales and arpeggios, trumpet excerpts, the *Waldstein* Sonata.

Dobson opened Demetra's office door and flipped on the light switch, an overpowering silage of her perfume as Simon entered, bookcases bulging with reference books and manuscripts, the delicate porcelain flower vase on the filing cabinet, everything in its proper place, disconcertingly familiar, though oddly unsettling without the focal point of the good doctor working away at her desk.

He looked around the room, imagining where she might have concealed the manuscript, making his way towards her desk beneath Dobson's scrutinizing gaze.

"Any luck?" Dobson called from the doorway.

Then he saw it, his valise beneath the window, breathlessly hurrying towards it, grabbing the handles, heartbroken by its appalling lightnesss, the sketchbook nowhere in sight.

"Mission accomplished?" Dobson asked, venturing another step into the room.

Wallowing in defeat, Simon shook his head.

Sensing what precious little time he had before exhausting Dobson's patience, Simon turned towards the filing cabinet, stepping forward to yank the top drawer handle, the drawer nearly relenting at first before resisting with a rigid click, Simon panicking, tugging at the drawer with greater force, the entire file cabinet juddering, the framed photograph and porcelain vase undulating, teetering, then tumbling to the floor in a percussive explosion.

"Hey, hey, now!" Dobson shouted. "Careful over there!"

"*Fuck*," Simon muttered, his neck and shoulders writhing, Dobson moving past him, frowning deeply as he slipped on a pair of work gloves.

"I got this," Dobson said, grunting, wheezing, stooping down gingerly to deal with the shattered glass and ceramic.

"I'm really sorry about that," Simon said.

"Man, oh man." Dobson released a little groan. "Looks expensive, too."

Indicating the file cabinet, Simon said, "I don't suppose there's any way we might get this open."

Dobson pushed out his bottom lip, coaxing glass fragments into a dust pan, placing a few of the larger shards upon the desk. He stared up at Simon.

"You know, Professor, it's one thing. Letting you prowl around Dr. Kouras' privacy. Sniffing around for whatever you claim you lost up here."

"I know," Simon said, "And I appreciate—Listen, if it wasn't urgent. But it's actually something I'll need tonight to prepare for my morning lecture."

Dobson narrowed his eyes. "That's one thing, snooping around a little. But, getting into someone's private possessions. Now that's a whole other thing."

Simon placed a gentle hand on Dobson's shoulder, gazing at the file cabinet. "I'd be willing to bet the document I need is locked in there."

Dobson glanced over at the cabinet, unconvinced.

"Fifty bucks says it's in that cabinet," Simon said. He forced a smile. "Look. I mean, *technically*. It *is my* document we're talking about, *my personal possession*." He laughed casually. "So, it isn't like we're actually doing anything *wrong*."

Staring up at the ceiling for a moment, Dobson exhaled heavily through his nostrils. "No, no, I got you. I hear where you're coming from." He drew in a deep wheezing breath. "But. Like I say." He shook his head. "Nope. Afraid, at this particular juncture, my hands are tied."

Simon tilted his head, placing his hands on his hips. "A hundred bucks says it's right there in that top drawer, Dobson. A quick look, and I'm on my way. Out of your hair."

"You understand what I'm saying," Dobson said. "That filing

cabinet. Now that's a whole 'nother thing. Mm-mm. That's just plain going too far."

Simon bent down to retrieve the photograph on the floor, Demetra's father with his arm around his daughter, glass shards everywhere.

"Look," Simon said, biting his lip. "This is *my* responsibility." He glanced at the photograph again. "No doubt about it, this is totally my fault." The photograph, demonic Demetra with coy smile, the ogre father with flat chin and slightly bored expression. Now it disgusted him. "I'll take care of all damages."

This seemed to reassure Dobson.

"But, Dobson, you know, what I'd actually, *really* like for you to do now is to see if we can get this file cabinet to open up." He nodded. "There might be a spare key lying around—I don't know—a key tucked away downstairs in Margaret's office or something."

"I'm sorry," Dobson said with a firm shake of his head.

"I've got to get that document."

Dobson licked his lips. "Yeah, I got you. Loud and clear, I got you."

Simon pivoted back towards the filing cabinet, exhaling loudly.

"Mr. Grafton?" Dobson said from the doorway, "I'm going to need to secure the room now."

Where would she think to hide a key? Simon wondered.

"Professor Grafton?"

"Please. Can you just see about a key?" Simon asked. "Please, Dobson. It's urgent. You know I wouldn't ask if it wasn't *absolutely* critical."

Dobson shook his head, stepping out of the room. "Truth of the matter? As it is, I've got to file a damage report." He sighed. "Man, I am *surely* not looking forward to *that.*"

Inside her desk. Is that where a key was kept?

"Time to go," Dobson said with greater urgency, "time to lock her up."

Without looking back, Simon nodded while Dobson flicked the lights off and on.

An image of Demetra's spiteful smirk slithered into his thoughts, an enormous bobble head come to mock him, Dobson meanwhile huffing, exasperated by how far behind schedule this had put him, as he shuffled away.

Alone now, he was confronted by her daunting bookcase, bookends of composer statuettes, the feverish wooden clock. Turning towards her desk, he yanked open a drawer, retrieving a pair of scissors, turning towards the filing cabinet to insert the scissors blade into the narrow crack between the top drawer and metal frame, forcing it in further, then violently jabbing, able to bend the top of the drawer slightly.

With all due respect, the bobble head mocked in a glassy, rasping voice while he worked the pair of scissors, *that sort of response is hardly professional.*

I need it back, he explained to the bobble head.

Needitbackneeditback!

Simon glared, baring his teeth, able to force the scissors in another half inch or so but unable to pry open the drawer or get the lock mechanism to snap. Out of his mind, he looked around her office wildly, pulse throbbing in his head, his gaze coming to rest on the Giacometti statue.

Slender, vaguely pouting and a little surly, the thin Woman of Venice appeared to flaunt her disapproval of him, the bobble head, meanwhile, dancing before him like a Petrushka puppet and mocking, *You don't really intend on threatening me.*

In his blind fury, panicked, out of his wits, he seized the statue from the shelf, its bronze weight frigid against the pulsating heat of his palm as clumsily, oafishly, he managed to jab the statue in head first, wedging it like a crowbar into the crude gap the scissors had made, leaning into it with his entire body, grunting, yanking down forcefully with everything he had as finally—*Sforzando!* —the lock relented and disengaged with an explosive snap. Heart in his throat, panting barbarically, he pulled open the drawer.

Nothing.

Files. Files stacked up against more files; more files still within drawers two and three.

Nothing!

Hahaha. the bobble head mocked. *Wouldja get a load of that, Bro? Zilch!*

Fuck fuck-fuck-fuck-fuck! No sketchbook!

The bobble head whispered in his ear, *I can assure you, it's absolutely safe.*

He squeezed his eyes shut, trembling, the Giacometti cudgel dangling in defeat from his arm.

Desperate, yanking open the bottommost drawer—his final hope—he surveyed the empty space, watching helpless as a lone, clanking thermos rolled side to side against the metal partitions of the drawer.

"Fuck!" he said under his breath, kicking the filing cabinet until his toes smarted, the bobble head reminding him with yet another sardonic *portamento* twirl, that *that sort of tough-guy aggression might wind up landing someone in a whole lot of trouble.*

With a startling click, the office door opened, Dobson standing in the doorway alongside a two-man posse of beefy and terribly put-out campus security officers.

"Show's over, Mr. Grafton," Dobson said glumly. "Time to call it a night."

With a sharp breath, Simon turned back towards Demetra's desk, trembling as he set the statue down, horrified by the gaping void where the Woman of Venice's head was supposed to be.

Tableau XIX

Igor

"We drive to Palmdale for lunch, spareribs in a cowboy-style restaurant, Bordeaux from Stravinsky's thermos. A powdering of snow is in the air, and, at higher altitudes, on the ground: Angelenos stop their cars and go out to touch it. During the return, Stravinsky startles us, saying he fears he can no longer compose: for a moment he actually seems ready to weep. Vera gently, expertly, assures him that whatever the difficulties, they will soon pass. He refers obliquely to the Schoenberg Septet and the powerful impression it has made on him. After forty years of dismissing Schoenberg as *experimental, theoretical, démodé,* he is suffering from the shock of recognition that Schoenberg's music is richer in substance than his own."

—Robert Craft, quoted in Jonathan Cross,
The Cambridge Companion to Stravinsky

Los Angeles
September 1947

The wooly mammoth terrorizes him, trapped in the midst of Los Angeles, captured for all eternity against the backdrop of swaying palm trees. Such a cruel fate, Stravinsky thinks, the doomed fiberglass replica's lower body submerged in primordial ooze, mouth agape in its bellow of torment, tusks pointed at the gods in a futile act of supplication.

Indian summer, sultry, the air dry and heavy. He and Vera have been strolling the grounds of the La Brea Tar Pits after his appointment with Dr. Rubel, the zealous dental practitioner, who this afternoon has undertaken elaborate bridgework, rendering Stravinsky numb and tingling.

Parched. His teeth hurt, an acrid stink, the trickle of viscid tar from softly burbling pits dotting the park. He daubs his brow with his handkerchief as Vera gently tugs his arm, coaxing him along the stone-fringed pathway, bougainvillea, birds-of-paradise, a row of slender sashaying palm trees, the iconic Hollywood sign looming from the hills.

Elsa's recent death, a mantle of distress and hopelessness he can't seem to free himself from, Vera equally devastated. These days, Marta and Ingo, Elsa's niece and nephew, spend much time at the Stravinsky home, everyone searching for any inkling of solace.

"*Impossible!*" he says in a quiet voice. Vera reaches for his hand.

Other irons in the fire. The excuse he was only too quick to offer Elsa a few years ago, the overweening response that continues to nag at him. Truthfully, there's been quite a parade of farces, false starts, near-misses. The version of the *Star Spangled Banner* he arranged for the Boston Symphony, re-harmonizing parts of it then, after the concert, practically getting himself arrested for breaking some arcane federal law forbidding any altering or tampering with the national anthem. And the circus polka—*good God!*—music for one hundred Barnum & Bailey elephants, a ballet project Balanchine pressed him to take on, insisting that the elephants happened to be young elephants. *Very well,* he'd said to Balanchine. *If they are very young elephants, I will do it.*

Meanwhile, the world took little notice of his *serious* musical ideas, wanting *commodity* music instead, elephant tunes, background music for the cinema, reconstituted anthems, utilitarian melodies and other propaganda, music that *sounded* like the old Diaghilev ballets, music created decades ago in an Old World across the Atlantic, familiar and comfortable, music he was no longer willing to write, or even capable of writing.

Schoenberg, meanwhile, continued to ride the vanguard of modernity, heading a compositional school whose avant-garde experiments the general public might have difficulty digesting but whose musical substance, as far as Stravinsky was concerned, remained persuasive and compelling.

Was Schoenberg, like the wooly mammoth, destined for obscurity? Such an ephemeral fate possibly awaited Schoenberg while also lending him a kind of victimized heroic valor. But the man plugged away, in any case, refusing to disguise his unique genius or kowtow to the culture industry, instead carving out, time after time, his dazzling diamonds.

Schoenberg. His cross to bear, eternal pebble in his shoe.

Vera touches his arm. "Igor, what is it?"

"Orpheus. The world's greatest musician," he's barely able to stammer as he turns away to place his face in his hands.

"What's all this about?"

"I see no way forward."

"You'll find your way again."

"Extinction," he mutters. "The bitter regrets along the way."

"You can only be who you are," she says. "No one else. You, Igor, are you." She kisses his cheek. "You're Stravinsky! You could never be *him*."

"Never," he says hoarsely, "in a million years, never."

from the journal of Jasper Grafton

Newberry Psychiatric Hospital
Los Angeles
September 1946

*Shelter for the afflicted. Bedlam. Dr. Pinkerton's facial tick scrubby
moustache spicy bodily scent pockets under his eyes hums the same
four notes Dah-dah-dee-dum taking hold of my eyelids wanting me
to look this way then that, coarse fingers push into my neck abdomen
shins Pressure's up! proud Pinkerton proclaims, terrible tea-stained
teeth hint of smirk informing me w/ glee a rejunvenating round of shock
treatments may be headed my way.*

*No appetite/ hole in the sock wants mending sewing sowing sighing
lonely lingering nights malingering in the metal chair by the window of
the common room, low ceiling, fireplace flame moving with her breath
her shoulder bare. Lone black piano single key unstruck & no one there,
watercolor, mirror at night, stars through the window dropping like
snowflakes one by one onto*

one-eyed toad turkey tail stinkhorn devil's fingers witch's butter
death cap bleeding tooth
Dry laughter static crackle from

the radio: Beethoven ich bin der
*Schneider Kakadu. The leaves outside, they refuse to rustle, serpentine
stripes along the snakebark maple*

greensilver trunk iridescent Acer davidii naked
branch limbs where sorrow grows, snakebark snakebite

cold chord discord Arepo
*guiding the wheels of his plow, secret-filled field to sow. Hole in the
garden gloomy*

glade of the dead, vines crawling the hoarfrost, honeysuckle,
Goldenrod Helena
* I failed to protect her when she stepped on a viper*
slipped through the stars through the
hole
in the sky, heavenward, air from other planets
while I wept & all the blue from your eyes faded but if you stay—

ocean crossing warm incubating train

underworld & no turning the clocks

back no turning back, Helena vanished but I stayed

       alive

Elsa visiting: don't be

              afraid, she holds the small boy's small hand, if

       you stay I won't be afraid. Haloed, Hold on

                 there, Chosper, we've come

to rescue you, bring you back &

              if you stay

I won't be afraid

SIMON

YEARS AGO, during their Rochester days, he and Francine discussed moving in together. But when her photography internship at Kodak concluded, suddenly she was off to Philadelphia to pursue photography at the Art Academy, leaving Simon alone at Eastman and missing her so badly he'd struggled to move forward with his doctoral studies.

These days he caught himself thinking about Francine all the time. He recalled the early days of their courtship, the footbridge over the Oswego River he and Francine had crossed, during a a day trip in frigid January, snowdrift scalloped along the river bank, placing his arms around her, pulling her close, the two of them, in puffy down coats, yoked together against the northeastern landscape.

Turning to him, taking hold of his hand, she'd said, *I'm glad we're here together.*

He couldn't recall what his response to this might have been.

Now, overcome in the silence of his motel room, he grabbed his phone and dialed home, surprised when Francine answered.

He asked how Luke was doing.

Recuperating, Francine told him, hanging in there.

"*God*, you have no idea how relieved I am to hear that."

"He's a strong kid. He was fortunate."

"We all were."

For a moment, the phone line went silent. He wanted to tell her how much he missed everyone, apologizing instead, expressing how sorry he was about Luke. About everything.

More silence.

"I've had a lot of time to think about things," he said. "I don't know what else there is to say, except to tell you how terrible I feel." He could feel his jaw tensing. "I'm a wreck, pretty much."

"I placed their lives in your hands."

He glanced up at the cracked ceiling, the absurd pair of giraffe and flamingo paintings over the beds.

Tense, he managed to say, "I'd like to come back." He listened to her breathing.

"France?"

"I'm not ready to go back to the way things were."

"I miss the boys. I want to be there to help out, help you guys." He closed his eyes. "It must be hard on everyone. Even just logistically, Luke getting around with crutches, getting in and out of the car." He expelled air forcefully. "I could help pick up groceries, help with errands, laundry, dinner."

"Carla's been helping out. She's been a real trooper, actually, fetching Lincoln from soccer and tennis, carting him over to his viola lesson. Shopping, fixing dinner. Around on the weekends to lend a hand."

He was tormented when he hung up, *grave e doloroso*, in his miserable dwelling at Guillermo's Roost, perusing the wad of paperwork—his walking papers—Boderman had handed him yesterday, *Official Notice of Intent to Terminate: Extreme misconduct, violation of University policies governing the professional conduct of faculty... ethical misjudgment in violation of standards of integrity and quality... in accord with the Commission of a criminal act within the workplace and educational setting...policy 4.7.2...* immediate dismissal, *based on the recommendations of the Divisional Committee on Privilege and Tenure...*

Boderman had pushed the paperwork into his hands, looking at him askance.

Jeez, Simon, seriously—breaking and entering? Seems you've managed to paint yourself into a fairly tight corner with this one. A swift and judicious resolution. That's what the provost is after. Willful destruction of campus property. Valuable personal *property as well. Criminy, Simon! You* get to take the hit on the personal property—take care of the bill on that one.

And Dr. Kouras was considering some sort of restraining order, it was only fair to let him know, Boderman had gone on to explain. *Timing stinks, Grafton.* Boderman wrinkled his nose. *I can't have a messy scandal playing out. Not while we're smack dab in the middle of a significant capital development campaign, donors arriving on campus from every corner of the globe, distinguished alumni, the chancellor, provost, regents, and president and, I mean, Christ on a cracker, Simon, you can't honestly expect me to play Johnnie Cochran over here, running our own miniature version of the O.J. trial.*

Now, Simon whisked Boderman's paperwork into the trash bin, glancing over at his father's journal on the nightstand, reliving the afternoon at Backyard Gates Nursery School when his father failed to pick him up, and a woman named Elsa showed up, finally, to retrieve him.

But where was his father?

What happened to you after that? he'd asked his father years later. *And what about the people I stayed with when you went away, that woman, Elsa, and her husband? What became of them?*

As Simon continued to read through the journal, he thought more about Elsa's tragedy and how Elsa's funeral could have become the nexus for three other lives—that moment a moment in time when the separate trajectories of Arnold, Igor, and his father all happened to cross.

He phoned home again, this time getting Lincoln.

"Mom says you need plenty of time to finish your project."

The sweet sound of his son's voice caused his throat to seize up.

"Things have gotten really crazy," Simon said.

"That's why you haven't come home."

"I miss you guys. I never really got to say *I'm sorry* to everyone."

"Miss you, too," Lincoln said. "Oh, hey, Dad, guess what? Some mega package came for you the other day. Stuart dropped it off."

Tableau XX

Arnold

"I have known for a long time that I won't live to
experience a wider understanding of my work, and my
much-acclaimed perseverance is an exigency based on
the desire to experience it after all. I have set my goal high
enough to assure that those who resist and even those who
oppose me will of necessity reach that point at some time."
—Schoenberg, writing to friends upon
the occasion of his 60th birthday (1934)

"I get along without you very well."
—Hoagy Carmichael/Jane Brown Thompson

"I am five feet three inches and weigh one hundred
pounds. These measurements were exactly the same fifty
years ago, but Schoenberg was shorter than I am."
— Igor Stravinsky

Los Angeles
September 1949

AT THE DAYLITE MARKET on La Cienega, Schoenberg stands in a
long line at the butcher department, waiting patiently to sort out the

mistaken meat order he holds in his hands.

The Jewish high holidays have gotten underway, the market swarming with shoppers in search of specialty items, kreplach, krupnik, kugel, kasha, kishke, knish, Harold, the manager, walking the floor with an affable smile as he greets everyone, pointing customers down the proper aisle.

Shifting his weight, Schoenberg surveys the brown paper packaging, the word, *Stravinsky*, scrawled across it. How is it possible he could have wound up with Stravinsky's meat order?

Verdi's *Nabucco Overture* plays faintly over the loudspeaker, the orchestral colors drowned out in the surrounding commotion.

"Aha!" a familiar voice hollers.

Turning, Schoenberg's startled to see Stravinsky standing beside him, shaking his own packaged meat order.

Stravinsky eyes him accusingly. "So, it was *your* name scribbled across the wrapping of my purloined sirloin."

For an uncomfortable moment, they stare at each other.

They both look away, watching the butchers behind the counter, barely able to keep pace with the slew of orders. There's a kid working alongside the the butchers, the name *Mel* printed on his nametag, scrambling against the blizzard of order slips, squinting as he tries to decipher the butchers' hastily scrawled directions.

Schoenberg huffs, dour, not entirely pleased about having to return to the store to straighten out his meat order as, softly, he hums along with the Verdi overture.

"But, imagine my own uneasiness," he says finally to Stravinsky, "returning home to sort out provisions, only to notice *Stravinsky* scrawled across the packaging of what I assumed were my short loins."

Short loin. Sirloin. Stravinsky. Schoenberg. Such things might easily be confused.

He steals a peek at Stravinsky, *the world's greatest living composer,* running off with his short loins. Which only further affirms how such a man could never be trusted. Not since Elsa's funeral two summers ago have they crossed paths, successfully avoiding one another that afternoon during the doleful proceedings, managing to steer clear of one another after that.

Meanwhile, Elsa's *Orpheus* project languishes—notations, dance configurations, outlines, musical sketches, summaries, synopses, scraps, odds and ends among the many other unclothed skeletons that populate his sketchbook—all of it gathering dust in his studio at home. What exactly is he supposed to do with the unfinished masterpiece that he and Elsa devoted so many hours to? What miracle would be required to bring the project to completion?

Elsa, Vivian. Loved ones dearly departed. He's lost other intimate friends as well: Helena, Werfel, Zemlinsky. Gershwin, Webern, Berg.

Now as the line inches forward, the clamor and turmoil abate a notch.

Static over the loudspeaker after the Verdi concludes, followed by the jarring crackle of an LP stylus fumbling for the vinyl groove. A moment later, transmitted over the Daylite intercom: Schoenberg's own *Transfigured Night*.

Suppressing a victorious grin, Schoenberg turns slowly towards Stravinsky, gloating to hear his own music playing, relishing the certain crestfallen look on his adversary's face.

Proud, overjoyed—vindicated in some small way—Schoenberg closes his eyes, rapturously alive to the soundtrack of his own story.

When the piece finishes, Stravinsky looks over at him with a shrug. "But I had no idea you were a customer here."

"A devoted one." Schoenberg points out that the selection of kosher items and Jewish delicacies the Daylite offers simply has no rival anywhere else in Los Angeles.

"Vera and I are not of the Jewish faith, of course," Stravinsky says, creeping forward a few steps in the line he's standing in. "But this Saturday we're expecting the Hersches for dinner. Maybe you're familiar?"

"Sol?" Schoenberg says. "Why, yes, of course! He advised me on the fingerings for the revised edition of my violin concerto."

"You don't say?" Stravinsky says. "He suggested fingerings and bowings for my violin concerto as well. And Sol certainly proved equal to the task—able somehow to figure out how to play the chord I wanted with the enormous stretch, even after everyone else had thrown in the towel." Smiling, he shakes his head. "It's a small world, after all."

Dear Sol. Who continues to pester Schoenberg about the Orpheus project, inquiring whether he's made any progress lately, encouraging him to keep going.

"That Sol's a good egg," Schoenberg says after he and Stravinsky exchange meat orders, preparing to go their separate ways.

Waving at Harold, Stravinsky holds the door for Schoenberg as the two exit the Daylite, stepping out onto the bustle of La Cienega Boulevard.

Coloring, Stravinsky says, "But perhaps. Later. After the holidays, you know, when you would have a little time perhaps." He swallows, surveying the busy street. "I would be curious, maybe to understand a little about the *Orpheus* project you and Elsa—"

Schoenberg shakes his head slowly. "I doubt there would be time."

"Everyone's terribly busy, I know," Stravinsky says.

"There just isn't time, you see. No time, whatsoever." He exhales, he can feel his body deflating slightly.

Stravinsky nods. "Busy, sure."

"In fact," Schoenberg says screwing up his face, "*it's later than you think.*"

Stravinsky raises his eyebrows. "Socrates?" he asks. "Kafka? Kierkegaard?"

Schoenberg sniffs. "Guy Lombardo."

SIMON

"Are you coming home to live with us again?" Luke asked excitedly, standing in the front doorway, balancing deftly on his crutches.

"I wanted to check up on you guys," Simon said. "And I needed to pick up a few items."

"Other stuff?" Luke asked. "You mean like the piano?"

Laughing, Simon shook his head. "Well, maybe not the piano. Not during this stop over, anyway."

Jabbing his crutches at the floor to anchor himself, eager to show off for his father, Luke circled, hopping back inside the house, calling for Francine.

"You'll never guess who came over to check up on us!" Luke hollered.

Francine, Lincoln, and Carla were seated around the table when Simon and Luke entered the dining room, Carla ensconced in *Papa Bear's* chair, Francine looking up with surprise.

"You're here!" Francine said, daubing at her mouth with a linen napkin.

Simon tensed. "I should have called."

Lincoln got up from the table, eyebrows knitted as he went over to Simon. "What are you doing here?"

"You don't sound all that happy to see me," Simon said with a mock-frown.

"I didn't mean for it to come out like that," Lincoln said. Simon ruffled Lincoln's hair, throwing his arms around him in a long embrace.

Francine stood. "Let me go grab that package for you."

When she handed him the oversized shopping bag he knew immediately what was inside.

"Is it a present?" Luke asked.

"Sort of," Simon said, setting the heavy bag down. "Just something I left behind at work,"

"Open it!" Luke shouted.

"Stuart filled me in a little on the situation at UCLA," Francine said. "I'm really sorry."

Such a *peety*," Carla said.

Sucking in his cheeks, Simon turned towards Francine. "I thought maybe we could talk." He shrugged. "In private, for just a moment."

Francine offered a pale smile. She looked tired still, worn down and a little older somehow, her brown hair pulled back into a ponytail.

Would Stuart have mentioned anything else to her when he'd dropped off the package? And what further acid might Mo have sprinkled on the situation? Would Demetra's name have come up at all, with Stuart maybe attempting to soft-pedal things, helping Simon to cover a few of his muddied tracks?

"Hey, Dad," Lincoln said, picking up on the dissonance between his parents. "This whole mess with the sleepover. It wasn't your fault." He swallowed heavily, looking over at his little brother with remorse.

"Actually, you know," Lincoln continued, "*we* were sorta the ones to blame." He swallowed again, cagy as he looked at his mother for acknowledgment.

"Sweetie—" Francine started to say.

"No," Lincoln said. "*We* were the ones who kept pestering Dad to let us go to the sleepover, right, mung?"

Blinking, Luke nodded.

"Linc, honey," Francine said, "that's very sweet. And I know we've gone over this." She sighed. "But, I think we—"

"He wasn't going to let us," Lincoln said with greater urgency, his eyes welling. "Dad isn't the one to blame! It was all *our* fault!"

Simon placed his arm around Lincoln's shoulder. "Hey, hey. It's okay, Linc. Don't worry about it. Everything's gonna work out." He looked over at Francine. "Your mother and I. We'll get things sorted and squared away. I promise."

A moment later, alone in the bedroom upstairs while gathering some additional clothing, Simon couldn't help but notice the feminine disarray—vestiges of Carla's presence, an overnight bag with a satin kimono folded over it, a silver compact kit beside a dog-eared bodice-ripper on the nightstand he had trouble believing Francine would be reading.

The room—*their bedroom*—felt foreign to him, their honeymoon portrait conspicuously missing from the wall, the bathroom cluttered with make-up cases, cold cream, and a teasing comb filled with alien reddish hairs, a lacy negligee draped over the towel rack.

When he returned to the living room he came upon the others, cross-legged on the carpet, huddled around the sketchbook, rapt as Francine, in the role of curator, turned carefully through the pages. Alarm on their faces when they looked up to see him standing there, Simon equally dumbfounded by the sight of the manuscript open on the living room floor.

Lincoln backhanded his brother. "Nice going, mung."

"Luke seems to have gotten into it and unwrapped it."

Wide-eyed, Luke stared at Simon.

"Wrapped packages, they can be so tempting," Simon said to Luke with a friendly wink.

Luke quivered, crestfallen as he stared into the carpet. "Great," he said softly, "now I'm probably gonna be ostrich-sized, too."

"Luke?" Simon said. "Hey, what is it, buddy? What do you mean?"

"Ostrich-sized," Luke muttered. "I heard Carla telling Mom, how no one likes being ostrich-sized."

Simon looked at Francine and Carla.

"Ostracized!" Lincoln burst out, giving Luke another backhand. "*Ostracized*, you mean, Mung; not *ostrich-sized*."

"Okay, sure, whatever," Luke muttered.

"Arnold Schoenberg?" Lincoln said to Simon. "Whoa, Dad, seriously? Man, this manuscript looks supremely important."

"Is it yours for real?" Luke asked. "It must be worth like a zillion bucks."

A few moments later Simon and Francine sequestered themselves on opposite ends of the sofa in the rear living room where Luke had been camping out.

"What can I possibly say or do to get you to forgive me?" he asked while Francine sat in stony silence, smoothing the tops of her corduroys.

"That's just it," she said with a shrug. "I can't just *put* things behind me. I'm not able to forgive you."

"When, though?" he practically yelled, getting to his feet. "It's been a couple of weeks." He looked over at her. "How long do we need to stay mad at each other?"

Francine stared mutely at the floor.

"How long do we need to drag this out?" he asked, frustrated about his confinement at Guillermo's Roost, missing the boys, more than a little bewildered by Carla. "Is there a rule book or something, so that we can maybe look up the penalty?"

"My God," she said. "*Breaking and entering*?"

"Things got complicated over there," he said, quick to defend himself. "I told you, work—France, it was nuts for me, the teaching, plus—"

"I keep asking myself what could have possibly convinced you to take your sons over to that house." Her look was bitter. "And then, to actually *leave* them there."

"I never had any intention of leaving them there, I swear."

"Mo said the two of you looked like a pair of lovebirds out on the town."

"Not even *close*," he said. "I mean—*really?* Jesus, France—"

"And after the two of you just happened to run into one another?" she said, starting to fume. "*Then* what?" She dug her fingers into her thighs. "Back to *her* place for more intimate discussions of *Schoenberg.* Was that how it went?"

He took in a slow breath.

"I told you," he said. "In terms of the document. There were specific questions I was dealing with. Which made it necessary for the two of us to meet in person." He sighed. "Extenuating circumstances. Of course, in retrospect, it's easy to see every glaring error made along the way, all the bad decisions."

"For God's sake, Simon. I want the *truth*."

"That's what I'm doing." He sniffed. "I admit it. The level of detail she and I were discussing—the information in the sketchbook she was able to decode. I can't begin to describe how paramount all of this is in terms of wrapping up my opera." He tugged at his beard. "God, France, you know how long I've been stuck. Three deadline extensions!" He shook his head in disgust. "But then, suddenly, a light at the end of the tunnel. Almost like a dream! Certain details within the sketchbook beginning to emerge.

"And so you slept with her?"

"Absolutely not!"

"A sort of thoughtful, *thank-you* present for helping you out. Was that it?" Groaning quietly, she removed her eyeglasses, closing her eyes and massaging the bridge of her nose.

"We had a few drinks," he said, wincing, squeamish, ashamed as the next two words flew from his mouth. "*We kissed.*"

Uh-oh. Now his neck was in the noose. Too afraid to look over at her, he swallowed, intent, though, on finishing his confession, no matter what.

"I kissed her," he said bluntly, watching as the pain registered over Francine's face.

"But, I swear," he said. "That's as far as anything went."

Getting to her feet, she moved towards the door.

"I never intended to hurt you. That's the last thing I'd do."

She stood at the door, shoulders slumped.

"So?" he hollered across the room. He slapped his thighs. "So, now what? A lawless kiss. One kiss and, *poof!* a decade of marriage suddenly up in smoke?"

Sobbing, Francine shook her head.

"I swear to God," he said, "if I could take it back—If there were any way to turn back—"

"But that's just the thing," she said, tear-streaked. "Don't you get it? We can't. There's no turning back. Things just don't work that way. We can never go back."

In his motel room, Simon leafed through the document, relieved to have it back, buoyed by its presence, despite the roadblock with Francine. Luke's stuffed penguin, Ned Spencer, was stationed beside him in the chair. Earlier, as Simon was departing the house, tail between his legs, Luke had bravely offered up Ned to his father, insisting he bring him along for company.

Now, smiling at the sight of the penguin propped up in the armchair, Simon placed a few of the items he'd grabbed from home into the motel room dresser, surprised to come upon one of Francine's old letters folded between a few of his Oxford shirts. He wondered how a letter could have gotten mixed in with his clothes. Was it simply another random happenstance, or could the kids (or maybe even Francine) have slipped it in?

Philadelphia-1983

Dear Simon,

My laundry is tumbling around in the dryer downstairs and I'm starting a letter to you. I am lying on the couch all wrapped up in my down blanket and my head is clear. I think I must smell of chlorine, gasoline, lotion and motor-oil (try and guess what I was doing earlier). Are these the scents that draw men to women?

Last night, leaving basic drawing class, Sally and I could see the full moon—yellow, larger than life, nebulous and frayed about the edges—rising from the direction of the ocean. We all stood around to have a look. It was magnificent. Like the entrance of the Queen of the Night or something. I helped Sally jump start her car—a common occurrence, since she is always forgetting to turn off the lights.

My turbulent (word of the day) physical state of missing you seems to change, intensify, metamorphose by the day. Let me rephrase this: before, earlier, missing you was just missing you. Now, it has become a physical feeling of loss, excitement, irony, agony, ecstasy, song. When I think about leaving Philadelphia and returning to Rochester to live with you, I am cautious in hoping, cautious of disappointment. And in saying that, doesn't it relay to you how much it would mean to me to be in the same city as you? In the same room, breath, conversation, caress, moment in time? I can't imagine it any differently than this. Because, then, I would really begin to dream of what it could be like to spend countless days and untold time with you. What say you to that, Mr. G?

Sweetheart, I am now going to bed. Take good care of yourself, Simon Grafton.

Love, Francine

Five days later his opera was completed. Within the meager

trappings of Guillermo's Roost, he'd been working like a man possessed, composing for nine, ten hours a day. He'd spent the morning relishing his victory, euphoric while flipping back through the score for one final review. He'd met his deadline by an eight-day margin.

Waiting in line at the FedEx store to mail the commission off to Santa Fe, nudging the package across the counter towards the cashier, he sensed an enormous weight lifted from him.

"Two hundred and thirty-five dollars and seventeen cents, boss," the kid behind the counter said. "That's the damage."

Simon turned to stare out the window. Wasn't it high time to head over to Flaherty's for a whiskey sour or something, raising his glass while saying a few well-chosen words to friends and family members who had been right there at his side the whole way?

But who exactly were these friends and family members he imagined addressing?

"Sir?" the kid behind the counter said. He had greenish-red liberty spikes, the sides of his head closely shaven.

Because. Hadn't he pretty much managed to drive all such people away, destroying everything he loved and everyone most dear to him?

"Will that be cash or charge today, boss?"

Heavy-hearted, Simon turned to stare at the kid, who was drumming his fingers on the countertop.

There was no one, not a soul left in his world to celebrate with.

The kid was squinting at him, shrugging at the other customers waiting in line.

"Know what?" Simon said. "Never mind. Change of plan."

Looking askance at Simon, the cashier nudged the package back towards Simon.

Turning to go, Simon said, looking over his shoulder, "Thanks, but I'll be delivering this in person instead."

BOOK VII

from the journal of Jasper Grafton

Sept. 1948

Soil, the living edge where earth & sky meet, life into death into life again. The skin surrounding the earth the place where life begins & finishes. The processes occurring within the top few centimeters of the earth's surface are responsible for all planetary life on dry land. Sator Arepo Tenet Opera Rotas. The farmer turns the plow, sows seed, looks after kith & kin, keeps the work circling. Sensing Helena nearby, I close my eyes, pressing the stone pendant gift into my palm, five engraved words—Sator Arepo Tenet Opera Rotas.

Something strange & delightful w/ Mr. Schoenberg yesterday. Knee-deep in soil & having it out w/ a mound of cheeseweed encroaching upon the hollyhocks, I'd been thinking of Milton's hell, the soil there constituting a sort of "underworld of the underworld(!)" where precious metals were sd. to be hidden, a terrain filled with gold that a brigade of fallen angels bearing spades & pickaxes goes about extracting.

Mr. Schoenberg stepped out into the garden wearing a blindingly shiny necktie affixed to his salmon-colored shirt, absorbed with his Orpheus score as the two of us engaged in some conversation I cld. barely keep pace w/ concerning composition techniques & tone rows.

The pedagogue in him perhaps compelled to highlight the four possible directions of the twelve-tone row—prime, retrograde, inversion, & retrograde inversion—the two of us seated beneath the generous shade of Quercus, the garden carpeted w/ blue-eyed grass, serenaded by the spotted towhee & lesser goldfinch, sweet breath of breeze, fragrance of lemon, peppermint, redwood, marigold, the sword fern, Polystichum munitum, w/ its dancing fiddleheads, woolly bluecurls, Elderberry, hyacinth & two small Schoenberg boys circling the yard on bikes, stopped momentarily at an impromptu toy traffic signal Mr. Schoenberg appears to have cobbled together from scraps of old wood, wiring & other odds & ends.

As Mr. Schoenberg delved further into twelve-tone explanations, image of the Sator Square suddenly came to mind, the embedded words in Helena's stone pendant. Like the tone row, the Square too is four-directional, readable in four directions. He was in mid-sentence when I stood abruptly from the table, colliding nearly w/ the two little boys while ravenously hunting about the garden for a stray stick w/ which to scratch the Square into a swath of dirt somewhere.

Schoenberg & sons observed me curiously, there among the billowy pink plumes & regal purplish leaves of the smoke tree, Cotinus, as I went about, in the most rudimentary fashion, carefully etching each letter of the Square into an unassuming patch of dirt. & when Schoenberg at last beheld what I had crudely done, a look of pure ecstasy came over him, a seventy-four-year-old man jumping for joy practically, or so it almost seemed & the boys likely convinced we were both of us a little daft & for a brief unbearable moment, I even suspected the indomitable magus might walk over & kiss me.

SIMON

"God, Linc, your voice," Simon said over the phone, "you sound so grown up," Lincoln quick to remind Simon that he *was* grown up. Simon asked how Luke was doing.

"Cast should be coming off next week," Lincoln said. "And, oh, hey, by the way! My viola recital's next week. The Hindemith piece I've been working on. Plus, Mr. Diaz is letting me play the piece I wrote, the original song for viola and piano."

"Fantastic," Simon said. The phone line went silent for a while.

"It sucks you're so far away," Lincoln said.

"I know," Simon said. "Believe me, I wish I could be there."

He missed his family. For the past several weeks, he'd been living in Santa Fe, housesitting for an out-of-town opera board member while immersed in the opera season's official opening, the premiere of *Arnold & Igor* only a few weeks away. Set design, costuming and lighting were in full swing, the cast of singers due to arrive for rehearsals, the orchestra expected not long after that. New squadrons of professionals seemed to be cropping up every few days to go over details of choreography and staging, untold numbers of people dedicated solely to the task of bringing Simon's artistic vision to fruition, Simon, meanwhile, engrossed in the endless details and steadily growing mania of the upcoming production, being introduced to directors and assistants, technicians, sound engineers, costumers, choristers, dancers and other supernumeraries.

Artistic Director Lindsay Tundler had taken him under her wing, inviting Simon to meetings with administrative staff and other key personnel, many of whom were now descending upon Santa Fe from the company's New York offices. Lindsay toured him around town in an air-conditioned Mercedes, pointing out the Palace of Governors, O'Keeffe and Folk Arts museums and various other local points of interest.

He went around to local schools, giving presentations to impressionable elementary students about his opera, students who reminded him of his own kids as he highlighted some of the challenges of being a composer.

Nestled against the snow-dusted Sangre de Cristo mountains and in close proximity to the historical state capital, pueblo architecture, gastronomic offerings, galleries and outdoor markets, he'd managed to find a kind of oasis among the mesas, far from all the madness of Los Angeles. He'd joined a meditation group through the Pueblo Temple community, hiking in the foothills on weekends and taking part in overnight retreats. He was eating healthier food, buying fresh produce at the local farmers market, managing his stress, attending to better self-care, and otherwise mindfully restoring himself, physically, emotionally, even spiritually.

But he also felt adrift, isolated from his family, biding his time while consumed with the ache of loss. He missed reading to his sons and putting Luke to bed. He missed the silly songs they liked to sing—*Do Your Ears Hang Low*; *Lolly, Lolly, Lolly, Get Your Adverbs Here*; and *All Together Now*. Playing HORSE with the boys on the basketball court, the spontaneous banter and guffaw around the dinner table and the boys saying the darndest things, Francine flashing him one of her furtive parental grins. He found he was homesick for the simplest, dumbest things—he and the boys constructing a secret cave out of bedsheets then crawling inside to pretend they were dinosaurs, bats, or venomous fart monsters. He missed the ridiculous Halloween costumes, glowy skeletons, bulky super heroes, Jedi knights. He reminisced about how he and Francine used to bathe their tiny babies in the kitchen sink, the care given to each puny, wrinkly digit, nostalgic for Indian Guides and Saturday morning soccer league; hands and feet imprinted into fresh cement along the driveway and for planting carrot seeds and checking too often to see whether they'd sprouted.

Yesterday he'd had a meeting with Mr. Vaughn, a vice president with the Chicago Lyric Opera, in town this week to attend a few of the early rehearsals while gathering further details of *Arnold & Igor* as potential repertory for an upcoming Chicago season. Mr. Vaughn proposed that Simon extract the Orpheus sections from *Arnold & Igor*, composing a follow-up companion opera to *Arnold & Igor*, Simon's own completed version of Orpheus as its own opera, a project that might morph, as Mr. Vaughn had intimated, into something significant. There were even rumors about potential interest at the Met in New York in a possible co-commission with the Lyric for such a work. *A career gamechanger*, Mr. Vaughn said. *This would really move the needle for you; you'd be pretty much set as a composer.*

But when would he be able to hold his boys again? That's the question that had been foremost on Simon's mind during their meeting, the nagging question he'd most wanted to put to the prophetic Mr. Vaughn.

Tableau XXI

Arnold

"Neoclassicism and serialism (or twelve-tone music) are
often considered polar opposites. The enmity between
Vienna and Paris, between the school of Schoenberg and
the school of Stravinsky, is a fact of history."
—Charles Rosen, *Arnold Schoenberg*

"Any composer who has not felt—I do not say
understand, but *felt*—the necessity of the dodecaphonic
language is useless."
—Pierre Boulez, 1952

Hollywood
February 1950

Schoenberg stands alongside Stravinsky at Sol's Music Store on La Brea. Two short men with hulking roman noses and pendulous ears glancing up at a framed photograph of the Gershwin brothers with an inscription, *Dear Solomon, to thee we sing! George & Ira.*

"*Ach*," Schoenberg says, wistful as he leans on the knob of his ivory walking stick, "George *vuss* a very dear friend."

Stravinsky offers a tepid smile. "And quite a talented composer."

"A true loss." Schoenberg clucks his tongue. "So young. Another loss. Often we played tennis together."

Sunlight illuminates the sign on the storefront window, *S. Hersch*

& Sons, Fine Violins. A calico cat dozes on the window sill, a horsefly drones percussively behind the louvers. From a small radio on the shelf, Beethoven's *Eroica* Symphony concludes, the two composers waiting expectantly for the classical station's next selection. Schoenberg conjures one of his own rousing compositions to be next up on the station's playlist—his *Five Orchestral Pieces* or piano concerto, for example, or his cantata perhaps, *A Survivor from Warsaw*—hoping to God it isn't that egregious, ubiquitous *Firebird*, or some other thumpingly dispiriting Stravinsky showstopper. When Ferdi Grofé's *Grand Canyon Suite* comes on—extolled by the radio announcer as among America's great musical gems—both composers' heads solemnly slump.

Schoenberg admires the assortment of glossy violins suspended by their scrolls from a high bracket overhead. The counters are heaped with sheet music, high cabinets bulge with orchestral parts and scores. Autographed photos line the walls, Heifetz, Menuhin, Piatigorsky, Rose, Feuermann, Stern, Horowitz, Milstein, Klemperer.

Across the shop, Sol finishes up a transaction with a customer, his work table nearby a hodgepodge of tweezers and small screwdrivers, machine oil tins, tuning pegs, cakes of rosin, bridges, and catgut string; a cigar box overflowing with bow components, whalebone wrap, abalone, mother of pearl, tortoiseshell.

"My friends!" Sol hollers, wiping his hands on a towel. He wears a Bermuda shirt, open at the neck to reveal a Hebrew *Chai* medallion nestled in a thatch of chest hair as he leads the two composers through the back of the shop and through a door bearing a mezuzah marked *Private*, the music studio where Sol teaches violin lessons and indulges in languid lunch breaks.

They enter the music studio, dimly-lit and drenched in an aroma of vinegar, garlic and cloves, an oily light over the baby grand piano from the patio's glass door. A sleek Bauhaus desk chair flanks the piano, a rosewood music stand, a well-worn Chesterfield and a Raytheon television set.

"*Shayna faigela,*" Sol says, pressing his face against a canary cage. "Why, hello there, Paganini!"

Crossing the room, he removes the weighty lid of a Dutch oven, smacking his lips. "Pickled ox tongue!" Sol announces. "Two weeks I marinated it."

The three lean over the Dutch oven, taking in the semi-submerged slab floating in viscid gray juices among bobbing carrots and mushrooms.

"But!" Sol raises a finger. "Today you will partake."

"My dears," Stravinsky says. "I may be speaking in tongues." He winces. "But I do not typically partake of offal or organ."

"With rye bread it goes nicely," Sol says, heading over to a small refrigerator in the corner and pulling out a pitcher of water. "I'll let the two of you get down to your business. But first, you shouldn't be thirsty. Some refreshing water, more than seven hours chilled."

"Water is for the feet," Stravinsky says. "A nice cognac, however—"

"Cognac it shall be!" Sol reaches into the liquor cabinet. "More than sixty years this Cognac has been aged!"

Alone with Stravinsky, Schoenberg painstakingly removes the sketchbook from his valise, setting it down among the coffee table's assortment of *Life* magazines *(Sir Laurence Olivier as Hamlet; Dodger Baseball Rookies; The War Memoirs of Winston Churchill)* and some old newspapers *(Israel Declares Statehood; Joe DiMaggio; Holland's Queen Wilhelmina Abdicates Throne).*

Collecting a stack of onion skin pages from within the sketchbook, he holds them up to show Stravinsky. "Elsa's dance notations. The sketches and notes she made for *Orpheus.*"

He lugs the sketchbook over to the piano, playing through some of the *Orpheus* passages, Orpheus' first meeting with Eurydice, Eurydice's fatal snake bite, intensely curious as to what Stravinsky's reaction may be, Stravinsky closing his eyes as he listens, his body very still, face expressionless.

When the final chord of Orpheus' descent into the underworld sounds, Schoenberg looks over at Stravinsky.

Stravinsky stares at his lap, folding and unfolding his hands.

"Impossible!" Stravinsky cries. "Impenetrable, this twelve-tone business of yours."

"I never claimed any of it would be easy."

Stravinsky snorts. "Too many rules."

"Constraint enables creativity," Schoenberg says.

Stravinsky throws down his arms. "Formalized cacophony! So dense, the texture! Stark, with so much— rubato! Nothing ever resolves. I fail to understand how you can abandon—*willfully abandon!*—*concord* in favor of *discord*." He removes his glasses to wipe his eyes. "How do you manage to sleep at night?"

"Dissonances are only different from consonances in degree," Schoenberg says calmly from the piano bench. "Essentially, nothing more than remoter consonances."

"Incomprehensible! Poppycock! Flapdoodle!" Flushed, Stravinsky hugs his arms in despair. "The music begs to resolve."

Schoenberg shrugs. "Not all conflict can be resolved."

"But we live in different *worlds*," Stravinsky says. "This pill you offer me. It's too bitter to swallow. I'm unable to hear music in such a way."

Schoenberg puffs his cheeks, determined to make his case. "But, really, Igor. Are you so addicted to old *habits*? True, this may *seem* like something radically new in its language and approach." He shakes his head. "Its content, however, is still organically linked to the past. Very much of a piece with German masters, Bach, Beethoven, Brahms.

"For the love of God," Schoenberg continues, blood racing to his head as he gets up from the piano bench. "You're no fool. Look around. It's everywhere, my method. Here and in Europe, worldwide—everywhere! It only continues to proliferate."

"Like the Spanish Flu," Stravinsky says.

It occurs to Schoenberg he's only wasting his time. And what difference can it make whether Stravinsky understands or appreciates what he's done?

"If I might perhaps share with you, though," Schoenberg says with great care. "The system I've come up with."

Stravinsky clacks his tongue.

"Because," Schoenberg presses further, lifting the sketchbook from the piano rack and bringing it over to show Stravinsky. "I think, once you see for yourself how elegantly it all works. Indeed, how beautifully it succeeds in bringing order onto chaos." Thumbing through the document, he comes upon a matrix he's written out.

"In any case," Schoenberg says, "you might as well learn it directly from—as they say—the horse's mouth."

Twelve rows, Schoenberg explains, "each row containing twelve pitches, the twelve chromatic pitches which comprise the octave, with the pitches organized in prime, inversion, retrograde and retrograde inversion." He smacks his lips. "One hundred forty-four pitches in total."

Stravinsky slaps his forehead with his palm, eyes rolling up in his head. "So many numbers!"

"The pitches can be manipulated," Schoenberg says. "Repositioned!"

Stravinsky pushes out his lip. "I should have brought along an abacus."

Taking hold of a pencil, Schoenberg scribbles something into the margin of the sketchbook.

```
S A T O R
A R E P O
T E N E T
O P E R A
R O T A S
```

"So, now I think you begin to see," Schoenberg says with fervor. "Permutated. Inverted. Transformed!" As he traces the Latin Square, his fingers begin to tremble. "Forwards, backwards, up, and down also." He rubs his hands together. "New rows sprouting everywhere like shoots. New shoots, yes. But which grow gradually into a complete tree! Organicism! Homology! Goethe's primeval plant, *Urpflanze*. Whose root is in fact no different from the stalk, the stalk no different from the leaf, the leaf no different from the flower, *und so weiter*. Variations on the same idea!"

He flashes an all-knowing grin at Stravinsky, barely able to contain himself. "And all of it emanating from the basic prime row of twelve notes!"

Later, the composers break for a round of table tennis out on the patio, their rubber paddles meeting the tiny ball with a rhythmic *pok!*

When Schoenberg whacks the ball directly into the net, he cries, "*Ach, Dummkopf!*" before proceeding to explain to Stravinsky exactly why the point was lost.

"Not a big deal," Stravinsky says with a wave of the paddle.

"On the contrary," Schoenberg says.

"But, it's only for fun we play."

"Eight apiece," Schoenberg says gruffly. "Your service!"

After table tennis, they return to the piano, seated side by side, Schoenberg playing an ostinato at the bass end of the keyboard while Stravinsky, stabbing fiercely, improvises a syncopated counterpoint.

They begin to tinker around with four notes—*E-G-Eb-A*, each creating variations and permutations, pausing to pencil ideas into the sketchbook.

Much to Schoenberg's delight, Stravinsky invents a variation on Schoenberg's *Orpheus Descending into the Underworld* motif, a pensive, lugubrious dirge.

"Write that down," Schoenberg says, "quick!" Pushing the sketch-book towards Stravinsky, he nods approvingly. "Ah, you see? Yes, now we're getting somewhere, now you're cooking with gas!"

SIMON

"*Now,* ARE YOU COMING BACK to live with us, Dad?" Luke wide-eyed and suited up in his argyle vest, asked Simon. Simon ruffled Luke's hair, amused by the blonde bangs, slicked with gel to form stiff peaks.
He and his family were seated in a booth at Swensen's ice cream parlor, enjoying banana splits in glass troughs. Almost as if nothing had ever changed.

Simon caught a flight from Santa Fe to LAX and had surprised them by showing up at Lincoln's viola recital and taking a seat at the rear of the church sanctuary. Several rows up, Luke and Francine's faces registered shock when they happened to glance back and notice Simon sitting there. Lincoln's performance brought joy, an exhilarating thing to behold, Lincoln beaming in his corduroy coat and clip-on necktie when he spotted his father in the audience, gracefully raising the viola and readying the bow for the Hindemith. Never more proud, Simon was bowled over by Lincoln's poise and natural expressivity, unable to fathom how this young kid of his could be mature enough to take on such a sophisticated and nuanced work, as Lincoln drew his bow deeply across the strings, shaping the tender phrases and coaxing the plangent music from the viola.

Now, from across the booth, Francine placed an arm around Lincoln, kissing his ear and telling him how wonderful he was, smiling at Simon across the table, the two of them sharing an unspoken moment.

Blushing, Lincoln jerked his head away, Francine laughing as she squeezed him all the more, leaning over to pelt the side of her son's head with kisses.

"That was really something," Simon said, beaming at Lincoln. "And that's no easy piece, the Hindemith. Your phrasing was beautifully shaped."

Lincoln shrugged, lowering his eyes while he murmured thank you.

"And then, my God!" Simon said, nodding, grinning, unable to contain his enthusiasm. "An original composition, as well—an opus one!" Simon laughed, joyful, pointing at Lincoln as he elbowed Luke. "Your brother, the composer!"

"When are you coming back to live with us?" Luke pressed Simon.

Glancing warily from Simon to Francine, Lincoln asked, "Are you, Dad?" Lincoln asked cautiously.

Francine and Simon looked away, a tense silence descending.

"My opera," Simon said, breaking the silence. "It's about to go into production." Francine stared down at her hands, the boys plunging their spoons into their ice cream.

Nudging his sundae aside, Simon looked around the table. "Guys, my opera's about to go into production."

"Right," Lincoln said. "That's amazing, Dad. But what about after that?"

"Sweetie," Francine spoke gently to Lincoln. "Your father and I—" Slowly, she looked up at Simon. "We're still trying to work through a few things." The boys were both staring at him. Simon chewed the inside of his cheek, unsure of what to say.

"I think. What Mom's trying to say." Simon drummed his fingers on the table. "People. Sometimes. I mean, there are times." He eyed Francine nervously. "When two people. Even though they still love each other—" Slowly, he shook his head. "Even though your mother and I—"

"Dad," Luke said with a stern look. "Use your words."

"Yeah, Dad," Lincoln said. "Try and focus."

Then Lincoln flashed a grin at Simon. "Oh, man. I still can't even believe you're really here."

"Wouldn't miss it," Simon said.

Lincoln looked over again at Francine, narrowing his gaze. "I vote we let Dad come home."

"I vote for that too!" Luke hollered. Francine smiled stiffly.

Simon nodded to his sons. "That's really sweet of you guys."

"I vote two times!" Luke cut in. They were all staring at Francine now, but she turned away, staring off at the line of customers at the take-out counter beside the door.

Lincoln gave Francine a snide look. "Looks like you're outnumbered, Mom. If Dad voted, the vote would wind up being three to one."

"You guys are too much," Simon said, hoping for levity, venturing a peek at Francine. "Listen, though. Mommy and I. We're still discussing—" He shook his head. "It's complicated. She and I are hashing things over, trying to work a few things out."

"It sure seems to be taking you guys a long time," Lincoln said.

"Yeah!" Luke said, nodding at his brother, "*eternally* long."

"We want what's best for you guys."

"*Best for us?*" Lincoln cried with a look of incredulity. He scowled at Francine. "I think you already know what that is."

"Yeah," Luke said, "probably best to just let *by-gods* be *by-gods*."

Simon laughed.

"*Bygones*," Lincoln said, rolling his eyes. "Jeez. Good grief, mung bean, I can't believe how dumb you can be at times."

"You're dumb!" Luke said to Lincoln. "You're lame. Sillier than a naked man in socks. Dumber than a doorknob."

"Doorknobs can't be dumb," Lincoln said hatefully, "only dumb little brothers can be dumb."

"Hey!" Francine said, giving Lincoln's arm a jab.

"See?" Simon said with a laugh, smiling at Francine. "You guys need me around." He nodded. "Mom needs a second referee on hand."

"Which Carla doesn't seem to get how to do," Lincoln said.

Francine and Simon bowed their heads.

"Hey," Luke said, "How 'bout we take another vote on allowing Dad to come home?"

"A recount," Lincoln said. "Now that all ballots have been cast."

"I'll bet even *Carla* might vote for Dad," Luke said, prompting an even longer and more uncomfortable silence.

Simon held his breath, mind spinning, strategizing, choosing his words with care.

"My opera opens in two weeks." He inhaled deeply. "They offered me a few guest passes. Best seats in the house." He looked at Francine. "I'd *really* like you guys to be there." The boys looked excitedly at Francine. "It would really mean a lot to me."

Francine tensed. "I just don't think we'd be able to swing it."

She handed the boys a few quarters to play an *Indy 500* video game in the arcade area.

"So, now what?" Simon asked. Francine shrugged. "This is killing me." He gnawed his lower lip. "And it can't be very easy on *them*." From a neighboring booth, they could hear a family laughing, making funny faces while pulling maraschino cherries from their bowls.

"We can't go to your opera," Francine said.

"I need them," he said, looking back at the boys, desperate, swallowing his frustration. "Just as much as you do."

"It's complicated," she said. "With such late notice, I doubt I could get time off from work."

"Can't we work together on this, France? Work *something* out?"

"Plus, even if we factored me out," she said, "I still wouldn't want the boys flying over to New Mexico by themselves. It isn't a long flight, but still—"

He watched Francine push aside her sundae dish.

"I know my actions—my mistakes—brought us to where we are now," he said. "Hell, I'm owning that." Nervously he folded and unfolded his hands. "I wish we didn't have to stay stuck like this, in a holding pattern."

"I'm trying," she said. "It may not seem like it to you. Or to the boys. But I am."

"Carla," he said. "Does any of this have anything to do with her?"

Francine shook her head. "She's been an amazing source of support for us. A true friend. There for me." She wadded up her napkin. "I honestly don't know what I would have done without her."

Heart in his throat, he reached across the table, gently placing a hand on her arm.

"I want to come back," he said, "home with everyone. Back to the way things used to be."

She allowed him to keep his hand over her arm for a moment.

"No more Santa Fe," he said bitterly, shaking his head, unsure about what he was attempting to propose.

Confused, Francine stared at him.

"If that's what it takes. "I'll do it. I swear to God, Francine, I'll do *whatever* it takes. No, listen. I've given it a great deal of thought." Anxious, he looked around the restaurant. "I'll just let Santa Fe know something came up at home. Something personal." He swallowed heavily. "I'm sure it won't be the first time someone's had to bow out during a premiere. One way or another, things will continue just fine over there."

Francine freed her arm. "I think what we all need is a little more time. I imagine things will become clearer. After a while. After this initial phase."

"*Initial phase?*" he nearly shouted. "Jesus, is that what you're calling it? My God, you make it sound like the process of grieving."

She placed her fingers around her water glass. "You've worked way too hard to throw this away."

"No!" he said, throat burning. "Don't you get it? None of this matters anymore. *None* of it." He shook his head. "I'm there in Santa Fe. My heart's not there, though, not in it. It's impossible. I can't be all in when—" He looked at her. "It's like I'm just going through the motions. Numb. Things aren't making sense. I have no idea what I'm doing half the time."

"I'm sorry to have to miss it." She scooted out from the booth. "The kids," she struggled to say. "Well, school, for one thing. Activities. Things going on in our lives."

Sickened, exhausted, he got to his feet. "I could fly to L.A." He was nodding. "I could escort the boys back with me for the premiere." He continued to nod. "A weekend. Two quick days and right back to you. We're talking about *two days*."

Francine glanced across the restaurant, searching for the boys.

"*Two days*, Francine. For godsakes."

"It's late," she said, frowning. "Way past their bedtime. School early in the morning. Work." She smiled. "It was thoughtful of you to be here tonight. Really. It means the world to Lincoln."

Giving his arm a pat, she turned to retrieve the boys.

Coda

SIMON

MOMENTS AWAY FROM THE curtain rise, he sat alone in his mezzanine seat, tense and thumbing through the printed program, the colors of the evening summer sky continuing to deepen through the theater's clerestory window and open sides. Crescendo of crickets, Simon nervously scanning the amphitheater while the crowd settled into seats. It made no sense that his boys weren't sitting here beside him.

The house lights dimmed and the audience fell quickly into a hush. From high up in the half-open, cantilevered roof, a spotlight shone as the conductor emerged in the orchestra pit for a bow.

Then, with a great sweep, the conductor gave the downbeat, Simon's entire body tensing, rapt, as the opening theme sounded, the Stravinskian motif from Tableau One. The curtain rose to reveal Igor at center stage wearing bow tie and oversized jacket, youthful and impassioned, wandering into a cloud of purple lighting for the premiere of Schoenberg's *Pierrot Lunaire*. As the trickle of Schoenberg's music began, the Stravinsky motif nosed up against it, weaving into it until the two separate Schoenberg/Stravinsky strands were juxtaposed. Then the orchestral accompaniment softened as the tenor, Russell Lowry, in the role of Stravinsky, intoned his opening line:

> *But what lurid sonorities/Dreamy, sinister,*
> *penetrating sounds encroach.*

Bewitching music, intoxicating perfume,
Oh, Schoenberg. Mastermind. Incandescent ge-
nius.
What can be done in the midst of such deluge,
against sheer force? Sheer force.
What can be done?

Later, during act one of *Arnold & Igor*, as Schoenberg and Vivian dream of creating an Orpheus project together, Simon felt the crushing force of Francine and the boys, Vivian singing wistfully to Schoenberg of Orpheus' tragedy.

Just as he turns to glimpse her, she slips from
his grasp. Orpheus has lost this great part of
himself, this other half in Eurydice. But, despite
whatever flights of fancy or musical charm, he
can never go back. Fate and the flow of time are
yet stronger forces. He can never go back.

During intermission, he planted himself beside a binocular rental stand, alone among the crowd to catch his breath after all the emotional upheaval of act one. He felt as if he'd been holding his breath the entire time, stiff in his seat, anxious, too tense to relax. Now, finally, he was able to take a few deep breaths while processing some of the overload: the stunning visual and auditory presentation; weeks of anticipation, leading up to tonight's opening performance. And the shower of applause—appreciation and approval from a few thousand people, something encouraging, no doubt, heartwarming even; though, with his family absent, something that also felt impersonal, intangible and incomplete.

A culmination, though, certainly. Real evidence that he'd managed to at least do *something* right. Watching the excited throngs pouring out from the theater and crossing the plaza, he was overcome by the experience of finally witnessing his artistic vision unfolding before a live audience in real time.

Then a flicker. A familiar flash of movement near one of the con-cession stands caught his eye, unconscious at first, but pulling him from his reverie.

Zeroing in on the motion, he was dumbstruck to notice the small tow-headed kid, grinning and gussied up in an argyle vest, Luke wav-ing at him, then waving with greater zeal, tugging at his mother's sleeve, Francine smiling faintly as she too spotted Simon among the crowd.

For a moment, they vanished, swallowed up by the passing throngs.

Then his boys emerged, rushing towards him, Simon kneeling to collect a boy in each arm, pulling them in close.

"You're here!" he said breathlessly, looking from Luke to Lincoln, kissing their faces.

"We came to see your show," Luke said.

"Dad," Lincoln said, glancing around, "this whole thing is amazing."

Simon hugged them again, glancing up to see Francine approach-ing, Carla trailing just behind, both dressed in light pastel sweaters.

Standing up, he took Francine's hand, moving closer, the hug she gave him somewhat stiff.

"Congratulations," Francine said. "This is really something."

"Truly remarkable, maestro!" Carla said. "You've outdone yourself."

"You're here!"

Francine smiled and nodded.

"And I absolutely love your new home!" Carla said, gesturing at the starry sky, silhouettes of mesas against the mountains.

"I can't get over how beautiful the opera is," Francine said.

"Yeah, me too!" Luke said.

"And I can't wait to find out what's going to happen," Carla said.

"Me too!" Luke said again with a little hop. "I can't wait to find out what's going to happen." He peered at his wrist watch. "Although, it's probably gonna take a while to find out."

Tableau XXII

Arnold & Igor

"An aged man is but a paltry thing,
A tattered coat upon a stick, unless
Soul clap its hands and sing."
—William Butler Yeats, *Sailing to Byzantium*

"*Moses und Aron* remains one of Schoenberg's most essential achievements. The internal conflicts that inhere within its germinal tone row are played out over the whole, generating the opera's personae, their driving forces, and their conflicting needs, abilities, desires, and destinies. Schoenberg's Moses is without final dramatic resolution, despite the composer's evident desire over many years to bring the conflict of the brothers to a close by Aron's death…I feel that Schoenberg had underestimated the importance of Aron. Perhaps he had underestimated or even repressed the importance of Aron-like tendencies within himself. More important, Schoenberg, as critic and theorist, had underestimated the power of his 12-tone method to resist musical closure. The instincts of Schoenberg the composer, however, could find no solution of closure. There was none to be found."
—Michael Cherlin, *Schoenberg's Musical Imagination*

Hollywood
January 1951

IN A SUNKEN BOOTH at the Brown Derby, Schoenberg and Stravinsky enjoy a leisurely lunch. Deep walnut paneling, candelabras and framed caricatures of Hollywood celebrities, waiters circulating in pressed white jackets and bow ties.

Schoenberg focuses intently on his boiled Catalina swordfish and side of marinated herring.

"I wish I'd begun earlier," he says.

Stravinsky looks up from his fried Eastern oysters and Cobb salad. "With lunch, you mean?"

"With lunch, sure." He indicates the massive sketchbook on the seat beside him. "I was referring to the *Orpheus*."

Stravinsky removes his bifocals, depositing them into an empty wine glass while Schoenberg fiddles with a hearing apparatus, tuning it before resecuring it inside the large cavity of his ear. He raises his Shirley Temple in a toast to *Orpheus*.

"And also to Elsa," Stravinsky says, clinking his martini glass with Schoenberg's.

"Vivian too," Schoenberg says quietly.

Lifting the sketchbook onto the table, Schoenberg eases it towards Stravinsky.

"Maybe you'd be willing to have another go at things," Schoenberg says.

Stravinsky's eyes grow big.

"My health. I'm forced to slow down." He nudges the sketchbook nearer to Stravinsky. "I'm not so sure how much more I can do with it."

He tells Stravinsky about the difficult year he's had, listing off a string of ailments, failing eyesight, erratic blood pressure, asthma attacks that rouse him in the middle of the night and force him to sleep sitting up in the living room armchair. He and his doctor continue to strategize against the ongoing barrage of nervous agitation, depression, physical frailty, shortness of breath, diabetes, pneumonia, kidney disease, hernia, dropsy.

"That's some list," Stravinsky says.

"And if this weren't enough," Schoenberg says, "I recently suffered heart failure. Cardiac arrest, brought on by a violent asthma attack. My heart actually stopped."

Stravinsky sets down his fork, raising an eyebrow.

"I remained for several minutes in some unknown region between life and death, resurrected finally—thankfully—by an injection to the heart." Schoenberg describes the ensuing days of delirium, the mad demons that appeared to take possession of him, resulting in a crazy sketch of a string trio, "a graphic depiction of my illness, as it were."

"Uncanny," Stravinsky murmurs.

Schoenberg taps the sketchbook. "So, here's what I propose. Take the sketchbook over to show Sol. He knows about the project already. Not to mention he knows every last person in the music world. Maybe Sol might be able to work a little magic, figure out how to help you along."

"But it's your work," Stravinsky says, nudging the sketchbook back towards Schoenberg. "Your brainwork, your sweat. I wouldn't have the faintest idea where even to begin."

"You'll figure it out," Schoenberg says. "You'll know what to do." He shrugs. "You always do."

It's already dark when they depart the restaurant, buttoning up their coats as they head away from the large derby hat atop the restaurant's brown dome and make their way along Vine Street towards Hollywood Boulevard. Stravinsky suggests C.C. Browns or Schwab's Pharmacy for ice cream, Schoenberg insisting they do a little walking around first.

The sketchbook is clasped beneath Stravinsky's right arm, Schoenberg's elbow clasped in his left.

They shuffle over pink terrazzo-and-brass stars along the *Walk of Fame*, endless celebrity names engraved into Hollywood Boulevard.

"Someday they'll have plaques here with our names," Stravinsky says. "Lovely Hollywood stars for each of us."

Glancing up from Gene Autry's star, Schoenberg nods. "It's nice we are remembered."

"And this?" Stravinsky asks, shaking the sketchbook. "What will the future make of this?"

Schoenberg snorts. "Let the world think what it wants."

But, even while savoring the halcyon moment, there's no way for Stravinsky to predict that in only a few short months the phone in his home will ring with news of Schoenberg's death.

Immediately, he'll draft a letter of condolence to Gertrud Schoenberg *(Deeply shocked by saddening news of terrible blow inflicted to all musical world by loss of Arnold Schoenberg)*, before falling into a gloomy silence.

Nor is Stravinsky presently capable of predicting that, on the evening after Schoenberg's death, he and Vera will be seated among dinner guests at Alma Mahler-Werfel's table where Alma's daughter Anna will unveil the Schoenberg death mask she's just created, not yet dried, Stravinsky too devastated to bid anyone goodnight, so overcome he'll need to make his excuses, as he gropes for Vera's arm to steady himself.

But for now, arm in arm, the composers resume their valedictory stroll, two quirky geniuses on Hollywood Boulevard conjoined at the elbow and beaming like schoolboys.

Acknowlegements

I'm grateful to the following for reading and responding to various sections, for reading the novel in its entirety, or for otherwise providing wisdom and encouragement: James Brennan, Debbie Cirimele, Kathy Cowan, Don Dickinson, Bruce Duffy, Janet Gregori, Isabel Halema, Mary Lou Holding, Mark Holzbrand, Samuel Jones, Philip Laird, Deb and Greg Lapp, Anne McMillan, Robert Matthews, Brenda Rappaport, Lisa Riley, Jennifer Robbins, Margaret Ross, Claire Schneeberger, Gerard Schwarz, Tom Smith, Robbie Stange, Leonard Stein, Brian Stone, Lawrence, Victoria, Linda and Stanley Trilling, Victor Urbanowicz, and Carol Zimbelman.

My heartfelt thanks to Donna Bister and Marc Estrin at Fomite.

I'm grateful to the writers community at Stanford University and Stanford's Online Writing Certificate in the Novel program, in particular, Ammi Keller, Angela Pneuman, and Malena Watrous. And thank you, Ron Nyren, without whose enthusiasm and lapidary faculty this book never would have been possible.

Works Consulted

Adorno, Theodor. 2016. *Philosophy Of Modern Music*. Translated by Anne G. Mitchell and Wesley V. Blomster. Bloomsbury.

Adorno, Theodor W. 2017. *Night Music*. Translated by Wieland Hoban. Seagull Books.

Auner, Joseph. 2003. *A Schoenberg Reader*. Yale University Press.

Bahr, Ehrhard. 2008. *Weimar on the Pacific*. University of California Press.

Bailey, Walter B., ed. 1998. *The Arnold Schoenberg Companion*. Greenwood Publishing Group.

Baum, Vicki. 2016. *Grand Hotel*. New York Review of Books.

Bernstein, Leonard. 1976. *The Unanswered Question*. Harvard University Press.

Boehmer, Konrad, ed. 1998. *Schonberg and Kandinsky: An Historic Encounter (Contemporary Music Studies)*. Harwood Academic.

Boretz, Benjamin, and Edward T. Cone, eds. 2015. *Perspectives on Schoenberg and Stravinsky*. Princeton University Press.

Brand, Juliane, and Christopher Hailey. 1997. *Constructive Dissonance*. University of California Press.

Bryn-Julson, Phyllis and Paul Matthews. 2008. *Inside Pierrot Lunaire*. The Scarecrow Press.

Cherlin, Michael. 2007. *Schoenberg's Musical Imagination*. Cambridge University Press.

Craft, Robert. 1958. *Conversations with Igor Stravinsky*. Faber & Faber.

Craft, Robert, and Igor Stravinsky. 1981. *Memories and Commentaries*. University of California Press.

Crawford, Dorothy L. 2009. *A Windfall of Musicians*. Yale University Press.

Cross, Jonathan, ed. 2003. *The Cambridge Companion to Stravinsky*. Cambridge University Press.

Davis, Mike. 2006. *City of Quartz*. Verso Books.

Dunsby, Jonathan. 1992. *Schoenberg: Pierrot Lunaire*. Cambridge University Press.

Ewen, David. 1937. *Twentieth Century Composers*.

Ewen, David. 1991. *The World of Twentieth-Century Music*. Robert Hale.

Friedrich, Otto. 1997. *City of Nets*. University of California Press.

Frisch, Walter. 1997. *The Early Works of Arnold Schoenberg, 1893-1908*. University of California Press.

Frisch, Waltern, ed. 2012. *Schoenberg and His World*. Princeton University Press.

Gould, Glenn. 1964. *Arnold Schoenberg, A Perspective*. University of Cincinnati.

Griffiths, Paul. 1983. *New Grove Second Viennese School: Schoenberg, Webern, Berg (The Composer Biography Series)*. W W Norton & Co Inc.

Harris, Donald. 1987. *The Berg-Schoenberg Correspondence: Selected Letters*. Edited by Juliane Brand and Christopher Hailey. W. W. Norton.

Hodson, Millicent. 1996. *Nijinsky's Crime Against Grace: Reconstruction Score of the Original Choreography for Le Sacre Du Printemps (Dance & Music Series)*. Pendragon Press.

Hodson, Millicent, and Kenneth Archer. 2014. *The Lost Rite: Rediscovery of the 1913 Rite of Spring*. KMS Press.

Igor and Vera Stravinsky: A Photograph Album, 1921 to 1971. n.d. Thames & Hudson.

Joseph, Charles M. 2002. *Stravinsky and Balanchine: A Journey of Invention*. Yale University Press.

Joseph, Charles M. 2008. *Stravinsky Inside Out*. Yale University Press.

Keller, Hans, and Milein Cosman. 1986. *Stravinsky Seen and Heard*. Da Capo Press, Incorporated.

Kelly, Thomas Forrest. 2000. *First Nights*. Yale University Press.

Lehmann, Lotte. 1938. *Midway in My Song, the Autobiography of Lotte Lehmann*. Bobbs-Merrill Company.

Newlin, Dika. 1947. *Bruckner, Mahler, Schoenberg*.

Newlin, Dika. 1980. *Schoenberg Remembered*. New York : Pendragon Press.

Pasler, Jann, ed. 2023. *Confronting Stravinsky*. University of California Press.

Peyser, Joan. 1980. *Twentieth-Century Music: The Sense behind the Sound*. Schirmer Books.

Posner, Sandy. 1945. *Petrouchka. The Story of the Ballet.* A. And C. Black.

Ringer, Alexander L. 1990. *Arnold Schoenberg. The Composer as Jew.* Oxford University Press.

Rosen, Charles 1996. *Arnold Schoenberg*. University of Chicago Press.

Schoenberg, Arnold. 1965. *Letters. Selected and Edited by Erwin Stein. Translated from the Original German by Eithne Wilkins and Ernst Kaiser*. St. Martins Press.

Schoenberg, Arnold. 1975. *Style and Idea. Selected Writings of Arnold Schoenberg. Edited by Leonard Stein. With Translations by Leo Black.* University of California Press.

Schoenberg, Arnold. 1988. *Self-Portrait*. Edited by Nuria Schoenberg Nono. Belmont Music Publishers.

Shaw, Jennifer, and Joseph Auner. 2010. *The Cambridge Companion to Schoenberg*. Cambridge University Press.

Shawn, Allen. 2003. *Arnold Schoenberg's Journey*. Harvard University Press.

Simms, Bryan R., ed. 1999. *Schoenberg, Berg, and Webern*. Greenwood Press.

Stravinsky, Theodore, and Denise Stravinsky. 1988. *Catherine and Igor Stravinsky: A Family Chronicle 1906-1940*. Edited by Neil Wenborn. Translated by Stephen Walsh. Schirmer Trade Books.

Stuckenschmidt, Hans Heinz. 1977. *Schoenberg: His Life, World, and Work*. Schirmer Books

Taruskin, Richard. 2016. *Stravinsky and the Russian Traditions, Volume One: A Biography of the Works through Mavra (Volume 1)*. University of California Press.

Thomson, William. 1991. *Schoenberg's Error*. University of Pennsylvania Press.

Van Toorn, Pieter C. 1987. *Stravinsky and the Rite of Spring*. University of California Press.

Wachtel, Andrew, ed. 1998. *Petrushka*. Northwestern University Press.

Walsh, Stephen. 2002. *Stravinsky: A Creative Spring: Russia and France, 1882-1934*. University of California Press.

Walsh, Stephen. 2006. *Stravinsky: The Second Exile: France and America, 1934–1971*. University of California Press.

Wellesz, Egon. 1971. *Arnold Schoenberg*. Translated by W. H. Kerridge. Greenwood Publishing Press.

Werfel, Alma Mahler. 1958. *And the Bridge Is Love*. Harcourt, Brace and Company.

White, Eric Walter. 1966. *Stravinsky: The Composer and His Works*. University of California Press.

Zweig, Stefan. 1987. *The World of Yesterday*. Pushkin Press.

About the Author

Howard Rappaport's work has appeared in *The North American Review*, *The Los Angeles Review*, and *The Madison Review*. *Arnold & Igor* was inspired by his work as a musician, educator and orchestral conductor. He lives in northern California with his wife and two children. This is his first novel.

Fomite

Writing a review on social media sites for readers will help the progress of independent publishing. To submit a review, go to the book page on any of the sites and follow the links for reviews. Books from independent presses rely on reader-to-reader communications.

For more information or to order any of our books, visit:
fomitepress.com/our-books.html

More novels and novellas from Fomite...

Joshua Amses — *During This, Our Nadir*
Joshua Amses — *Ghats*
Joshua Amses — *How They Became Birds*
Joshua Amses — *Raven or Crow*
Joshua Amses — *The Moment Before an Injury*
Charles Bell — *The Married Land*
Charles Bell — *The Half Gods*
Jaysinh Birjepatel — *Nothing Beside Remains*
Jaysinh Birjepatel — *The Good Muslim of Jackson Heights*
David Brizer — *Victor Rand*
L. M Brown — *Hinterland*
Paula Closson Buck — *Summer on the Cold War Planet*
Dan Chodorkoff — *Loisaida*
Dan Chodorkoff — *Sugaring Down*
David Adams Cleveland — *Time's Betrayal*
Paul Cody— *Sphyxia*
Jaimee Wriston Colbert — *Vanishing Acts*
Roger Coleman — *Skywreck Afternoons*
Stephen Downes — *The Hands of Pianists*
Marc Estrin — *Hyde*
Marc Estrin — *Kafka's Roach*
Marc Estrin — *Proceedings of the Hebrew Burial Society*
Marc Estrin — *Speckled Vanities*
Marc Estrin — *The Annotated Nose*
Marc Estrin — *The Penseés of Alan Kreiger*
Zdravka Evtimova — *Asylum for Men and Dogs*
Zdravka Evtimova — *In the Town of Joy and Peace*
Zdravka Evtimova — *Sinfonia Bulgarica*
Zdravka Evtimova — *You Can Smile on Wednesdays*
Daniel Forbes — *Derail This Train Wreck*
Peter Fortunato — *Carnevale*
Greg Guma — *Dons of Time*
Richard Hawley — *The Three Lives of Jonathan Force*
Lamar Herrin — *Father Figure*

Fomite

Michael Horner — *Damage Control*
Ron Jacobs — *All the Sinners Saints*
Ron Jacobs — *Short Order Frame Up*
Ron Jacobs — *The Co-conspirator's Tale*
Scott Archer Jones — *And Throw Away the Skins*
Scott Archer Jones — *A Rising Tide of People Swept Away*
Julie Justicz — *Degrees of Difficulty*
Maggie Kast — *A Free Unsullied Land*
Darrell Kastin — *Shadowboxing with Bukowski*
Coleen Kearon — *#triggerwarning*
Coleen Kearon — *Feminist on Fire*
Jan English Leary — *Thicker Than Blood*
Diane Lefer — *Confessions of a Carnivore*
Diane Lefer — *Out of Place*
Rob Lenihan — *Born Speaking Lies*
Colin McGinnis — *Roadman*
Douglas W. Milliken — *Our Shadows' Voice*
Ilan Mochari — *Zinsky the Obscure*
Peter Nash — *Parsimony*
Peter Nash — *The Least of It*
Peter Nash — *The Perfection of Things*
George Ovitt — Stillpoint
George Ovitt — Tribunal
Gregory Papadoyiannis — *The Baby Jazz*
Pelham — *The Walking Poor*
Andy Potok — *My Father's Keeper*
Frederick Ramey — *Comes A Time*
Joseph Rathgeber — *Mixedbloods*
Kathryn Roberts — *Companion Plants*
Robert Rosenberg — *Isles of the Blind*
Fred Russell — *Rafi's World*
Ron Savage — *Voyeur in Tangier*
David Schein — *The Adoption*
Charles Simpson — *Uncertain Harvest*
Lynn Sloan — *Midstream*
Lynn Sloan — *Principles of Navigation*
L.E. Smith — *The Consequence of Gesture*
L.E. Smith — *Travers' Inferno*
L.E. Smith — *Untimely RIPped*
Robert Sommer — *A Great Fullness*
Tom Walker — *A Day in the Life*
Susan V. Weiss — *My God, What Have We Done?*
Peter M. Wheelwright — *As It Is On Earth*
Peter M. Wheelwright — *The Door-Man*
Suzie Wizowaty — *The Return of Jason Green*